A SERI
PARADISE

A Tom Morton Novel

MARK HAYDEN

**PAW
PRESS**

www.pawpress.co.uk

Cover Design — Rachel Lawston.
Design Copyright © 2017 Lawston Design
This edition published 2017 by Paw Press:
www.pawpress.co.uk
Independent Publishing in Westmorland.

ISBN-13: 978-1535185110
ISBN-10: 1535185112

This book is dedicated to the memory of
Kate Burge

1972-2014

Acknowledgments

This book would not have been written without love, support, encouragement and sacrifices from my wife, Anne. She agreed to carry on full time work and let me step down so I could write. I also do the cooking and ironing, so it's not a one-way deal. Since the first edition came out, she has retired, but somehow I'm still doing the ironing.

Although Chris Tyler didn't get to see the draft this time, his friendship is a big part of my continued desire to write, and thanks also due to the fellow members of Kendal Writers' Café. Their critique of my opening chapters is always both merciless and justified.

A SERPENT IN PARADISE

Chapter 1

The police were waiting for them as they turned off the bypass.

Blue lights emerged from the hidden farm track and Lucy grabbed her brother's arm before he could put his foot down to race them.

'Gianni, no. Enough. You're not even speeding.'

She saw him glance ahead. It was half a mile to the 7Bridge Estate entrance and the Maserati would easily outrun the police over that distance.

'No,' said Lucy. 'It's too important to risk an arrest. Just pull in.'

Gianni slammed on the brakes and cut into the side of the road. Behind them, the police car went into a skid and came to rest half over the white line. If someone had been coming out of the Village...

'Don't get out,' she pleaded, but Gianni wasn't going to miss the fun. He threw off his seat belt and leapt out, just in time to watch the police car reverse from its dangerous position in the middle of the road and tuck itself behind Gianni's vehicle. There were two officers inside. That could make things awkward, because the driver had been embarrassed in front of his colleague. Or her colleague. Lucy slipped out of the car as well, and tried to be inconspicuous.

They were both men, and they both approached the Maserati in silence. Lucy noticed that the non-driving policeman had three little silver stripes on the shoulder of his hi-viz jacket. When they got closer to the car, Gianni squared up to them, an insolent grin on his face.

'Is this your vehicle, sir?' asked the younger policeman.

'*Non sono inglese*,' said Gianni, offering them his driving licence.

The officer looked at it and passed it to the sergeant, who tapped it against his hand. 'This is a full UK licence, sir. You must have learnt English to pass the test.'

'*Non capisco.*'

The constable turned and whispered to his sergeant, but Lucy could still hear him. 'Sarge, even if we don't arrest him, this will still get back to their security people.'

The sergeant's face set in a grim expression. 'You should have thought of that before you started to chase him.'

Lucy decided to intervene. 'Excuse me, officers, but if you want to question my brother any more, you'll have to arrest him and get a translator. He's done nothing wrong today, so just breathalyse him and let us go. It is Christmas, after all.'

'Who—? The younger officer started to speak, but the sergeant held up his hand.

'Thank you, Ms Berardi.'

'My name's Lucy White. Gianni's my half-brother. I live in the Village, not on the Estate.' She wanted to make it clear to the officers that she wasn't part of *that* world. Not any more.

The sergeant tapped the licence against his hands for a few seconds more. A gust of wind blew Lucy's coat open, and she shivered. Finally, the sergeant made up his mind. 'It's gonna snow soon,' he said. 'There'll be crashes all up and down the M6. There always are on Boxing Day. C'mon, take his reading.'

The constable reluctantly pulled out an intoximeter and gave Gianni the instructions. In English. He complied without going through the farce of waiting for a translation from Lucy. Two minutes later, they were on their way.

'*Cornuto*,' snarled Gianni.

'Don't,' said Lucy. 'You'll say that to their faces one of these days. A lot of people know what it means now.'

'That's what he is: his dick is small and his wife sleeps with the postman.'

'Are you going to tell Max Nolan about being stopped?'

Gianni drove carefully towards the Village, then turned into the Estate access road. 'Of course I will tell him. This is more harassment from the police. What else do we pay security for, if not to sort out our problems?'

There was no sign on the turning, nothing to announce it as the entrance to Cheshire's largest and most exclusive gated community. It had been over a year since Lucy had entered the 7Bridge Estate this way, through the residents' entrance. Although her family still lived here, and she had spent Christmas Day with them, she always walked through the Village and signed in at the security gate in the service area.

The drive to the residents' entrance was long, too long to walk, and was lined with trees on both sides. Among the trees were the CCTV cameras. They picked up the Maserati's number plate, and the security system recognised it as belonging to an official Resident of the Estate. By the time they arrived at the bridge, the way was clear, and they crossed into 7Bridge, waving to the patrol officer on duty.

Any vehicle not on the system would have been greeted by a ram-proof barrier and a patrol officer. Attempting to skirt the barrier would land the driver in the river. The patrol officer would direct the vehicle back through the Village to the service area. There were no exceptions: only full residents could nominate vehicles to pass through here.

Given that the footballers, boy-band stars, hedge fund managers and entrepreneurs who lived in 7Bridge often drove up in new vehicles, they were quite often stopped at the barrier. It was one of the many things that Lucy's father had to sort out for them, though he usually delegated this one to his assistant, Lucy's friend Grace. There was other business with cars, which Lucy handled, but she was getting fed up with that.

Gianni drove slowly through the Estate. He may have escaped the police, but he wouldn't risk the wrath of the Estate patrol: a formal warning from the head of security, Max Nolan, was much worse than three points on your licence. Lucy checked her phone. The Japanese guests were due to arrive in fifteen minutes, which gave her just enough time to calm her brother down.

They crossed over the mound, and Gianni stopped the car next to the visitors' reception. The Ikedas were rich, but even they had to arrive at Visitor Reception next to the service buildings and be signed in at the security desk.

Paul Warren, her father's attorney, was waiting on the other side of the security fence, stamping his feet against the cold.

When they had passed through security, Paul gave Lucy a hug and wished her a Merry Christmas; he was Dad's oldest friend, and also Lucy's godfather. Lucy had a lot of good memories of Uncle Paul. The bristles from his moustache tickled, like they always did, and Lucy was glad that he was going to the match with Gianni. He might keep her brother in check.

The service area was even more exposed than the lay-by where the police had stopped them. Lucy pulled her woollen scarf higher. A stray gust brought the odour of cooking oil from the Hartley Catering building. 'Why am I doing this?' she asked. 'It's Boxing Day.'

Gianni grinned at her. 'What would you rather do, *cara mia*. Spend the afternoon with our stepmother, or take Signora Ikeda to the 7Bridge Spa? When was the last time you went for a full afternoon of *la dolce vita*, eh?'

'Before I moved out, that's when — and you know it. I can barely afford the Village Café these days. That's why I was hoping to be invited to watch the Trafford Rangers game with you and Dad. I haven't missed a Christmas game in years.'

'Signor Ikeda could be a big sponsor. That is why Papa is paying you to take Signora Ikeda to the Spa, and why Holly is paying you to babysit tonight.'

'I'd rather go to the Nugent Ball than look after the Nugent children.'

'No, you wouldn't. You cannot say you are poor and then go to the ball. You are not Cinderella.'

'Now then, you two,' said Paul. 'I think I can see lights. What is it we do again, Lucy?'

'We bow first, then you say *Konnichiwa, Ikeda-san,* because Gianni can't pronounce it.'

Paul practised the phrase as a stretch limo glided towards them.

Football fixtures are governed by many factors, but the biggest is television. On Boxing Day this year, Trafford Rangers had played at lunchtime and Chelsea were playing later; the rest of the Premier League, and all the divisions below them, had kicked off at the traditional time of three o'clock.

Salton Town FC, newly promoted to the Championship, had made the relatively short journey from Cheshire to Burnley. They were now about to leave.

The seats at the back of the team bus were known as Cripple's Corner because they were reserved for the walking wounded after the game. Dean Rooksby was there because he'd bashed his shoulder into the goalpost. His left arm was strapped across his chest, and the painkillers were threatening to send him to sleep. His head jerked up as the rest of the squad piled on to the coach. Leading the charge was his best mate, Travis, a bottle of beer in one hand and a teddy bear in the other — a teddy bear swaddled in a Salton Town FC scarf. Just behind him was Dean's central defensive partner, Ricardo 'Rich' Menghini.

'You all right, Deano?' said his friend.

'No, I'm not all right. I'm going to miss the cup match, not to mention the derby.'

'Eh? Is not good,' said Rich.

'Did you hear?' said Travis, pointing to the Italian. 'He got another yellow card after you were taken off.'

Dean tried a smile. 'Careful, Rich. They can't do without both of us.'

Menghini made a violent gesture towards the window, '*Arbitro cornuto!*' he said.

'Yeah, we know,' said Travis. 'All the refs pick on you because you're so attractive and they're jealous.'

'Is true. This referee… he is so ugly, no woman goes near him.' With that assertion, Ricardo went back to his seat.

'This is yours,' said Travis, placing the teddy bear on the empty seat next to Dean. 'That fat blond bird who's always waiting outside said she hopes you get well soon.'

'Leave off, Travis. Her name's Emily, and she's the supporters' club secretary. She interviewed me last season for the newsletter. She's really nice.'

Travis thought for a second. 'Yeah… she was really sweet, actually. She still ate all the pies, though. C'n I get you anything, man? Beer?'

'Naah. I can't drink with these pills, but can you get my phone out? It's in the locker.'

Their manager, Gus Burkett, was very strict about rules on the bus. On the way to games, all electronic devices had to be locked away. Travis fished in the locker and handed Dean his phone.

At the front of the coach, Gus's well-padded figure mounted the steps. 'Seats, lads,' he said. That was another rule: sit down when arriving and departing.

Dean had been Man of the Match again today — not bad for a teenage centre half. His heroics with the goalpost had cleared a shot off the line and earned them a hard-fought draw with Burnley, one of the promotion favourites. He'd been stretchered off after making the clearance.

'Cheer up, mate,' said his friend. 'You'll be playing in the Champions League with Trafford Rangers next year.'

'Maybe,' said Dean.

Travis waved to him and swayed back to the table where they normally sat together. The lights dimmed, and the coach pulled out of Turf Moor.

With some effort, Dean unlocked his phone and saw a message from Madison: *Hope you're OK. Call me when you can.* He dialled, and she picked up on the first ring.

'Dean, love, what's happened?'

'Did you see it?'

'Yes, I bloody well did. Three times. Twice in slow motion. No one knew if you'd broken it or not.'

'The physio doesn't think it's broken, but I'll need a scan tomorrow to check it out.' He sighed. 'I'm gonna be out for a couple of weeks at least. You can practise being a housewife. For when we're married.'

'Lay off, Dean. It's not funny seeing you on a stretcher like that. Do you want me to stay in tonight and look after you?'

In the pause after her question, Dean could hear the sound of a hairdryer and a girly laugh: Maddi was already round at Holly's, getting herself glammed up.

'You go and have fun. Not too much fun though. I'll be asleep when you get back.'

'Thanks, love. Text me when you get home.'

'Yeah. Love you, fiancée.'

'Love you too.'

Concentrating on his phone had made his shoulder ache. Dean had no idea whether he could even undress himself, never mind get something to eat. He called Gary White, his agent. Injury clearly brought privileges, because Gary himself took the call and asked how badly he was hurt.

Dean filled in the details and then, with a little hesitation, said, 'Gary, you know Madison's going to this do in Chester?'

'So are we. Robyn's just getting ready.'

'It's just that Mum and Dad have gone abroad for Christmas, and I don't think I can look after myself tonight.'

'Don't worry, Dean. That's what living in 7Bridge is all about. I'll put in a call to Natasha. Personally. There'll be a nurse waiting for you in Salton. It'll have to be a bloke, though: you might need lifting. He can drive you to 7Bridge and look after you. Besides, I don't want Madison coming home to find a hot Filipino in your bedroom.'

'Cheers, Gary. It's a good job I'm not gay, then.'

'Don't even *think* those thoughts. Gotta go.'

Dean relaxed properly for the first time since the goalpost had brought his afternoon to a premature end. He swiped his way through to the *Salton Advertiser* match report on his phone. They had given him 8 out of 10 for his performance — making him the top of the paper's player rankings, much to the skipper's annoyance. Dean grinned. His finger hesitated over another website. Should he read it? No. He'd find out soon enough what the Mother Superior was saying about his fiancée on that website of hers.

Mother Superior. Maddi had said it was irony or something. Dean didn't see what was ironic about a super-heated gossip queen calling herself after a nun. Sometimes he didn't get the references on the *SeenIn7Bridge* website, and Maddi had to explain them. No, it could definitely wait until he got home. He looked at the lights of Manchester, and remembered the diamond sparkles in the engagement ring. He fell asleep with a smile on his face, and the phone slipped from his hand.

Down the coach, Travis heard the clatter when the phone hit the floor, and peered over his shoulder to see if Gus was watching. With the coast clear, Travis sneaked back and did what any good friend would do: he picked up Dean's phone, placed the teddy bear on Dean's lap, and then took a picture. Using Dean's own Twitter account, he posted the picture with this message:

Feeling better now I'm curled up with Teddy from @EmilySaltonTown. Love you Blondie!

Travis had done his good deed for the day, and felt much better when he sat down.

At the back of 7Bridge, lights were shining in most of the service buildings, including the Estate Office. The Estate manager, Saul Blackstone, had the top floor to himself. Half of it was office, and half of it was a small flat where he had spent too many nights. Including this one.

He was in the tiny kitchen making coffee when he heard his name called.

'I'm in the flat, Max,' he shouted back.

When Max Nolan, the security ops manager, came through, Saul asked what he always asked: 'Status?'

'Calm on the Estate,' said Max, and handed over three days' worth of reports covering the meagre Christmas break that Saul had allowed himself this year. He did not want to be back at work on Boxing Day, but he didn't have any choice.

'I should hope it's quiet: it is Christmas.' Saul pointed to one of the coffees, took the other one, then flicked through the reports on the way to his office.

'There's been another incident with the police,' said Max.

Saul glanced at the police incident: *A 7Bridge Collective car, travelling below the speed limit, was pursued and stopped for no reason. The driver was breathalysed. Negative. He reports that the attitude of the police was confrontational and that they only backed off when they realised there was a non-resident witness.*

'Who was driving the car? And who was the witness?'

'Giovanni Berardi was driving. His sister was the passenger.'

Saul grunted and tossed the reports into his out tray. This was getting out of hand. A lot of the talent liked fast cars but didn't like getting points on their licence. Their agent's attorney had come up with a scheme, which Saul would have vetoed if it weren't for the fact that Gary White, super sports agent, was a resident of the Estate and owned 20% of the Estate holding company.

White's attorney, Paul Warren, had set up a company called the 7Bridge Collective, which was the legal Keeper of all the fast cars, the Keeper being distinct from the owner. The residents owned the cars, but the 7Bridge Collective was responsible for them legally. Every time one of the cars tripped a speed camera, Paul Warren would ask for pictures. The driver was usually unrecognisable, so Paul would declare that the company was unable to say who was at the wheel, he would be summonsed to court and he would stand impassively in front of a furious magistrate and be fined £1,000. A corporate body does not have a driving licence, so no one got any points.

Shortly afterwards, the real guilty party would make an anonymous cash payment to the Collective, routed via the books of White-Berardi Sports Management. A £1,000 fine would discourage normal people, but these are not normal people: for most of them it was less than 1% of their weekly wage. The police knew exactly what was going on, and they had started lying in wait for every fast car in north Cheshire.

Last week it had come home to roost when a squad car chased a Maserati down the access road and nearly crashed into the ram–proof barrier. Max's patrol officers had stood their ground, and the policeman had had a screaming fit, threatening to arrest them, until he realised that he was on HD CCTV.

Saul would have to do something, but not until after the holidays. There was a more pressing problem to attend to.

'Is Hoskins here yet?' he asked.

'I left him in the lobby, to keep him out of the way.'

'Let's get the show on the road.' Saul picked up his iPad and went out to the lobby, where their newly engaged cyber-detective was waiting.

They had emailed and spoken, but not met before. Hoskins might sound like a geek, and talk like one, but he looked like a teddy bear, right down to the fluffy sweater that must have been a Christmas present from his mother. Saul looked again: the man had a wedding ring. Good for him. Saul still reckoned that his mother had bought the jumper, though.

Max made the formal introduction. Saul said, 'Thanks for coming on Boxing Day. I know we're paying you handsomely, but it's still a big sacrifice for you.'

'My youngest is only one,' said Hoskins. 'Too young to know what's going on, but old enough to get completely hyper. I'm glad of the break.'

Saul would have liked to have a one-year-old again, but that was unlikely at the moment. Perhaps next year the lawyers would stop holding him and Miriam to ransom, and let them divorce each other in a civilised way.

The preliminary contact with Hoskins had been all about his credentials, and Saul had not been willing to discuss specifics until he had a signature on the confidentiality agreement. That had arrived in the last post on Christmas Eve.

'I'll put this in very simple terms, Neil,' said Saul. 'Princess Karida, who represents the Estate's majority shareholders, and who lives in Sevenbridge Hall, has ordered me to stop the Mother Superior.'

'Who's the Mother Superior?'

'Let me show you.' Saul opened his iPad and flicked through to the *SeenIn7Bridge* website. Hoskins showed no sign of recognition. 'This website is written by someone in or from the Estate. She calls herself the Mother Superior. It's been unpleasant for some of the residents and staff for some time, but things are getting worse. This is the straw that broke the camel's back.'

He clicked through to a posting from five days ago, and they all crowded round the screen to read this message:

Happy Winter Solstice! Today is the shortest day of the year, and it's also a pagan festival. A little bird told me that 7Bridge has its very own pagans.

A series of grainy pictures accompanied the post, showing the Christmas tree on the green and the surrounding grass covered in snow. Across the images a group of women, naked apart from their running shoes, were seen to race each other round the tree. All but one of the women had their faces digitally covered with black squares. The one woman whose face was visible raised her arms in triumph in the last picture. Clearly she had won the race.

'Who…?' said Hoskins.

'Doesn't matter who the woman is,' said Saul. 'You can look it up later. What matters is that these images were taken just across the green, from inside a holly bush.'

'As soon as this was posted online, I went to see where it was taken from,' said Max. 'The ground was frozen, and I found a deep indentation. Whatever these ladies were getting up to, someone knew about it in advance and planted a camera there.'

'Nasty,' said Hoskins. 'Can't you just go after the website?'

'We tried that last year,' said Saul. 'Unfortunately, they've done nothing that's actually criminal. We got a court order to force the web hosts to take it down, but couldn't get one to force them to reveal the site owners. All that happened was that a really scurrilous web magazine took over: *Hot & Viral*. We can't touch them.'

Hoskins stroked his beard. 'I see.'

'You probably don't see, yet. I need a name. If it's an employee, I can sack them and sue them. If it's a resident, they'll get thrown off the Estate. The residency agreement allows me to revoke their residency status for this sort of thing.'

'There are privacy issues to consider,' said Neil.

'Not on this Estate,' said Max. 'So long as we use a reputable third party – that's you by the way – we can sniff around the Estate's Internet links.'

Hoskins smiled. 'The fact that you've brought me down from Cairndale says that this is a priority.'

'Princess Karida is paying,' said Saul. 'You have the wealth of the Ghar'aan royal family to draw on.'

'I'll start in the morning,' said Hoskins.

Lucy White strode along the footpaths through the 7Bridge Estate, whistling along to the music in her earphones, secure in the knowledge that no treacherous ice lay in wait around the corners. This wasn't because the Estate was immune to nature, though it sometimes felt like that. It was because the residents paid so much in management fees that there would be an uproar if unauthorised ice were discovered on the footways. Not only that, if one of the talent hurt himself, the court case could cost tens of millions. It was the blessing and the curse of 7Bridge: complete service with no hint of spontaneity. On the whole, she was glad she had moved out.

The earmuffs kept out the cold, but trapped the music inside, making her head echo with the beat. She broke stride to dance a little, then did a shuffle, snapping her fingers and coming to rest under the streetlight when the music stopped. She looked up at the CCTV camera and pointed into the lens. 'Yeah! That's right!' she said to the camera, just as the red light winked into action. Damn. Someone really was watching her now — perhaps even Sergeant Nolan himself. She flinched, but held her ground for another second to show she meant it, then turned slowly towards the Visitors Gate. Instead of passing through, she waited in the shelter of the building.

Despite the cold, Lucy felt good: a whole-body massage, a steam room and an essential oils head massage will do that to you. She had enjoyed the company, too — Mitsumi Ikeda was a lot like Lucy (if six years older). Mitsumi had been an unmarried elementary school teacher in Miyagi, until one day a former pupil had come to endow them with a new building, and he had fallen in love with his hostess.

Kaito Ikeda was a *lot* older than Mitsumi, but she said that was okay because he was a big kid, and she just treated him like one of her students, and now they were on their honeymoon. Mitsumi had insisted that they spend Christmas at a country house hotel in the Lake District. She had been to England as a student, and wanted to go back to a happy place. That's what she'd said: a happy place. She said the hotel had made her very happy.

Kaito was happy too. He had spent the afternoon watching Trafford Rangers at Barton Bridge stadium, enjoying the hospitality of the White-Berardi executive box and wearing his gift: a blood-red Trafford Rangers shirt with *Ikeda* and the number 7 on the back. Trafford Rangers had beaten Arsenal 2-1.

Tonight was the highlight of Kaito and Mitsumi's visit, and Lucy was waiting with the special pass to get them into the Estate. Right on time, the car pulled in a monstrous stretch limo, big enough for eight. Lucy leaned in to the security office and handed over the pass, then walked up to the limo.

This car came with a footman (it was the only word she could think of to describe a man whose job it was to leap out and open doors). He was already in place before she got there.

'Evening miss.'

'Hi. I'm not going to the Ball, you know.'

'I guessed. Enjoy the ride, even if it is only round the bend.'

She climbed in and joined the Ikedas at the back. Kaito half rose from his seat to bow, and Lucy managed the same before collapsing into a padded chair.

'I had to stop him bringing the shirt,' said Mitsumi. 'He wants John Nugent to sign it, but I told him that was rude.'

Gianni would have arranged a good deal more than a signed shirt, so Lucy just smiled. Kaito looked smart in his tuxedo, except for the wild hair. Mitsumi looked … well, put it this way: Mitsumi didn't scrub up quite as well as her husband. When they had arrived this morning, Mitsumi had been shrouded in the most beautiful Hermès scarf, a Christmas present from Kaito. Lucky her. In her winter coat and boots, she looked chic and well-polished. She hadn't made the transition to evening wear so comfortably. Lucy and Mitsumi were the same height (five foot four), and Mitsumi had gone for something that only a much taller woman should have attempted. *Never mind*, thought Lucy. *No one will say anything except to ask who designed it.* The answer, of course, was Dior.

The limo had started moving without Lucy noticing — and then it swung to the right and they were there, pulling into John and Holly Nugent's residence. The footman was at the door before they'd stopped moving. How did he do that?

'Please,' said Lucy. 'After you.'

Mitsumi nudged her husband and he moved first. '*Arigato*,' he said, giving another bow.

Gianni was waiting outside, and her brother led the Ikedas towards the front door. Lucy gave them half a minute, then slipped out of the limo. The footman hadn't moved.

The others had disappeared, so Lucy walked into *Casa Nugent*. That's what she called it, because what else would you call a Spanish-style mansion stuck in the middle of a Cheshire snowdrift? The main doors were thrown open to the night. When you don't pay your own heating bills, it's easier to leave them open.

Inside the hall, she levered off her boots, slinging them to one side to land under the second-largest Christmas tree in 7Bridge (the largest was on the green). The hall was like something out of an opera. In fact, the stage at La Scala Milan seemed shallower than *Casa Nugent*.

A marble staircase descended from a colonnaded gallery to meet the black and white tiled floor. Short passages led back to the catering kitchen and the family kitchen, and to either side of the hall were double doors: stage left to the family quarters, stage right to the party room.

'Auntie Lucy!' Peeking round the door to the family room was Holly's oldest child, Ellie. She beckoned furiously for Lucy to come over.

'Wow, kid,' said Lucy. 'Love the outfit.' She wasn't Ellie Nugent's real auntie, of course, but she had known the Nugents since both families had moved into 7Bridge when Lucy was eleven, which is why Lucy was babysitting tonight. Holly had an au pair, of course, but she also practised what she preached: family values. The au pair was with her family in Poland and not due back until Sunday, so Lucy was the most trusted stand-in.

Ellie was wearing a blue dress that came to just below the knee; anything shorter would have emphasised just how thin her legs were. Her waist-length hair was kept in check with a matching Alice band, and the only thing missing for the full *Through the Looking Glass* effect was an apron. At twelve years old, Ellie was going through a growth spurt that, with the black heels, made her almost as tall as Lucy.

Ellie stood with her feet in first position. She hoped to be a ballerina. Lucy hoped she'd grow out of it soon.

Ellie disappeared into the squashy, comfy, childproof family room, and Lucy followed. When they were out of earshot, Ellie said, 'Tell me who those people are. The…' she searched for a politically correct description.

'You mean our Japanese guests?'

'Stop teasing me. Yes, I do. Why are they here? And why are they going to the Ball? Mum's never taken anyone except Sheena, and this year she's taking Madison and these people.'

'*These people* are Kaito and Mitsumi Ikeda. I think they've come over to sort out something with your dad. Anyway, Kaito's a big fan of Trafford Rangers, and Mitsumi thinks your mum walks on water. Much prefers her to Victoria Beckham.'

Ellie's face fell. She sat on the only upright chair in the room, sweeping the skirt of her dress out of the way without thinking. When Lucy sat down like that, she always thought about moving her skirt afterwards, not before. Away from the cold, she dumped her coat on a beanbag.

'I thought they might be someone different, you know?' said Ellie. 'Someone from outside 7Bridge and football.'

'They'll be gone soon, and then we can enjoy ourselves.'

'That's right! Now they're here, I can get changed.'

Ellie jumped up again and clattered into the hall. On the way upstairs, she passed her mother coming down.

Holly Nugent still had her ash-blonde hair in giant rollers, and wasn't wearing her shoes yet, but otherwise she was ready for the ball — the fourth Nugent Boxing Day Benefit Ball.

'You look great,' said Lucy. 'The empire line always works for you.'

Holly made a slight grimace. 'You mean I've got big tits, big hips and I've eaten too much turkey.' She waved her hand. 'Thanks so much for tonight. I'm surprised that

Robyn allowed you over here to babysit when she's going herself.'

It was Lucy's turn to grimace. 'One of the perks of living in the Village instead of on the Estate is that my stepmother is no longer my keeper. She asked me to babysit, but I said that you'd got in first, and that you paid better.'

'You can't put a price on peace of mind,' said Holly, and Lucy felt as if her life was on elastic. One minute she was being treated by Ellie as if she were a responsible adult, an Auntie, and the next minute she was being paid to babysit as if she were still a teenager. *I'm twenty-six*, she thought. *I have my own business*. When her bad angel started to remind her that the business was hanging on by a thread, and was underwritten by her father's money, she screwed up her eyes and tried to forget.

'Have you done story-time yet?' she asked Holly.

'Going to do it now.' Holly checked the time on her Rolex Pearlmaster, and had to hold her arm away from her body to get the hands of the watch in focus. 'We've got to leave in half an hour, so I'd better get a shift on. You go ahead and make yourself comfortable – and listen – I think I've got another client for you. One of the African players has his family over for Christmas.' With that, she headed back upstairs, a lot less elegantly than her daughter.

There was a blast of noise from across the hall and the doors to the party room opened. The sound resolved itself into the commentary from Stamford Bridge, and John Nugent was standing in the doorway.

'Hello, Lucy,' he said. 'Are they anywhere near ready, yet, do you know? I'm struggling with small talk in here.'

John Nugent, captain of Trafford Rangers and England, was already in his evening dress. It was bespoke, to fit across his shoulders, and it barely creased when he lifted his arm to drink from the bottle of San Miguel. John Nugent was the first man that Lucy had formed a crush on (with millions of other girls), and he was even more handsome now that his stubble was flecked with grey. He took a step towards her and reflections glittered from his watch, his earring and even his shoes. Lucy felt a shiver that was only partly from the breeze from the wide open doors. Another man appeared behind him — John's teammate, Murray Cavendish. He was thinner and shorter than John and had a high-pitched Edinburgh accent and red hair. He had only been with Trafford Rangers a few years, and because he wasn't one of her father's clients, Lucy didn't know him very well. His tuxedo was expensive but off the peg, and his shoes weren't shoes at all — they were black leather trainers.

'Good result this afternoon,' she said to the men.

John waved his hand dismissively. 'Should have been easier. Two years ago we'd have cruised through a game like that. Have you seen Holly?'

'She's reading the boys a story. She said they'd be down in less than half an hour.'

He took another step forward and looked over his shoulder. 'I'm used to fans, but not in my own house. I'm not sure who's worse — Mr or Mrs.'

'You mean the Ikedas?'

'Yeah. Whatever. When Gianni introduced them, I thought Mr Ikeda was gonna topple over, he bowed so low. He kept saying my name, too. Then he says things in Japanese and she translates them. That's when she's not staring at the door waiting for Holly to appear, like the second coming.'

Murray took another swig of beer, and appeared to be enjoying every moment. 'Ikeda said that my cross for the second goal was driven by a divine wind. I like that.'

'Shut up, you. You're not helping,' said John. He turned back to Lucy. 'Neither is your brother. He keeps saying how good I'll look on posters in Tokyo.'

'Mmm. You will,' said Lucy. 'Especially stripped to the waist. You might have to dye your chest hair, though. Or finally get it shaved.'

John went back into the party room, and grabbed Murray's hair on the way. 'At least it's not ginger,' he said.

Murray winced with pain, and sloshed beer on his trainers. He cursed, and saw a discarded Santa sack under the tree. Without thinking, he polished his shoes and threw the sack into a corner. A roar from the crowd drew his attention back to the game. Lucy shivered on top, but could feel the underfloor heating toasting her feet.

'I don't like him,' said a voice from the stairs. 'That was Jack's Santa sack from Granddad Nugent. He uses the same sack every year, and now it's got beer on it.' Ellie had changed from Disney princess back to little girl. Her hair was loose, and she was sporting pink pyjamas under a towelling dressing gown. Her face was barely visible over the double duvet she was carrying.

'Careful, love,' said Lucy. 'Don't trip on the stairs.' She dashed up to take the duvet from Ellie before there was an accident. 'Who's this?' she asked, spotting the five hunky faces on the duvet cover. It looked like a boy band, but not one that Lucy had seen before.

'Five Dimensions,' said Ellie over her shoulder. 'They're going to be *massive* this year. They were in the grand final of *Sing for Glory*. I thought you'd know all about that.'

Lucy tossed the duvet on to the couch. 'Why would I? Some of us are allowed out on Saturday nights. Right, what's it going to be?'

Ellie flung open the cupboard under the massive TV and pulled out a stack of DVDs big enough to equip a small shop. They were rooting around and arguing about which film to watch when Lucy heard voices from the hall.

'Let's go and check them out,' said Ellie.

'Why not? C'mon.'

They went up to the double doors, and Lucy peered round. Ellie peered from underneath her arm.

The hall was big enough for John, Murray, Gianni and Kaito and Mitsumi Ikeda to form a reception line at the bottom of the staircase with the Christmas tree as a backdrop. The two footballers were waiting with their hands folded in front of them, as if they were defending a free kick. Gianni was next, and then the Ikedas. Mitsumi's hands were clasped to her mouth, her eyes riveted above. Her husband was still looking at John. That was weird. Heels began descending the staircase, and Kaito finally looked up.

Holly was in white — a sweeping gown that emphasised her cleavage. Sheena Cavendish had gone for red (which clashed horribly with her husband's hair), and she had neglected the legs *or* cleavage rule. The third woman was Madison Greenwood, fiancée to 7Bridge's newest resident, Dean Rooksby. She was younger than Holly and Sheena, younger even than Lucy. The green floor-length gown suited her perfectly.

'Have you heard what happened to Dean?' whispered Ellie. 'She shouldn't be going out when he's injured. She should have gone to Burnley.'

Lucy didn't care whether or not Madison neglected her boyfriend, but she did care that the red carpet for the Nugent Benefit Ball would be papped all over the Internet. *No one will notice the handbag*, she thought, and tried to forget the sight of Madison leaving the house with a Paola Berardi clutch.

John and Murray took their wives' arms, and Gianni did the same to Madison. Lucy liked Maddi. In fact, Maddi was putting together a refurbishment plan for the House of Lucia, her shop. Not that Lucy could afford it, but Maddi was an intern with the Estate's interior designer, Anthea Godfrey: the House of Lucia project was a practice assignment. Gianni had arranged the internship, and brought Maddi round to the shop. Lucy hoped that he wasn't going to get too close.

At the last moment, Holly turned and gave a little wave to her daughter. Ellie beamed back.

'What's that about Dean?' asked Lucy.

'He damaged his shoulder this afternoon. Madison should have been with him.'

With Dean being one of her dad's up-and-coming young clients, Lucy was surprised she hadn't heard. And what was with Ellie's attitude? 'Did you work that out for yourself — that Madison shouldn't have gone out tonight?' she asked.

'Sort of. It's what the Mother Superior said.'

'Aah.' That would be the anonymous author of the *SeenIn7Bridge* blog. She called herself the Mother Superior, and every female who set foot on the Estate was a target: resident wives, visiting girlfriends, the senior support staff — all were fair game, and there was a lot of detail that only an insider could know about. Everyone said that the Mother Superior was a complete bitch, but they all read the blog and spent hours discussing who the author might be. Apparently.

Lucy tried to ignore it, mostly. Now that she lived in the Village, the blog rarely mentioned her. While Ellie made a final choice between three DVDs, Lucy looked up *SeenIn7Bridge* on her phone, and read the latest entry:

*Let's hear it for early kick-off times! WAGs with men at Trafford Rangers can get home in plenty of time to put their slap on before the red carpet bash in Chester. Who has a ball on Boxing Day? HOLLY NUGENT, of course. She's persuaded the B-listers from our favourite soap MERSEYGATE to grace her charity bash, which means that Holly may not be the oldest person there! I hope you laid off the Christmas Pudding, Holly — a moment on the lips, and all that.

*BTW, a little bird tells me that MADISON GREENWOOD will be there too. Why isn't she going to support Dean at Turf Moor — especially now they're engaged? Well, who'd want to be seen in BURNLEY when there's a red carpet and paparazzi in Chester? Just because you can, Maddi, it doesn't mean you should. Try being more supportive next time.

Ellie really shouldn't be reading this, but Lucy wasn't going to suggest that Holly took her daughter's phone away. Or her iPad, or her MacBook.

Lucy was still worried about potential pictures of Madison, though. The handbag that Maddi was carrying tonight was one of Mama's designs. Gianni and Lucy's mother lived in Italy, and she supplied a lot of Lucy's designer stock. Gianni had bought one of the bags, and said that he was going to give it to Dean for him to pass on as a gift. Lucy would have loved the publicity, but if Gianni had actually given the bag himself, someone would say something on Dean's Twitter feed, and then there would be trouble.

On the table in front of the couch was a variety of snacks and treats, most still in their supermarket packages. 'Didn't you get Sonia to do the feast?' she asked Ellie.

'I wanted this to be special. We have Sonia's food all the time, but I wanted the things I really like.' She held up a DVD box. 'We'll watch this one.'

Lucy accepted the box from Ellie, checked the age rating, and put the disk into the machine. Ellie worked the remote, and Lucy slipped off her pullover and socks, then spread the duvet over the couch. As the menu came up on the screen, Lucy and Ellie snuggled up under the quilt.

'Will you put my hair into a braid?' asked Ellie. 'Now that Christmas is over, it's such a pain having it loose all the time.'

'I'll do it before you go to bed. Now pass the gummy bears,' said Lucy. 'You're nearest.'

Chapter 2

Sunday 29 and Monday 30 December

Detective Chief Inspector Tom Morton was both a respected police officer and a qualified solicitor, and had recently arrested a deputy chief constable, cracking open a multinational money laundering conspiracy in the process. He was also divorced, homeless and living with his parents in York. After the big case he had been given extended leave, so he was enjoying the rugby on television while his mother fretted and his father prepared for an emergency hearing in the morning. Even judges sometimes had to work over Christmas.

Tom's father wouldn't be Mr Justice Morton for long: he would soon be Sir Thomas, knighted for services to the law. Tom could then stop being Tom Junior — something he'd been waiting thirty-four years to happen. Why couldn't his names have been reversed? Why couldn't he have been Alexander Thomas Morton, instead of vice versa? No one would have confused him with Granddad.

The future Sir Thomas was in his study with the case papers, and the future Lady Morton was reading the details of his investiture. It was still three days until the official announcement (they didn't call it the New Year's Honours list for nothing), but Valerie Morton had been basking in reflected glory all over the holiday period.

'This is going to cause problems,' she said. His mother was sitting forward on the couch with official documents spread in front of her. They were headed with the Cabinet Office logo and various heraldic insignia. 'We can only have three guests,' she continued.

Tom knew that she had been angling to get her own MBE for charity work. If the archbishop retired soon enough, his successor would probably have to go one further: his mother was determined to finish her career as Dame Valerie.

'What's the problem? Fiona, Di and me. That makes three.'

'Unfortunately, this is your father's show, not mine. I have to count as a guest.'

Tom sat up. This could be serious: all three siblings would fight to be the one left out, so that they could play the martyr. Tom wasn't bothered either way, but he wasn't going to let Fiona or Di take the moral high ground. Then a thought struck him. 'It's got to be Gran and Granddad. They risked a lot to put Dad through law school and subsidise his pupillage — and this is the culmination.'

'You're right, of course. Don't tell Fiona or Diana yet.'

Tom subsided back to watching the rugby, and his mother cleared the papers away, then left to get some tea. Tom had made his New Year's resolution in advance this year: to get fitter. He had been working too hard even before the explosion, and the holidays had only made it worse. When he had decided where to live, he might even look for a rugby club with a dodgy fifth team that needed a veteran fly half. He heard the phone ring in the distance, and turned up the volume on the TV. Irwell Mancunia were pressing Newcastle hard, and a try was bound to come soon.

When his mother returned with the tea, she had the same troubled look she'd worn on Boxing Day, when they all realised that Granddad's chest infection wasn't clearing up properly. The sooner his grandparents left the farmhouse to Uncle Peter and moved into that bungalow, the better. Peter had been running Rooksnest Farm for years, and it was about time he lived on the job as well.

'That was Russell Lonsdale.' She sighed. 'He's heard from the Middlesex coroner: the French won't release

Kate's body until *after* the inquest into that psychopath Offlea is concluded. It could be months. Poor man.'

Tom expressed his sympathies but didn't take the conversation any further. He wasn't looking forward to meeting Kate's father. The rugby finished (Irwell did score that try), so he turned off the TV and turned to face the table.

His father joined them. Thomas senior always knew when there was a pot of tea on the go (Tom had inherited the trait). Valerie poured, and asked half-heartedly if anyone wanted cake. Tom expected her to say something about the investiture, but she looked from him to his father and said, 'Darling, is there nothing you can do to get Tom out of London? He's been so much happier since he's been up here.'

Thomas put his cup down. 'The chief constable would listen to me, I'm sure. Tom would do very well in North Riding Constabulary.' He paused. 'There's a lot to be said for going out on top.'

Alarm flashed into Valerie's eyes. 'What do you mean?'

'I couldn't possible keep sitting as a judge when my son is on the local police force. The first time he was in court, the defendant's barrister would say, "My client can't receive a fair trial when the judge has dinner with the senior officer's father." I'd quite like to step down now.'

Tom couldn't stop himself grinning. His mother looked appalled at the notion of her husband retiring, but Thomas hadn't finished yet.

'The Justice Department were in touch again before Christmas, you know. They need someone to chair that enquiry in Lancashire. The one about shale gas. Should last a couple of years.'

Valerie put her own cup down and fished out the investiture papers. 'I'm sure Tom will find something, dear. Now, how do you feel about Grandma and Granddad being your guests when we go to Buckingham Palace?'

Is this what it's like to be old? thought Dean, shuffling in his chair. The high-backed orthopaedic chair was like the one his grandfather sat in at the nursing home, except that his grandfather had better mobility. Dean had tried to sit on the couch, but it was way too low: within ten minutes the ache in his shoulder had driven him outside for a walk around the estate, until he realised how cold it was when you walk rather than run. He was tired but restless, doped up on pills but still in pain, and above all he was hungry. He went to switch on the TV: it would be kick-off time in Spain. You can't get enough football on a Sunday.

The TV was showing *Grand Designs* from the Lake District, one of Madison's favourite programmes. She loved their new house. Well, she loved the fact that it was in 7Bridge, but it wasn't very *distinguished*, according to her. She had been around the Estate with someone and discovered that there were still a few places available for new-builds. It had been her dream, ever since then, to design their own place. According to Gary White, you needed at least two million cash for the smallest plot, so that was another dream on hold. Like the wedding.

On the telly, Kevin McCloud was showing exactly why this couple had spent more on glass than his parents had ever spent on a car. The couple on screen also owned their home, which Dean definitely did not. Although he still played for Salton Town he had been signed last summer by Trafford Rangers and then loaned back to his old club for the year. If he continued to improve as a player, one day he would join John Nugent, Murray Cavendish and the others in playing with the big boys. At the moment, all he shared was an address: 7Bridge.

Their new home belonged to Trafford Rangers. The club had insisted that he move into the exclusive 7Bridge Estate when he signed for them. Gary had told him that it was the UK's biggest gated community, and had more

MARK HAYDEN

millionaires than anywhere outside London. Dean was a long way from being a millionaire, partly because Trafford Rangers deducted the rent and service charges from his salary. Gary had been forced to sit them both down and explain why they were overdrawn at the bank.

'You may be rich, Dean,' he had said, 'but you're not wealthy.'

'You what?' said Maddi. 'That doesn't make sense.'

'Look at this,' Gary had said, brandishing a printout. He called it a spreadsheet, and Madd seemed to understand what he meant. 'This is your salary on the top line,' he continued. 'And this is the deduction for your residency at 7Bridge.'

'And what's that?' Maddi had asked.

'Tax.'

'Wow? Why do we pay that much?'

'Because you have to, and because 7Bridge isn't tax-deductible. Yet. Look here: this is what's left after all fees.'

It was a big sum. Bigger each month than his father had ever earned in a year, but it didn't go far when you have expensive tastes: Maddi's tastes had become very expensive.

'Just lay off the credit cards for a month or two,' said Gary. 'It'll come right again before Christmas. Sooner, if Gianni can get you a decent endorsement or two.'

So far, things hadn't got any worse, but they weren't much better. He had been forced to get an advance to buy the engagement ring.

He flicked over to Real Sociedad vs Atletico Madrid, and had almost forgotten the pain when Maddi came home from a visit to Holly Nugent. He heard a male voice in the hall as well, and pressed the mute button on the remote.

'Guess who I met at the gate? It's Gianni. He's got some news.'

Dean had forgotten the pain, but not his hunger. It took priority over Giovanni Berardi. 'Can you ring Sonia for me? I'm famished.'

'Sorry, love, I can't. You've already had your rations.'

Dean was starving. Absolutely starving. His body still expected over 3,000 calories a day, and because of his injury, the physio had instructed Sonia to send him only 2,000 until he was back in training. If he had been at home in Stoke, with his parents, he would have raided the fridge. Having your food delivered by Hartley Executive Catering was all very well, until they said 'No'. 'Is there no breakfast cereal? I know we've got milk.'

Madison shook her head. 'You know I don't eat it. I'll get you a Diet Coke … help to fill you up.'

'What's Berardi doing here?' asked Dean. Maddi didn't answer.

Gianni Berardi was 100% Italian, from his haircut to his silk socks. His job was to negotiate the extras — sponsorship, endorsements, promotions and other stuff. So far, he had delivered his 'n' hers Range Rovers: a Sport for Dean and an Evoque for Madison. He had also got Madison that internship with the designer woman. Unpaid. Unless he delivered soon, Dean was going to complain to Gary, even if Berardi was his adopted son. Or something like that. On the other hand, Berardi had come up with that handbag from his sister's shop for Dean to give as a Christmas present. Dean would never have thought of that on his own.

Madison returned with two glasses of wine. Berardi was behind her, holding the bottle and carrying a can of Coke.

'It's brilliant news,' said Madison. 'Tell him, Gianni.'

'I have some news for you and for Madison,' said Giovanni. 'For you, Dean, I have the watches. All the Trafford Rangers players who are out on loan to other clubs get a watch from Sandero of Geneva, and a group advert. It will say, "Ready for when their time comes."'

'That's not the best bit,' chipped in Madison. 'It's going to be in every edition of *Eurotrend*. You're going to be seen all over Europe!'

'Great,' said Dean. 'How much?'

'Dean!' said Madison. 'He's done you a big favour.'

'It's my job,' said Gianni. 'It is all about money. Of course he should ask me.'

'It's not *all* about money,' said Maddi. 'It's about being associated with the right brands. Sandero of Geneva is exactly who you should be seen wearing.'

Dean wasn't sure you could wear a *who*, rather than a *what*, but if Maddi thought it was right, then she would be spot on. She always was.

'Eight thousand, plus the watch,' said Gianni. 'The watch costs twelve thousand in the shops — but is very good for tax.'

It could have been better, it could have been worse. Madison was on the edge of her seat, expecting more.

'Do you remember that Madison was in *Hello* magazine after the ball?' said Berardi.

Dean wasn't going to forget that: the magazine had only come out yesterday, and the picture was taped to the fridge. Maddi was going to put a framed copy of the page in their bedroom when Housekeeping reopened tomorrow. He nodded.

'Well, the magazine owes me a favour because I get them exclusive on the ball.'

'Didn't they have to pay?' asked Dean.

'The fee went to Holly's charity,' said Madison. 'They didn't pay much at all.'

'I have also talked to my father,' said Berardi. 'He will get permission for a big tent — a marquee? Yes, a marquee to go up on the 7Bridge Green. The magazine will pay big money to cover the wedding … Sonia will give good discount for catering … you can get married this summer. It's good, no?'

'That's brilliant!' exclaimed Madison.

This was everything Dean had wanted, but why was Berardi doing it? He tried to find a flaw. 'Will all our guests be allowed into the Estate? Family, friends, the lads from Salton Town?'

'If Gary is behind you, that's no problem.'

'Holly's already said her daughter can be bridesmaid,' said Madison.

That seemed to settle it as far as Maddi was concerned: Holly Nugent was going to be at her wedding. Dean wondered if he need turn up at all.

'And I tell you, this is provable harassment,' said Saul. He was standing in his study, looking out of the window at more snow, and rapidly losing his temper with the professional standards unit of South Lancs Constabulary.

'This has been investigated before, Mr Blackstone, and there is no case to answer.'

Saul did not give up easily. He was not going to let the situation escalate until the media were involved. 'Where do I go next? It was only a sergeant who investigated last time.'

'But his report was signed off by the deputy chief. If you're still not happy, you have two choices. If you think there is a statutory issue, you can go to the IPCC.'

'I've already been in touch with them. It could take years, and this has got to stop soon. What's my other choice? I didn't think there was one.'

'The law changes on the first of January. You can take your complaint to the Central Inspectorate of Professional Policing Standards — CIPPS. The only trouble is that they will recover costs, and they won't take the case unless you can afford it.'

'What was their name again, and where are they based?'

The voice on the line spelt out the title, and said they were based in Lambeth. Saul jotted it down and finished the call. He took the note through to the main office and looked around. His PA was off, and so was almost everyone else. Tiffany, the youngest permanent member of staff, had been forced to cover the gap between Christmas and New Year. Saul went up to her and smiled.

'See this lot here…' he said, pointing to the note. He waited until Tiffany had understood his handwriting. 'Ring them up and find out who the most senior person is who's on duty. There must be someone.'

She looked around the empty office. 'You mean you don't want to speak to the apprentice then?'

'I'm here, aren't I? I bet their boss is in too. Book me a call with them, and say that we have a job for them.'

'What about Mr Hoskins?'

'What about him?'

'I messaged you ten minutes ago. I don't know who he is, but he's waiting outside.'

'You're supposed to come and see me when we have visitors, not just message me.'

'I didn't want to disturb you in the flat.'

'Send him through.'

The living quarters at the top of the Estate Office were not generous. Saul would have called them monastic if he had been given to religious metaphors. There were some nice features: the bedroom had an emperor-sized bed, and the study had views towards the Peak District. It also had the legal status of being a domestic space: that meant that the workplace smoking ban didn't apply.

He took out a cigar and was tempted to just light it, but held on for a second until Tiffany and Hoskins appeared. 'Do you smoke?' asked Saul. Hoskins looked horrified, and shook his head. Tiffany was screwing up her face. 'Pity. Could you bring us some coffee, Tiffany?' The assistant left. 'I wasn't expecting you. It's only been four days, and two of those were the weekend. What have you come up with?'

Hoskins looked over his shoulder, and waited until the coffee had been served and the door closed. 'I've got something and nothing.'

'The Princess won't like the "nothing" part. It's getting worse.'

'I can report three things with confidence.' Hoskins drank his coffee and took out a single sheet of paper. 'First, the website is definitely being updated from 7Bridge.'

That was a relief to Saul. If it was all off site, it would need a much more shadowy figure than Neil Hoskins to crack it. He nodded, and Hoskins continued.

'Second… I'm fairly sure that two different people are involved, one of them relatively recently. The third thing is less promising: the traffic is quite well encrypted. It'll take me longer, and more entries need to be posted before I can get an answer. I will get there, but not for a while.' He hesitated.

'Go on,' said Saul. 'I won't hold you to anything, or repeat it.'

'At least some of the traffic, perhaps the bulk of it, is being routed via 7n1 — that covers this building, the Spa, the Hall and all the service buildings. Only some of it is coming from 7n2, the residents' network.'

Saul stood up and massaged his back. 'I'm going on holiday next week,' he said. 'To Florida. With my parents. Don't be frightened to call me if you get a definite lead. Nothing in writing, nothing that could be traced. Okay? If you need practical help, talk to Max.'

'Of course.'

As soon as Hoskins had left, his phone rang. 'I've got Leonie Spence, Deputy Director of CIPPS waiting in her office for you to call,' announced Tiffany. 'Shall I get her?'

'Yes, please.'

Saul lit his cigar while he waited for the connection.

Chapter 3

Monday 6 January

Back to school, back to work: the first Monday in January is no one's idea of a good day, except for those going on holiday. Tom had been off work for nearly two weeks, and finally felt ready for a new start with a new case. His office was technically in London, but he had only been there once. He had been planning to drive down on the Sunday, until his boss had sent him a text on the Friday: *See you Monday for Lunch. Tell Lady Morton to go to that deli. Loved the Quiche. Happy New Year. Leonie.*

Leonie Spence was his boss at CIPPS. That she was going to be in York was strange enough — that she would return to the Cloister for another round of sparring with his mother was stranger still. The only sensible thing to come out of the text was that she wanted to avoid his mother's cooking. Everyone tried to do that.

Tom texted back: *Don't call her Lady M. See you Monday.*

When Leonie arrived, Tom didn't rush to answer the door. He thought it would be more fun to watch his mother.

Valerie had fine control of her eyebrows: only one of them rose with interrogation when she saw Leonie. She stepped back to admit their guest, and Tom could see what the issue was. Instead of a tailored suit, his boss was dressed for the mountains: shapeless coat over a tight-fitting base layer, rumpled trousers in some water-repellent fabric and Goretex boots. Only the blue clip holding up her fringe had survived.

'Don't tell me you're dressed to do some actual police work,' said his mother. She blamed Leonie for Tom having been blown up. It was easier than blaming her son. Leonie didn't blame herself, though.

'No, Valerie, I'm on my way to Scotland. On holiday. I thought it would be nice to brief Tom on the way, rather than make him go to Lambeth.'

'Very thoughtful. Come in, come in. No need to take your boots off. They don't look dirty.'

Everything his boss was wearing looked brand new: Tom knew for a fact that Leonie's idea of the Great Outdoors was Kent.

Having made her point, Valerie was much nicer over lunch. She left them in peace over coffee, and headed out to check that the Archbishop hadn't ordered the tree to be moved too early.

'Do tell,' said Tom when they were alone. 'There must be a very, very good reason for you to buy Berghaus in the sales instead of Prada.'

She looked down. 'It's a younger woman,' she said. 'I had to agree to a walking holiday in the Cairngorms or she was going to dump me.'

Aah. That explained a lot. 'You haven't left her in the car, have you?'

'God, no. She did Hogmanay in Edinburgh while I was holding the fort in Lambeth. I'm collecting her on the way to the mountains. For the second week, we're chilling in a remote cottage. Talking of Lambeth, I've got a new case for you, up north. Saves you going back to London.'

Tom sipped his coffee. When Leonie offered something with one hand, he always looked behind her back to see what was in the other one.

'That's not all,' she continued. 'I guarantee that there will be no bombs, ex-IRA men or renegade soldiers in this case.'

Tom rubbed his arm where the skin graft was still healing, weeks after the blast that had blown him halfway across the pub car park in Blackpool. He barely noticed he was doing it any more. 'What about golf?' he said. 'I'm not touching anything with a golf course in it.'

'I doubt there'll be golf,' she said. 'Everyone in this case has too much taste.'

'What, then?'

'Have you heard of 7Bridge? — that's with the number 7.'

'No.'

'It's a very exclusive gated community for footballers and other mega-rich people. It's technically in north Cheshire, but it still falls under the jurisdiction of South Lancs Constabulary.'

'I thought you said it was up north.'

'Whatever, Tom. It's not in London or Earlsbury. Be thankful.'

'What's their problem?'

'The naughty boys in 7Bridge are at war with the traffic division. I want you to see if there's a mutually agreeable solution.'

'I'm a detective, not a diplomat. Surely there can't be any issues for us in this one?'

Leonie took the clip out of her hair, and the rogue fringe fell over her eyes. Tom had seen her use that lock of hair to flirt, to change the subject and to give herself thinking time. Today it looked like nerves, for some reason. He hoped it was the thought of winter in Scotland rather than his case.

'They're paying,' she said. 'The Estate Manager is paying for us to investigate the SLC's own professional standards report. I've told their Deputy Chief that we'll do that, but we'll also try and knock some heads together.'

Towards the end of the Operation Jigsaw case, Leonie had gone to a lot of trouble to let him attend a victim's funeral. She could be very generous, even when it cost her something. She could also be vindictive. Tom's father had once said to him, 'If you're going to fight a battle, make sure it's worth winning.' This was not that battle.

'You've talked me into it,' he said. 'But if you're going to start hiring me out like this, you need to include all the costs — I want a DC attached as support. I couldn't have cracked the Jigsaw case without Kris Hayes' local knowledge, and I need the same here.'

'All right, all right… I'll get you a DC. It might be a man this time, though. I can't keep providing you with pretty young things.'

'Not now you've got one of your own, you mean.'

She gave him a warning look, and stood up. 'I need to shift if I'm going to get to Edinburgh. The files are in the car.' As they walked out, she continued. 'The Estate Manager is on holiday. You can start with their head of security, and with the SLC traffic people. I'm going to be out of contact: there's no phone signal or Wi-Fi in the mountains or the cottage.'

'I'll try not to get blown up until you're back in circulation.'

When she had handed over the files, she looked at the overcast sky. 'Is your mother really religious?'

Where did that come from? 'Yes. She's deeply involved in cloister politics, but that's built on a foundation of faith. My sisters are the same, though only one of them is a Christian.'

'Well, ask Valerie to pray for me while I'm in the Cairngorms. I might need it.'

Also back at work on Monday was DC Elaine Fraser, but she was starting a new job completely.

Warrington is famous for many things, one of them being a complete accident: it's halfway between Liverpool and Manchester. For this reason, the South Lancs Constabulary (SLC) had built its headquarters opposite IKEA on the Gemini Retail Park; it was one of many gestures to prove that the force could serve both cities equally. After being kept in reception for an hour by his assistant, Elaine reported to ACC Nick Schofield's office.

She had never been inside a command officer's den before, and was vaguely disappointed with Schofield's: it looked just like any big office she had seen on TV. He was reading her transfer request as if it had landed on his desk that morning and not five months ago. At least he waved her to a seat instead of making her stand to attention in front of him. She toyed, just for a second, with the idea of sitting at one of the two easy chairs near the window, but resisted. The force may have approved her transfer application, but that didn't guarantee her a posting in CID.

He put down the folder and looked at her. From her treatment so far, she had been expecting hostility. Maybe he didn't like successful women. Maybe he didn't like her being so young (she was the youngest detective constable in Leicester for a decade). Maybe he was gay. Instead of anger, what she got was irritation. Waves of irritation and tetchiness emanated from the Assistant Chief Constable, like a Dalek who's been foiled by the Doctor.

'There's no point in calling this an interview,' he began, 'because I've got no choice but to accept you. This stinks.'

She had already bitten her lip metaphorically. Now she did so for real.

'The sooner they abolish these bloody police and crime commissioners, the better for everyone. If they'd given us that man's salary, and the cost of his office – and the cost of the election that no one voted in – I could have had another ten detectives.'

The commissioner for SLC was on the board of Irwell Mancunia rugby club. When the club offered Elaine's husband a five-year contract, he'd only agreed because they promised to smooth Elaine's transfer from Leicester. She had thought there might be a comment or two, but she hadn't expected this.

She cleared her throat. 'I'd be willing to transfer to a suitable uniformed division, if it would help, sir.'

'Hah! That would be even worse. Do you know how many front-line officers I've had to lose since these cuts came in?' Elaine treated the question as rhetorical. 'If I allowed you to transfer into uniform, I'd have the Federation on my case before you could say *ring-fenced position*. The only wiggle-room I've got is for specialist officers. The trouble is… your only specialism seems to be violence.'

'Sir! That's—'

'…true. Unfortunately. You have one complaint on your record for use of excessive force, and one chief constable's commendation for bravery.'

'The complaint was dismissed, sir.'

'I know. To be honest, I've got three myself.' He threw himself back in his chair. 'I'm not saying you won't be a valuable addition, but I could do without having to squeeze you in right now.'

'Sorry, sir.'

'At least you're from Lancashire. I dread to think what they'd make of a Cockney. OK, leave it with me, and I'll find something for you. Go and see HR on the way out, and get them to sort out your warrant card, et cetera.'

'Thank you, sir,' said Elaine, rising as she spoke. The last word was delivered to Schofield's lightly gelled hair. As he bent down to scrawl on her folder, she could make out the grey roots.

Trafford Rangers wanted to protect their investment, so Dean had been summoned to their training ground for tests and treatment. Salton Town were a progressive club with a good academy, but they weren't in the same league as Rangers, in all senses of the word. It was Dean's first visit since his medical last summer, and it was a bit like going to hospital: he had to sit in the waiting room with assorted reserves and youth team players.

They told him that he was making good progress. The senior physiotherapist said that he would email a recovery plan to Salton. 'We need to keep up your core strength and cardio fitness,' he said. 'But we'll need to incorporate balancing measures too.'

'Oh,' said Dean.

Madison had driven him to the Trafford complex, and she was going to be ferrying him to Salton until he was fit to drive on his own. While he was being prodded and stretched, she had spent the time emailing people about what date they should have the wedding. It was going to have to be fitted in between the end of the season and the start of the European Championships, and Salton Town might be going on tour to Germany.

'Try and talk to Gus,' she said. 'He might know.'

Dean snorted as they headed for the M6. 'Gus is the last one to know about things like that. I doubt that the chief executive will rearrange the tour to fit into your wedding plans.'

'*Our* wedding plans. Don't you want Travis to be your best man?'

'Sorry, babe, I just want to get back in action. This is killing me.'

She continued to tell him about Anthea helping with the design of the marquee interior, and other details, until they arrived at Salton.

'I'm going to source some sample fabric for Lucy's shop,' said Madison. 'But I'll be back to pick you up.'

He gave her an awkward kiss across the gear lever, and climbed out.

Inside the treatment room, the physio was reading the email from her counterpart at Trafford Rangers. When she'd finished, Dean discovered what "balancing measures" really meant.

He was going to be doing his work in a straitjacket.

'Nice view from here,' said Rob Fraser.

'Mmm,' said Elaine.

'You're not looking.'

'Oh, yes, I am.'

Elaine and Rob were standing at the bottom of a rock face. Rob had been looking out over the dale towards the distant fells of the Lake District: Elaine had been looking *up* the rock, towards the Lycra-clad buttocks of the Irwell Mancunia rugby team. Seen one mountain, seen them all, but she didn't often get a good look at so many fit arses struggling upwards. Rob realised what she was looking, at and gave her a playful slap on the backside.

'Oi, you,' he said. 'You're here to work.'

'I am working,' she said, then cupped her hands round her mouth to shout. 'Johnson! Take the route to the left.'

The Premiership rugby season was on hold for a month while the Six Nations took place, and, with no game to prepare for, the head coach had decided that a round of adventure activities was in order. Elaine was in limbo, waiting for SLC to find her a job, so she had arranged some rock climbing. Her friend from the ULIST climbing club was at the top of the rock: she was assisting at the bottom.

Rob was guarding the mobile phones in case one of the national coaches rang. Eight of the Irwell players were in with an outside chance of an international call-up, including Rob. He had played for Scotland last year, but his only start had been in a heavy defeat to Wales. Elaine desperately wanted him to be selected, but she didn't want him to disappear for weeks when they were starting a new life in Lancashire.

A ringtone sounded. He glanced at the phones laid out on the grass and frowned. None of them were lit up, then they both realised: it was hers. 'Where's your phone?' he asked.

'In that bag.'

He scampered to retrieve it, and took the call before it went to voicemail.

'Hello?' He frowned, then held out the phone. 'For you,' he said. 'Work, I think.'

She took the phone and identified herself.

'This is ACC Schofield's assistant. Please hold.'

Elaine pressed her lips together and said nothing. Ten seconds later, Schofield came on the line.

'Morning, DC Fraser. Sounds like you're outside.'

'Yes, sir, I am.'

'Can you talk?'

Elaine looked up at the climbers. 'Yes, but I may have to break off.'

'I won't keep you, then. Can you report to Detective Chief Inspector Morton at two o'clock tomorrow afternoon? Thanks. I'll put you back to my PA.'

The line went dead while Elaine's mouth was forming the first of many questions. Schofield's assistant came on the line. 'DCI Morton will be in an office at Lyme Court Buildings. It's by the Macclesfield Canal, just north of the town. You should find it easily enough.'

'Macclesfield?' Elaine had never been, but she was sure it wasn't in Lancashire.

'Yes. Take the M56. DCI Morton will explain everything.'

The call disconnected, and Elaine's mouth was still open when the screen went dark.

'What's up, hen?' said Rob.

'I don't know.' She stared at the phone. 'But I think I might have been given a transfer before I've even started.'

The bag was packed and standing by the door. The taxi was ordered, but Lucy had an hour to kill, which was why she let Madison Greenwood into the shop. The younger woman had called last night to say that she had some

48

thoughts — and did Lucy have the time to give them the once-over?

Madison unpacked her portfolio while Lucy made the coffee.

'Do you mind if I ask a daft question?' asked Maddi.

'Only if you don't mind a daft answer.'

'I wondered what your name was. It's just that Gianni always calls you Lucia, but I was talking to Dean yesterday, and he called you Lucy. I don't want to offend you or anything.'

'You don't speak Italian, do you?' said Lucy, bringing in the coffees.

Maddi shook her head. 'I thought about learning, in case Dean gets transferred to Italy one day.'

'You know that Gianni and I have the same mother but different fathers? Mama insisted that because I was born in Italy, I should be registered as Lucia, but Dad's always called me Lucy. Mama said that Italian teachers couldn't cope with English spellings. She was right. So… I've always been Lucy in English, and Lucia in Italian.'

Madison blew on her coffee. 'Do you think in Italian or English?'

That wasn't a question she expected from a WAG. Many people had asked it over the years, but Madison was the first resident of 7Bridge to express such curiosity. 'At the moment, English, but by tonight I think I'll be half-and-half, once I get to Mama's house.'

Lucy looked at her watch, and Madison got the message. There were several sheets of A3 paper on the coffee table, all face down. Madison put her coffee out of the way and said, 'I know you're not planning any changes at the moment.'

'You mean I can't afford them.'

Madison blushed a little.

'Sorry,' said Lucy. 'I didn't mean it to come out as a whinge. Go on. I'm interested.'

'I was just going to say that … if you could go back to when you fitted out the shop, what would you do differently?'

'That's a good question. I don't know. A bit less silk, maybe?'

'What sort of look were you going for?'

'The sort of look that would appeal to my target market.'

Madison was nodding in agreement. 'Who do you see as your market?'

Lucy took a sip of coffee. 'People who come to Sevenbridge Village expecting to find it full of boutiques and famous people.'

'Like I want to be? Is that what you're saying?'

It was Lucy's turn to blush. 'I knew from talking to Holly that none of the 7Bridge talent ever comes into the Village, but I knew that lots of other people do. That's my market.'

'Talent? Is that what you call us? What they call us?'

'This is going to sound really insulting, Maddi, but it's true. People on the fringes of 7Bridge, people like me — we call the wage earners *the talent*. You – and Holly – wouldn't be there if it weren't for Dean and John. My stepmother wouldn't be there if it weren't for Dad, come to that.'

'Harsh, but fair.' Madison looked around the room, as if seeing it anew. 'I think I'm going back to the drawing board,' she said. 'I don't think this would cut the mustard.'

Madison turned over one of the pages and revealed a perspective drawing of the back wall. The mirror was still there, but around it she'd sketched a completely new look, and pasted on some pictures of new furniture. The theme was very contemporary, with pale woods and black detailing.

'That's…lovely,' said Lucy. 'It's very close to the design I rejected two years ago. You've got talent, Maddi.'

'I may have talent, but I'm not *actually* talent. Is that what you're saying?'

'Oh God, I sound like a right moody cow.' Lucy threw her arms up. 'It's just the way it is, that's all. I really want to see what you've done, Maddi. Honest.'

Madison shuffled the papers together and put them away. She took out an iPad and unlocked it. She hesitated for a second. 'This really hurts, you know,' she said, offering the tablet to Lucy.

On the screen was *SeenIn7Bridge*. Lucy hadn't checked it for a few days, and she looked at one of the entries:

Another little hobby for MADISON GREENWOOD. She has started carrying ANTHEA GODFREY's bags for her. We know all about Anthea's designs: the ex-hippie who embraced Scandi-chic. But what will Maddi do to poor ex-SoDoF, LUCY WHITE? We love the tart's boudoir look in her cute little shop. Don't spoil it, Maddi.

'Bitch,' said Lucy. She shifted in her seat, and had to resist the urge to chuck the iPad across the room. With a deep breath, she handed it back.

Madison put the iPad away. 'What's a "SoDoF"?' she asked.

'It's the Mother Superior's word for Sons and Daughters of the Famous.'

Maddi sat still. Unused to the silence, Lucy looked at her, and she met Lucy's gaze. 'Who is it?' said Maddi. 'Who is this woman?'

'I don't know. I wish I did. We thought it was Robyn at first, because that's just the sort of thing my wicked stepmother would do. But it isn't: Gianni and I hacked into her laptop, and she's not bright enough to have hidden her tracks that well.'

'She's getting worse,' said Madison. 'If she carries on like this, she'll push someone over the edge.'

A car horn sounded from outside: the taxi was here, and Lucy was off to Milan. It turned out that Dean had given the bag to Maddi himself, and the publicity had led to a sudden rush of sales. As well as seeing her mother, Lucy was going to restock her shop.

Elaine was always thankful for small mercies: Lyme Court Buildings were easy to find, but they were very much in Cheshire. She should have contacted ACC Schofield again, to find out what was going on. Rob said that she'd bottled it, but she'd responded that she couldn't afford to antagonise a command officer any further.

What was going on? There was no DCI Morton in SLC, or anywhere, according to Google. She had found a Detective Sergeant Morton working for the City Police a while ago, but that couldn't be him: no one goes from DS to DCI in a year, disappearing without trace in the process. Rob had quoted Sherlock Holmes to her: "When you have excluded the impossible, whatever remains, however improbable, must be the truth." In that case, it was impossible for a DS from Economic Crimes to appear in Cheshire, and it was impossible for a command officer to play a practical joke (no sense of humour). Therefore, the utterly improbable explanation was that she was being dumped into a special mission for SO15 — the Counter Terrorism Command.

Lyme Court was pleasant enough on the outside. Anywhere with a car park always scored highly in Elaine's opinion, and they had even gritted the approach road. She paused outside the foyer and another piece clicked into place: the whole building was given over to short-term office rentals. Perfect for a discreet operation.

'I've got an appointment with Mr Morton,' she told the receptionist, who was actually a security guard. Another sign. Elaine had deliberately left out Morton's rank.

'First floor, up the stairs. Suite 12.'

Next to the desk was a board with a list of all the office spaces. Some had slide-in labels identifying the tenants: a mix of Hi-Tech startups and a national chain of solicitors. There was no listing for Suite 12, nor, when she climbed the stairs, was there anything outside the door. There was a glass panel which she peered through, and saw an empty office with a clear desk. Elaine gave the door a knock and tried the handle. It opened.

'Hello?' she said.

'Is that DC Frazer?' came a man's voice from her left. She went inside and saw a further office, from which her new boss was approaching, his hand extended and a smile on his face.

They shook hands, and he offered her one of two visitors' chairs in front of his desk. At least this part of the suite looked occupied, with an open laptop and papers strewn about. Without asking, he started to pour tea from a very dodgy-looking brown teapot.

'Sugar?'

'No thanks, sir. Just milk.'

She took a good look at him for the first time. He was about average height, had light brown hair in a sort of public school quiff and he was wearing a very decent-looking blue pinstripe suit. His shoes looked handmade, though he'd obviously walked through some snow since they were last polished. His age was more difficult to tell, but she had a horrible suspicion that he wasn't a DCI at all. If ever a man looked like a DS from Economic Crimes, it was this man Morton. *Bloody hell*, she thought. *Please don't let me be sent to fraud. I hate fraud.*

He turned round and gave her another smile, setting down the mugs and taking a seat behind the desk.

'Okay then, DC Frazer. Who have you upset?'

'I... err...' Elaine took a deep breath. 'Are you Detective Chief Inspector Morton? Sir.'

His mouth twitched at the corner. 'Also known as Tom.'

It was him, from the City Police.

Morton took a sip from his tea and said, 'My last DC upset the apple cart, and got sent to me as a punishment. I was just wondering why you were here.'

'But I haven't upset anyone. This is my first day.'

'First day as what? A detective?'

'First day with South Lancs. I've just transferred from Leicester. To be honest, sir, I have no idea what I'm doing here at all.'

'Aah. That explains a lot.' He stood up again and went to shake hands again. Ingrained politeness, and the fact that he was her boss, meant that Elaine found herself on her feet without knowing why. 'Welcome to CIPPS,' he said. 'I hope you enjoy your time with professional standards.'

Oh shit, was Elaine's first thought. She could feel her smile freezing into a grimace. She had forgotten that there were worse things than fraud, but only because the thought was too painful. If it got about in SLC that she was in professional standards, it would be next to impossible to find another posting.

'I can see you're thrilled,' said Morton.

'Sorry, sir. It's come as a bit of a shock.'

He folded his hands, and the look of amusement vanished off his face. 'You've got two choices, Frazer. You didn't volunteer for this, and I don't want a conscript who resents being here. I can send you back to Warrington right now – no harm, no foul – if that's what you want, or you can stay. If you stay, then I expect one hundred per cent commitment.'

Elaine blew out her cheeks. She was very tempted to get back into the car and disappear up the M56. It's what Rob would do: *Never settle for less than what you want* was one of his mottoes, and he'd said it on their first date. Morton was waiting, his hands flat on the desk, and it was the thought of ACC Schofield's assistant that made up her mind: she was more scared of going back to Warrington and explaining herself than she was of staying here. She took a deep breath and picked up her mug. 'What's this job all about, then?'

Morton closed his eyes, and seemed very relieved. He picked up his own mug and sat back in his chair. 'Before we get on to that, tell me what you're bringing to the party.'

'What do you mean?'

He picked up a Post-It note and passed it over. 'This is all I know about you.' The note said: *DC Frazer will be with you two o'clock Thursday.*

Elaine ventured a smile. 'In that case, I'll be going. Mistaken identity.' Morton frowned. 'My name is Fraser. With an "s". Elaine, if you like.'

Morton screwed up the note and dropped it in the bin. 'That's a start. Tell me more. Graduate?'

'Yes. Degree in geology from ULIST in Cairndale.' A small shadow passed over Morton's face. Most people hadn't even *heard* of Cairndale: whatever had happened there must have been bad. She pressed swiftly on. 'I joined Leicestershire Constabulary because my fiancé got a job down there, and I've transferred up to SLC because he's transferred too. But I'm a serious copper, sir. That's why they accepted me into CID.'

He nodded thoughtfully. 'I guessed as much... not that I'm allowed to ask your age.'

'I'm twenty-five. If we're still working together in March, I'll give you fair warning of my birthday so that you can get me a present. Rob might forget.'

'Rob Fraser? As in Irwell Mancunia and Scotland?'

Things were starting to look up — Morton was a rugby fan *and* he made a decent cup of tea. 'He got the call-up yesterday. He reports to the international squad on Sunday.'

Morton nodded his approval and said, 'I was a qualified solicitor before I joined the Met. After two years I moved to Economic Crimes and climbed up to the dizzy heights of DS. I joined CIPPS partly because they offered me an inspector's rank. Have you got any special strengths?'

'According to ACC Schofield, I'm good in a fight.'

'That's reassuring: you never know when a disgruntled inspector is going to give you a black eye. Well, if you're married to a professional sportsman, you should be right at home on this case: we're going to 7Bridge.'

Elaine spluttered into her tea. 'He's a rugby player! He doesn't earn that sort of money!'

Morton raised his eyebrows.

She had thought things were looking better until he mentioned money. Okay, technically it had been her. She hated people thinking about Rob's salary instead of what she could offer. On the other hand, it looked like Morton valued openness. 'He's on £250,000 this year. He might get another £100k if he makes the final Scotland squad.'

'Only six times my salary, then.' He smiled at her. 'I won't mention it again if you don't… down to business. Did you say your husband was off on Sunday?' She nodded. 'I'm going to Earlsbury tomorrow on an old case, so you take a long weekend. Just make sure you read all the files today, tomorrow and Monday, and I'll see you here first thing on Tuesday morning. I'll be travelling down from York on Monday.'

'Is that another old case? In York, I mean.'

'No. I'm living with my parents in York at the moment. I did live in Surrey, but I got divorced last year. I was ill before Christmas, and I went home to recuperate. Then it was the holidays, and then Leonie Spence assigned me this case. I think she might try to keep me away from Lambeth for a while longer.'

'Don't you get on?'

'Like some married couples, we get on fine when we're apart. I was brought into CIPPS by an old mate called Sam Cohen — and by keeping me away from London, Leonie limits his influence. Not just that, she has plans for CIPPS to be a truly national organisation. I think that I'm being groomed to lead her northern hit squad.'

Elaine laughed. 'A one-man rapid reaction force?'

'One man and one woman. If you're not careful, you might find Leonie offering you a job.'

'That's not funny, sir.'

'It is from where I'm standing. When I make a joke, you can call me Tom.'

'When you make a joke, I will.'

Then he handed her some files. Pinned to the top was a list of things for her to look up. It was the perfect end to a bad day: she was now working for a fraud detective, in professional standards, and he wanted her to memorise Section 172 of the Road Traffic Act 1988. And that was only the start.

Chapter 4

Tuesday 14 January

The weather had certainly changed overnight. Dean looked out on to curtains of rain demolishing the last of the snowman he had made on Christmas morning — that was nearly three weeks ago, when he still had a working shoulder. Since then, he had rested for two weeks, suffered a week with Helga and only yesterday had he been re-admitted to the first team squad for light training. He also had to do a run every day, but he was getting better slowly. Behind him the microwave pinged, and he took out his porridge. He was still waiting for it to cool when Madison came in, half dressed and looking at her phone.

'Urrgh. There's no chicken in that, is there?'

He just stared. It was too early in the morning for a discussion on why there was no animal protein in his oats.

'Check out the Mother Superior,' she said, by way of explanation. 'She's gone too far this time. When Princess Karida hears about this, she'll order Max to tear the Estate apart until he's found out who's behind it.'

Maddi wandered out, and Dean switched from the *Daily Mirror* website to *SeenIn7Bridge*. There were four new entries this morning.

*If you're about to enjoy one of SONIA HARTLEY's cooked breakfasts, you might want to pause a moment. The butcher who supplies Hartley Executive Catering has been busted by trading standards. It seems that not everything in those sausages is pork, and very little of the breast makes its way into her chicken burgers. You don't want to know where the chewy bits come from.

We all know about PRINCESS KARIDA's ban on all men in the Hall and the 7Bridge Spa - so who cleans the pool? In these days of equality, women plumbers and electricians are easy enough to locate, but there's something about being a pool guy that makes it VERY unattractive to us ladies. I hear that security only discovered the engineer was in drag when MAX NOLAN (chief thug) asked him/her on a date. No one has told the Princess yet that a man with a cheap wig has been hanging around the changing rooms.

Is there a pile of fluff in your house (apart from your useless husband)? That might be because the Border Force has been in action. A whole van load of NATASHA THOMPSON's cleaners were made to produce their documents, and some of them were led away. If you've got a dust-accumulation issue, that may be because Natasha's short handed. Rumour has it that two of the mop-wielding illegals are actually doctors from Africa. Instead of deporting them, perhaps they could be trained up as pool technicians.

Dean looked down at his congealing porridge. Madison would have tipped it in the bin, but not Dean. He stirred in a little milk, then starting eating. Far too good to waste.

He put the bowl in the dishwasher and shouted to Madison, who shocked him by appearing from another door. He still hadn't got used to the house having a passage for servants. She was buttoning up a blouse, and he realised that the necklace disappearing under the buttons wasn't one that he had bought. Where had that come from? He'd ask her later.

'I'd better get going, babe. What are you up to today?'

She frowned, still looking at her phone. 'I've been trying to get hold of Lucy, but she's not answering her phone or returning my texts. I'll keep trying this morning, then I'll go to Anthea's place this afternoon.'

'Do you think that stuff about the tranny in the pool is true?'

Madison looked up at him. She seemed far more troubled than she should be. He put his hands on her shoulders and said, 'Look, babe, you've got to ignore it, okay? People say stuff about me all the time, yeah? Just ignore it.'

'Yeah. You're right. Go on… you'll be late.'

She gave him a peck on the cheek, and headed back towards the dining room, which she had commandeered as a design studio. He felt his pockets. Damn. No money. He saw her bag on the stairs in the hallway and looked in her purse. He took a twenty pound note, just in case… and when he pulled it out, a black credit card fell on the floor.

That was new. How had she got that? According to Maddi, they were maxed out on all their cards and could only use debit cards until February. He looked at the front: it was in the name of G Berardi.

Dean looked at the dining room door. This needed some serious discussion — but he had never been fined for turning up late at training, and he wasn't going to start now, not when he was trying to get back his place in the first team. He put the credit card back in her purse and dashed off into the rain.

Half way to the M6, the hands-free phone burbled to notify him of an incoming call. The screen on the dashboard read *STFC*. It was the club calling.

'Hello, Dean?'

'Yes.'

'This is Gus's assistant. North West Tonight want to do an interview this morning, so he's moved training to the afternoon. I rang you first because I know you leave earlier than the others.'

'Thanks. I'll turn around and go home.'

'Gus has a message for you. He said you have to do your run this morning, and he said, "Tell Dean… no slacking." Sorry.'

'You're all right. I'll go and get it over with now.'

He disconnected, and did a U-turn at the next roundabout. He used the residents' entrance to get into 7Bridge and, on an impulse, he pulled into a space just over the bridge. This way, he could get straight on to the running track without having to see Maddi, and the last half of the circuit would be downhill. Then he could drive home. Neat. Then he could ask Madison what the credit card and the necklace were all about.

This was 7Bridge, so he just left the keys in the ignition. He carefully stretched his shoulder, his quads, his hamstrings, and he rotated his spine. The rain was already running into his eyes. He jogged on the spot for a few seconds, set the timer on his watch and kicked off into the downpour.

Tom could have afforded a bigger office in Lyme Court, but he had decided that the view from Suite 12 was more important than the space on offer in Suite 23. Besides, he could then spend the difference on a better hotel. He did feel ever so slightly guilty about using the 7Bridge money this way, but not so guilty that he was going to give up the vista of snow-laden fields and clouds of steam from the barges as they made their way north. That, however, was last week. It was raining so much this morning that all the snow would soon be gone.

He hadn't seen or spoken to Elaine Fraser since Thursday afternoon, but she seemed both keen and efficient so far, and he had the tea steeping in the pot when she walked through the door at half past eight.

'Put your stuff on the desk out there,' he said when she breezed in. She started to unpack a rucksack, and he took another look at her. On Thursday, she had worn a grey suit and white blouse which were so new he could almost see the holes where she'd removed the tags. Today she had a completely different look, from toe to top.

On her feet were a pair of serious Doc Marten boots. Not the slip-ons, but proper lace-ups. He hoped that they didn't visit any houses requiring footwear removal. Elaine was very thin, but in a sporty kind of way. She wore a pair of jeans that were tucked into the boots, and under the bright red Helly Hansen waterproof she was wearing a green Leicester Tigers fleece over a black roll-neck pullover. Her long, dark brown hair was pulled back in a ponytail.

After she had unpacked, he waved her into his part of the suite and gave her a mug of tea. She looked at it suspiciously. 'I thought inspectors never made the tea because they were too busy,' she said. 'Oh, yes… Good morning, sir.'

'It's part of my strategy. I always make the DC two cups of tea. Gets them hooked, and avoids accusations of exploitation. I'll brief you on tea-making later, but for now we need to actually start some police work.'

'Ready when you are, sir.'

'I've arranged a meeting between representatives of the two sides: the senior Traffic sergeant is coming to represent South Lancs Constabulary. On the phone I got the impression that he has better uses for his officers' time, and that he wants this sorted. The 7Bridge Collective are sending their director and company secretary.'

Elaine looked at her notebook. 'As far as I can see, the 7Bridge lot are within their rights. So long as the law stays the same, they can carry on doing this forever, so what's your plan for them?'

An excellent question: she's thinking strategically, thought Tom.

'It's an arms race,' he said. 'When the Traffic patrol car tried to enter the Estate, 7Bridge Security stopped him – quite legitimately – because no one was suspected of a proper criminal offence. We can't access the Estate without a warrant.'

'Which we won't get.'

'Not directly. We're not the United Nations here, we don't have to rely on diplomacy alone. We're more like NATO: we can use our big guns if we want.'

'Have we got any?'

'I sent the 7Bridge director a message. He's a lawyer, and I told him to look up R v Chris Huhne & Vicky Pryce.'

'Oh. I see. Going for the nuclear option then, sir?'

'It's a deterrent. Come on, let's go.'

They met on neutral ground, in the Sevenbridge Village café. Tom and Elaine were first there, having allowed extra time because of the rain. Although the lights were on, the door was locked. The owner heard it rattle and dashed over to unlock it.

'Ooh… come in, love. You must be soaked.'

'Thanks. I'll try not to drip on your nice clean floor.'

'Are you with Paul?' asked the owner.

'I'm meeting Mr Warren from White-Berardi.'

'That's him. I've got the table at the back for you. Tea or coffee?'

'Tea, please, for both of us. My colleague is just parking.'

'Coming up.'

The owner disappeared, and Tom hung up his dripping overcoat. Elaine came in and did the same. The bell chimed, and a tall man with a leftover Movember moustache took a pace inside before shaking out his umbrella. Tom hoped the facial hair was a leftover, because it did nothing for the man otherwise.

'DCI Morton?'

'You must be Paul Warren.'

The handshake was civilised on both sides, and Warren shouted for a pot of coffee before leaning in and whispering, 'Their pastries are to die for, but hell on the waistline.'

'I'll be careful. This is DC Fraser.'

Warren greeted Elaine, and said, 'The company secretary will be here in a second. You wouldn't think she lives two doors down.'

Elaine spoke up. 'In that nice-looking boutique? The House of Lucia?'

'That's her. She lives over the shop. What time is Sergeant Marsh due?'

'I thought we'd have a chat first. He's coming in half an hour or so.'

As they sat down, Elaine pulled out a radio and said, 'I've had SLC control on the phone. Technically, we're in South Lancs territory here, and I either have to leave the radio switched on or hand it back. It's keyed to me, so they won't bother us.'

'Fine.'

The final person appeared — not through the front door, but out of the kitchen. She was quite young: probably too young to be the owner of the boutique. She was quite short too, certainly shorter than Elaine, and she had a curvy figure. Not fat, but definitely a woman. Her very dark hair, just on shoulder length, was naturally curly and glistened with moisture, matching her dark eyes. She was wearing a tunic dress, pulled in with a belt to emphasise her waist. She must prioritise comfort, he thought, because most women of her height would wear boots with heels, rather than damp ballet flats. She must have run out of her digs without a coat or an umbrella.

The owner placed a large cafetière of coffee and a very enticing plate of croissants on the table, then left them to it.

He was on his second circuit of the running track, and he was making good time despite the rain. Dean had just crossed over the central road, and was now climbing up the gentle slope away from the river. Madison loved this part of the Estate, because the oldest and biggest houses were here, and they had the best views. Water was splashing up every time his feet hit the ground: he kept his head down to focus on his rhythm. Football pitches don't slope, and this was getting steeper.

He nearly slammed into a figure coming down the hill. The other man was using an umbrella, and Dean had to swerve on to the grass, where he slipped in the mud and landed on his back.

'Oi! Watch out,' he said.

'You watch out,' said the other man. The way he stretched the "out" gave away his identity. It was Giovanni Berardi.

Dean rolled on to his side and got carefully back on to the running track. Berardi was about to walk away, but Dean said, 'Here, hang on.'

'What's the matter, Dean?'

'I think Maddi's got something of yours.'

Berardi laughed. 'What's that?'

Something about his laugh made Dean clench his fists. 'Why has she got a credit card with your name on it?'

'She must have picked it up by mistake in a shop. She tried to use her own, but it was declined. You are not paying your bills, Dean. I had to pay, but it was nothing. You don't need to pay me back.'

Berardi was still sheltering under the umbrella. He was wearing a smart winter jacket and hadn't even got his shoes properly wet. Dean could feel the water running down his nylon sleeves, and it had soaked into his neck half a kilometre back. With the bobble hat, he knew he must look ridiculous, and that only made him angrier.

'What were you doing shopping together?'

Berardi made a circling gesture with his hand. 'I was showing her some of the shops for her business. She bought some material with a special pattern: it's called *il cornuto* in Italy.'

It was also what Rich Menghini called the referee. Dean knew exactly what it meant. He stepped forward and knocked the umbrella out of Berardi's hand. 'What the fuck are you saying?'

'Hey! Back off.'

Dean advanced another step. Berardi retreated. 'Have you been shagging my fiancée?' He pushed Berardi in the chest.

'*Vaffanculo*,' said Berardi, and he made the sign of the horns. 'You can have her back now.'

Dean went to kick him in the balls, but Berardi twisted away. Dean swung a punch at his smug Italian face, but Berardi was expecting it, and he let Dean connect, because he was making a grab for Dean's left arm. Berardi pulled down and twisted.

Dean would have ridden with it, but the running track was too grippy. His feet stuck to the rubber and his body weight resisted against the arm. Berardi pulled again and Dean felt something pop out of his bad shoulder.

He dropped to his knees in pain, and couldn't move his left arm. Tears joined the rainwater in his eyes, and he didn't see Berardi's fist coming towards him until it was too late. The knuckles smashed into his nose and he heard the crunch. Berardi took a step towards him, but this time it was Dean's turn to lean in.

He was much taller than the Italian, and his head was above the other's groin. Dean opened his mouth and bit into Berardi's crotch.

The other man screamed, staggered back and tripped over, hitting his head on the rubber surface. Holding his left shoulder with his right hand, Dean levered himself upright and kicked his opponent, hard. Berardi rolled to his side, and Dean kicked him in the stomach. As a fight, it was over. The Italian curled into a ball.

There was still punishment to come, though. Dean placed a few more kicks into Berardi's back and head, then he stamped hard on his ankle. The pain made Berardi try to get up and crawl away. Dean gave him a final kick to propel him off the track and into a melting snowbank.

Dean had never seen a dislocated shoulder, but that's what he had. It was the only explanation for the pain. He probably had a broken nose too. The car. His phone was in the car. He could call an ambulance. Or he could cut through the Estate and get Madison to call one. At this point on the track, it was a lot nearer.

He tried to jog, but every time he put his left foot down, the pain shot through him. He hobbled, dripping blood from his nose, through a gap between two houses and on to the central road. Another hundred metres and he was at his gate. He punched in the code, his fingers shaking and slipping on the buttons, and he staggered down the drive. The dining room window was nearest, so he just banged on the glass. He could hear Madison scream through the double glazing.

She ran out with no shoes on, then helped him into the hall. He saw the stairs and collapsed on to the third step.

'Call an ambulance, Maddi. I've dislocated my shoulder.'

'What's happened?'

'Just call an ambulance, all right?'

'Tell me what's happened, Dean.'

'I've just met your boyfriend.'

Her hand flew to her mouth. 'What have you done? Is he okay?'

'Never mind him. Are you going to call me an ambulance?' The pain overwhelmed him for a second when he shivered with cold. He screamed.

Madison ran into the dining room and came back with her phone. She held it towards him, but just out of reach. 'Where is he?'

Dean tried to grab the phone, but she snatched it away.

'Where is he, Dean?'

'He's on the running track.' Dean didn't want Madison to find Berardi too quickly, so he lied. 'He's down by the river, near John and Holly's place.'

She threw the phone at him, and ran through into the kitchen. There was a pause, then the back door opened and slammed shut. Dean dialled 999, and asked for an ambulance. When he'd finished, he looked at Madison's contacts. There was one that he didn't recognise: TIS. Looking at the messages, it seemed that TIS stood for The Italian Stallion. His shoulder spasmed, and he threw up his porridge on to the tiles.

While Paul was pouring their coffee, Lucy studied the two police officers across the café table. The woman was about her age — but already had lines around her eyes, and very dry skin. Pulling her hair back like that didn't do her any favours, though it went with the outdoor-living look. Her boss was older, and quite well dressed for a policeman — in an agricultural sort of way. He was fiddling with the teapot, and then he looked straight up at her. He had very sad eyes, but they seemed to twinkle when he spoke.

'And how do you fit into things, Miss White?'

'I organise things for the Collective, that's all. It's only a part-time job.'

DCI Morton looked at some papers. 'Last month, police stopped a Giovanni Berardi, who you stated was your brother. Your name is White, and Mr Warren here works for White-Berardi Sports Management.'

Paul was about to get huffy, but Lucy stopped him. 'It's not that unusual: my dad is Gary White. He adopted Gianni when he married our mother, Paola Berardi. She lives in Italy now, and Dad has a new family.' She turned to Paul. 'He could find out all that in ten minutes on Facebook.'

'I'm sure he could, but the fact that DCI Morton is being paid by the Estate is nowhere on social media. Yet.'

This didn't seem to faze Morton at all. Maybe that heavyweight suit had sewn-in armour plating. 'Do you know what Saul Blackstone has paid for?' he asked. Paul shrugged, unwilling to commit himself. 'He's paid for a review of the SLC professional standards enquiry. I could do that without talking to you, or to the Traffic officers – and I'd probably rubber stamp it – but we at CIPPS like to offer an extended service. Putting it simply, Mr Warren… this has got to stop.'

Paul pursed his lips, and Lucy had to look at her coffee to hide her smile: whenever he did that, the bristles on his moustache went up his nose.

'Is that why you're threatening us with conspiracy to pervert the course of justice?' said Paul.

'Not my decision. I'm just saying that the public are fed up with rich footballers getting away with murder. If the press get hold of this story – that money is being used to buy off traffic offences – the media outrage at SLC would be so strong that they'd go for the weakest link. I think that would be you and Miss White. It's largely down to Sergeant Marsh that there's been no leak to the press.'

Lucy was enjoying this. She took one of the pastries and bit into the warm sweetness.

'If this is your idea of a discussion, Chief Inspector, we're going to drink our coffee and leave.'

'If I said that a conspiracy charge was the least desirable outcome for me,' said Morton, 'then we might have a better starting point.'

'Go on.'

Morton opened his mouth, then nearly jumped out of his skin when the policewoman's radio burst into life.

'*Control to all units in Division 2 south.*'

Lucy dropped flaky pastry down her dress, and Paul looked like he'd been given an electric shock. Only the policewoman didn't flinch.

'That's us,' she said. She picked up the radio and keyed the button. 'Alpha Oscar three niner. Location Sevenbridge Village. Over.'

'Report of suspicious death in 7Bridge Estate. Possible homicide. Over.'

DC Fraser was half way to the coat stand already. 'Show us attending. That's Alpha Oscar three niner and DCI Morton from another force. Over.'

Lucy and Paul looked at each other in dismay. DCI Morton took a second to lean over and say, 'We'll sort this out later, okay?' Then he was gone.

Paul looked at his watch. 'It's almost time for the café to open to the public. Let's get back to the office before we start ringing anyone.'

They abandoned the table and only paused to let Paul open his umbrella. Lucy's feet were squelching before they got to the White-Berardi offices. Paul dumped his umbrella in the downstairs lobby and dashed up ahead of her. It was only when she went through the door that she remembered: Dad was working from home, and Gianni had met the Ikedas for breakfast at the airport. Only Grace was in the office.

Paul was decisive. 'I'm going to ring security. You ring your dad. Grace, can you call the Estate office?' Grace's mouth was an O of surprise. Paul added, 'Someone's been killed in 7Bridge.'

'What? Who?' said Grace.

'We don't know. That policewoman got a message on her radio, and they ran off. ' Paul lowered his voice. 'The message said it was a suspected homicide.'

Lucy tried her Dad's number: *This is Gary. Sorry I can't take your call right now…*

Chapter 5

Tuesday 14 January

Outside the Village Café, Elaine was already heading for her car, so Tom ran after her. He dived into the passenger seat with one arm still out of his coat sleeve. Elaine paused with her fingers on the ignition key.

'Do you know where the service entrance to the Estate is?' she said.

He pointed to the other end of the village. 'That way, but turn right after the houses.'

The acceleration jerked him back into his seat. She didn't change up from second gear, and the engine screamed as she threw it round the corner. He gave a sigh of relief when they emerged from trees into a mini industrial estate. 'Over there,' he said. 'Security office.'

Elaine did an emergency stop in front of a hefty barrier, then blew the horn. A security guard was waiting in front of the cabin, and she lowered her window. 'Police. Raise the barrier.'

The guard leaned forward. 'If you let me in, I'll direct you.'

'The Estate's not that big, is it? Just let us in and tell me which way to go.'

'I think it would be best if you let me show you.'

Tom put his hand on Elaine's arm. She got the message, and flicked open the central locking. The guard climbed in the back. Only when he had closed the door behind him did the barrier rise.

'If you drive straight ahead, you'll see my colleague waiting for us.'

Elaine shot forward into the 7Bridge Estate. *So this is how the other half live*, thought Tom. The first part of the road led up and over a small mound. The regular shape of the embankment made him wonder if it had been built specifically to hide the cluster of service buildings and car park behind them. On the other side, the road wound pointlessly through walls and hedges. All he could see of the houses were the gates in front of them: wrought-iron statements of wealth, all of which were closed. There were a couple of side roads and a few footpaths, but nowhere was there a sign of life until they came round a corner and an open expanse of green was revealed. The road split to circle round it, and the guard told them to head left. The green was just that — an open space of grass, with a small children's play area and a large pond which was partly fenced off. The deep end, presumably.

Ahead of them, he could see another guard — a woman this time, with the hood up on her coat. Their escort told Elaine to pull in by his colleague. 'You can leave your car here, for now,' he added. Elaine gave him a look and jumped out of the car. When they went down a footpath between two walled-off properties, both of the guards accompanied them, the woman taking the rear.

At the end of the path was another track. Tom paused when he put his foot on it, and tried again. It was rubberised. Elaine was already off to their right, heading towards a large group of people, all of whom seemed to be security guards, forming a ring around something. As they approached, the circle parted to reveal a rapidly-melting mound of cleared snow just off the path, and a pool formed in a dip where the grass had sunk. Next to the water was one man lying on his back and another standing two feet away. The man on his back looked dead, even at this distance.

The standing figure was wearing the same waterproof as the other guards, but his hood was down. Water ran off his bald head like a billiard ball in a shower. He was the only one not wearing black trousers and boots. This was the boss.

'DCI Morton, Metropolitan Police. This is DC Fraser of South Lancs. I assume a regular SLC patrol will be here shortly. What's happened?'

The other man didn't offer to shake hands. In a clipped voice, he gave the facts: 'I'm Max Nolan, Ops Manager, 7Bridge Security. One of my men on patrol saw the victim…'

'…Victim?' said Elaine, clearly itching to put someone in their place.

'He was face down in six inches of water, and someone had pulled a chunk of hair out of his scalp to hold him there. Yes, I'd say victim.'

Tom jumped in. 'What did your…man do next?' He was reluctant to call the security guards "officers", because they weren't, but so far they had been more professional than some police patrols he had come across.

'His top priority was to see if he could give first aid. However, he did activate his chest-cam before touching anything. The footage will be made available as soon as you ask.'

'Chest-cam?'

'All my patrol officers – they're called POs – wear webcams that they can activate.'

'Did he try first aid?'

'Yes. He said that when he felt for a pulse, the man was still warm, so naturally he did what he could. But not for long.'

Before asking another question, Tom took a long hard look round the scene. Elaine had already been doing that. The victim was blue in the face, and his features were locked in a grimace. Small cuts were all over it, probably from being ground into the soil. He wore a light overcoat, with no hood: hardly the best choice for walking out here. Tom made a mental note, then looked more closely at the snow. A small red stain had pooled in a crevice. Carefully, he put on some gloves and knelt down by the victim. The coat did not come much below the waist, and Tom found a tear in the fabric by the man's groin. There, and down the legs was quite a lot of blood, standing out in colour against the monochrome grey wool.

'Fraser, look,' said Tom, pointing to the evidence. 'Whoever did this must have been injured in the fight. Quite badly, judging from the amount of blood.'

The running track sloped down, away from them and towards the river. As Tom stood up, he heard footsteps coming up the path towards them. A young woman, with no coat at all, ran towards the line of POs protecting the scene. A female officer put out her arm, but didn't have the confidence of a police constable. The woman smashed past her, then stopped abruptly and put her hand to her mouth.

'Oh, my God, Dean… What have you done?'

Nolan had his finger to his right ear, pressing an FBI-style earpiece in place. He was looking at the young woman, then leaned towards Tom. 'The Service Gate officers have just admitted an emergency ambulance for Dean Rooksby, Madison's boyfriend. They say he has a dislocated shoulder.'

'Elaine!' Tom's voice stopped his partner from taking the young woman's arm, and he waved her back. He made sure Nolan was listening. 'A suspect is about to be loaded into an ambulance. One of the POs will show you to his house.' Tom paused, and Nolan nodded his understanding. 'Take a good look, and if he's showing blood, arrest him on the spot and go with him in the ambulance. We need all his clothes and his phone: we need swabs and samples. Give me your radio, and I'll arrange for SLC to meet you at A&E, but you need to secure the chain of custody.'

'Right,' said Elaine, handing over the radio.

Nolan pointed to a young PO and shouted, 'Rooksby Residence.'

He shot up the track, Elaine in hot pursuit. When Tom looked round, the young woman had disappeared. It didn't look as if anyone had followed her.

'Do you know who it is?' asked Tom, pointing to the body.

Nolan wiped the rain away from his face. 'Yes. It's Giovanni Berardi. Gary White's son. He's a resident.'

They stared at Gianni for a second. Tom's last case had been littered with bodies, but he wasn't inured to death: he felt it acutely that he was in the presence of a life cut short by violence. After establishing that Elaine's ambulance was on its way to Wythenshawe, he gave a summary of the situation over the SLC radio. The control room went silent as it digested his news, then sprang into life.

'Control to Inspector Morton. A traffic patrol will be with you in two minutes. MIT have been alerted and will respond. Over.'

He looked around the track, beyond the impassive ring of patrol officers. The slope down was a straighter section than most, and he could see a couple of lamp standards with what appeared to be CCTV cameras on them. There was another one uphill. He waved towards them. 'Is this area covered by CCTV?'

'Yes and no. The running track forms the outer perimeter of most of the Estate, but those cameras are set to face the fence and the woods.' Nolan turned towards him. 'I'm going to have to be up front about this, Inspector. The whole of 7Bridge is private property – every single square centimetre – and one of the main things that residents buy is privacy and security.'

'Isn't there a conflict between the two?'

Nolan gave a grim smile. 'Yes. That's 90% of my job, balancing residents' privacy against their security. When it comes to stalkers and the paparazzi they're often the same thing, but I'm under strict instructions not to open the Estate to the police except as required by law. That means your officers will be escorted on and off site, and warrants must be obtained for all premises, except where they relate directly to the scene of crime, which is here.'

Tom snorted. 'I'm glad this won't be my job, then. I'll be handing over to an SLC major incident team in the near future. I'll have to ask… are you ex-job?'

'Army.'

'Oh.'

'Here's the cavalry,' said Nolan, jerking his head towards the path between the houses. Two uniformed officers, resplendent in fluorescent jackets, were being escorted towards them.

Tom took out his warrant card, and walked to meet them. He identified himself and said that he was waiting for MIT to take over. The senior officer recognised him.

'I'm Sergeant Ryan Marsh. I was on my way for that meeting. Is there anything we can do, sir?'

'Yes. Your colleague can join Mr Nolan over there in keeping watch on the victim. You're coming with me to notify the next of kin.' Tom took a last look around the crime scene. 'Where is everyone?'

'Sir?'

'Nothing.' He turned to the nearest PO. 'Escort to Gary White's house, please.' The officer looked at Nolan, who nodded. 'Lead the way, then.'

They cut back between the houses towards the green. On the way through, all had been peaceful (if wet), but now the residents (or should that be Residents?) had emerged to see what was happening. The entry to the shortcut was guarded by POs, which explained the lack of attention at the crime scene — and a scattering of people, almost all of them women, were huddling under umbrellas. A couple of them had pushchairs with transparent canopies raised against the rain.

'We'll take a buggy,' said their escort.

Tom's brain connected the word "buggy" with the children's carriages, then the PO pointed to a couple of golf carts sporting the 7Bridge logo. 'Is it far?'

'Far enough. The Estate can be very deceptive. I can see the top of Mr White's residence from here, but it would take us ten minutes to walk there, at least.'

Tom let the traffic policeman get in the back: his jacket and belt of equipment would have become tangled with the patrol officer's only slightly smaller rig if Marsh had tried to sit up front. The civilian patrol officer had no handcuffs, but he was equipped with a police issue baton. Tom looked more closely at the cross-over strap on, and saw a white patch with a tiny camera stitched into it. 'How do you activate the chest-cam?'

'Like this.' The PO slapped the patch, and it bleeped. A red light came on. 'You are now being recorded, sir. This recording will be retained by 7Bridge Security. Shall I leave it on?'

'Why not?.'

The buggy moved swiftly down the road for a couple of hundred metres. The watching women had recognised the uniformed policeman as being a real copper, and several fingers pointed at their backs. Two were filming them on their phones. They went round two corners, and Tom was lost. He suspected that the road layout was designed for some purpose, and wondered if any of the residents used it as a racetrack. They passed a lamp post which was taller than the ones on the running track, and a light started shining on the dome above it. More CCTV.

The driver stopped when he saw a man running towards them, with a hastily-donned waterproof unfastened over his suit. 'That's Gary himself.'

Tom hopped down and held up his warrant card, and the man stopped. He had a shaven head, like Nolan, but everything else about him screamed *resident*: winter suntan, rings, watch, suit, a smooth face and smoother shoes. At this point, Tom hadn't decided whether Nolan was a servant or a jailer. He was about to identify himself when White interrupted.

'The cleaner says you've found my boy. Is that true? Is he all right?'

'Are you Gary White?'

'Of course I am. Have you found Gianni?'

'Perhaps we should go back to your house, then I can explain things.'

'Have you found my boy: yes or no?'

White was a big man, and Tom couldn't see any fat on him. The PO wouldn't restrain him, and White knew the Estate. If he ran, he might break through to the crime scene before they could catch him. Tom gave the traffic officer a hard stare. The message must have got through, because Marsh took two steps to the side and put his hand discreetly on to the handle of his baton.

'Mr White, if you want to know what's happened, the best place to go really is back to your house.' As he spoke, Tom held out his hand towards the buggy. White's eyes flicked from Tom to the police sergeant, then the patrol officer.

'Oi you,' he said. 'You're not supposed to record residents without telling us.' The PO stammered an apology and slapped his camera. It gave a lower-toned bleep. White climbed into the front of the buggy. 'Come on. Hurry up.'

They climbed back on board. This time Tom was half on the running board, as there was only room for one buttock on the back seat. The PO made double time to yet another imposing set of gates, then stopped. He took some sort of remote control out of his belt and keyed in a number: the gates swung open, and he drove them through.

The White residence had another turn in its own drive, so that the house was invisible from the road and hidden behind some conifers. Those trees weren't here when the Estate was built, and they were too mature to have been planted as saplings. More extravagance. And then he saw the house.

The last series of *Dallas* had aired in 1991 (he discovered later), and Tom had never watched it, but everything about the building in front of him said 'Howdy!' in a broad Texan accent.

'Isn't that—?' he said aloud, without meaning to.

'Southfork? Yeah. Paola was a big fan,' said Gary. 'Robyn hates it. We're gonna pull it down one day and start again.'

The buggy pulled up under a covered portico, out of the rain. The front doors were wide open. Tom hopped off, and they followed Gary into the hall. A staircase on the right curved up to a balcony. Tom had no idea whether it was faithful to the TV show, but the rest of the decor had a distinctly French accent, possibly *Louis Quinze*. The PO reached for his boots.

Tom and Marsh followed Gary into a den, trailing mud behind them.

'Right. Cut the crap and tell me what's going on.'

White was standing in front of a wall-mounted TV set, arms folded and legs braced. Tom took out his warrant card again.

'I'm DCI Morton, of the Met, but I was nearby.

Recognition flared in White's face. 'Aren't you the one who…'

'Yes, I am. I was in the café with Mr Warren. I think you should sit down, Mr White.'

'Just tell me.'

'Please… For Lucy's sake.'

'How dare you? I—' White stopped abruptly and sat on a leather couch.

'Mr White, I'm sorry to tell you that we've found a body, which Mr Nolan has identified as your son, Giovanni Berardi. Several other people recognised him too. Do you know what he was doing on the running track?'

'I have no idea. What happened? The cleaner said he'd been murdered. *Murdered*, for God's sake.'

How did the cleaner know? Did they have radios? Was she in the house when the body was discovered?

'Do you know a man called Dean Rooksby?'

'Dean? Of course I do. I'm his bloody agent. Was it him who found Gianni?'

'Do you know of any reason why Dean would want to hurt your son?'

Gary looked around wildly, as if his world had come loose from its moorings. 'No. No, it can't be him. Not Dean.'

Tom judged it was time to put things on a more formal footing. While White was distracted, Tom turned to the others. He looked at the 7Bridge patrol officer and hooked his thumb towards the door. The man left. Without being directed, Marsh took a position to Gary White's right. Tom sat in an armchair and took out his notebook.

'I'm sorry for your loss, Mr White, and one of my colleagues from South Lancs will need to speak to you later, but it would really help us if you could think of anything that Gianni and Dean might have quarrelled about.'

'Have you arrested him? Dean?'

'My DC has gone with him to the hospital.'

'Hospital?'

'Mr Rooksby called an ambulance, saying that he had a dislocated shoulder.'

It looked like White's brain had short-circuited when it tried to put Dean and Gianni together. Tom changed tack. 'When did you last see your son?'

Paul Warren looked at Lucy as if, just by sitting in her dad's chair, she could take on his authority; Grace was enjoying every minute of the drama, her eyes wide with excitement. Paul shook himself and pulled up a chair for Grace, then one for himself. 'The players are all at training. Who do you know on the Estate?' he asked Lucy.

'Holly. Holly will be there, I'm sure.'

Lucy looked up the contact and pressed *dial*. It rang a couple of times, then she answered. Lucy could hear outside noises: wind, chatter, rustling clothes.

'Lucy… where are you?'

'I'm in Dad's office. What's happening?'

Holly's voice caught in her throat. She started to speak then broke off to take a deep breath. 'Is Gary there?'

'No, he's at home, and Robyn's out with the little ones. We can't get hold of him.'

'I'm on the green with Sheena. I'll go to your dad's place and get him to ring you.'

'Thanks, Holly.'

The line went dead, and all they could do was wait.

'I haven't seen him,' said Gary. 'Not since yesterday morning. Gianni didn't come home last night. He texted me to say he'd be here this morning, but he never showed up.'

'Do you know where he was last night?'

White shook his head.

'Where would he have been coming from, to be using the running track?'

'Out of here. All the residences have gates that lead on to the track.'

Tom frowned. 'But you just said you didn't see him this morning.'

'He didn't come to the house. Gianni's a resident, you know.'

'A resident?'

'Yeah. He pays his own site fees, and he has his own Residence. It's a wooden building in the garden.' Gary shook his head, like a dog. 'Lucy… Lucy's in the office. I need to go and see her before someone else tells her.

God… and Paola. I need to ring her before it hits Twitter.
I've got to go, Inspector.'

'Of course, sir. PC Marsh will go with you. Do you have
a key to Gianni's … residence?'

'What for?

'I need to take a look, just to see if anything's happened.'

'I get that, but you won't need a key. This is 7Bridge: no
one locks their doors.'

From the hall, they heard the PO saying, 'I'm afraid you
can't…'

A woman in a knee-length padded coat pushed into the
room. 'Gary… I'm so sorry,' she said. 'I've had Lucy on the
phone.'

Tom took a step forward, and quickly checked the
woman's coat. It was very wet, so she'd obviously been out
in it for a while and hadn't got changed. There were no
blood or mud stains. 'I'm DCI Morton. You are?'

'Holly Nugent. Old friend. We've got to go and see
Lucy.'

'Will you come with me?' asked Gary, wiping his eyes.

'I've got my car. I'll drive. Come on.'

White realised that he was about to cry in front of a
woman, and pulled himself together. 'There's something
else,' he said to Tom. 'Have you arrested Dean? Tell me.'

'Yes. But that's just a precaution.'

'Well, you'd better get him a message. I'm terminating
his contract with immediate effect. The pampered arsehole
will have to find his own lawyer.'

Holly Nugent put her arm around Gary and led him out.
Marsh followed discreetly behind, and the patrol officer
looked confused, turning from one to the other.

'They're leaving the Estate,' said Tom. 'You come with
me. And put your chest-cam on.' The PO did so, and
looked very embarrassed when he repeated the warning that
Tom was being filmed.

Tom took the patrol officer outside, and followed the most obvious path to the right. The path hugged the building round the corner and then round the back. At the side of the house was a small artificial grass pitch, with two five-a-side goals: at the rear was a large patio, the furniture piled together in the middle and covered in plastic sheeting, waiting for spring. The area was flagged with York stone. Tom leaned down to run his fingers along it. No, it wasn't concrete: it was the real thing, probably stolen from some back street in Bradford. At the corner of the patio was a small brick shelter protecting a gas barbecue with more rings than his mother's kitchen.

'Any idea where Giovanni's residence is?' asked Tom.

The PO pointed towards a low extension at the other end of the house. 'There's a path to it by the pool.' Of course there was an indoor pool: Tom should have expected it.

As they passed the extensive poolhouse windows, Tom tried to peer in without looking as if he were doing so. There was too much rain running down to get a good idea, but it seemed big enough for proper swimming, not just splashing around. The promised path zigzagged through some rhododendrons and then forked, the left-hand trail ending at a door in the garden wall. The running track must be through there. Tom made another mental note.

To their right was a building which might have started life as a wooden summer house, but only in the designer's head. Once it hit the ground, several extensions had been added, and the original wooden framed structure was like the facade of a railway station — a fig leaf to cover the brutal reality behind it. This far from the main house, some of the trees were clearly original native specimens. Stark branches loomed over the summer house, one of them rubbing against the roof in the wind. It must be very dark in summer, when this lot were in leaf.

There was a small deck before the door. Tom climbed up. 'How good is the microphone on that camera?'

'Pretty good. It picks up most things within about ten feet.'

'Following a statement by Gary White, I am now entering the Residence of Giovanni Berardi. If the door is unlocked, that is.' It was.

The old summer house had been turned into an intimate seating area around an oak coffee table. The chairs looked old and comfortable and well stuffed, old enough to have been chosen originally by Paola. Had they been exiled to the outbuilding when Robyn redecorated Southfork? Tom stuck his head into a tiny galley kitchen through the left-hand door. There was an unwashed plate and mug on the draining board: it looked like Gianni had come home this morning. The smell of marijuana also lingered in the kitchen. Coffee, toast and a joint. The perfect breakfast.

He was halfway into the main living room on the other side of the building when his phone rang: it was Elaine. Before answering it, he told the PO to walk round the living room with his hands in his pockets and film everything. Tom stepped on to the deck outside and took the call.

'I've been relieved, sir. A sergeant and two DCs from MIT are here. They've taken over.'

'How's Dean Rooksby? Who's Dean Rooksby?'

'A footballer. He's on the books at Trafford Rangers, but he's on loan to Salton Town. Look, Tom… sorry. Look, sir, I'm…'

'Come on, Elaine. Spit it out.'

'I don't think he did it.'

'I'm listening.'

She hesitated again. 'He was going into shock when I got to the ambulance. They'd already put him on a chair, and the paramedics were about to give him oxygen. He'd got a broken nose, blood everywhere and cuts on his knuckles. I asked his name, and he answered clearly enough, so I arrested him. He was expecting it, right up until I said the word *murder*. Then he started saying, "No, no. He's alive."

'Are you sure it wasn't just denial?'

'No. It was disbelief. I finished reading him his rights, and one of the paramedics actually pushed me out of the way so they could get him in the ambulance. I almost had to force my way inside.'

Tom would not have liked to have been the paramedic who tried to stop Elaine Fraser.

'They put an oxygen mask on him, and we left. He'd been holding a phone, and he dropped it. That seemed to wake him up, especially when I put it in my pocket.' She sighed. 'He lifted the mask off his face and insisted on admitting to me that he had been in a fight with Berardi. He says he left the victim alive and in agony. And I believe him.'

From inside the summer house, Tom heard the PO shout 'Inspector.' He turned around, and the patrol officer was waving him towards the living room. He went in.

To Elaine, he said, 'If you believe him, then I do too.'

'There's another problem: he also gave me a motive. Berardi was having an affair with his fiancée, Madison Greenwood. She was the girl who came up to the crime scene. It was her phone that Dean was using, and there's enough evidence on it to drive any man to murder.'

'Not any man, Elaine. I didn't murder my ex-wife's lover.'

He made the last comment sotto voce, because he was in the living room and the PO was pointing to a glass dining table in the corner.

Elaine continued, 'MIT are going to lock us right out of this case, sir. They'll send him to court, and no jury's going to find him not guilty.'

'Go back and see him, or get MIT to give him a message. His agent has sacked him: he'll need to arrange his own lawyer. Oh… hang on a sec.'

Tom lowered his phone to stare at the dining table.

'I think I know a way of keeping us on the case,' he said to Elaine.

'How's that? There's no professional standards issues. Yet.'

'But there's something else I'm good at: money laundering. I've just found a large pile of £20 notes in Giovanni's living room. Grab a taxi and get back here.'

'Sir.'

'And that's not all,' said the patrol officer. 'I haven't touched it, but you should look at the laptop.'

Tom glanced at the screen. He suspected that the PO had nudged the mouse to unlock the screensaver, but he didn't blame the man. Tom looked closer.

'What's *SeenIn7Bridge?*' he asked.

Chapter 6

Tuesday 14 January

They had tried ringing everyone they knew in 7Bridge, but all the lines were engaged or went straight to voicemail. Lucy had even tried checking Twitter. Whatever had happened was clearly so bad that none of the usual suspects wanted to share it. Yet.

Grace turned her head to look out, and Lucy looked up: there was her father and Holly. Paul stood up and opened the door. 'Come on, Grace.'

'But…'

Paul propelled her out of the door, and left it open for Dad and Holly to come in. Lucy went round the desk to give Dad a hug. He whispered into her hair. 'It's Gianni, love. He's dead.'

She squeezed her father as hard as she could. 'No, Dad. No.'

'I'm so sorry, love.'

She squeezed again, and pushed back. Her dad let her go, but kept his arms on her shoulders.

'Paul says he's been murdered. That can't be right. Not in 7Bridge.'

'It's true.'

Her vision swam, and she felt Holly take her by the hand, lower her into the couch, and hand her a tissue. Holly sat next to her and squeezed her hand.

'What about Mama?' said Lucy.

'I'm gonna call now,' said Dad. 'Are you all right to stay here, in case she needs to speak to you? You know what her English is like when she's stressed.'

Lucy smiled in spite of herself, and Gary picked up the cordless phone from its cradle. He lifted the phone to his ear and waited.

'Paola, it's me. I've got some bad news about Gianni.' He paused while Mama said something. 'No. Paola, there's been an accident. Gianni's dead.'

Lucy could hear the scream from across the room. Whether or not Mama had started in English, she was now shouting in Italian. Dad passed her the phone.

'Mama. It's me.'

'*Bambina mia…*'

As her mother started to ask a hundred questions, Holly kept a grip of her hand. Her father walked out of his office and started talking to Paul. Something inside her made her baulk at using Italian.

'Mama, it's true,' said Lucy.

'Control to Inspector Morton. Please supply your exact location. Over.'

'I'm at the victim's residence, on the 7Bridge estate. Over.'

'DCI Stamp is arriving on site shortly. He has asked you to meet him at the crime scene. Over.'

'I'll be there. Out.'

When he had walked out of the summer house to talk to Elaine, Tom had seen something in the back of the outside door: a key. Clearly Berardi had valued his privacy, if not his security. He summoned the patrol officer and told him to check for other entrances.

'There's a fire door in the gym. You can't get in that way. All the windows are closed.'

'Thanks. We'll lock up and go back via the running track.'

A gym? Tom would have to stop being surprised if he were going to be spending much time here. He turned the key and took a final look at the car-crash house. It was almost childish in its terrible collision between the witch's cottage in *Hansel & Gretel* and the *Young Architect's Book of Concrete Blocks*.

The PO touched his sleeve, gently, when they came to the gate in the wall. 'Look — the lock's been tampered with.'

Tom looked more closely. The gate had a strong spring and a simple catch: he could tell from here that it was supposed to be an exit-only gate. Someone had broken the hasp on the catch, and added a hi-tech lock underneath. A little red light glowed in the gloomy well next to the wall.

'Strictly illegal, that,' said the PO.

'Hardly illegal. It's his house: he can do what he wants.'

'Not really, sir. Continued residency is subject to complying with security. A well-known singer was forced to leave last year because she wouldn't follow the rules.'

'What's Berardi done wrong?'

'These doors are for exit only. A lot of residents go running or walking. The exit-only gates are to ensure that their security is maintained. They sometimes prop them open when they go out. If we're on patrol, we close them and log it.'

Tom shivered. Max Nolan and his patrol officers were getting much closer to "jailer" by the minute. 'Does it open without a remote?'

The patrol officer fiddled with a catch, and pulled the door open. Beyond it, a gravel path led to the running track. The woods were quite thin at this point, and Tom could see through the bare branches to the river. Between the track and the woods was a short space of grass. A low wooden fence separated the grass from the trees. Tom pointed to the left. 'Crime scene that way?'

'Yes. About ten minutes by foot.'

The rain had eased a little, but only at the expense of rising winds. Tom pulled his collar up and set off. It was his breathing that made him realise they were climbing a slope.

Which way had Berardi been walking when he met Rooksby? Did Rooksby catch up with him, or did they meet face to face (assuming that Dean was running)?

Another slight bend and Tom could see where Gianni Berardi was lying. The ring of patrol officers had dispersed, though several were still standing in a knot. They had been replaced by crime scene technicians, as yet unencumbered by the paper suits. A uniformed police officer (female) was stationed in front, her clipboard covered by a plastic sheet.

'Thanks for all your help,' he said to the PO. 'Are you sticking around?'

'Breakfast. Finally. I won't be having the chicken, though.'

'Chicken? For breakfast?'

'You'll see what I mean when you read *SeenIn7Bridge*. Good luck, sir.'

Tom showed his warrant card to the woman on duty. She peered at it carefully before transcribing his details on to the sheet.

'I'm here to see DCI Stamp,' said Tom.

She looked behind at the activity surrounding the mound of snow. 'I think that's him, wearing the parka.'

Tom walked over to a grey-haired man who filled his parka. 'Are you Morton?' Tom nodded. Stamp raised an eyebrow, but made no comment about Tom's relative youth. He stuck out a hand. 'Rod Stamp. I can see why you're in professional standards.'

'Oh? Because I annoy people.'

'No, because you've done everything by the book. If you hadn't responded, and made that decision to arrest Rooksby, we might have lost all sorts of evidence.'

'Have you spoken to Max Nolan?'

'Just finished. Did he give you any grief? Because I've just had my ear burned. There was nearly a riot when I pitched up at their barrier. Good job I'm not on armed response.'

'I played nice. I thought it wouldn't help you if I started a fight before you got here.'

Stamp harrumphed. 'Early days, Tom. Did you find anything at Berardi's house?'

'They call them *residences*, not houses, apparently. Yes, I did. It's going to make your life very difficult, I'm afraid.'

'Oh, God. What? Another body? Illegal immigrants chained to the kitchen sink? This has got to be simple.'

'What makes you say that?'

'The violence. This sort of violence doesn't go with a complicated crime.'

Now was not the time to question Stamp's first impressions. 'No bodies at the Berardi Residence, but there was £200,000 in cash, on the table.'

'Dinner money? A bung for some manager?'

Tom shook his head. 'I used to work economic crime, in London. I'm up here on a case which touches on Berardi's sister … half-sister. If you hand over the money issue to your financial team, you won't hear back from them until next Christmas. If you ask your boss to co-opt me, I promise to have a full report by Monday.'

'Are you volunteering?'

Tom laughed. 'In the sense of "doing it for nothing", then no, I'm not. Four days' pay, plus expenses, and the services of DC Fraser. But she's already on your books.'

'I'll ask the ACC as soon as I'm done here. Leave it with me.'

'I'll leave this with you too,' said Tom, offering the key to Berardi's residence. 'It's a shame he's dead, otherwise you could prosecute Giovanni for crimes against architecture.'

'Not you as well… I've already had my sergeant talking about decadence and decay when she saw the set-up here.'

'One last thing. If your search team don't turn up a hat or umbrella nearby, get them to look again.'

'A patrol officer told me they'd found a big brolly— a freebie from some cognac firm. It's been logged.'

'Oh… and if you find a remote control in his pocket, it works the back gate. You might need it.'

Stamp lifted his hand in acknowledgement, and Tom headed towards the path to the green. When he moved, a PO detached himself from the group and tagged along. When they emerged from the cut, a buggy was dropping Elaine off next to her car. The PO dropped back, and Tom went up to his DC.

'Are you okay?'

'Yeah. At least I'm mostly dry. That coat of yours looks soaked, sir.'

'It's dry on the inside, and wool doesn't burn like that nylon stuff you're wearing.'

'It's Goretex, and I'm not planning to enter any house fires.'

Tom didn't elaborate. He'd tell her about the bombing one day, but not today. He checked his watch: eleven-thirty. 'Let's go to the White-Berardi office.'

Elaine popped the locks and climbed in with a frown. 'Will they let us in? We don't have any jurisdiction there, surely?'

'I've got us in on the case. We've got four days to find an angle that will point to the real killer.'

She seemed surprised. 'You agree with me? Thanks, sir. And how did you get us attached. I thought MIT were like MI5: they don't play well with others.'

'Stamp seems reasonable, for now. You and I are going to follow the money, because no one else wants to.'

Elaine groaned. 'No spreadsheets, please. I hate them.'

'Remember the Economic Crimes motto: *To err is human, but to really foul up, you need Excel.* We're going to White-Berardi because I want to talk to Paul Warren, and because we can't go to the café, the press will be all over it, and I need a cup of tea.'

Elaine started the engine and did a circuit of the green, so that they could head towards the service entrance. As well as the pond and play area, there was a burnt patch of ground where a bonfire had been, and other signs of communal activity. *Who organises all that?* he wondered. *Is spontaneous enjoyment included in the residents' fees?*

The residents themselves had all disappeared. Between the green and the exit, they saw no one except police officers and patrol officers. 'There's something else you'd better do, sir,' said Elaine.

'Hmm?'

'Ring your boss.'

Tom laughed. 'We're on our own, I'm afraid. Leonie's in the Cairngorms, and I'm not going to bother the Director with this. Yet.'

It was the screaming that got to him. In rooms around him, women were crying in pain as their contractions got closer together. Dean was in the maternity unit.

The bone was back in its socket, but the doctor had told him that there was a good chance he'd need surgery. Something called the labrum might be torn. He had been going for ultrasound when the police had finished arguing with the hospital about him. In the meantime, he tried to relax, but it wasn't going to happen. There was a pillow between his arm and his chest, and various bits of strapping holding him together. *Don't move* had seemed like an easy instruction at the time. Now he wasn't sure if he could.

The consultant had called it a *reduction* when he manipulated Dean's shoulder. He wasn't the first doctor to see Dean, but he was the last so far. When the A&E guy realised that they had a Trafford Rangers player in casualty, with a police escort, he had bottled it, and telephoned the general manager. The orthopaedic consultant appeared shortly afterwards. The consultant wasn't happy to be dragged down to A&E, but he was nice to Dean.

'You won't play again this season, I'm afraid,' he had said. 'But you're young. With the right treatment, you should make a full recovery.'

'Haven't you heard? I'm under arrest.'

'Not my business: I treat the person, no matter who they are, or what they've done. Unless they're drunk, of course. Then I make them wait. How bad is the pain, on a scale of one to ten — where ten is unbearable agony?'

It sounded like the women around him were coming up to eight or nine on the scale.

The hospital wouldn't give the police a secure room in A&E, so they started to block off the whole corridor, asking for other patients to be tipped out of bed. The general manager had arrived by then, and said that there were private rooms in maternity. So here he was.

A nurse came in and checked him over, with the police watching from the door. She left and told the copper that the patient was going to radiology in ten minutes, followed by a trip to fix his nose.

When Dean closed his eyes, he couldn't see Berardi's face. He couldn't remember the fight. All that came into his head was the image of Maddi running away to find her lover. Could she be the one who finished off the slimy bastard? Someone had, and it wasn't him.

Two minutes before the porter arrived, the policeman came in. He was wearing a really cheap suit, and looked like he ate too many pies. His eyes were cold, as well.

'You are under still under arrest, Mr Rooksby, and you do not have to say anything…' The rest of the words slid over him. It was the fourth time he'd heard them today. He tuned back in when the copper said something about Gary.

'What was that?'

'I said that you will need to make other arrangements for legal representation. Mr White has informed us that your contract with him has been terminated. Not surprising, really, given that you killed his son.'

Dean clenched his jaw.

'I am also advising you that the police surgeon has said you will be fit to interview this afternoon. You will be taken from here to a police station. If you do not have a solicitor of your own, one will provided for you.'

'Hang on,' said Dean. *Think…think. Who can you call*, he thought. When he signed on the dotted line for the Salton Town Academy, his father had signed them up to White-Berardi, and Dean had followed suit on his eighteenth birthday. Since then, Gary had arranged everything. Everything. The police wouldn't explain the situation to his father properly. They'd lie, because that was what they did. There was only one person who might help him. 'Call Salton Town FC. Get Gus Burkett, the manager, to ring me.'

'You're under arrest, Mr Rooksby. No one will be calling you for a long time.'

Dean mashed the sheet with his right hand. The throbbing in his nose felt like it might be bleeding again. 'Call them anyway. Tell Gus what's happened. Tell him I need a brief.'

'They're only called "briefs" on TV, but I'll give the club your message. You'll have to hope they pass it on, won't you?'

Hope. Dean had never thought of it as a commodity before: something you could have, like money in the bank. He had very little of either at the moment.

There was only one space left in the Village car park. News was already getting about, and they had passed the first TV truck as they left the service area of the Estate. There was no one loitering by the White-Berardi building, but surely they wouldn't be long when they saw the security guard outside. Tom showed his ID, and they went into a tiny lobby which was mostly staircase. Sergeant Marsh was occupying the only chair.

'I didn't expect to see you again, sir.'

'Nor me you. This isn't your normal job.'

'I'm just waiting for the DCI to sort out a family liaison officer. They're all upstairs — Mrs White arrived a few minutes ago with three children and a nanny. I had to help them carry the buggy.'

'Not very accessible, is it?' said Elaine. 'Shouldn't they have a lift?'

Marsh grinned. 'I doubt that many of their visitors have disability issues.'

'Thanks,' said Tom, dragging Elaine out of the way before she got side-tracked again.

Most of the upstairs was laid out as an open-plan office with several desks. A spare corner had been turned into a crèche, and the only person sitting at his desk was Paul Warren. A young woman with long hair, a short skirt and too much make-up was running between the kitchen and a private office, where Tom could see four people. Lucy White was sitting on a small settee with Holly Nugent, Gary was behind his desk — and a new figure, presumably Robyn White, was standing with her hands on her hips. Tom caught the last part of what she said:

'… not staying with us. Why can't she use Gianni's place?'

'That's a bit insensitive,' said Holly. Tom guessed they were talking about Paola. It was an interesting dynamic, and one that Tom would have liked to have observed for longer, except that Gary noticed him and stood up. 'Inspector Morton,' he said loudly. The other three turned to look.

'I'm sorry to intrude,' said Tom. 'I've come to see Mr Warren, but if I could just ask you one question?'

Lucy was looking at her dad, Holly was looking protective and Robyn was determined to assert her authority. 'You shouldn't be bothering us at a time like this,' she said.

'As I said, I'm sorry. The family liaison officer – the FLO – will be with you shortly, and all further contact will be through them. That's why I only need to see Mr Warren. Apart from the one question.'

Gary White squeezed past his wife and came out of the office. He waved them to seats in front of Warren's desk, and called over the young woman. He introduced her as his assistant, Grace Revell. 'Take their coats and get them a drink,' he told her. 'They must be frozen.' Grace ran to the kitchen, hesitated, and came back for the coats. Tom handed his over, but Elaine shook her head and draped her waterproof on the back of the chair.

'Tea?' asked Grace. Tom nodded.

'I'm Gary White,' said Gary as he went to shake Elaine's hand. 'You went to the hospital with Dean, didn't you? Did he have anything to say for himself?'

'That's a question for the FLO, I think,' said Tom. 'I wouldn't want to step on anyone's toes. I'm sure you'll understand.'

'Of course. What was that question for me?'

'Before I ask it, I should tell you both,' he looked at White and Warren, 'that we've been attached to the major incident team to look into your son's finances.'

'What for?' said White. 'He got into a fight with Rooksby, for some reason. Shouldn't you be looking at his personal life, not his money?'

Elaine had her notebook ready. 'Is there a reason we should look at his private life?' she asked.

Tom cringed, and jumped in before White could open his mouth. 'As I said, that sort of question will come through the FLO, not from us.'

White and Warren looked at each other, then at Tom and Elaine. Tom thought he was starting to build a team with Fraser. There was clearly work still to be done. Elaine herself had gone red and was staring at the blank page in her notebook. Tom moved on. 'Mr White, is there any reason you know of that could explain the large amount of cash in your son's residence?'

'How large?'

'I think there's £200,000, but that will be verified by the crime scene manager.'

Gary whistled, and Paul's moustache did a tango with his nose. 'We don't do cash in this business,' said White.

'Forgive me, Mr White… but have you never made a rendezvous with a football manager, in the service station, carrying a brown envelope?'

'Ha! Only in the Sunday papers. I might have, once upon a time, but not any more. If you do finances, Inspector, you must have heard about offshore accounts.'

'Indeed I have. It's on my list of things to talk about with Mr Warren. So, to be clear, you know of no reason connected with the business why your son should have that money.'

'I do not.'

'Thank you. Once again, I'm sorry to intrude.'

Grace had been hovering in the background, carrying two Trafford Rangers mugs. When Gary went back to his family, closing the door behind him, she put the drinks down on the desk, and went over to the nanny in the corner.

'Why *do* you want to look at Gianni's finances?' said Warren. 'I only ask because most of the material here is covered by commercial confidentiality. There is a very clear limit as to what I can disclose without a warrant.'

'I understand. I did work in the economic crimes unit for many years, so I know the rules.' Warren looked slightly disturbed when Tom mentioned that part of his CV. During his career, he had met two types of white-collar criminal: those who knew they were robbing people, and those who genuinely believed that their activities were a legitimate expression of capitalism. If there was anything shady in White-Berardi, it would be under the latter heading. 'I'll keep it simple, or try to. First, what was Giovanni's relationship to the company? Second, what activity was he working on at the moment? Third, what do you know about his personal situation? Where did he bank? What property did he own, and so on?'

Warren blew air through his moustache. 'That's hardly simple, Inspector.'

'Then start with the easiest question, as you see it.'

Grace returned with a plate of chocolate biscuits. All three of them helped themselves. Elaine was the only one who dunked. Tom was worried that Warren would get crumbs in his moustache, but the lawyer popped half a biscuit into his mouth as if firing it from a cannon, then he rubbed his hands and leaned forward.

'Giovanni is – was – a director of White-Berardi Sports Management Ltd. He also owned 25% of the shares. His mother made them over to him some years ago. Strictly speaking, he did very little work for Sports Management Ltd, and that was mostly connected with hospitality events. Gianni's main job was chairman of White-Berardi Image Rights Ltd. He had 49% of that, and SM Ltd had the balance. In reality, it's all part of the package. When a client joins us, they sign several contracts: the main one is with Sports Management Ltd, and another is with Image Rights Ltd.'

Elaine looked at Tom, and nodded as if to say, *It was the same for Rob*. Tom gestured for Warren to continue.

'With new clients, Gianni always got a few deals sorted out quickly: sponsored vehicles, equipment endorsements — boots, golf clubs, that sort of thing. After that, he tended to work with the sponsors and then look for the right fit to the client. Most of Gianni's money came from our percentage of the contracts.'

Elaine made a note. Tom nodded, and said, 'What was he working on at the moment?'

'I was trying to explain. He could be working on any number of deals. We all have to use Outlook for our diaries and calendars, so if your techie people could come over, I will authorise an export of Gianni's individual account.'

It was Tom's turn to make a note. He would have to get Stamp to move quickly on that, or he could be spending most of his four days waiting for the information. Before Warren could move on, Tom had another question. 'What about accommodation? A lot of your clients seem to live in 7Bridge.'

'Only the biggest, and only the ones in the north west. That wasn't part of Gianni's role, though you have reminded me of something. Grace!'

The young assistant was looking more harassed by the second. At the sound of Warren's voice, Lucy came out of the office and spoke up. 'Leave her alone, Paul. She's not a robot. Gianni worked here, and so does she. Grace has lost a friend.'

'It's okay, Luce,' said Grace. 'I'd rather keep busy.'

'I know, but we're not going to exploit you.' Lucy White folded her arms and planted her feet in front of Warren's desk. 'I want you to get on to the agency, and get a temp over here now. No... get two.'

Warren gestured towards Tom and Elaine. 'The police...'

Lucy marched towards them, determination fighting with grief on her face. When she got closer, Tom could see her swollen eyes, and a smear of mascara on the left sleeve of her dress. He also noticed the way her hips swayed, and closed his eyes for a second.

'Give me their number.'

Tom opened his eyes to see Lucy holding out her hand to Paul Warren. The attorney capitulated and looked at his monitor. He clicked the mouse, then wrote something on a Post-it note. Lucy took the note and moved towards an empty desk. At the last moment, she swerved away: that must have been where Gianni had sat. Lucy plonked herself in Grace's chair and picked up the phone.

Grace herself had been hovering behind her friend. Blotchy, dry skin was visible where she had rubbed off some of the foundation on her jaw. 'Did you want something, Paul?'

'Yes. Thanks, Grace. When Lucy's finished with your phone, could you ring Saul? Someone has to break it to Madison that she can't stay in 7Bridge any longer, now that Dean's residency has been revoked. Normally we'd handle that, but in the circumstances…'

'Erm, had you forgotten? Saul's in Florida.'

'Damn.'

'I can get Tiffany in the Estate Office to do it. I think she's been round a couple of times.'

'Fine.'

'I'll do it.' They all looked up. Holly Nugent was standing in the doorway of Gary's office. 'I think I'm closest to her, out of the residents.' Lucy had finished on the phone, and Holly said to her, 'Will you be all right?'

Lucy nodded, and Holly started to collect her things. The trio round Warren's desk refocused on each other.

'Whose decision was that?' asked Tom. 'To expel Dean and Madison from paradise.'

Elaine looked at him in much the same way that he had looked at her. Perhaps Tom was overstepping the mark, but he was the boss. Paul Warren looked embarrassed at the question, so Tom had made the right decision.

'I had a message from Max Nolan,' said Warren. 'Dean had a personal contract with the Estate company for residence, but the rental agreement for the property is with Trafford Rangers. Max must be in touch with Saul by phone. He told me that they were revoking Dean's residency with immediate effect. It's their choice — but if they hadn't, I imagine that Gary would have been on the phone screaming at them.'

Revoking his residency. Tom changed his internal metaphor... 7Bridge wasn't a jail, or a paradise garden: it was an early experiment in gated sovereignty. He wondered if, in the near future, a bill would be presented to Parliament allowing some communities to opt out of Britain, to become a sort of inland Channel Island with their own tax and justice systems. He shook his head and focused on the issue at hand.

'Paul, are you Gianni's personal attorney?'

'Yes. Because he was a resident at 7Bridge, and because he rented from his father, I handled a lot of his business. When he became a resident, Gary insisted that he make a will. I've got that too. As far as his financial affairs are concerned, I'm afraid that our investment guru is away. Could you give me a moment?'

Warren got up, and started moving around the office, opening filing cabinets and accumulating paper. Tom turned to Elaine. 'Anything you want to ask?'

'Lots, sir, but I'll wait until later. That way I can run my questions past you first.'

Tom would deal with that later, because Paul was returning.

'I'll just copy these myself. I've got Gianni's financial details here, and his will. You don't want the originals, do you?'

Tom shook his head, finished his tea, and went up to the window at the front of the building while he waited for Warren to copy the files. There was a TV crew ensconced outside, and several other reporters.

'There's a back way out, you know.'

Tom flinched. He hadn't heard Lucy come up behind him. 'Thanks,' he said. 'It's good of you to think of us. I'm not expecting to be anyone's favourite person at the moment.'

She touched her hand to his sleeve and leaned towards him. 'It's Tom, isn't it? While no one's listening, and nothing's on the record, can you tell me what's going to happen? To me, I mean. It sounds selfish – what with everything that's been going on – but I just want to know, one way or the other, whether you're going to arrest me for the 7Bridge Collective stuff. When I know, then I can focus on Dad. And Mama.'

Tom looked down at her. This close, he didn't have an option. 'I'm afraid that with me, very little is off the record, but if you resign as company secretary to the Collective, I won't be pursuing anything retrospectively. If they start this nonsense again after today, that's another matter.'

Warren was coming slowly towards them. Lucy came closer to Tom so she could whisper. 'Leave the Collective to me.' She stepped back.

Tom nodded to her. Warren handed over the copies, and Tom was about to leave when the main door opened and two detectives came in. Tom could tell they were detectives because they were both holding up their warrant cards. Paul, Lucy and Grace all looked at Tom.

He took two steps forward and held up his own ID. 'DCI Morton… I'm just leaving.'

'What are you doing here?' said the woman.

'And you are…?'

'I'm the FLO. Who are you?'

'DCI Stamp asked me to handle the financial enquiries. I was just getting some paperwork. From their lawyer.'

'I'll need to see that.'

'Are you sure? It'll be in HOLMES 2 by this evening, but if you want to start looking now…'

'You said you were leaving.'

'I think what you meant to say was, "You said you were leaving, sir."'

The woman's colleague had been trying to edge back out of the door, then froze in position. There was a long pause, which was broken by Paul Warren.

'I'm the family's legal representative,' he said, moving to shake the FLO's hand. 'Shall I make the introductions?'

Tom collected Elaine and his coat, and left them to it, via the back entrance.

'Pub. Lunch,' he said to Elaine.

Chapter 7

Tuesday 14 January

Even though the January transfer window was wide open, Isaac Redmond had no one to go to lunch with. That was why he took Gus Burkett's call.

Redmond's office in north London was close to the Emirates and to White Hart Lane. He did business in both places, but rarely with Gus up in Salton. He knew that Salton Town weren't in the market to buy, and he knew that Gus tended to steer his best young talent towards Gary White. On the other hand, Gus had never lied to him or messed him around.

'Gus! Happy New Year.'

'No, it isn't.' Isaac heard the intake of a deep breath. 'Look, it's going to be on the news in a minute, but you need to act fast. Do you know Giovanni Berardi, Gary White's lad?'

'I know of him. Seen him a couple of times in the distance. Why?'

Isaac knew Gianni a lot better than that, but he wasn't going to give the game away.

'He's dead,' said Burkett. 'Murdered. And Dean Rooksby is under arrest for it.'

Isaac stood up and banged his desk, then waved his arms frantically towards the open door.

'Gus? Are you kidding me?'

'Wish I bleeding well was. Straight up, Isaac. Dean's in hospital, under arrest. The police rang the club just now. Not only that, Gary's terminated his contract. That lad needs help, and you're the best person to give it. Whatever it costs, I'll pay myself in the short term.'

Isaac's PA/daughter had run in as if her boss/father were having a heart attack. 'One second,' he said to Burkett, then covered the mouthpiece. 'Sara — get your mother's cousin Daniel on the phone. You know, the one in Manchester who's always after extra tickets for Trafford Rangers. No matter where he is, get him on the line.'

He shooed the woman away, and spoke to Gus. 'Where was he arrested? Do you know which police force it was?'

'He was arrested in 7Bridge. It must be South Lancs.'

'I'll sort it, Gus, don't worry. The best criminal lawyer in the north of England is going to drop everything and get over there. Do you know what happened?'

'Haven't a clue. Thanks, Isaac.'

'Don't worry.'

They hung up, and Isaac Redmond stared into space while he waited for Sara to get hold of Daniel. There were plenty of Dean Rooksbys in this world. Isaac had four boys like him on the books, but Gianni Berardi was irreplaceable. What was he going to do now?

Elaine couldn't say that her boss was opaque, but he didn't give much away until he'd finished mulling things over. They walked in silence from the centre of the Village, over the quaint humpback bridge, and towards the pub. The sign displayed a stylised river with a group of little stone bridges receding into the distance. Gold letters attached to the brick declared it to be the Seven Bridges Inn.

'My ex-wife once consulted a spiritualist,' Morton announced. 'She came back and told me that my lucky number is seven, and that one day I would cross water to find happiness. If ever there's a place to get lucky, it has to be here. Mind you, I'm not sure whether I need to cross *in* to Sevenbridge to find luck, or cross water going *out*. If we're really lucky, they'll serve decent food and Thwaites Lancaster Bomber in here.'

'Not for me, sir. The beer, I mean.'

'We've just seen a man's most precious gift stolen from him.'

Elaine wasn't sure, but she thought he meant Berardi's life. She hoped he didn't mean Dean Rooksby's residency at 7Bridge: that would be too gross. Then again, people would kill for what Dean had.

'We're police officers, not soldiers,' continued Morton. 'We're not in a combat zone, and if we're going to help out, we need a drink. Unless you're teetotal, of course.'

'No. I just don't normally drink at work.'

'My last DC was an evangelical Christian. She prays. I drink.'

They had gone through the doors and in to the pub. From the look on the face of the landlord, he was slightly panic-stricken at being understaffed for the hordes which would soon descend. He put down his phone and asked her boss what he wanted. Morton pointed to one of the beer pumps, then turned to face her.

'Vodka + Red Bull, please,' she said to the landlord.

When they had settled in a corner, Morton said, 'It's Tom in here, okay?'

Elaine nodded, and raised her glass. 'To Giovanni Berardi.'

Tom seemed to approve. 'May he find peace, and may he be remembered well.'

Elaine swallowed, and spoke first. 'I don't think he'll be remembered that fondly by Dean Rooksby.'

'Go on. Tell me from the beginning.'

She went back over the journey to the hospital, and how she had seen the bewilderment in Rooksby's eyes when she arrested him for murder. 'It just can't be faked, Tom. If Berardi had died of an aortic aneurysm, or something … fair enough. But he didn't, did he? He was held face down in the water, deliberately and brutally. If I hadn't been there to see Dean's face, I wouldn't believe it either, but that lad is innocent of murder.'

Tom drank again. 'I believe you. I bet the post mortem will show that Berardi is covered in bruises and maybe has broken bones — but he wasn't killed by the person who gave him that kicking, whom we know is Dean. Let's order before the kitchen gets swamped.'

While they waited for the food, Tom told her about Berardi's house and the money he had found there. 'Even for these people, £200k is a lot of cash,' he said, waving his arm towards the Estate. 'Was it coming or going, or both?'

'Drugs are the obvious source. Or destination,' said Elaine.

'I agree, but I saw no other evidence. Dealers always keep their cash near their stash, and there were no scales, no bags, no cash-counting machines.' He paused when their meals arrived, and where Elaine would have pushed hers aside to continue the conversation, Tom stopped until he had sampled the food and pronounced it good. If he was this deliberate in all his actions, she was going to get very impatient very quickly. Someone had been murdered, and they had to sort it out before it was too late for Dean Rooksby. He was about to say something, but his phone vibrated. He glanced down and frowned at the message.

'Damn,' he said. 'I've got to go outside in a second.' He continued eating for a minute, until most of his gourmet burger was demolished. 'There was something else in Gianni's summer house that seemed very interesting to the patrol officer. I'm going to talk to the jet-setting Mr Blackstone. When I get back, I want to know all there is to know about a website called *SeenIn7Bridge*.'

Saul Blackstone was not one of life's natural travellers. He liked to put down roots, and even a temporary relocation was not something he took in his stride. Abandoning nearly all his luggage in the holiday apartment was therefore fairly traumatic. His mother would pack it, and the concierge would ship it, but that didn't make it right. His journey back to 7Bridge was not one he was going to enjoy, and starting with a three-hour wait at the airport didn't help. Finishing with a 2 a.m. taxi from Heathrow wasn't going to help either. At least he could work his phone while he waited.

Max had so far failed to get the senior police officer's number, and Saul had nothing to say unless he was saying it to the chief. This DCI Morton was a different matter: they had already spoken, and Max had told him that Morton was first on the scene. Not only that, here was Morton returning his call.

'Mr Blackstone … DCI Morton here. I understand you're abroad.'

'Yes, worse luck. I'm on my way back, but won't get there until the early hours. I believe you've arrested Dean Rooksby.'

'Not me … South Lancs, but they have asked me to look into Mr Berardi's finances. And one other matter.'

'Aren't you part of the investigation, to make sure things are done properly?'

'That would be very rude of me. DCI Stamp is the SIO; I'm just a hired gun, or hired calculator, to be exact.'

'But you were there. Max told me.'

'Indeed I was, and afterwards I searched Mr Berardi's residence.'

'Hah! The Swiss Cottage. How Gary ever got away with that, I'll never know.'

'That's something we can agree on. I went round with one of your patrol officers. He showed a very great interest in two things, both of which I'm sure you know about already.'

'I'm in Florida. I have no idea what's going on. That's why I've rung you.'

'I think you know exactly what's going on. You've already terminated Dean's residency.'

'I had no choice.'

'Perhaps. I'll need to see you when you get back, but I want to ask about something I saw in Gianni's house.'

'You mean the money?'

Morton laughed. 'Suddenly you do know what's going on. Not that, Mr Blackstone. Something else. The patrol officer who accompanied me was very, very interested in Gianni's computer, especially something to do with a website. If he's interested, Mr Nolan will be interested, and if Mr Nolan is interested, then so are you. What's going on?'

That was a tricky one. Max had more-or-less fingered Berardi as being the Mother Superior, based on the evidence from the patrol officer's chest-cam — but Saul didn't believe it, or didn't believe that Gianni was acting alone. Max had also told him about Gianni and Madison Greenwood (and that Max had known for a while). If Dean had found out, no wonder he'd killed him. Saul didn't want any unnecessary complications, and he didn't want Neil Hoskins giving a statement to the police. Saul tried to think innocent. What would he say if he had nothing to do with it?

'That website is nothing less than online stalking. I'm glad to see the back of it, and so will a lot of other people, but I don't know any more than that,' he told the detective.

'Have a safe journey. I'll be in touch.'

While her boss was outside making a call, Elaine ate her salad and acquainted herself with the Mother Superior. After five minutes, she pushed her salad aside having lost her appetite: this woman was poison. She didn't notice Tom coming back until he sat down, plonking a bottle of sparkling mineral water and two glasses on the table. He too pushed the remains of his meal away. Elaine would never have left that many chips.

'Before we go on,' he said, 'I want you to know that I trust you, and you have to trust me. I pulled you up in the office because you asked a question that was inappropriate. I hope you learn from that.'

'Sir…'

He held up his hand to stop her. 'I know I can sound patronising sometimes, but you've got the same right to speak to me.' The hand he had used to forestall her was now rubbing his left shoulder and the top of his left arm. That wasn't the first time he'd done it, but he didn't seem to have the same sort of muscular pain that poor Rooksby was suffering from. 'I make the decisions. I carry the can. That's what I'm paid for.'

Elaine looked at her empty vodka glass, and made a connection. 'You said your last work partner was teetotal. Did she have other faults? Because I'm not her.'

He snorted, and finished his beer. 'I'm in no danger of confusing you, Elaine. For one thing, Kris plays football. Tell me about *SeenIn7Bridge*.'

Okay, thought Elaine. *Conversation over. Change the subject … move on*. Before speaking, she sat back. 'If Rob gets selected for the next rugby World Cup, I'll be over the moon, I will.' This time it was her turn to hold up a hand, because she suspected he was going to make some Scott-ist comment. That was her job. 'But there's one thing I'll hate: the wives' photograph. It's in his contract, more or less, that we "ladies" have to turn up and pose for the camera. I'll do it, they'll put a caption saying who I am… then I'll go back on duty, wherever that might be.'

Tom nodded, and Elaine realised that she was getting a bit too worked up about this. 'Sorry. I don't like being labelled a WAG. I don't do Twitter, and most of my Facebook friends are from the ULIST Climbing Club.'

'Aah. I thought you were an athlete of some description. I'm not, in case you hadn't noticed.'

'It's different for footballers' wives, especially in the Premier League, but it's still a choice. All the women who live in 7Bridge have chosen to be WAGs, and they should have thick skins, but this…' She waved her phone at him. 'This is beyond the pale. It's malicious, hurtful, and worst of all, it looks like it's all true. Listen to this, from a couple of months ago:

'*Practise what you preach: always good advice. Someone should give it to ROBYN WHITE. It's all very well being patron of the local dogs' home, but getting your husband to put down the family pet because it chewed your Louboutins is a bit rich. P.S. Dear readers, don't tell her kids: they think it was ill.*

'There's a picture to go with it: the dog's basket is out by the rubbish.'

Tom looked hurt, but that might be in sympathy with Robyn or the dog. 'Is there any form of comeback on this website?'

'No. Strictly read-only. No comments. And it's not just the WAGs. The staff get it too. This is the next item:

'*Talking about the doghouse, that's where we'll find BETH PEDLEY.* Apparently, she runs the spa or something,sir. *We hear young beauticians may be in short supply in future now that the internationally renowned educational institution SALTON COLLEGE has withdrawn its apprentices from the 7Bridge Spa. Something to do with a culture of bullying, perhaps?*

Tom nodded, lost in thought. Elaine put down her phone, and waited. He snapped back into the present, and said, 'I'll need to think about that. Thanks. The reason I wanted to know is that Berardi had this website, or some entries from it, on his computer. Let's start with what we know and move slowly. From what you've seen so far, tell me what you think happened to Gianni Berardi today.'

The pub was getting more and more crowded. Elaine saw at least two people she recognised from the local news: the sports editor and the chief reporter. She moved her chair closer to Tom. 'We know that Berardi was having an affair with Madison Greenwood, Rooksby's fiancée. When Dean was in the ambulance, he more-or-less admitted that the fight was about her. He definitely admitted to giving

Berardi "a good kicking". During the fight, Dean had his nose broken and his shoulder dislocated. In fact, I'm not entirely sure that he would have been physically able to hold Berardi down, but that's another matter. Dean needed urgent medical assistance, so he went home. The patrol officer said that his phone was in his car on the other side of the Estate. Madison came looking for Giovanni afterwards, so he must have said something to her.'

'I agree with you so far.'

'The next bit is the difficult bit for Dean's defence.'

'Why?'

'Because the jury will never believe it. The window of opportunity for the murderer was tiny. If it wasn't Dean who killed Berardi, it was someone who witnessed the fight or who came round the corner while Berardi was still incapacitated. The blood on that snowbank you spotted proves that: Berardi hadn't moved from when he fought Dean.'

'You're right. Thank you.' Elaine was only human. Recognition from the boss was always welcome. She took a swallow of mineral water to stop herself looking smug.

Both of their phones vibrated, and they both checked their notifications. Elaine's was a selfie of Rob with a cheerleader in the smallest kilt ever. She'd get him back for that. Tom's appeared to be work-related, so she put on a serious face.

'We're in,' he said. 'That was DCI Stamp. We've been assigned to investigate Berardi's finances and produce a report. It has to be with the major incident team by Monday morning. But they're only paying me – and you – until Friday. No overtime, I'm afraid.'

'It was me who said Dean was innocent, sir. I'm not going to clock-watch now. Besides, Rob's away, so I've got no one at home to cook for me.' As soon as she spoke, she realised what she'd said, then she dug herself in deeper. 'Well, he's not that good a cook. I'm sure your mother's a great cook. Not that it's the same, or anything… Sorry. I'll shut up.'

Morton sighed. 'Elaine, if your husband isn't a better cook than my mother, divorce him now. As far as our mission is concerned, we've got five days to find someone who hated Berardi enough to kill him, and who is also mad enough to be outside during a downpour in the middle of January. Should narrow the field.'

'Is there anyone sitting here? Do you mind if we share your table?'

A young couple hovered over the two empty chairs next to them.

'We're off,' said Tom. 'Back to work for us.'

It was grey and cold outside, but not raining. Tom buttoned his coat as they walked. 'Your job this afternoon is to attach yourself to the MIT. Sort out HOLMES2 access, and find out what they're up to. Make yourself useful, and discover anything you can about the 7Bridge Estate that's not going to be in the reports.'

'Right. Where will I get you?'

'I'm going back to Lyme Court. There really does have to be a financial report, and I'm not sensing any enthusiasm on your part for writing it.' Elaine shivered at the thought. 'I didn't think so. When you've had enough, bring your favourite takeaway back. And don't forget the receipt.'

As they crossed the bridge, they huddled into the parapet when a grey van passed by. The sign on the side said PRIVATE AMBULANCE. Tom looked at her, and she nodded back. Giovanni Berardi was taking his penultimate trip. The next one would be in a hearse.

Chapter 8

Tuesday 14 January

Back to Southfork. Home, really. Part of Lucy had never left the place. Part of her doubtless never would — but here she was, and she probably wouldn't be staying anywhere else for a while. Dad had gone first with Robyn and the kids in the BMW with the blacked-out windows. Lucy had followed in the Mercedes S-class, crossing her fingers that she didn't crash the enormous great thing before she got it through the gates. Dad and Robyn were still arguing when she got through the front door.

'This is only a four-bedroomed house,' said her evil stepmother. 'The kids can't all share one room. Paola and Lucy will have to double up. I still don't see why…'

Robyn stopped speaking when she realised that Lucy was behind her. Dad gave her another hug. 'I've just heard,' he said. 'Paola's arriving in Manchester at 1725. Will you come with me to collect her?'

Over his shoulder, Lucy thought that Robyn was about to suggest a taxi, but threw her arms in the air and stormed off to the kitchen. 'She doesn't mean it,' said Dad. 'She's just worried about the impact on Phoenix and the boys.'

'She does mean it, Dad. That's the point. I don't blame her for it, though. I'll sleep in the conservatory. That inflatable mattress is fine for me.'

'Nonsense. Hang on a minute.' He took out his phone and dialled. 'Natasha? Gary here. Get someone up here with a spare bed. Only needs to be a single … I don't care … just get them up here, and tell them to put it in the formal dining room. Gianni's mother's arriving tonight.' He disconnected. 'There, love. A bit of peace and quiet for you.'

There was a knock on the open door. The squinty-eyed family liaison officer stood at the threshold. Lucy smiled to herself when she remembered the way that Tom Morton had faced her down.

'Robyn's in the kitchen,' said Dad.

'It's you I'm here to see, Gary,' said the FLO. 'My colleague will be here shortly to take a witness statement from you.'

'You go and help Robyn sort out some tea,' he responded. 'I'll be in the den with Lucy. Let me know when you want me.'

The FLO took a step forward, but Dad put his hand in Lucy's back and took her through to his den, shutting the door behind them. 'She's like a limpet, that one,' he said. 'I know she means well, but we're here for each other, Luce.'

Lucy couldn't care less. All she wanted to do was flop down — so she did, kicking her shoes into the corner. Dad came and sat next to her. 'It's a mess, love. It's a real mess.'

Into the silence that followed, Lucy could feel the snow melting inside her, like it had melted outside on the green. The tears started, and he put his arm round her. Gianni was the most infuriating big brother in the history of infuriating big brothers, but he was *her* big brother. No one had the right to take him away. Hadn't he come back to England to be near her, when he much preferred living in Italy?

Italy… Mama… The chain of memories pulled her upright. When Lucy was sixteen, Paola had discovered Dad's affair with Robyn, and flown off to Italy in a rage, dragging Gianni with her. Lucy had stayed here, in Southfork, gritting her teeth for two years until she had left school. Rebellion took her to university in Milan, but the welcome there was frosty. After a year, she transferred to Manchester. Home again. Gianni had come back four years ago, and G White Ltd had become White-Berardi Sports Management.

'What's up, love?'

Lucy wasn't entirely sure. She opened her mouth to say something about Mama, but there was a knock on the door, and Holly came in with a tea tray. The FLO was behind her.

'How's Madison?' asked Lucy. She couldn't help but think that the teenaged Madison Greenwood might be the one most cut off from everyone right now.

Holly looked at the FLO. 'Can you excuse us? Robyn will get you a cuppa.'

'It's not the tea I'm after,' said the policewoman. 'I'm just reminding you that you haven't made your statements yet.'

'You what?' said Dad. 'Are you trying to suggest that we might be in a conspiracy or something?'

Someone called out from the front door, and the FLO reluctantly left them in peace.

Holly poured tea, and Lucy accepted because it would have been rude to refuse. She wasn't going to drink it, though. 'Maddi's gone with the police,' said Holly. 'They were searching the house when I arrived, and she was hiding in the dining room.' She smiled at Lucy. 'Surrounded by all her designs for your shop, she was, but she hadn't even got her phone. She'd given it to Dean so he could call an ambulance. To cut a long story short, I phoned her mum and they're on their way up from Stoke. They're going to collect her from the police station and take her home. I threw a few things in a case for her.'

'Poor Maddi,' said Lucy.

'Yeah. Poor Maddi,' said Dad.

'She's innocent,' said Lucy. 'It's not her fault.'

'Well, that's what I've come about,' said Holly. 'I wanted you to know first, before the police tell you. When I found Madison, she was in tears. Said it was all her fault. I said, "No it isn't," and she said, "Yes it is. I was having an affair with Gianni, and Dean found out."'

'The two-faced bitch.' Gary almost spat the words, and went red with anger.

'What about Gianni?' said Lucy. 'I bet she didn't throw herself at him. He was going behind Dean's back in a big way.'

'That's as maybe, but…'

The FLO didn't knock, she just came in with another woman. 'Gary, the sooner we get your statement the better. Shall we go somewhere else?'

'You can take Lucy's statement and mine together. In here. There's plenty of chairs.'

Holly gave Lucy a squeeze on the leg, and whispered, 'Don't be shy about coming round. Ellie could use the company, if you need a break.'

It was nice of her to say that. It wasn't so nice to think about why she needed to say it.

It was the silence that got to him. From the moment the radiographer told him that he would need an operation, to the moment that he was pushed towards the custody desk in Wythenshawe police station, no one spoke to him. Not one word, not even when they handed him a plastic bag full of prison clothes to wear. The last time he had been treated like that was at school.

The police sergeant behind the desk was no better, at first. He listened to the detectives without making eye contact with Dean, and then pointed to a notice on the desk. 'Those are your rights,' he said. 'Can you read them?'

'Yeah.'

The sergeant read them out anyway, and then started asking questions. Things were going fine at first, because Dean knew his own name and date of birth. They got more difficult when he was asked his address.

'Homeless.'

'Are you not Dean Rooksby of The Maples, 7Bridge Estate, Cheshire?'

'I'm Dean Rooksby, but I don't live there. Didn't they tell you? I'm barred.'

'This isn't funny,' said one of the detectives.

'And I'm not laughing.'

The custody sergeant picked up a piece of paper. 'There's a solicitor in reception. He says he's been retained to represent you.'

Thank God for that. Gus had come through for him.

'His name is Daniel Abramovitz.'

The detectives looked at each other. 'You can ask for the duty solicitor if you want,' said one of them.

'Why would I?'

The policeman raised his fingers to make quotation marks. '"Daniel Abramovitz. I represent the unrepresentable." Don't go to his office. One of his other clients might try to sell you half a tonne of cocaine.'

'Or just stab you,' said the other detective.

'Does he get them off?' asked Dean. Their silence was all the answer he needed.

He didn't get to meet his potential saviour until an hour later, after food. He was taken out of his cell, and escorted to a tiny room with nothing but two chairs. The sign on the door said Duty Solicitor - Private.

Abramovitz was a big man, in all sorts of ways. He had a bushy beard and bushy black hair, where it wasn't being held down by a skullcap. 'Are you Jewish?' blurted out Dean. 'Sorry.'

'What's the problem?'

'No problem, honest. I've just never met anyone Jewish before. Not proper Jewish.'

'My mother says I'm not proper Jewish, so maybe you still haven't. Where are you from?'

'Stoke-on-Trent.'

'Aah. I've never met anyone proper Jewish from there either. Just don't offer me a bacon sandwich and we'll get on fine. Sit down. We haven't got long.'

Dean sat. 'Did Gus send you?'

'Not really. I'll explain. You have many problems, Dean, but the biggest problem is that you don't have an agent any more.'

Dean snorted. 'I'd say the murder charge is a bigger problem.'

'You haven't been charged yet – and besides, that's what I'm here for – and you can pay me from your wages.'

'Have I still got a job? No one's telling me anything.'

'Trafford Rangers can't sack you unless you're convicted, and they won't sack you because you might be innocent. They don't throw away assets like you. You need help, Dean, and I have a cousin who can help you. Do you know Isaac Redmond?'

'I've heard of him. Murray Cavendish is with him, isn't he?'

'He is. Isaac is a big fan of yours, Dean. He's willing to take a risk with you.'

'Really?'

'Really.' Daniel opened his briefcase and took out some papers. 'I've got a contract here, if you want to sign it now.'

Dean took the lawyer's pen like it was a rope thrown from a lifeboat, and signed five pieces of paper without even glancing at them. Only when he'd finished did he remember to ask something. 'As my lawyer, would you have advised me to do that?'

'I don't give advice: people never listen to it. I just carry out instructions. Now… about this fight you had with Berardi. Allegedly.'

Before Dean answered, something struck him about Abramovitz's tie, which was mostly obscured by his black jacket. 'Is that a Trafford Rangers tie?'

'It is. Not all Jews support Tottenham, you know.'

The cells in Tom's spreadsheet were starting to develop a life of their own. When he looked away from the screen, they were overlaying themselves on papers, on his desk and even on the teapot. He gave a huge sigh of relief when Elaine breezed in with some food.

'Is Indian okay? I thought we deserved something better than pizza.'

'We do. Let's eat.'

Between mouthfuls of biryani and rogan josh, she told him what had been going on at Wythenshawe police station. She summed it up like this: 'Lots of forensics putting Dean on the running track, an admission from Madison Greenwood that she *was* having an affair with Berardi — but no witnesses, no CCTV, no murder weapon (because there isn't one) and no confession.'

Tom chewed on a piece of lamb. It was tasty, but he could feel the bits getting in his teeth. 'Do they have a timeline on Berardi's movements?'

'Sort-of. Lucy White said he had a breakfast meeting at Manchester Airport with a potential sponsor — if you can call five o'clock breakfast. I'd call it a late-night snack. His BMW was registered on the system leaving the Estate yesterday, then coming in at eight o'clock this morning. Putting together all the other evidence, he was in the fight at around 09:15, and was dead by 09:30, when the patrol officer found him.'

'Was he definitely at the airport? Who were the potential sponsors?'

'They're making enquiries with airport parking and security. The sponsors were a Mr and Mrs Ikeda of Japan. Mr Ikeda owns …' – she consulted her phone – '… the Miyagi New Engine Corporation.'

'I'll try to contain my excitement.'

She held up a finger. 'Wait … all is not what you think. They don't make physical engines. He's a software developer … they make games engines.'

Tom had a flashback to his younger sister's loft in Hackney, where he used to go to escape his studio box. Kate Lonsdale, just back from an undercover adventure in

Dublin, was telling them about her client and the video games they produced, while Diana wanted to know about her sexual conquests.

He hadn't thought about Kate all day, so far. Then there was this spike of sweet memory. Was this what grief was all about? Slow forgetting punctuated by stabs of loss?

'Tom? Are you okay?'

'Sorry. Phantom memory. Is it for JRPGs?'

Elaine was impressed. 'I had to look that up. Don't tell me you play them.'

'No. I do not like computer games.'

'Good. Japanese role playing games – JRPGs to those in the know – is how the company started, but they've just developed a new system for sports action games. Again, according to Lucy White, Mr Ikeda is a lifelong Rangers fan, and he wanted to sign John Nugent to be their front man when they try and sell it to the console developers.'

'I'm guessing that the Ikedas were on their way out of the country.'

'Correct. They had been in the UK for two weeks, and they are now continuing their honeymoon in the USA. Have we got any dessert?'

'Did you bring one?'

'No.'

'That'll teach you to think about the big picture. Let's clear up.'

Tom wanted the fresh air, so he volunteered to take the bin bag outside. He didn't want the office to smell of curry: they might not give Leonie her deposit back when the rental period was up. He returned to his desk. Elaine had made a very acceptable pot of tea.

'What news on the interview with Rooksby?' he asked.

She pulled her face. 'That's the one fly in the SLC ointment. Out of nowhere, Dean has conjured a shit-hot criminal lawyer. I heard the sergeant talking — even before they got him in the interview room, the lawyer had pointed out that the CPS could only prove GBH if they could establish that Dean was not acting in self-defence.'

'I'd have thought that the kicking he gave Berardi would establish that he wasn't acting in self-defence.'

'Dean had a broken nose and a badly dislocated shoulder. Apart from Berardi being dead, you could say that Rooksby came off worse.'

'Hmmph. I like that lawyer's style. So … it's murder or bust.'

'That's about the size of it. They're interviewing Dean about now, and again in the morning. I suppose they might release him on police bail.'

'They won't,' said Tom. 'Because there's not going to be any new evidence, no matter how long they wait.'

Elaine put her mug of tea down on one of Tom's printouts. He moved it out of the way.

'Dare I ask how you got on?' she asked. 'Please keep it simple. It's too late for VAT.'

'My boss used to have a poster in his office that read, "And Jesus said, The Geeks shall inherit the Earth." Remember that, DC Fraser.'

'I'll try not to.'

Tom passed over a piece of paper, which was now embossed with a brown ring. 'I've been able to establish that there is no legitimate private reason for Berardi to have £200k in his house. His income is high, but his assets barely cover his liabilities. He doesn't even own that house. I need to push Paul Warren a bit more. If I can get proof that White-Berardi and its subsidiaries really don't deal in cash like that, there's going to be a question mark hanging in the air. It might be small comfort, but Dean's lawyer would be able to exploit that in a trial. That's not the most interesting thing, though. Have you checked *SeeinIn7Bridge* tonight?'

'No. Hang on.'

While Elaine looked it up, Tom refreshed his memory. At 18:45 that evening, this post had appeared:

*Some of you are waiting for the inside story on today's events in 7Bridge. One of my fans on Twitter is even calling it "Death in Paradise". The Mother Superior may be super-human, but she's still human. Our thoughts and prayers tonight are with Gary, our old friend Paola, Lucy and all the others who are devastated by Gianni's death. Especially MADISON GREENWOOD. Oops! Have I said too much?

'That didn't take long to become public,' said Elaine.

'It doesn't mention Robyn White,' said Tom. 'And do you notice the reference to Paola Berardi? According to one of the reports, she hasn't been resident in 7Bridge for nine years.'

'This new stuff proves that it wasn't Berardi writing it.'

'Not alone, at any rate. You won't have seen this, yet. Those chest-cams the patrol officers wear are very detailed.'

The security team at 7Bridge had insisted on a memorandum of agreement. They were willing to hand over specific bits of information, on request, without a warrant. That included chest-cam footage of the officer who found the body, and the other one who had accompanied Tom on his visit to the summer house. He turned round his laptop and played it from the beginning.

'Get you, sir. I hope this goes on YouTube; you could single-handedly bring waistcoats back into fashion.'

'I've got some footage of you picking your nose at the crime scene.'

'No you haven't.'

He gave her an enigmatic smile, and paused the footage when the PO jiggled the mouse on Berardi's computer and brought the screen to life. 'Look at that.'

She squinted at the screen. 'It's this morning's entries from *SeenIn7Bridge*.'

'What do you notice?'

She looked more closely. 'It's not from the website! This is in a text document.'

'There's more, but you need to compare it to the published version.'

She got out her phone, and compared the two. It took her two minutes to discover that after "MAX NOLAN" the words "(Chief Thug)" had been added when the site went live.

'Thoughts?' said Tom.

'This was being sent to Berardi for approval. To show that he'd read it, he added those words.'

'I agree. First thing tomorrow, you go to Wythenshawe and get access to that laptop as soon as you can. I've got this report to finish in the morning, then we've got a meeting booked with Paul Warren and Lucy White in the afternoon. I'll see you in the Seven Bridges Inn at two o'clock. The rush should be over by then.'

'Are we meeting them at Lucy's house or the White-Berardi office?'

'Neither. To avoid the media, we're meeting at the House of Lucia, but we have to use the back entrance.'

Chapter 9

Wednesday 15 January

There were no dreams when he was asleep, but Dean was starting to dream of Gianni Berardi when he was awake. All last night, and again this morning the police had been at him: *Describe the fight … tell us how you held his head under water … did you suspect they were having an affair?* They had even asked about whether Dean had given Berardi any money. Dean had told them it was supposed to be the other way round — and no, Berardi had never given Dean or Madison any cash.

When they left him alone, he kept seeing Berardi's face, just at the moment when Gianni put his hands over his head to protect himself. If only he'd stopped there. If only he hadn't kicked the shit out of the slimy bastard, Berardi might have been able to walk away. Drowned in a puddle … what a way to go.

His head fell on to his chest, and he jerked awake. *Oww.* Every time he moved his shoulder without thinking, it hurt. He moved into the corner of his cell and rested his head on the wall. He jerked again when the guard put the key in the door.

They took him back to the same interview room, and Daniel was waiting.

'I'm sorry, Dean. I tried, but no use. They're going to charge you.'

'Hmmph.'

'You'll get off at trial. Don't worry. The most important thing is to get you bail this afternoon.'

'Do you think you can?'

'Leave it with me.' Daniel had learnt not to pat Dean on the shoulder after the second time he had screamed, so Daniel patted him on the hand instead.

'Are you going?'

'You're doing great, Dean. You don't need me here. You need me down the magistrate's court getting ready for the bail hearing.'

The detective sergeant came in and told Dean that he was going to be taken back to the custody suite, where he would be charged with murder.

Despite his hasty departure from Florida, Saul had found room in his case for a box of the finest corona cigars. Three were already gone, and he was rolling the fourth in his hand, but he couldn't smoke it until Max had left.

'Status?' said Saul. Max managed a smile. In all their years together, Saul couldn't remember a worse time — not even when Holly was nearly raped on the green by an intruder.

'Did you get any sleep?' asked Max. 'Because you look even more like shit than usual.'

'At least I haven't lost any more hair. Yes I did. Thanks for asking. I slept on the plane and in the flat, but my body clock says it's five in the morning. I'll be okay until tomorrow, then I'm in trouble. I've read all the reports. Has anything new happened?'

'They've charged Rooksby with murder, and their forensic team returned the keys to his house this morning.' Saul grunted his acknowledgement. 'Before we get on to the other business, there's something else I've heard on the grapevine. Rooksby has signed a new deal, with Isaac Redmond.'

'Bloody hell. Gary won't like that. Not one bit.'

To remove temptation, Saul gave the cigar one last sniff and put it back in the box, and put the box in a drawer. While he did so, Max had took out a notebook from his coat pocket. Everything else on the Estate was documented online.

Max waved the notebook at him. 'I had to ask Tiffany for this. It's a free sample from somewhere.'

'And what does it say?'

'Berardi was definitely the source for some of the Mother Superior's stories. Now that he's dead, a few tongues have loosened. I had a word with Beth, who had a word with Vanessa. It seems that the legionnaires' disease certificate on the pool was in trouble, and they either had to get a man in or close the pool. That's *get a man in*, literally. There really weren't any female technicians with the necessary skills or registrations. Neither of them is admitting to be the one who suggested cross-dressing, but they both admit talking about it during the staff party before Christmas. Berardi was there.'

'What was a resident doing at the staff party?'

'He's shagged so many of the staff, he almost counts as one.'

'Please, God, deliver me. Have any of DCI Stamp's team shown any interest in the Mother Superior?'

'No. Not at all.'

'And did you find out about Morton's status? He's definitely interested in our little problem.'

'Apparently, he's looking into Berardi's financial position, and that's all.'

'Good. Thank you. Now, Hoskins … is there anything physical on site that could compromise his work if the police found it?'

'Yes. There's a gizmo – don't ask for details – in the junction cabinet on the green, and one downstairs in our server room. He's on his way down this morning to remove them.'

'Just make sure you escort him on site yourself, and put him in some overalls before you let him loose.'

'Right,' said Max, getting up to go.

'How did you hear about Isaac Redmond taking Rooksby under his wing?'

'His secretary rang Vanessa to arrange access for a removal firm to Rooksby's house. She mentioned it to me, and I did a little digging of my own.'

'Keep me posted.'

There was nothing else to do that required his immediate attention, and nothing to stop him doing what he tried to do once a day: walk the estate. It was his only real exercise, but Saul valued his hour spent on the running track and round the paths. Not only did it keep him fit, it kept Max's people on their toes.

He would have to pass the spot sooner or later, so it was time to see where Berardi had been sent to meet his maker.

'Did you have a cooked breakfast this morning?' asked Elaine as they walked into the pub.

'What if I did?'

'You're going to have lunch now, and I'll bet you have dinner at the hotel tonight. Why don't you put on weight?'

'Careful. You'll turn into the Mother Superior. Anyway, it's not about how many meals you eat. It's about how much of them you leave behind. Mineral water?'

'Yes, please.'

She picked up a menu and found them a seat in the corner. They both ordered the vegetarian risotto, then exchanged news. Apart from the murder charge, nothing new had come up this morning. Elaine was beginning to doubt herself. The longer she lurked in the MIT office, the clearer it became that the Estate had more security measures than an army base. There was no evidence at all of anyone near Giovanni Berardi except for Dean. To suggest that someone else had done it – that someone else *could* have done it – was beginning to sound like it was beyond reasonable doubt … something the prosecution would no doubt emphasise. Unless she and Tom could find something soon, Dean's future liberty could be down to which side had the best barrister when his case came to trial. Either way, if it went to court, his life would be ruined.

Just before the risotto arrived, a woman approached them. Elaine had half noticed her looking around the pub — a well-built woman in her thirties, with long blonde hair. She was wearing a padded coat with something on the front that Elaine didn't recognise. As the woman approached them, she saw a crest, with a white triangle and a football, and STFC underneath. Salton Town Football Club. She nudged Tom, who flinched way too much.

'Are you really police, or are you the press?' said the woman.

'Do we have to be either of those?' said Tom, far more politely than Elaine would have done.

The woman tried a smile, but didn't have the courage for it. 'I saw that sign you put in your car when you parked in the *No Parking* zone. It said police. The press often do that.'

'If I were a journalist, would I admit it now that you've told me what you know?' Tom was enjoying himself. Elaine was hungry.

The woman tried to smile again, and shifted her weight from one foot to the other. She didn't look like she enjoyed standing up very much. Tom put her out of her misery by briefly flashing his warrant card. 'How can we help? I presume you don't really want to criticise my parking.'

The woman flushed bright red, and twisted from her hips as if to offer a handshake, but thought better of it. Instead, she pulled a business card from her pocket and offered it to Tom. 'I'm Emily Miller, secretary to the Salton Town FC Supporters' Club.'

Tom took the card, studied it, stowed it, and said, 'DCI Morton … DC Fraser. I don't want to sound rude, but we're about to eat those risottos.' Tom pointed to a waitress who was bearing down on them with two plates. 'If you're quick, go ahead. If it's very urgent, go ahead — but otherwise I'll happily see you later this afternoon.'

Elaine expected the woman to crumble, but she didn't. She planted her feet firmly on the carpet, and spoke as if she were giving evidence. 'Dean Rooksby is not a killer. He is a good man. No one who cares for people like he does would take another life. I know the real Dean.' She stopped. The waitress had been hovering, and Emily moved to one side. 'That's all,' she mumbled.

'Thank you, Emily,' said Tom. 'This isn't my case. Not really. DCI Stamp is the senior officer, but I'll tell him I've met you. If you really want to help Dean, contact Daniel Abramovitz — his lawyer, and whatever you do, don't start an online campaign to support him.'

'Why not? I've already started one.'

'Stop. It won't make any difference to the trial, and it will bring you so much pain and grief that you'll regret every second. If you've got any influence with the club – and it's a small club, so you might have some – get them to allow him back in training after the operation.'

Her eyes widened. 'What operation?'

'He's going to need serious surgery on his shoulder. Support his right to a fair trial and fair treatment from behind the scenes, not in public. Let his agent handle that. He'll thank you more in the long-run.'

Tom smiled, and picked up his fork, as did Elaine.

Emily backed off, mumbling her thanks, then stopped. 'Salton Town is not a small club,' she said, and left them to their lunch.

'Are you really going to tell Stamp about her?' asked Elaine.

'Not really. I'll log it in HOLMES2 and he can pick it up if he wants to. Let's change the subject. How's Rob doing?'

The risotto was good. Elaine was already halfway through hers. 'All right, I suppose. He'll get in the squad, but he's no nearer the first team. There would have to be a spate of injuries for that to happen. Or for Scotland to get thumped in the opening fixture.'

'Who are they playing?'

'Italy.'

'If they don't win that one, he might as well come home. They won't win anything after that.'

'Don't tell him, but I think you're right.' Magically, Elaine's plate was empty. Tom left about a quarter of his portion.

'Going back to the case...' she continued, '...there was an issue with the laptop. He had an Outlook client which duplicated his work emails, but there was an encryption program too: he used webmail for contact with the *SeenIn7Bridge* hosts. It was pure chance that we found that text document open. Why are you so interested in the Mother Superior? No one kills over what gets said on the Internet.'

'If it were just Berardi, I'd agree, but there's something else going on here. Something much bigger.'

'Why do you say that?'

'I told you I was once a lawyer.' Elaine nodded. 'When I was at law school in Durham, we had all sorts of special sessions to prepare us for practice: professional conduct, equality and diversity — you know the sort of thing. Well, one day we had a woman from the Plain English Campaign.'

'I'd have said that was a bit of a lost cause, with a room full of potential lawyers.'

'That's what she said, but she was very good. She made us do exercises and tried to make us see how easy it was to slip into obfuscatory and sesquipedalian terminology.'

Elaine spluttered into her mineral water. 'Please, Tom, do not tell me what that means. I don't want to know.'

'I will one day, when you can't get away from me. The real point is this: most people use very few long words.

That website uses a *lot* of long words, in case you hadn't noticed.'

She hadn't noticed. Elaine had felt there was something not-quite-WAG about the website, but couldn't put her finger on it.

'Everyone says that Gianni Berardi was very Italian, and that shows in his emails — I finally got to see them, by the way. His written English was good, and he knew his stuff, but the only polysyllabic words he used were related to business. There is at least one other person involved in that website, someone with a gift for parody who puts a consistent, acid-rich varnish on the gossip.'

'I won't argue, but you'll have to convince me it's relevant.'

'You're right. The cash is far more likely as a motive for murder, but why was it still there? Come on. Let's go.'

On the way out of the pub, Elaine held the door open to a cheerful man with a beard. When she caught a whiff of his aftershave, it triggered a memory — a memory of meeting another bearded man, who wore the same aftershave as an ironic comment. Or was it the same man in a completely different setting? She looked at his figure as it headed towards the bar, and it nearly came back to her. She let go the door and hurried after Tom.

'You can't go out there looking like that, Dean.'

'But I want to tell everyone that I'm innocent.'

'That's what Daniel is for. You look like a sick convict. You're wearing prison clothes and your arm is in a sling. Is that the image you want to give to the world?'

Dean was being processed at the back of the magistrates' court. Instead of his lawyer, he was accompanied by his new agent, Isaac Redmond. When he had first met Gary White, there was no doubt that Gary had once been a professional footballer. You could see it in his build, in his walk — but Redmond had probably never played football in his life. He looked like a well-off lawyer, which he probably was. He also looked Jewish. Possibly. But not proper Jewish like Daniel: no skullcap.

'Put your foot on the stool,' said the security guard. 'I need to fit the tag.'

Dean raised his left leg and plonked it on a fixed metal step. The electronic tag clicked on to his ankle, and he was given an instruction booklet, then he was told to go back out through the front of the building.

'The TV crews will have gone by now,' said Isaac. 'Once they've got Daniel waxing lyrical about your innocence, they'll have all they need. Just put your hood up and no one will recognise you amongst all the other hoodies.'

Dean thought about saying something, something like: *Not everyone who wears a hoodie is a delinquent.* Then he realised where he was. The proportion of non-delinquent hoodie-wearing young men in a court building was probably very small.

On their way through to the front door, Isaac told him about the arrangements he had made to empty the house in 7Bridge and remove the contents to his parents' place. 'Good job we didn't have much,' said Dean. 'Mum and Dad don't have a lot of room. They said they weren't going to build an extension until I got into the Trafford Rangers team. They might have a long wait now.'

'Next summer, you mark my words. Another year on loan at Salton and you'll be summoned to Barton Bridge.'

His parents were waiting in the lobby. Seeing his father in the public gallery – giving him the thumbs-up – was the best thing that had happened to Dean all day.

'Before I go, take this,' said Isaac. He was holding out an iPhone. 'It's all sorted, all set up. You've even received a tweet already.'

Dean took the phone, then realised it was hard to work one-handed. He made it through to the Twitter app, and Isaac was right: *STFC supporters call on the Club to honour their*

commitment to Dean and support his recovery #innocentuntilotherwise
@EmilySaltonTown.

'She's toned it down a bit since this morning,' said Isaac. 'Sounds like the sort of person you'd want in your corner.'

'Yeah,' said Dean. 'I'm gonna need them.'

Chapter 10

Wednesday 15 January, continued

There was desperation emanating from the House of Lucia. Heavy, close-slatted shutters were down. There was no need for the note saying *Closed due to family bereavement.* Tom and Elaine lowered their heads as they passed it, and the White-Berardi building next door.

They turned down an alley just past the Village Café, then left again to retrace their steps along the back of the buildings. Most of the structures had been extended at some point, and the White-Berardi building had been extended so far that its Victorian frontage was little more than a facade.

By contrast, the House of Lucia was almost as the builder had left it, apart from new windows and doors on the projecting kitchen/bathroom extension. Its back yard had been cannibalised for White-Berardi's car park. Did Gary White own both buildings? Was the House of Lucia a hobby for his daughter?

One door was labelled *Flat*, so he presumed that the other was the shop, especially as it was propped ajar. From inside, he could hear music and a rushing, mechanical noise. 'Hello? Miss White?' he called, and opened the door.

There was a toilet to the right, and to the left a galley kitchen with no cooker. It would have been quite spacious, except for the cupboards and shelves full of stock. Lucy was boiling the kettle and moving to the music of a mini sound system.

'Oh! Morton! I mean… sorry.'

'I'm the one who should apologise. I didn't mean to disturb you.'

'Come in.'

She led them through into the shop, and Tom stepped into a world he hadn't entered since his marriage broke down: the world of women's desires and needs, made real in the silk hangings and accentuated by the lighting. The fact that the shutters were down made it the most intimate and inappropriate place in which he had ever conducted an interview.

There was a counter by the door with the card machine and wrapping equipment. To the left was a dressing table, with beauty products in glass cases for customers to try then buy. Beyond that was a window covered by floor-to-ceiling curtains … no, it wasn't: Tom had seen the outside of that wall, and it was brick. *Something* was behind the curtains. His gaze continued round to the fireplace wall, where the glow of coals was replaced by rows of shoes and a big display of handbags.

Over the handbag section was a small wooden plaque with yellow italic lettering: *Paola Berardi. Exclusive by Design.* The yellow of the letters was echoed in many of the bags — sometimes in a strap, sometimes in a stitched-on detail. Was that what they called *appliqué*? Pride of place was given to a stiff, almost retro bag, wholly in yellow crocodile skin apart from upright handles in shiny black. If the queen of a wasp nest owned a handbag, it would be that one.

In front of the glass cabinet were two intimate leather settees facing each other, one of them containing Paul Warren. He looked more out of place than Tom felt, and he struggled out to shake hands.

Tom saw that Elaine's visual inspection had continued beyond his own. She was studying a carousel of scarves by the front door when Warren greeted her.

'Would you like coffee?' asked Lucy. 'We're all a bit Italian — we don't drink much tea, but I do have it.'

At this point, Elaine was getting ready to sit down, so Tom said, 'I'll make it, don't worry,' and headed back to the kitchen. Lucy White followed him, and bustled around a two-cup Nespresso machine, but she didn't actually make the drink. Tom was faced with a choice of herbal teas.

His heart was sinking when Lucy said, 'Look behind them.' An unopened box of English Breakfast was lurking behind the nettle and raspberry, and Tom sighed with relief.

He poured the water, then turned around. 'How's your mother? I understand from the FLO that she wasn't … composed enough to be interviewed last night.'

She cocked her head on one side, and scooped her hair into a twist. With her hair up, she had quite a round face, he thought. 'Do you know everything about us?' she said.

'Far from it. It's just that I'm allowed to read the reports online. It's none of my business, really.'

She turned back to the coffee machine. 'Mama's always been a bit of a drama queen, especially in England. She's different at home. Her home. Much more reserved. But over here, she likes to play the extravagant Italian.'

'That doesn't mean she's not devastated, though.'

Lucy turned back, the coffee still unmade. 'Of course she is.' She looked up at him, and he realised how small the kitchen was. 'It's not just Gianni she's lost. It's the last link to Fabrizio.'

'Sorry?'

'Gianni's father. He was killed when Gianni was a baby.'

'Killed…?'

'Oh, he wasn't murdered, but it was bad. He was the manager of a tanning factory. There was an industrial accident. Gianni was the spit of him as a young man: I've seen the pictures. How long do you leave the tea bag in? It's been in there ages already.'

Tom looked at the steam coming off the mugs. 'I aim for five minutes, but I don't always get there.'

'Ugh.'

They both jumped when the music system burst into life. 'Damn,' said Lucy. 'I only pressed pause; it re-starts after five minutes.' She turned it off. 'Probably not your thing, dance music. You must like music of some sort.'

'I hope you don't think all detectives like opera. That was my ex-wife's thing. I really, really hate Wagner.'

'Wasn't he a Nazi? Wagner, I mean.'

'Perhaps in spirit, but he was a bit before their time in the flesh. I find that people like the music their parents like, but updated. My mother took me to a lot of choral evensong at the Minster.'

The look on her face suggested that she had absolutely no idea what either of those terms meant. 'The Minster is the cathedral in York; I like church music, but I'm not religious. My dad liked folk music when he was younger, and when I was eighteen he dragged me down the club for some male bonding.'

'My mother used to take me to the opera in Milan, sometimes, but that was more about being seen than watching the show. It didn't do much for me. Has anyone ever told you you're a young fogey?'

'I'll take that as a compliment. The "young" part. This tea should be ready.'

He ejected the teabags, and Lucy pressed the button on the coffee machine. Tom carried his brews. Lucy put hers on a tray, with sugar.

'I hope you weren't harassing my god-daughter,' said Warren.

'We were talking about folk music,' said Tom.

'Folk music!' said Elaine, in a completely inappropriate way. They all stared at her. 'I've just remembered something. I'll tell you later, sir.'

They settled down, and Tom and Elaine adjusted themselves on the sofa. If he leaned on the arm of the couch, and Elaine did the same, their hips came together. She was making the notes, so Tom sat up straight.

'I've read your statements,' he said. 'And thanks to Mr Warren, I've been able to piece together Giovanni's

139

financial situation, but that doesn't explain the £200,000 on his dining table. If I looked at the accounts for White-Berardi, and all its subsidiaries, would I find any large cash movements?'

Warren pursed his lips. 'No. I said that yesterday.'

'I don't want to press things, so I'll settle for a signed statement. What about you, Miss White? I know Giovanni is your brother, and I know you were close. Do you have any idea what he was doing with the money?'

'No.'

Elaine's hip bumped into his again. They had both seen the evasion in her eyes. Even Warren folded his arms defensively. 'It was from a bank,' Tom continued. 'It was still in paper wrappers.' He left the statement to hang, and hoped Elaine would keep her peace. She did.

'He used to gamble,' said Lucy suddenly. 'Cards, horses, football. Especially football. Dad had to bail him out a couple of years ago. Gave him a last warning. I haven't seen him bet since.'

'Mr Warren?'

'I didn't know him socially.'

That was a real lawyer's answer, but Tom let him get away with it for now. 'As I said, I've got access to all your witness statements, but the only person who mentioned Mr and Mrs Ikeda is you, Miss White. At the moment, they are the last people we know of who spoke to your brother. Could the money have come from them?'

Warren bristled, his moustache especially. 'Ikeda-san is a very respected businessman. His business is online, not cash.'

'And I can't see Mitsumi letting him carry that sort of money around,' added Lucy.

Tom turned slightly, so that he was facing her rather than Warren. 'Perhaps you could give me more of an insight into the negotiations. You seem to have been round them a lot.'

'It was a job. That's all. Dad paid me a small retainer to entertain Mitsumi a little, and we discovered that although her English was good, she found Gianni's accent difficult to deal with.' She took a deep breath, remembering her brother. 'It *was* difficult, but we were used to it. Mr Ikeda wanted to sign up John Nugent in all his roles, especially as captain of Trafford Rangers. We can't sell that. I had to explain to Mitsumi, who translated into Japanese, that if John went to work for Miyagi Engine, he couldn't put on a Rangers shirt. Or an England one.'

'Was the deal concluded?'

'I think so,' said Lucy. She looked at Warren. 'Did you get the paperwork, Paul?'

'Kaito emailed it from the airport, with his digital signature. It's binding.'

'How much?' said Tom.

'That's confidential.'

Elaine had her pen poised over her notebook. 'If you tell me now,' said Tom, 'it's off the record. But I will pursue this.'

'It's not the money that's confidential. It's the terms.' Warren leaned forward, or did his best. 'You were bandying around terms like *perverting the course of justice* yesterday. Here's one for you: *misconduct in public office*.'

Tom sat back. That was harsh. He hadn't been bandying anything: he'd made a veiled threat. Elaine bumped him with her hip. 'R v Bembridge, 1783,' said Tom. 'In case you'd forgotten, I do work for professional standards. It's my favourite offence.'

Did Lucy stifle a snort? While he was fencing with Warren, she had let her hair down.

Elaine had finally had enough of biting her tongue. 'I don't work for professional standards,' she said. 'I just *am* professional.'

Lucy coughed.

Warren wiggled his moustache. 'The Miyagi New Engine Corporation will pay John Nugent £450k for six months, with an option to extend. But the contract doesn't start until next year. This is the confidential part: John's standing down as England captain after the Euros this summer. Most people are expecting that, but he's leaving football altogether next year. Mr Ikeda gave him a full-time contract.'

'What?' squeaked Lucy. 'No one told me.'

Tom couldn't resist it. 'You'll have to hope that Miss White is bound by the ordinary standards of confidentiality.' Warren went red in the face and sat tight-lipped. 'Thank you for that, Mr Warren. One final question: what was the firm's commission on that?'

'It was £75k,' said Lucy. 'That much I do know.'

'As you can see,' said Warren, 'there's no scope for a cash payment in a confidential agreement that doesn't come into force for eighteen months.'

'Quite. There's one more question, on another matter. Based on evidence at Giovanni's residence—'

Lucy interrupted. 'It's his house, not his residence. I hate them being called that. And his name was Gianni. No one called him Giovanni if they knew him.'

Tom paused for a moment. 'We found his laptop. Next to the cash. There was evidence that he was a contributor to *SeenIn7Bridge*.'

'No,' said Lucy, emphatically.

'No,' said Warren, but with a salacious edge to his voice. 'Really?'

'Really, I'm afraid. This isn't easy, Miss White, but do you know who the other contributors might be?'

'No, I don't. And I don't care, either. It certainly isn't me. Look. Take it.' She squirmed in her seat and pulled out her phone, thrusting it towards Tom.

'No thanks,' said Tom. 'You would need a laptop, at least, not a phone. I think we'll leave it there, for now.'

He had to lean on the arm of the chair to lever himself out of it. Without thinking, he offered his hand to Lucy. She accepted, and he lifted her upright.

'They're a bit cosy, these chairs,' said Elaine, with a pointed look at her boss. She didn't need any help to get out.

'What's behind the curtains?' said Tom.

'Watch,' said Lucy. She still had her phone in her hand, and pressed it a few times. The curtains glided apart to reveal a full-length mirror with an ornate frame. Lights came on overhead. Elaine was nearest, and Tom noticed that she turned her back firmly to the mirror before picking up her coat.

He should have expected it: people love a memorial. The spot on the running track where Giovanni Berardi had been murdered was already marked by several extravagant bunches of flowers, much to Saul's annoyance. He didn't like that sort of thing, and he didn't like having it on the Estate. The flowers should go to Gary or Paola. Other than a muddy patch on the grass, the flowers were the only thing that gave the game away. Under no circumstances would he ever allow a permanent marker. That's what graves are for.

'Has anyone said anything about wanting extra security?' he asked the junior patrol officer who was with him.

'No, sir. Because Dean has been arrested, I don't think the residents see it as a security issue. Put it this way… there's no fewer joggers than there were.'

Saul grunted — and realised that he had lingered just a little too long, because coming up the hill, in a totally unauthorised buggy, were Gary White, his ex-wife and Lucy. Saul turned to the PO. 'Thanks,' he said. The man got the message and left him to it.

He composed himself, and folded his hands in a respectful position. The original architect of the Estate had insisted that the track have no lighting, so as not to spoil the views. It was a decision he had supported when some of the residents tried to get it overturned a few years ago. After Gary's intervention, they had compromised on movement-activated lights. One of them flicked on as the buggy went by. Paola Berardi looked ghostly under the LEDs.

When the buggy stopped short of the exact spot, Saul bowed his head. Gary gave him a brief nod in response. Duty done, he turned and walked back up the hill. As he made to turn left, his phone vibrated: Max.

'I'm on the running track,' he told his head of security.

'Our visitor is just leaving,' said Max.

'Any problems?'

'No. He says that now he knows Berardi was one of the contributors, he can get a fix on the type of encryption that's being used. If the other party is doing the same, it shouldn't take too long to track it down. He wants to wait a week, then put something in the cabinet by the main road.'

'Is he allowed to do that?'

'No. When I say, "He wants to do it," what I really mean is, "He's going to give me a box and some instructions." It's up to you then.'

'Perhaps. In a week or so. Call by my office at the end of the day.'

'Will do.'

Saul triggered the motion sensor himself when he moved on and a sudden shadow appeared before him. A sudden shadow, from nowhere. He took out his phone again and dialled the last number

'Max? Before you come and see me, can you sort out the CCTV footage for yesterday morning? There's something I want to check.'

'Will do, but I've watched it four times. So has my best pair of eyes, and the police have it too.'

'I'm not you, and I'm not the police. And one other thing: send a PO round to Southfork to get that buggy back off them.'

'I think there's a shortcut back to the bridge this way,' said Elaine when they left the House of Lucia's back door. Tom nodded. Should she say something? Elaine didn't want to get on the wrong side of her new boss, but he'd sailed very close to the wind with Lucy White. She zipped up her coat, and looked him in the eye. 'She's a nice kid, but you came on a bit strong there, sir.'

Tom lowered his face and blew air out of his nose, a little like a bull snorting. 'She's a year older than you. She's not a kid, even if she was flirting a little.'

'A little? At least you acknowledge it. She is a kid, though. Daddy's shop. Daddy's mansion, Daddy's money. She's just lost her brother, if you can believe it.'

Elaine realised she'd gone too far. Again. Tom Morton was the most even-tempered man she'd ever worked for, and she had started looking for aggro. Why did she do it? After three seconds of his silence, she wondered if he was going to send her back to ACC Schofield.

After five seconds, she couldn't take it any more. 'Well?'

'I'm waiting for you to tell me why the thought of folk music made you jump. Repressed childhood trauma, perhaps?'

'Do you always do that? Deflect the personal with a joke?'

He shoved his right hand between the buttons of his coat and rubbed his left arm. Again. He'd done it twice during the interview. Did he have eczema?

'It worked, didn't it?' he said. 'Lucy White was dancing when I first walked in. She's doing her best not to think about the fact that her mother and stepmother are refighting the battle of Gary White, and that she's lost her closest ally. That shop is obviously her haven — her port in the storm of life. The more she relaxes, the more I could push her. Do you think she's the Mother Superior?'

'No.'

'Neither do I, but I wouldn't have been certain otherwise. Now… folk music.'

Elaine started walking. 'There were two main groups in the ULIST climbing club. One did it for the thrills and for the adrenalin; the other group did it to be with nature. The first group was into hardcore techno or thrash metal. The second was into folk.' She looked up to see that he followed her. 'I was more sympathetic to the first lot, but the beer and the company was better at the folk club. The president was a guy called Neil Hoskins, a lecturer. He was going into the Seven Bridges when we were coming out.'

'Oh. I was expecting something more … interesting.'

'Bear with me. Neil was a lecturer in cyber security, and I think he did consulting work too.' They had crossed the river, and Tom was opening his car. It was nearly dark already. 'I think it might not be a coincidence that he's here. Do you mind if we do a PNC check?'

'Hmm. If he's any good, there might be a security flag on his record, and I don't want another encounter with Mr Lake in the near future. Would Mr Hoskins by any chance be a … well-padded gentleman with a beard?'

'Yeah.'

'There can't be too many of them driving bright red Porsche Cayennes. He looked most embarrassed when he got out of it, as if he knew that the car was designed with a different customer in mind.'

They got in Tom's BMW, and he started the engine. 'Are we going back via the Estate?' asked Elaine.

'Naturally.'

As Tom drove carefully through the village, Elaine said, 'What do you reckon about that money, then? Do you think it might be gambling?'

'Metaphorically, perhaps. I told Warren and Lucy that it was straight from the bank. That's not strictly true. The paper wrappers were generic: they could have come from anywhere. Can you do me a favour tomorrow? Get the actual physical evidence and look for any bundles of uncirculated notes.'

'How can I tell they're uncirculated?'

'As well as looking new, the serial numbers will be consecutive. Make a note of any you find.'

They had arrived at the Estate service area. The Porsche might not have stood out on the Estate itself, but in the service area it was a bright red beacon amongst the modest family cars. Tom pulled in and turned off the engine while Elaine made a note of the registration number. As she did so, two figures appeared through the security gate. 'Isn't that—?'

'Max Nolan. Yes. I take it the guy carrying the box and wearing overalls is your Mr Hoskins.'

'He wasn't dressed like that in the pub.'

'No, and judging from the way that those buttons are straining over his gut, those overalls don't belong to him.'

'Who's Mr Lake? You said you didn't want another encounter with him.'

'John Lake is a security liaison officer at the Home Office. He's a bit like the angel of Death: nothing good comes after a visit from him.'

They watched Hoskins put his case in the back of his car, and strip out of his overalls, hopping on leg as he did so. 'It's your lead,' said Tom. 'If you want to go to Cairndale tomorrow and tackle him, you're more than welcome.'

She thought about it for a second. 'Are you seeing Saul Blackstone soon?'

'Tomorrow afternoon, I hope.'

'Then let's save it for now. We can get hold of Neil at any time.'

Lucy had grabbed a scarf on her way out of the shop. Talking about the Ikedas had reminded her of the way that Mitsumi had struck a colourful note with the scarf fluffed up around her neck. Sadly, the House of Lucia didn't run to Hermès, but she chose something bright, in Mama's signature yellow. Thanks to her father, Uncle Paul had a permanent visitor's pass to the Estate, so he was able to drop her off by the house. As soon as she walked through the gates, she saw them, arguing under the portico … Mama and Papa, going at each other as if the last nine years hadn't happened.

Dad saw her first, and pointed. Mama saw and strode forward to embrace her. Naturally, she spoke in Italian. 'It's so terrible, Lucia. We can do nothing. We cannot even see him until tomorrow. We must go and honour him.'

Dad manoeuvred himself round to the other side so that he could give her a kiss without having to touch Mama. 'You've been ages,' he said. 'What did the police want?'

'I'll tell you later.' She addressed her mother, in English. 'What do you mean about honouring him?'

Paola stuck to her guns: it was Italian for her, no matter what. 'We must go to the place where he fell. We must show that we remember him. They will not let us say goodbye to him until tomorrow.' She sniffed. 'The autopsy. They have not finished. Gary, get us a cart.'

Like Lucy, her father stuck to English. 'I've told you, love, we can't use the carts any more unless we buy our own. Insurance.'

'And can we not drive?'

'No.'

'Then get a cart. I don't care about the insurance.'

Lucy took a step away from her mother. Mama could be difficult, especially when she wanted something, but she wasn't normally given to full-on diva strops, not like this. Was something the matter? Apart from the obvious.

Her father rolled his eyes in Lucy's direction and went inside. He emerged a few minutes later with a security radio. 'Gavin's on patrol in the East Section,' he said. 'I've promised him tickets if he lends us a buggy.'

Mama seemed to understand that okay. She went back into the house. Clearly they were expected to call her when the transport arrived.

'Were the cops okay?' he asked. 'They didn't harass you or nothing, did they?'

Thinking about the way that Paul had tried to protect her as well made her smile. Not that she needed protecting from DCI Morton. She wasn't sure about his sidekick, though. 'It's about the money, Dad.' She left a pause to see if he had anything to say. He didn't. 'And about the Ikedas…. These two detectives are trying to find out why Gianni had that money in his house, and what he was doing at the airport with the Ikedas. Paul had to tell them about John retiring in summer next year.'

Gary pulled his chin. 'That could be awkward.'

'Don't worry. Paul made sure they'll keep it to themselves. Look, Dad, is there anything you're not telling me? About Gianni and the money.'

Did she catch just the flicker of something in her Dad's eyes? 'I don't know, Luce. He's been playing his cards close to his chest for a while now. Maybe even literally. I've tried to get hold of him a couple of evenings recently — and he's been off the Estate, phone switched off, always vague about where he's been afterwards. That deal between John Nugent and Miyagi Engines … or whatever they're called, that was nothing to do with me. I've been trying to get John to plan ahead for months now. He should either finish his coaching badges or start doing more media work. He can't just let it drift like this.'

'If it's a full time job with Kaito, he'll have to go to Japan, surely?'

'It isn't.'

'Then Paul's just lied to the police. He told them that John was going there full time.'

Dad was about to say something, but the electric whine of a security buggy interrupted him. 'Go and get your mother,' he said. 'I'll deal with Gavin.'

Lucy went into the house, and called out. Mama emerged from the formal dining room, carrying the most enormous bouquet of flowers Lucy had seen outside La Scala. The core of the display was white lilies, just opening, and they were surrounded by more white flowers. To emphasise the contrast with her all-black Prada outfit, she wasn't wearing a coat. The heels on her boots were way too sharp, but Lucy wasn't going to say anything. She wasn't sure she knew the Italian for *rubberised running track*.

Paola handed Lucy the flowers, then allowed Gary to hand her in to the back of the buggy. Lucy put the flowers in the carry basket, and got in next to Dad. He drove at a sedate pace, going the long way round to get to the track rather than cut up through the green. As they drove up towards the place where Gianni had died, Lucy caught sight of Saul Blackstone. After bowing to them, he left them in peace. *He'd get on very well with Kaito*, thought Lucy. *That was a very accomplished bow.*

It was much more exposed out here, and the sun had already gone down. Lucy shivered while she waited for Dad to help Mama out of the buggy, and she turned her face resolutely away from the place they'd come to visit. The spike heels caught in the track almost immediately, and Paola would have fallen over if Gary hadn't been there to steady her. Lucy retrieved the flowers, and handed them over. Finally, she turned round.

It wasn't the sight of the other flowers that made her cry, nor was it the thought of Dean Rooksby's violence. It was the thought that she wouldn't be able to sneak into Gianni's house for a joint and tell him what a fool Robyn looked. Lucy wiped the tears away with the back of her woollen gloves which were typically practical, like her coat and her soft boots. Mama stretched out her black leather hands and moved two other bouquets aside so that hers had pride of place. When Mama stood up, Lucy was wiping her eyes again and nearly missed it. Mama stood with her head bowed and placed her hands on her abdomen. No, lower. She was holding the spot above her womb.

She turned to Lucy and said, 'You must come home with me, darling. You have no life here.'

Dad stiffened. He had understood that all right, but he said nothing.

'Let's not talk about this out here,' said Lucy. 'Let's go back.'

'You must come home. You must help me.'

Lucy looked at Dad; he was giving her his poker face: Paola wouldn't get the satisfaction of seeing him beg. For once, she wished he would. Lucy switched to Italian. 'Of course I'll help you, Mama. You know I will.' She switched back to English, because there is no Italian word for *home*. 'But this is my home.'

Paola didn't flinch. 'You must come with me. Enrico will not know what to do when the time comes for me to go into hospital.'

Both father and daughter reached out their hands. 'Mama?' said Lucy. 'Are you ill? Why didn't you say anything last week?'

'What's up, love?' said Gary.

Lucy's mind flashed back to her visit. Was it only two days since she'd come back? Mama had been preoccupied, certainly, and a little bit more emotional than normal, but she'd put aside a whole evening for them to be together, and cooked all her favourite dishes.

'I had to come here,' said Paola. 'To show the baby where his brother died. For him to meet his spirit.'

Oh, my God. That's gross! Mama liked to lie about her age, but all the family knew she was forty-seven. How had this happened? Was it just luck, or had she been having IVF?

'What the f…?' said Dad, tailing off into thunderstruck silence.

'Is it true?' said Lucy, blushing because her voice had come out like a little-girl squeak.

Mama placed her hands where they had been before, where soon there would be a bump. 'Be happy for me, Lucia. For both of us.'

That explained another unusual thing about last weekend: it hadn't been antibiotics that had made Mama abstain when Lucy hit the Prosecco. It had been concern for her unborn child.

'Did you say "he"?' asked Gary.

'Yes. For Lucia and Gianni … a brother.'

Dad offered her his arm, and Mama high-stepped her way back to the buggy.

'I'll see you back at the house,' said Lucy. 'I'm just going to spend a moment here.'

The paparazzi had missed him in Wythenshawe, but they were waiting in Stoke. Everyone in court had heard the bail conditions: reside with his parents, curfew at nine o'clock, wear a tag. The only exception was for in-patient treatment, notified in advance.

Dean had called ahead on his new phone, and his little brother had said that they were camped outside. When something like that had happened before, he always called Gary. Would he get the same service from Isaac? He tried the preprogrammed number.

'Dean? I only said goodbye to you half an hour ago. What's the problem?'

'It's the media. Mum and Dad only have an ordinary house. There's no gates on the drive or anything. The press are standing blocking the way.' He lowered his voice. 'It's not me: it's them. If Mum has a panic attack, Dad might get carried away and run one of them over.'

'Already sorted, my boy. Just tell him to sound the horn twice – short blasts – when you get close to the house.'

He passed the message on, and his father sounded dubious. 'I think you might have been a bit hasty, signing a new agent when you were in prison,' he said. 'We don't know anything about this Redmond.'

'He got me a good lawyer.'

'We'll see,' said his mother.

They could see the scrum of reporters and cameras from the top of the road. Dean's father slowed down a little, then sounded the horn. Like the Red Sea, they parted, moved gently aside by the biggest security guard Dean had seen since the last time he went clubbing in Manchester. Standing just on their driveway was a policeman.

His father drove steadily through the press of bodies with flash lights blacking out the windows and shouts ringing in their ears. Dean pulled the hood over his face. From the safety of the driveway, his mother scuttled inside the house. Then Dean did the same, hiding behind his father's outstretched arms.

As well as his brother, they found a young woman in the living room. She was bright, blonde and had a good dentist. Dean had met hundreds like her, right down to the sub-designer suit. His brother was standing behind her left shoulder. *Put your tongue away*, thought Dean. *Have you never seen one of these before?* Then again, his brother was still at college, so he probably hadn't.

'Hi,' said the woman. 'Isaac sent me. I'm your new PR.'

'Do we have to do this now?' said his mother. She had wanted to burst into tears the minute she crossed the threshold. It was what usually happened after a bad day.

'Yes, Mum,' said Dean. 'We have to get a narrative together, don't we?'

'We certainly do,' said the PR.

'Let me get out of these clothes first. They stink of the cells My brother will make us all some tea.'

153

'That would be lovely.'

Dean had only moved out of his parents' house seven months ago, and there were still plenty of his clothes in what was now his little brother's wardrobe. He suspected that they were given regular outings, but he didn't care. He took a quick shower first, and sprayed the electronic tag to see if it short-circuited. It didn't. On his way downstairs, still towelling his hair, he heard the landline ring.

'Dean?' said his mother. 'It's Maddi.'

Over her shoulder, he could see the PR watching him, one perfectly sculpted eyebrow raised in query. He could read the message: *Up to you, Dean.*

'Who?' said Dean to his mother.

'It's Madison. She says she wants to talk.'

'Never heard of her. Must be a wrong number.'

He chucked the towel to his brother. 'Let's go into the front room,' he said to the PR. 'Is there anything I can say before the trial?'

'Not really, but "Sources close to Dean Rooksby" can say quite a lot,' she said, closing the door behind her.

Chapter 11

Thursday 16 January

The door to DCI Rod Stamp's office was always open, literally and metaphorically: it was wedged firmly into position. That was part of what made him a good boss, though in a completely different way to Tom Morton. Elaine had spent quite some time in the MIT room, running errands, entering data and snooping around. She had followed Tom's lead and made lots of cups of tea: two of the team had already said they'd miss her, but they were men. The linchpin of the group – and Stamp's second in command – was DS Julia Jepson, a stocky woman in her early forties who dressed in blue and had pictures of two teenage boys on her desk. There was no sign of the boys' father. Someone had said in passing that Julia would have been the DCI if she hadn't taken a career break.

During Elaine's time in the MIT office, she had seen many colleagues dash into the SIO's lair, give their reports and dash out again. Usually, they left with a curt but sincere "Great" in their ears; twice, she had seen – and heard – an almighty bollocking.

Now that Dean Rooksby had been charged with murder, the operation was winding down. Detectives assigned from other teams had been returned to their normal duties, and a double murder in Ashton-under-Lyne had taken two from Stamp's own squad. Elaine was alone in the main office with Julia, who had stayed behind to watch Elaine sort through the money. It was partly for the chain of evidence, and partly to weigh it back into the evidence room afterwards.

None of the paper wrappers had the name of a bank on them. They were all yellow, with a large "£20" and a smaller "£1,000" printed on them. That made two hundred bundles to flick through. She was on to her tenth bundle (no consecutive serial numbers yet), when Stamp's phone rang. By bundle thirty, she had found two suitable packets, and Stamp's voice was getting louder. Two bundles later, both she and DS Jepson stopped what they were doing and listened to Stamp ranting at the phone.

'… My team are all police officers, not press officers. If you want someone to do that, you can … I don't care, sir, we've got better things to … with respect … What? Why? … No. Absolutely not… If you make it a direct order, then I've got no choice, have I?' There was a longer pause, and they heard the phone go down. 'Julia! Get in here now. Who else is here? Anyone?'

Jepson was scurrying towards the inner sanctum, 'Only DC Fraser, sir.'

'Good. She's a woman, isn't she?'

Julia Jepson, Elaine had discovered, was not someone to let even a hint of sexism go unchallenged, but this one passed her by.

'Get her in here too,' added Stamp. Elaine scrambled to her feet and joined the other woman in the doorway.

Stamp pointed at the phone as if it were alive. 'That was ACC Schofield. I have been ordered, would you believe…? *Ordered* to send a woman detective to see the Princess, and give her an update on the case.'

'I hope he said "female detective", not "woman detective",' said Jepson. 'I detect men as well as women.'

'Don't push it, Julia. Not today. Take Fraser with you and don't hang about. And before object, DC Fraser, your boss will approve. Now go. Both of you.'

Elaine curled her toes up inside her boots, and closed her eyes. 'Sorry, sir,' she said. 'We've signed out Berardi's money. We can't leave it in the office.'

'How much longer do you need?'

'Ten minutes should do it.'

'You can have five.'

With Julia's help, Elaine found five bundles of notes with sequential serial numbers, and took quick photographs of the top note. It would have to do.

Julia signed the chitty, and returned the cash to the secure room. They took their coats and headed downstairs. 'I'll drive,' said Elaine. 'If you can get a lift back.' Julia nodded. 'You must trust me: you didn't weigh the notes.'

'You don't need the money,' said Julia. 'I've heard about your husband.'

Shit. Was this how it was going to be? No one in Leicester had minded. They were either pleased to know a local sporting hero's wife, or they couldn't give a damn.

'I'm not judging you,' added Jepson. 'I'm just saying, that's all.'

'Sounds pretty much like a judgement to me. What does your husband do? If you've got one, that is.'

Julia stopped at the bottom of the stairs. 'Sorry. That came out wrong. Rod – the boss – doesn't often get worked up like that.'

Elaine was about to say that a proper apology was owed, then she thought about next week: Tom Morton would be off to pastures new, and she would be unattached. A recommendation from Stamp and Jepson could make a huge difference to her next posting. 'Come on. Let's go.'

On the way to Sevenbridge, Elaine asked about the Princess. There had been almost no references to her in the HOLMES2 reports, and Elaine thought that what little which had been added might have been sarcastic.

'She's a real princess, right enough,' said Julia. 'She married the Crown Prince of Ghar'aan.' Elaine racked her brain to remember why that name rang a bell. Julia supplied an answer. 'It's that little island in the Indian Ocean with big oil.'

'I know that. I was trying to remember what I know about the Crown Prince.'

'A victim of democracy.'

'Come again?'

'The sultan created a popular assembly to try and move the country towards a constitutional monarchy. In the first session, a suicide bomber blew up twenty people, including the Crown Prince. His widow was already pregnant, and the Sultan shipped Princess Karida out to England.'

'That's it!' said Elaine. 'They own 40% of Trafford Rangers, don't they?'

'And 80% of the 7Bridge Estate: it was originally developed by the Sultan's brother, who's the chairman at Rangers. When the Princess moved into the Hall, she built the Spa on to the back of it…'

One of the *SeenIn7Bridge* entries came into Elaine's head. '…And it's women only, all through the Hall, isn't it?'

'That's right, except for the Princess's son. They're a very Anglophile lot, the royal family. Even the Princess was educated over here. The Sultan wants the new Crown Prince to look west, not east.' She paused. 'Mind you, whether the people of Ghar'aan feel the same way is another matter.'

The Hall and Spa had their own security gate, further on from the back entrance to the Estate. The guard told them that they should report to the Spa reception. Elaine drove into the car park and admired the back of the Hall, which had been totally remodelled when the Spa extension was added, not that it looked any less palatial.

'Tawdry,' said Julia.

'You what?'

'Look at the columns: all fake.'

'No, they're not. That's Portland stone: you can tell by the pitting. All the fossils.'

'Well, they're not original.'

Only the Earth is original. All else is man-made. It was one of the ULIST Geology professor's sayings. Another of his favourites was: *If you don't think the Earth is alive, try dancing on a volcano.*

Elaine let Julia have the last word, and followed her into reception. There was a kid in uniform on the desk itself, and hovering behind her was a woman in a suit who came forward to greet them. At least she didn't say *Dressed like that, you must be police*, though that's how Elaine felt. All around them, tanned and toned women drifted between the lounge and the treatment rooms.

'I'm Beth Pedley, Spa Manager and House Manager in the Hall. I'll take you through, if you wouldn't mind showing me your ID first.'

Beth was in her late thirties, and obviously used her staff discount on the tanning facilities in the Spa (though judging from the line on her neck, it was spray rather than sunbeds). Her hair was one shade lighter than jet black.

'The Princess asked me to invite you this morning because she's concerned about the community here.' Elaine looked at Julia, whose mouth was turned down. It didn't feel like anyone had been invited. They stopped at a white panelled door, which filled the whole end of the corridor and had a security box next to it. 'There's only one rule in the Hall, if you don't mind: could you leave your shoes inside the door?' Pedley pressed her thumb to the box and a light turned from red to green. A heavy click sounded from within the door. Pedley took the handle and pulled lightly. The door glided open without a whisper.

On the other side, a woman wearing a headscarf over a green sari and green trousers was waiting for them. Her features, as well as her dress, suggested that she was from the subcontinent rather than the Middle East.

'You'll be coming out this way,' said Pedley. 'I'm sure you don't need an escort off the premises.'

Neither Elaine nor Julia felt the urge to thank her, but Pedley wasn't finished asserting her authority yet. She spoke to the Princess's maid. 'Alia, take these officers to the Morning Room.'

It was obvious that Alia had been given exactly the same instruction already, but she bowed her head and said, 'Yes, Miss Pedley.' She moved out of the way and invited them inside. Elaine prepared for the worst.

In two seconds, Julia had placed her zip-up boots on to a rack; Elaine had only just undone the first knot on her DMs. She knelt down and worked as fast as she could, but it felt like hours; Julia started tapping her fingers on her notebook. Then Elaine noticed something.

When she had finished, she stood up and whispered, 'Did you know you've got odd socks on?'

'Shit.'

The sergeant wavered between going barefoot and sporting one blue sock and one black one. She opted for the latter. The maid led them through wide corridors with gilded lamps and dense carpet, then ushered them into a shrine to good taste.

Princess Karida's Morning Room was intimate rather than overwhelming, but the level of decorative finish was intimidating to anyone who furnished their house from IKEA. From the four-armed chandelier to the marble fireplace, everything had been designed to give a message: this person had a good eye and a great budget. Neither of the officers wanted to sit on the delicate sofas, so they admired the view.

A gap in the clouds had allowed through some sunshine, and what remained of the original gardens was lit up below them. Beyond that, rolling fields led to the low hills that marked the start of the Peak District. It was there that Tom had rented an office, and the thought of him toiling over his spreadsheets reminded Elaine of something.

'Sorry, Julia,' she said. 'I need to text the boss.' She took out her phone and sent over the pictures of the £20 notes, with a message: *Been pressganged to accompany DS Jepson on visit to Princess.* She got a reply almost immediately: *Inquest opens 1400 Wythenshawe Town Hall. Be there. Thanks for the pics.*

They both jumped when Alia reappeared behind them. 'Please sit down and help yourselves,' she said, placing a tray on the table between the couches. Steam rose gently from matching tea and coffee pots. Instead of cups and saucers, there were delicate porcelain mugs. Next to the sugar bowl was a pair of black socks. 'The Princess will be with you shortly.'

Julia looked at the socks, then looked up. 'Go for it,' said Elaine. 'They look like silk to me.'

Her colleague plonked herself down and stuffed her mismatched footwear in a coat pocket. Then she stood up and removed her coat. Elaine did the same (with the coat) and sat down to take charge of the tea tray. While she was pouring Julia's coffee, she noticed that the spoons had hallmarks, and a shiver ran down her spine: *This is what a gilded cage looks like*, she thought.

The captive bird floated in shortly afterwards. She was about the same age as Elaine. Her thick black hair was loose. She wore no headscarf and no Arab dress: Princess Karida was a fan of Gucci, and bling. A delicate row of pearls stood out against the coral-pink blouse, matching the pearl earrings; the coral was echoed in her fingernails and toenails. Bare legs emerged from a fitted black skirt with a woven jacquard pattern, and stones glittered in flat sandals. They couldn't be diamonds, could they? Whatever, the Princess wasn't dressed for the outdoors.

'Call me Kari,' she said. 'I don't have a title here, and I wasn't born with one, despite what you may have heard.' She shook hands with the detectives before pulling up a low chair and pouring herself coffee. There was no sign of the maid.

Julia introduced herself and Elaine, then opened her notebook. 'What is it you want to know?' she asked.

'I understand that poor Paola's son was having an affair with Madison,' said the Princess carefully. 'I have never met either Giovanni or Madison, but Holly Nugent has told me some of the details. Was that the motivation for what Rooksby did to him?'

Elaine was glad she didn't have to answer that question: it cut to the heart of the way they worked as police officers. No matter how rich the Princess was, she was still a civilian in their eyes.

Julia took a sip of her coffee. 'Under British law, the police investigate crime. We give the evidence to the Crown Prosecution Service, and they decide how to use it in court.' She paused. 'We have evidence that Berardi was having an affair with Miss Greenwood, and we have evidence of a fight between Berardi and Mr Rooksby. I'm sure that will be at the heart of the prosecution case.'

Ten minutes on the Internet would have told their hostess exactly the same thing, and there was an iPad in a jewelled case on a side table. Kari evidently had some contact with the outside world.

'I have heard something else,' said the Princess. 'I may not see Saul Blackstone very often, but we message each other. That's how I run the Estate. He tells me that Giovanni was involved in the *SeenIn7Bridge* website. Is that true?'

Julia shifted uncomfortably in her seat. 'There is evidence to that effect.'

'And how are your investigations proceeding into the other people behind this vile filth?'

'There's a lot to sort out,' said Julia.

Kari smiled at her. 'Are you telling me that it's "one of a number of lines of enquiry"? Because if you are, that means you're not doing anything. Please… be honest.'

Julia flicked through her notebook, paying special attention to the blank pages. If she admitted the truth, it might rebound on DCI Stamp like a poisoned boomerang — and if he got it in the neck, Julia would be next in line for his anger. She opted to say nothing.

Elaine sat on her hands to stop herself butting in.

The shapely legs crossed themselves, and the Princess considered the silence. 'I see. Perhaps a little background would help. Ghar'aan is going to have problems. Big problems. By the time my son becomes the sultan, the oil will be running out. If my father-in-law and his brothers cannot make a home worth going back to by then, I want my son to have a life here, but I would prefer him to go home. I did not expect to be handed a happy marriage on a plate: I expected to work for it, but I didn't expect to be a widow at nineteen.

'They told me that I had two choices: live as a widow in the royal palace, or leave my son behind and make a new life for myself. I told them there was a third way: I could live as a widow in 7Bridge, and make sure that the Crown Prince grows up to be a good Ghar'aanian. He starts learning Arabic and the Koran next year.'

It was only at that point in the conversation that Elaine realised her hostess spoke with a British public school accent.

The Princess continued, 'There are many voices in Ghar'aan who would condemn me, and I have to be like Caesar's wife.' That went straight over Elaine's head. 'If I want to carry on living here, and I do, then this website must be stopped.'

Julia sat as rigidly as she could on the couch. 'That's not how we work in this country.'

'Don't give me "free speech", detective. I know exactly how things work in this country, and I will not tolerate a cobra in my nest. Saul has tried to uncover the author, but to do so would break the law. I would have thought that it was a *very* legitimate line of enquiry, given that Giovanni was murdered.'

Aah, thought Elaine. *That's what Neil Hoskins was doing here.*

The Princess's attitude had pushed Julia to the edge. 'We've exhausted our lines of enquiry, and I'm afraid that your problems are a civil matter.'

Damn. It was official now: Dean would go to trial, and the MIT weren't interested in anyone else but Dean Rooksby. Elaine looked from the Princess to the policewoman, and decided to gamble her future. 'You must be very worried about your son, Kari,' she said. The other women stared at her. 'Please forgive my ignorance, but is Ghar'aan a friend of the UK?'

'Where are you going with this, Constable?' said Julia, warning signs writ large across her face.

'Up to a point,' said the Princess.

Elaine ploughed on. 'I was thinking that there may be a security issue here.'

'I doubt that very much,' said Julia.

'It doesn't have to be our decision,' said Elaine. She reached down to the side of the chair and fished around in her coat pocket. There. She had stuffed Tom's business card in there after their first meeting, and took it out. She jotted another name on the back. 'I'm sure you can find this gentleman, or your embassy can find him,' she said, pointing to the name. 'Tell him that DCI Tom Morton is already investigating the case.'

Julia's face was a mask of fury. She stood up and turned her back on Elaine. 'Thank you for the coffee. If you're in touch with Mr Blackstone so often, I'm sure he can keep you abreast of any further developments.'

Princess Karida put Tom's card down carefully on the tray, and stood up herself. She slipped the thinnest mobile phone out of the waistband of her skirt and pressed a number. 'Alia, please show our guests back to the Spa,' she said into the phone. 'Thank you for taking the trouble to see me,' she said to Julia and Elaine. By the time they reached the door to the Morning Room, Alia was waiting to show them out.

Julia said nothing until they reached the security door that led back into the Spa. Instead of a digital lock, this side of the door just had a red button and a small camera. Julia leaned down to retrieve her boots, pressed the button, and swept out of the Hall before Elaine could say anything.

She turned to the maid. 'Were they your socks?'

Alia smiled. 'No. They were Karida's. I hope your colleague appreciates them.'

Elaine hefted her Doc Martens. 'I'll put these on outside… save you waiting.'

'A lady should always be ready when she walks through a door. Put them on here.'

Elaine toyed with saying something about not being a lady, but decided it would be rude to Alia, and shoved her feet into the boots. They were easier to lace up than get undone. As she tied the last knot, Alia pressed the button and disappeared.

This time, Elaine took a proper look round the reception area. There were even more women in Spa robes, mostly her mother's age, though they didn't have anywhere like this in Bacup. The decor was much less opulent than the Hall — mostly polished wood and glossy tiles with underfloor heating. On a whim, she asked the receptionist for a brochure.

'We're a private members' club,' said the girl. 'You have to be nominated by an existing member, or signed in by one as a day visitor.'

'Let me guess,' said Elaine. 'If you have to ask, you can't afford it.'

A voice from behind her said, 'We hear that a lot. Our rates are very competitive on an annual basis.' It was Beth Pedley. 'Your colleague seemed in a rush to get out, but now she's stuck outside.'

It was true. Julia Jepson was standing to one side of the front door, on the phone, looking annoyed. 'How did it go with Princess Karida?' asked Pedley.

'Fine,' said Elaine with a smile. Beth got the message.

The burst of sunshine that had illuminated the view from the Morning Room had given way to drizzle. Elaine looked at her watch: there was time to grab a sandwich, but not to go back to Lyme Court Buildings. She walked up to Julia. 'I'm going to the inquest. Do you want a lift back to Wythenshawe?'

She hadn't seen that the other woman was still on the phone, until Julia raised it and said, 'Don't bother. I'll come back with Fraser.'

They walked up to Elaine's car, but she didn't pop the locks. Instead, she leaned on the roof. 'I'm sorry for butting in there. I really didn't mean to tread on your toes.'

'That didn't bloody well stop you, did it? Are you on some sort of power trip, just because you're running errands for Posh Boy from CIPPS?'

That hurt. That really hurt. She was going to stand up for Tom, but realised he didn't need her to fight his battles. Not yet. 'I was thinking of you and Stamp. I've met Schofield, and I wouldn't want him on my back. If the Princess goes elsewhere for help, it'll keep Schofield off your boss's back, and it'll keep Rod Stamp off yours. Look, I'm not even going to tell DCI Morton about this morning. Unless I have to.'

'You can tell him what you like. Are you giving me this lift or not?'

Elaine drove them back in further silence, while Jepson answered her emails. When they got close to the police station, Julia said, 'Drop me here. You won't be welcome in the MIT office in future unless DCI Stamp invites you.'

Julia Jepson was a DS. Sergeants always had the last word. Elaine drove to ASDA and bought a sandwich.

Paola had refused to go to the inquest, and she had begged Lucy not to go either, until she discovered that Robyn would go in Lucy's place, then Paola insisted: 'You must go to this inquest. You must be there for Mama.' And that was that.

Mama's news had detonated around Southfork like a bomb. Last night had been very tense all round. Over the course of the evening, Lucy had managed to determine that although Mama really was pregnant, she was much less advanced than she had led them to believe: her confident assertion as to the baby's sex was based on a feeling, not a scan. All Lucy's other enquiries, no matter how gentle, about IVF and whether Enrico was the father, were met with vague assertions that the baby was the "Will of God".

Even the status of Paola's relationship to Enrico was unclear. She assured them that he was going to propose marriage, but obviously he wouldn't do so now — at least not until after the funeral. First thing in the morning, the FLO was on the doorstep asking if Gary could go to the hospital to formally identify Gianni, and if he could attend the inquest that afternoon? At first, Lucy thought that her mother wouldn't have the stomach to go to the hospital, but she did. When they returned, her father had said that she had cried, a lot, but that there had been no hysterics. On the way back, they had stopped in the Catholic church to light a candle. Lucy wondered if she should do the same.

No one had much lunch, except the kids, then Gary and Lucy left in plenty of time to get to Wythenshawe Town Hall. Paul drove them, and dropped them near the doors. He was going to wait in the car park. She wondered if the media would be there, and she had given her hair an extra brush just in case, but they were alone. A young man who looked like a reporter from the local paper was there, along with an older man who must have been from the press agencies. They were swapping notes outside the door. Dad started making phone calls until the FLO came up and escorted them into the building.

There were more people inside than Lucy expected, including several of the police officers who had been involved. For some reason, Tom Morton and his sidekick were a long way away from DS Jepson and her boss. Max was there, as was the patrol officer who had first come across Gianni. There was no sign of Saul. The FLO showed them to reserved seats near the front, and the coroner stepped into the room.

The FLO had told them what to expect: only two people would have to say anything at this stage. Gary would have to give evidence as to Giovanni's identity, the pathologist's report would be taken as read, and then DCI Stamp would say that police enquiries were continuing. Apart from the fact that the coroner was very sympathetic, she was spot on.

The only thing the FLO hadn't explained properly was that the coroner could issue an Interim Certificate. When DCI Stamp had finished saying his bit, the coroner turned to Dad and said, 'I've received a statement from defence lawyers stating that they do not wish to arrange their own post mortem examination. This means that I can issue an Interim Certificate, and that you can go ahead with the funeral arrangements. You should make an appointment with the registrar, and they can help you.' And that was it.

The journalists left the room milliseconds after the coroner, and were nowhere to be seen outside. When they got back on to the street, a man who had been at the back of the chamber came forward. He made eye contact with Lucy, but hesitated. Lucy instinctively moved closer to Dad, but he didn't notice and turned away to summon Paul for their lift home. When Gary's back was turned, the man came over.

'Miss Lucy White?'

'Who are you?'

'I'm sorry to intrude, but I'm your brother's lawyer.'

'No you're not. Paul Warren is Gianni's lawyer.'

'Perhaps I should say that I'm your brother's new lawyer. He instructed me a couple of months ago.'

'Oh.' Lucy reconsidered the man. She hadn't noticed him because he looked so normal … about Dad's age, and wearing a respectable suit. It went with his respectable haircut.

'This may come as a shock, but I believe that I have the most recent copy of your brother's will. I would have said something before, but it's irrelevant in these cases until the Interim Certificate has been issued. Under the terms of this will, you are the executor and sole beneficiary. I won't keep you, but I strongly advise you to get in touch with me. Here's my card.'

He handed over a business card, and backed away. There was no sign of Paul, and Dad was still on the phone. She looked around the pavement: the only other people lingering were Tom Morton and his partner, who took out some car keys and walked away. Lucy looked at Dad, then walked up to Morton.

When Tom Morton had arrived for the inquest, Elaine had grabbed his arm, and he had winced. The pain wasn't physical any more, but anyone touching the top of his left arm made him flinch with the memory.

'Before we go in, there's something I need to tell you,' she had muttered. 'About DCI Stamp and his team.'

'Where have you been? What's happened?'

'I went to see Princess Karida with DS Jepson. You remember her, don't you?'

'Of course I remember her. What's happened?'

'I don't think we'll be very welcome in the MIT office any more. I won't at any rate.'

Good heavens above, what had she done now? Tom's mind was boggling. They had to go into the court, and all further conversation was suspended until after the inquest had been opened and adjourned. Throughout the hearing, not one single police officer had looked in their direction, though they were clearly aware of them. Elaine was no more forthcoming afterwards.

'It was something Jepson said, sir. They've officially closed down all enquiries except to complete the reports. They're going to move on as soon as ACC Schofield gets another big case.'

'That doesn't explain why we're *persona non grata*, Elaine.' He was tempted to make a joke about excessive use of the baton on a member of a foreign royal family, but he restrained himself. Elaine was worried, but seemed more concerned about what he was going to say rather than what she herself had done.

'We can't talk here. I'll tell you everything back at Lyme Court.'

Elaine had left, and now Lucy White was walking towards him. He was going to be very careful about what he said. Not only was Elaine warning him off for flirting, Stamp could get very prickly about contact with a witness that hadn't been arranged through the FLO.

'Have you got a second?' she asked, and drew her hair away from her face. The first time they had met, in the Village café, she had obviously plastered on the make-up to face the police. Was that only two days ago? Since then, perhaps to avoid smudging with the tears, her face seemed bare, but he knew from being married to Caroline that this only meant that Lucy was being subtle. Or she had very good skin.

'I've got to get going,' he said. Something flickered in her eyes: it wasn't the reception she had hoped for. 'But not just yet. Is there something you want me to explain? About the inquest, I mean.'

'I got all that. It's that man.' She turned and pointed to a guy trying to cross the road. 'He says he's a lawyer and that Gianni made a new will, without telling anyone. He gave me this card.'

Tom looked at the card. The lawyer's own name meant nothing, but the name of his firm was ringing bells: Abramovitz & Co. It was unlikely to be a coincidence. He passed the card back.

'Thank you for telling me. That's very … interesting. Why did he come to you and not your father?'

'He said I'm the executor and sole beneficiary.'

That was even more interesting, but he didn't say so. 'You're obviously close to Mr Warren. When you've told your father – I assume you're going to do so – you should tell him, too. Let him find out what's going on. You've got enough on your plate, but I wouldn't leave it too long. I hate to say this, Miss White, but things could get complicated.'

'Call me Lucy, if you're allowed to. How could they get any worse?'

'If this lawyer is telling the truth, you're going to be responsible for the funeral.'

She gave him a bitter smile. 'You're not big on good news, are you?'

'Story of my life. I could do with some myself.'

They stood, two feet apart, with nothing more to say. Over her shoulder, he could see her father frowning at him. She still had the lawyer's card in her hand. Tom dug out one of his own. 'Take this. If anything else comes up relating directly to your brother's finances, get one of your lawyers to call me. I think your father's ready, Lucy.'

She looked behind her. 'I might call you myself. Thanks, Tom.'

Warren had pulled up on the double yellow line, and Gary hustled his daughter into the back seat. Tom didn't envy her that conversation. He could have told her about the link between Abramovitz and Dean Rooksby, but he might have been wrong. For all he knew, there could be dozens of Abramovitzes practising law in Manchester.

He set off towards the car park, but hadn't got far before his phone rang. The display said *Incoming Satellite Phone*. What was Kate doing calling him from Afghanistan? Halfway to answering it, he remembered: Kate was dead. When he took the call, his voice caught in his throat, and he had to repeat himself.

'What have you got yourself into this time?' It was Leonie. What on earth was she doing calling him from the wilds of Scotland when she should be on holiday?

'Are you all right?'

'I am now. My … friend answered the door in her pyjamas a short while ago, and found herself face to face with a uniformed constable clutching a satellite phone and asking for me.'

Oh, my God, thought Tom. *What's happened? Mother? Father? Why else is my boss ringing me?* Leonie liked to keep people off balance. She had rung him, but given no verbal clue as to why. Tom cleared his throat and returned her serve. 'You survived the walking holiday, then. Well done.'

'Only just. I almost enjoyed it towards the end. When the blisters healed up. Why are you still in Manchester? This was a week's job, maximum.'

'Haven't you heard? We were first responders at a murder scene. SLC hired me – us – to write a report into the victim's finances. I'll be finished on Friday.'

'What are you not telling me?'

'I don't know. That black doesn't suit you? That I sometimes wish I was back in the fraud squad? Give me a clue, Leonie.'

'Very funny, Tom. The nice Scottish constable had a message to go with the satellite phone: *Ring John Lake on this number.* The only person I know who's had contact with Mr Lake is you. Why does a Security Liaison officer want me to call him when I'm on holiday?'

Tom looked around him. A few well-wrapped shoppers headed for the indoor market, and a council employee clutched files to her chest as she scuttled into the Town Hall. There was absolutely no inspiration for an answer to Leonie's question.

'Sorry, boss. I'm stumped. Honestly. Not a clue.'

'This call is costing someone a fortune, and Hamish Macbeth will be round to collect his phone soon, so I'd better get off the line and call him, hadn't I?'

'I suppose so. Enjoy the rest of your holiday.'

'Hmm. Were you serious? About me not looking good in black, that is.'

'Never take fashion advice from me, or cooking tips from my mother.'

'Goodbye, Tom.'

He had been thinking about Lucy when he made the comment about not looking good in black, which was almost as disturbing as the call from Leonie. He scratched his head and headed for his car.

On the way to Lyme Court, his contact from the Bank of England Counterfeiting Unit called him. His name was Frazer Jarvis - definitely with a "z". They made polite conversation for a few seconds, then Tom got down to business.

'I wondered if you could help me, Frazer. Does the Bank still keep records of the destination of new notes?'

'What's going on Tom? You can't have found me another counterfeiting gang.'

'I hope not. It's something completely different. A murder victim had a lot of cash — £200,000 worth in fact. It would really help if I knew where it came from.'

Frazer Jarvis exhaled noisily. 'De La Rue keep records, but we don't have direct access to them. Do you need this officially? It could take a while. If you can make do with an unofficial, non-admissible answer, then I know someone who should help.'

'Off the record will do nicely. It may be nothing: it might help prevent a miscarriage of justice.'

'You don't need to justify yourself. We owe you big time for cracking the Jigsaw case.'

'I'll text you.'

There was no afternoon sunshine today. By the time he got back to the rented office, all the street lights were on. While it was fresh in his mind, he forwarded Elaine's pictures of the £20 notes to Jarvis before leaving the car. His antennae quivered as soon as he walked through the door: Elaine had bought cream cakes and made the tea. Whatever she'd done, it must be bad. She gave him a nervous smile as he hung up his coat.

'What have you done?' he asked.

'I think I may have brought the Angel of Death down upon us.'

'There'd better be a good reason.'

She opened her mouth to explain, and his phone rang: it was John Lake.

'That's a very enterprising constable you've got there, Tom,' said Lake.

Tom gave Elaine the darkest possible look. She bit her lip.

'So it would seem. So enterprising, in fact, that she hasn't told me why you're on the phone.'

Elaine cringed.

'Oh. I'm sure she'll bring you up to speed. Has Leonie been in touch?'

'Only to say, "Why have I got to ring John Lake?"'

'Then I'll be brief: the Foreign Office have agreed to pay CIPPS for you to sort out Princess Karida's problem. One week to start with. I doubt there's a real security issue here — but at the sniff of anything Islamist, let me know.'

'I'll make sure to check the back seat of my car. Or get DC Fraser to do it. Just one thing before you go: is a man called Neil Hoskins on your radar?'

'Erm…' Tom could hear the sound of computer keys. 'Aah, yes. He's a friendly asset. Does some consulting, and he's a useful source on radical campus groups.'

'Thanks. Put us down as starting on Monday.'

Tom placed his phone carefully in the centre of his desk.

'Tea? Cake?' said Elaine hopefully.

'Explanation,' said Tom.

'What were you talking to Morton about?' asked Lucy's father when they had settled in the car. He turned round fully to look at her in the back seat.

'I was talking about that man. The one who accosted me while you weren't looking.'

'That's below the belt,' said Dad. 'I only turned my back for a second. Was he bothering you?'

'He's a lawyer, Dad. He said he was Gianni's lawyer.'

'What?'

'Eh?' said Paul and Dad together. Lucy wasn't sure she should be telling them both, but whoever she told first, the other would be aggrieved. On the whole, it was better that Paul was driving, then Dad couldn't blow up and hit something.

She took a deep breath. 'He said that Gianni made a new will. He said that Gianni left everything to me, and that I'm the executor.'

'What the…?' Dad's voice trailed off. He just stared at her.

Paul stepped into the silence. 'Did he say how recently this was?'

'Last couple of months.'

Paul grunted. 'Easy enough to verify.'

Dad rounded on him. 'There's more to it than that, Paul. This changes everything, don't you see? Does Lucy have to accept this?'

'Dad! What's the matter?' Lucy sat wringing her hands. Her father ignored her.

'Well?' he said to Paul. They were crossing a roundabout. Paul took his time answering.

'No beneficiary has to accept their bequest, but if they decline, the procedure isn't simple. If this other lawyer is halfway decent, he will have said, "What are your wishes if - God forbid - something happens to your sister?" And Gianni will have said, "I want the money to go to…" He could have said, "I want the money to go to the dog's home," for all we know. It's the same with the executorship. If Lucy declines, I suspect the other lawyer will act.'

Dad mulled this over for a second, then turned back to Lucy. 'I'm sorry, love. This must have come as a shock, but I have to think of the whole family. Including your mother.'

'But, Dad, that's not the worst bit. He told me I'm in charge of the funeral.'

He put out his hand, contorting himself round the seat and taking hold of her shoulder. 'Easy, love. Don't worry. You're only in charge on paper. I'll handle everything, and I'll even talk to your mother. Paul can sort out the legal stuff, too. You'll just have to sign the probate at the end.' He ventured a smile. 'Just make sure you read it first, eh?'

'Thanks, Dad.'

The feel of his arm on her shoulder, rubbing it up and down, ever so slightly, was as reassuring now as it had always been. Gary White wasn't the best husband, but she knew he was the best Dad ever.

Paul coughed. 'Bit of a problem there, Gary.'

Dad frowned. 'No problems today, Paul.'

'Minor detail, that's all. I can't act for you both. It really would be better if this went to someone else.'

Dad took his hand off her arm, and gave Paul the slightest tap on the shoulder. 'You're family, Paul. We keep this in the family, eh?'

Lucy could just see the side of Paul's face as he did the moustache tango. 'Only if Lucy's happy,' he said.

Dad raised his eyebrows. Just like last night, when he wouldn't beg her to stay in England, he was leaving it up to her. Paul might not have any choice, but she did.

'Can you get in touch with him?' she said to Paul. 'Find out if it's all true, as soon as you can. Then can you tell me what needs to be done?'

'Of course.'

Dad nodded. 'Good. You know what this means, amongst other things, don't you?'

'Sorry, Dad. My brain's at saturation point. That's why I went to the police with the news: I just wanted to offload it.'

'I'll forgive you, especially now that you're my biggest minority shareholder.'

OMG. She'd forgotten about the shares. 'How much?'

'If this new will is kosher, you now own 25% of White-Berardi Sports Management, and Gianni's operation, too. You even own 25% of the loan to theHouse of Lucia.' He turned to the side. 'I reckon it's time she came on board and joined the business, don't you Paul?'

'If that's what you want, Lucy. If you don't take over Gianni's work, we'll have to go outside to replace him.'

Lucy had no idea what she wanted. She had done Grace's job for a while after university, but soon realised that very few women make it to the top in any football-related activity, and you wouldn't want the ones who did as role models. That was then, however. Now is different. Now means barely scraping by on sales from the shop, taking babysitting jobs and living in a dump.

'I don't know, Dad. I really don't know. I might … I might not. Let's see what happens, eh?'

'You can't say fairer than that, Gary,' said Paul.

'Of course, love. The door's open. Just push when you're ready.'

'Thanks. For everything.'

He put his hand back through the gap and squeezed her fingers.

There were four cream cakes on the plate. Tom pulled it towards him and ate three of them while Elaine told her story. Should he chew her up, like the cakes? What she had done was to take all control of the investigation out of his hands: he was now answerable to the Foreign Office. She had, of course, also bought them time and authority to poke their noses into things. Halfway through her account of life in Sevenbridge Hall, his phone pinged: Frazer had come up with the goods. He now knew which bank had received the £20 notes on Gianni's table.

He looked at the last cake. If he ate that one, it would be purely out of spite. His mother would have done it to make a point, as would Caroline, his ex-wife. He slid the plate over to Elaine. 'Do you think the website has anything to do with Berardi's murder?'

She looked down, turned the plate round with her finger and picked up the cake. 'I honestly don't know,' she said, and started to eat the cake.

'Neither do I, but it's one of two solid lines of enquiry.'

She licked her fingers. 'It's more solid than the cash angle.'

'Not any more. We're going home now. Tomorrow morning, you're going to Cairndale to put the squeeze on Mr Hoskins. I'm going to do the same to a bank in Leeds.'

'Do you think we can do it, Tom?'

He took longer to reply than she expected, judging from the way she was twisting a tissue. 'You'd better hope we had,' he said at last. 'For your sake, as much as Dean Rooksby's.'

'Why's that?'

'A good result will help your application to CIPPS enormously.' She opened her mouth in astonishment. Tom leaned forward. 'You don't seriously think you've got a future with South Lancs after this, do you?'

Chapter 12

Friday 17 January

Most people have heard of Cairndale, even if they couldn't place it on the map. If they are suddenly sent there on business, they get a shock when they see how far north it is. Elaine had a good start getting out of Manchester, and was soon stopping at Charnock Richard for a bacon sandwich. Why not? That's what expenses are for. She drove further up, past Preston and past Lancaster. Just when motorists are thinking of the drive through the Lakes, there is a turn-off to Cairndale. She turned off the slip road on to the A6, for the first time in four years, despite her promises to keep in touch with old friends.

The town sits on the river Cowan, and straddles the border between Lancashire and Westmorland. Just before the river, she turned right at the lights and into the University of Lancashire Institute of Science and Technology campus: ULIST, her *alma mater*, as Tom would no doubt call it.

She should have phoned Van Darracott, and arranged for a coffee, but she told herself she was too busy. That hadn't stopped her contacting the IT department, though. Hoskins was on site and expecting a visit. She had to think about where to go: IT was a foreign country, mostly. It was also on the top floor of the old building — and had its own lift, its own receptionist and its own security doors.

Hoskins hadn't shown any sign of recognition when she bumped into him at the Seven Bridges Inn, and he showed no more when he ushered her into his office and offered her a seat.

'I see you're still into folk music,' she said, pointing to a framed poster of John Renbourn's album *The Nine Maidens*.

Hoskins paused, half seated, half standing. 'You have the advantage of me, as they say. Are you an ex-student I should remember? If so, please forgive me.'

'Sort of. I was in the climbing club with Van. I was Elaine Bradbury then.'

'Of course. Sorry. You've grown your hair since then. Weren't you going out with…?'

Elaine held up her ring finger. 'Four years now.'

'Still a novelty then. I don't go to the folk club so much since we had our second child. What brings you back to ULIST?'

That was clever of him: he'd got one up on her by boasting about his kids, then changed the subject. Elaine smiled. 'I wondered if you could tell me about your work for the 7Bridge Estate security division.'

He didn't jump or flinch, but he did stroke his beard, just like Tom rubbed his left arm. She'd have to ask Tom about that soon, before it drove her mad.

'Why on earth should I do that?' he said.

Elaine slid her warrant card across the table. 'Because the Foreign Office have asked me to help find the Mother Superior. I reckon you're on the same mission.'

He scrutinised her warrant card carefully before passing it back. 'I'll have to check, of course.'

'Tell your contact to verify it with John Lake from Liaison. I'll grab a coffee and come back.'

'Ask Melanie to get you one. She's the admin assistant in the general office. I'll find you there.'

When she saw the jar of instant coffee on Melanie's desk, Elaine opted for tea. She was checking her emails when Neil summoned her back.

'How much do you know about Gianni Berardi?' he asked.

'I was first to the crime scene with my boss. We've been looking into a related matter, and the Princess called in a favour to put some urgency into things.'

'Saul won't like it,' said Neil with another rub of the beard. 'He's been trying to keep things as private as possible, but if the Princess wants police involvement…' He shrugged, then he went to a steel cabinet, put his body in front of the lock to hide something, and quickly removed a small box from inside. He put it between them on his desk.

'I've got nothing I can tell you, really,' he said. 'To get something more definite, you need to fit this packet sniffer to the cabinet by the bridge.'

'I understood "bridge". The rest … not so much. You do mean a real, over-the-river bridge, don't you?'

He laughed. 'Yes I do, in this instance. The network bridge is in Saul's building, but I've already done that one. Can you get a warrant?'

Elaine waved her hand from side to side: maybe.

'Without one, nothing will be admissible — and once you've played your hand, they'll route things elsewhere. It's up to you.'

She picked up the box. 'I'll need more than a warrant to fit this. I'll need some help.'

'Get a warrant, and the telco – the service provider – will fit it for you. If you go ahead without one, talk to Max.'

She put the device in her pocket. 'I get the impression that my boss doesn't like this sort of thing. He called it *intercept*.'

'That's a GCHQ term. Is he MI5 or ex-army?'

She snorted. 'Hardly. He's ex-fraud squad, and proud of it. Perhaps there's another way. What's your gut reaction, Neil?'

Another stroke of the beard. 'Saul asked me the same question. I told him that the most likely source for the non-Berardi data was his side of the fence. In order of probability, I'd say: first, the Spa, then his office, then the other service buildings.'

'Not the Hall itself?'

'No. Definitely not, unless one of the servants nips in to the Spa to use their terminals.'

Servants. That's what they were, she supposed. It was very *Downton Abbey*. 'What about the Estate? Are you ruling out the residents?'

'No, but if it's one of them, they've hidden their tracks very, very well.'

He opened the pen tray in his desk. 'Here's my private number and email address.'

When she had signed out of the IT suite, she hesitated by the lift. Should she nip along to the media department? No. Not enough time. She pressed the button for the ground floor.

'Who's she?' said Madison.

She was the woman standing next to Dean, his PR, whose smile didn't crumble in the face of Madison's aggression. Would anything make her crumble? She had pulled out all the stops this morning when they met at the entrance to the Trafford Rangers training ground. Her suit was an immaculate pale grey, with just a hint of black thread, buttoned over a black blouse. Even Dean had noticed the shoes: gleaming black leather and high enough heels to tower over Maddi. Not many women could do that. The PR tossed her hair back into place and waited for Dean to say something.

'She's helping me. Like you should have been doing. She's got something to show you, too.'

They were in the waiting room at the treatment centre. Dean had been for a scan, to assess the damage to his shoulder, and he was waiting for the specialist to come back with the results.

'Let's sit down, shall we?' said his PR.

She had advised him against meeting Maddi at first, until Dean's mother had intervened. There had been a tense discussion behind closed doors in the kitchen before his PR emerged and said that she'd arrange things, but it had to be on her terms. She now proceeded to spell out her terms to Madison.

'Today's meeting is strictly confidential, and subject to you signing this agreement.' There was no piece of paper offered. It was all on his PR's iPad. 'What you're agreeing to is this: we reckon your story is worth £5,000 to the press, once the trial is over. We'll pay you that amount now, and the same again six months after the trial if Dean is found not guilty. In return you ensure that not a single word goes to the press. Anywhere.'

Madison managed a smile. 'What if he's found guilty?'

The PR's shoulders lifted ever so slightly, disturbing the seam of her jacket but not the blonde hair lying on top of it. 'You can do what you want in that case.'

Madison looked at Dean. 'Is this what you really want?' she said.

The PR interrupted. 'It's what he needs, Madison. Take it or leave it.'

'Dean?'

He pointed to the tablet. His PR offered Madison a stylus. She signed.

'I'll leave you to it,' said the PR. 'But Daniel has asked me to remind you that it would be contempt of court to discuss the case.'

She clicked out and left them. Madison waited until the sound of heels on the corridor had faded completely. 'I'll stand by you, Dean. I mean it. I can't forgive myself for what happened.'

He stared at her. 'I didn't kill him.'

'I know you've got to say that, but…'

'But nothing. I kicked the shit out of his greasy arse, that's all. Someone else finished him off.'

She flinched back. 'How…?'

'I don't know, or care. Good riddance. Maybe one of your other lovers did it.'

He was hurting her. He could see it in her red eyes, in her hands, even in the shabby clothes she was wearing. No more designer threads for Madison Greenwood.

'I'm sorry, Dean… so sorry. He was so nice to me, I just couldn't think straight with everything that was going on.'

This was shit, and Dean wasn't having any of it. 'We were a team, Maddi. Together, forever. I gave you everything you ever wanted, and you threw it back in my face.'

He nearly lashed out when she smiled at him, but that would have been giving away an own goal.

'Oh, Dean,' she said. 'You just don't get it, do you?'

'I get this,' he said, standing up and leaning towards her. 'In six months' time, I'm going to walk out of that courtroom a free man, and I'm going to go back to Salton Town, then to Trafford Rangers, and you can watch me on TV when you get home from stacking shelves in the supermarket. Spend that money wisely, Maddi. It might be a while before you get any more.'

She started crying, fighting to hold the sobs inside herself. She fumbled in her bag for a tissue, but instead, she pulled out an envelope. She took out the engagement ring and held it out towards him. He straightened up and took a step backwards. She dropped the ring on the chair and fled. As she ran down the corridor, her sobs echoed until the outside door slammed.

Dean stared at the ring. He heard someone coming — a man's footsteps. The consultant. He slipped the ring in his pocket. He'd decide what to do about that later.

Praed's bank had not exactly made Tom welcome. Not only had he been made to wait nearly half an hour, but the regional manager hadn't taken him up to his office: he squeezed them into a tiny interview room with nothing but a desk, a computer terminal and three chairs. There had been no offer of refreshment.

Tom took his time removing his coat and draping it over the back of the chair before giving the manager a list of serial numbers.

'What makes you think our bank had these specific notes?' asked the regional manager.

'I am a detective,' said Tom. 'I detected. Have a look at this.' He showed the man two pictures. First was the stack of notes on Berardi's table, then a close-up of the serial numbers. 'I asked the Bank of England where those specific notes had been dispatched to. They told me the name of the security courier, and they told me that it was here.'

'Once notes have been delivered, we don't keep a track of the serial numbers.'

Tom leaned back and crossed his legs. 'That's a shame. You know, up until the 1950s, banks wrote down the serial number of every five pound note, in and out.'

'I did know that. We've still got one of the registers in the archive. I don't think I'd find it a very fulfilling job.'

'Perhaps you're right. Do you pass large volumes of notes between branches?'

'Sometimes. Most of the cashpoints are stocked by a security company that picks them up from here, but your pile of cash didn't come from a cashpoint. If a branch is short, we sometimes top them up.'

'We'll keep it simple,' said Tom. 'I have two questions. First, have you reported a large cash withdrawal to the National Crime Agency recently? Say, between the ninth and fourteenth of January? And if not, why not?'

'I'd have to look that up.'

'You can use this terminal here. And while you're at it, you can answer the second question: do any of this lot bank with you?'

He passed over a second piece of paper with Berardi's name, along with the Ikedas and their company.

'You don't have a warrant.'

'That's because I haven't asked you to tell me about their accounts, just whether or not they bank with you. I can call your compliance officer in the City if you want. He never said No to me when I worked in Economic Crimes.'

'It's not up to him,' said the regional manager, but he didn't show Tom the door. Instead, he logged on to the terminal, turned the screen towards himself and started searching. 'We reported a withdrawal of £250,000 on Friday 10th January. We flagged it as low risk.' There was more clicking and tapping. 'None of those names bank with us, not at this branch or nationally. There's a Mr Ikeda in London, but he has a different first name, and a different wife.'

'How long has he banked with you? Roughly.'

'Decades.'

Oh. Damn. That wasn't good. *Where the hell do I go now?* thought Tom. The man opposite was making no secret of his impatience, and Tom didn't blame him. He reckoned that he was good for one more try, then it was bye-bye Leeds, hello dead end.

'John Nugent. *The* John Nugent, or his wife Holly.'

The man didn't even look at the screen. 'Oh, yes. They bank with Praed's. John still has an account with this branch from his days at United. I know that because I've just been looking at a cash withdrawal from it.'

'You've been more than helpful. I'll remember that.'

Tom shook hands and left.

The roadworks on the M62 were so bad at the moment that he had caught the train to Leeds. He had half an hour before the return journey began, so he settled down in his favourite chain store coffee shop and sent Elaine a text: *Don't rush back to Lyme Court. Interesting news from bank. Going to give DCI Stamp last chance to reopen case. Meet me in Seven Bridges Inn.*

Lucy would have preferred to get out of Southfork to talk over Gianni's will, and to do it alone, but Dad had insisted: there should be a full family conference, including Mama and Robyn. That could only happen in the formal dining room.

The biggest fight was over who was going to enter last. Robyn led, by playing the children card. 'I'll be with the kids, Gary. Let me know when everyone's here.'

Paola trumped that easily. 'I have to take great care of the child. I must lie down.'

When Paul arrived, Lucy went to the playroom first. 'He's here,' she said.

'Let me know when Paola's come down. She'll insist on getting dressed, and that could take an age. I don't want to waste time sitting in there when I could be helping Arthur with his shapes. He's learning so quickly now.'

And he'll learn just as fast if the nanny teaches him, thought Lucy, *which is what happens most of the time*. She settled for something more straightforward. 'No,' she said, and walked out.

Mama was lying on the bed, fully dressed, reading a magazine. 'What have they said already? Is it true about Gianni's will?'

'No one's said anything. You know what Paul's like: with that moustache, you can never tell what he's thinking.' She sat down on the bed. 'Look, Mama, this is going to be bad enough. Do you want me to translate?'

Mama patted her hand, and switched to English. 'Don't worry. I will make the effort.'

Robyn lost by nearly five minutes. Despite waiting an absolute age, she still appeared ahead of Paola. They had all digested the news of Gianni's bequest last night. Mama had taken it better than expected. Lucy had been afraid that she might try to get her to go to Milan again, or to give up the shares, but she just nodded and said that Lucy should make up her own mind about it. Perhaps she had got the message: her daughter was going to be neither an unpaid childminder nor a pawn in the battle with Dad. Perhaps Mama was just tired.

When Paola finally arrived, Gary spoke first. 'Paul's been busy this morning, sorting out all sorts of stuff. What've you got?'

Paul cleared his throat. 'The solicitor from Abramovitz & Co was telling the truth: Gianni did see them and make a new will. He faxed me a copy and the original is coming later. It's very simple, and it does what he said: Gianni has left everything to Lucy. In the event of her predeceasing him, it was all to go to Paola. That's it. As for his estate, that's almost as straightforward. He had no house, and the Maserati was on a lease and has already gone back. That leaves the shares, his Audi and his personal effects. His other assets will cover his debts and the cost of the funeral, but only just.'

Paul had something else to say. 'Before anyone asks, the £200,000 in his house is rather problematical. There's no proof that it was legitimately his, but so far there's no proof that it isn't. It could take months before the police decide what to do with it.'

'Is it all right for me to sort out the funeral?' said Gary.

'He must lie in Italy. With his father,' said Paola.

'I thought about that,' said Paul, the second Paola had finished. 'You would need a certificate from the coroner, and one from the local authority, and permission from your own registrar in Milan. I called the coroner's office and they said that permission would be needed from the defence too.'

That wasn't going stop Mama. Those arrangements were issues she would expect someone else to sort out for her. What Lucy hadn't reckoned on was Dad, who had been gritting his teeth during Paul's speech.

'I'm his father. He took his first communion at St Saviour's, and I think he should rest there, near where he lived.'

Paola had one last card to play. 'It is for Lucia to decide, no?'

She rested her hands in her lap and looked from one to the other. 'He was my brother,' she said, 'but I'm only his sister. You're his Mama, and you're his Papa. You should agree on this, if nothing else.'

Mama blinked first. 'I have to think of my child. It is easy for you, Gary, with so many to run around after you. I must go home to the doctor, and it will be too risky to fly again. If I cannot take Gianni home with me, I will return alone. Book me on the afternoon flight. I will send flowers next week for the funeral, and pay for masses to be said. Now I must rest.' With that, she was gone.

'Dad, can you sort everything? Church, undertaker, reception and stuff?'

'Of course.'

'Thanks.'

Robyn looked at the door where her rival had disappeared, and then spoke for the first time since Paola had entered the room. She addressed her comments equally to her husband and to Paul. 'Why did he do it, do you think? Why did Gianni go to this other lawyer?'

It was the question that had bugged Lucy the most. Under the terms of the original will, Gianni's shares were to go to Dad, although it was understood that things would change if he got married. She remembered the way that Paul had not been keen on acting for both her and Dad. If Gianni had wanted to make changes, he might have realised the same thing. But was the new will the only reason that he had gone to Abramovitz & Co?

Paul looked at Gary. Gary shrugged. 'I don't know, love. We all know he's been a bit furtive lately, but I have no idea why. Perhaps it was to do with that money.' He looked at

Lucy. 'Or perhaps it was old habits coming back,' he said darkly. Everyone knew what he meant: gambling.

'I need to see Holly,' said Lucy. 'I'll come back before Mama goes.'

'What do you need to see Holly for?' asked Robyn.

'I'm sure she's got her reasons,' said Dad.

Lucy did have her reasons. She smiled at Dad and Paul, ignored Robyn, and left Southfork as quickly as she could shove her feet in her boots and grab her coat. In a normal estate, Holly would live three doors away, but in 7Bridge, it was a ten minute walk round the bend, up the hill, down the slope and back on yourself. She sent a short text on the way, and Holly had the coffee ready. Her youngest was at nursery today, so for once they were alone in *Casa Nugent*.

'You're a lightweight, you are,' said Max. 'You've only been doing a couple of hours. Try doing it all day.'

Saul grunted. He reckoned that his brain wasn't temperamentally suited to watching hours of nothing.

'Could you at least tell me what you're looking for?' said Max.

'I won't know until I see it.'

'Then you won't see it, because there's nothing there.'

Max was standing over his shoulder, watching him watch the Estate CCTV footage from the morning of Giovanni's murder, especially the cameras which covered the perimeter — the ones that showed nothing of the running track.

'I've triple-checked,' said Max. 'The nearest camera to the crime scene doesn't show the fight, or Berardi's last moments. The angle's just too obtuse.' He paused. 'Hang on. Didn't you know that you can use the keyboard as well as the mouse to do this? Here. Watch.'

With a few flicks of the Ctrl button, Max showed him how to fast forward and slow down. Much easier.

'Thanks,' said Saul. He looked at his watch. 'You'll have to excuse me. The Princess wants to FaceTime.'

'Must be important. See you later.'

The Princess rarely talked over the secure vidcon system (which everyone called FaceTime or Skype, but was neither): she preferred the in-house messaging system for day-to-day discussions. In fact, the last time they had talked in vision, it had been Christmas Eve. He opened a window on his computer and waited for her to call him. When she came online, she was wearing a veil, as usual.

'You know the police came to see me yesterday,' she said.

'At your request, ma'am, I understand.'

'Yes. When you told me about Gianni and the website, I had to find out more.'

If it please you, God, let her forget about this soon. It wasn't quite a prayer, but Saul sincerely wished that the Princess would let sleeping dogs lie: the Mother Superior hadn't posted anything since the update on the day that Berardi died.

'Were they able to tell you anything?' asked Saul.

'No. In fact, the sergeant from the murder enquiry told me that they are closing things down now that Dean has been charged. Very unsatisfactory.'

'I agree, but that's good news, in a way. Now that the police are going to leave us alone, I can get on with the electronic tracing. Mind you, I think that Berardi might have been the senior partner in this. Have you noticed that there haven't been any postings lately?'

The Princess waved her hand in front of the screen dismissively: the camera struggled to cope with the movement as the gemstones on her ring flashed in the light. Saul could see enough of her forehead above the veil to recognise a frown.

'She's keeping a low profile,' said the Princess. 'She'll be back soon. There was another policewoman with the sergeant, and she was much more helpful.'

Saul groaned inside. This was not what he wanted to hear.

'Have you met a DCI Morton?' asked the Princess.

'We've spoken a couple of times. He was the first officer on the scene. Max has had more to do with him.'

The Princess's face retreated from the screen. She was sitting back and crossing her legs. He could make out the top of a white blouse below the veil. 'It seems that Morton's name is trusted in some quarters. I spoke to my friend in the Embassy, and she agreed: we need to take more aggressive action before the website causes problems in Ghar'aan. The British Foreign Office have agreed that Morton and his associate will stay on another week to look properly for the Mother Superior.'

There was no point trying to hide his displeasure. 'This could have a seriously destabilising effect on the Estate. And don't forget, once word gets around, the Mother Superior could easily set up a campaign against police harassment. The public don't like the idea of the police being used to sort out … our kind of problem.'

Was that a smile behind the veil? 'You were going to say "Rich people's problems", weren't you?'

'It's what the papers will say.'

'Only if word gets around, and that will only happen if they need to talk to the residents. I want you to make sure your staff treat any enquiries as a matter of the utmost confidentiality. Is that clear? Any leaks from staff should be treated accordingly.'

Saul liked the Princess. She could be funny, and was always self-deprecating, but when it came to anyone except the residents, she was a Princess through and through: she might like him, but he was a servant, and servants had to toe the line. Even him. Especially him.

'Of course. I will make sure that they know your will in this matter, and render all assistance I can to the police.'

'Good. I will see…' She looked down at something, and her hair slipped out of its hold. 'I will see Elaine Fraser and then you can give me updates. This must not go through Beth. Get Max to give Fraser access to the Hall, and you can text me when she's coming.'

'Are you sure you want the police to have access?'

'I'm sure she won't abuse it.'

'As you wish. I'll be in touch.'

In the houses of most rich couples, the family's commitment to domestic values is confirmed by the kitchen. Things are a little different in 7Bridge.

Lucy's family was one of the first to move in, and despite the overall horror of Southfork, it had a very Italian family space at the back — and Lucy really did have happy memories of the family sitting around a battered kitchen table, summoned by the smells of Mama's cooking. Then Robyn took over and pointed out that highly nutritious food was available 24/7 from Sonia Hartley's catering operation, and that she had more important things to do than cook. Most of the other houses had been built with fairly small kitchens because the occupants planned to eat in front of the TV, but Holly was different.

Casa Nugent had two kitchens. One for use by caterers, the other for Holly to do actual cooking: she didn't allow eating in front of the telly. When Lucy arrived after the White-Berardi conference, she followed the smell of coffee into the family kitchen and took a seat at the family table.

Holly was wearing her domestic outfit — a shapeless pullover and jeans with slippers. As Lucy crossed the kitchen floor, she saw her neighbour/friend/employer giving her the usual critical appraisal. It was only when she had finished telling Holly about the funeral arrangements that a verdict was given.

'Is it going to be traditional, the funeral?'

'Pretty much. The priest doesn't like pop songs or anything.'

'So it's black, then.'

Lucy nodded.

'It doesn't do much for you. I hope you've got something better than that.'

Lucy had been wearing the same jersey dress for two days: it had long sleeves and took a belt nicely. It was also the only black thing she had taken with her to Southfork from the flat over the shop. 'I haven't. Not really. They're all too short, or they make me look like a waitress.'

Holly stirred her coffee. 'For most young people's funerals, it tends to be colours these days. That would work much better for you. If you're both in black, people are going to think that Robyn is Gianni's sister.'

'I can live with that. So long as they don't think I'm his mother, I don't care.'

'Lucy, you can't say that. These pictures are going to be in the nationals.'

They both looked towards the French windows and the world beyond 7Bridge. You could just see it peeking over the trees. Sergeant Nolan and his patrol officers were very good at their job: not a single reporter had managed to get on to the Estate, so all the media interest in Gianni Berardi had been focused on Dean Rooksby, his killer, not his family. It would change for the funeral.

Lucy asked after Ellie (doing very well), then took a deep breath. 'Listen, Holly, when I saw DCI Morton on Wednesday, he told me something about Gianni. He said that he had been submitting articles to the Mother Superior. I'm sorry.'

Holly flinched. 'How did they find that out? I thought the Mother Superior must be a woman.'

'There was something on his computer, I think. They also said he wasn't acting alone, so the real Mother Superior is out there. I'm really sorry. I hope he didn't write any of the things about you.'

There were home-made flapjacks on the table. Holly rarely ate things like that, and Lucy didn't have the appetite. Holly pushed the plate aside. 'I try to ignore it, I really do. The trouble is …people keep referring to it on my Twitter feed. I can't stop people following me, but I got the PR company to block everyone who uses *#seenin7bridge*. That helps, but it isn't easy to get your message across when most of the Internet is full of shit about my hips, my boobs and whether my daughter is anorexic, for God's sake.'

Holly was patron of a women's shelter in Manchester. When she first took on the role, she tried to campaign against domestic violence: *#noexcuses* had trended for a while, but when the misogynist counteroffensive started, Holly had to step away for a while. No woman wants to be on the receiving end of tweets saying *#deserveseverythingshegets*.

'Did you know about Gianni and Madison?' asked Holly.

'Why do you ask? I didn't, as it happens. They had better places to get it together than my flat.'

'I suspected,' said Holly. 'I saw him coming out of their house once too often. He used the gate to the running track, and I can see that stretch from my study upstairs.'

'Were you looking on the day that…?'

'No. I was in here. Besides he … the place where it happened … that was on the other side of the Estate.' She stood up. 'Come on, Luce. Let's get you sorted.'

'Wha—?' Holly had already gone out. Lucy followed, and because Holly was halfway up the stairs, she indulged herself with a sliding turn on the polished floor, grabbing hold of the newel post as she slid past. 'Where are you?' she called from the landing.

'Dressing room.'

Oh no. Don't tell me she's going to offer me something to wear for the funeral. Lucy padded into the dressing room and found

Holly already holding out three black dresses. Too late. 'This didn't work last time,' she said.

'That's because we didn't get them taken up properly. We'll choose two and I'll get the au pair to run them into Knutsford this afternoon.'

Lucy slid back one of the wardrobe doors on the opposite side of the designer hanging where Holly was looking. Lots of jumpers, neatly folded, were in one section — and in the other, nightwear. One of the silk robes had an oriental pattern, and Lucy lifted it out. 'Is this your kimono?' she asked. 'For when you move to Japan.'

'How did you know? Who's been talking?'

'It came out in the police interview. What's going on, Holly?'

Her arms dropped, and the black dresses slumped to floor. 'It's John and Ellie. Mostly John. He can't bear the thought of retiring at thirty-four, which is what he'll be after the Euros this year. He doesn't want to go down a division, either: he's had a decade of being the best player in the country, and he can't give it up, so he's going to change country.'

'That's not what…'

'Only Gianni knew the real truth. That's why John signed the deal with the Ikedas, to get a foot under the table. We're going on holiday to Japan after the Euros, and he's going to talk to some clubs. Their season starts in March, so we might leave next Christmas. Please, Lucy, don't tell your dad. Not yet.'

Lucy could think of at least five players who had been better than John Nugent for some time, but she let it go. 'Wow, Holly. That's amazing. Are you really going too, or is he going on his own?'

'John has stood by me through everything. I wouldn't let him down. Besides, it means that Ellie can go to the International Ballet School.'

Lucy swallowed her anger. They weren't going to Japan for another year, and there was plenty of time to fight that battle later. 'Never too late to change, eh?'

'Let's try these on,' said Holly, marching through to the bedroom.

On the way out, Lucy went to put the dressing gown back, and overshot with the sliding door. In the wardrobe at the end was a series of slimline dresses that would not have fitted Holly for years, hanging next to three vibrant Indian saris. What was that all about? Was Holly going to a fancy-dress party or some sort of community liaison event? She shrugged and closed the door behind her.

To say that Tom wasn't looking forward to his little chat with DCI Rod Stamp would be an understatement. DS Jepson clocked him the moment he entered the room, and her eyes bored into him all the way across the space to Stamp's office.

'Sit down, Tom. You'd better close the door,' said Stamp. At least Tom was being given the time of day. That impression didn't last long. 'What the hell is your DC doing? I nearly had a mutiny on my hands yesterday.'

'Elaine doesn't have good timing, I admit, but she was using her initiative.' Tom took a deep breath. 'I hate to say this, Rod, but she thinks that Rooksby didn't do it, and I'm inclined to agree with her. I was going to lay it out with the report this morning, but Elaine jumped the gun.'

Stamp looked down at his desk, and swivelled slightly in his chair. He tapped the ends of his fingers on the edge of his desk, once, twice … then he beat out a quick rhythm. 'You're a difficult man to track down. I had to ring several people last night to find out about you.' He paused. Tom let him finish at his own pace. 'You haven't been with CIPPS long, so you've still got something of the real copper left in you. That's why you're still here. You've got two minutes.'

'Your team have done a superb job of tracking down every lead, Rod, but there's one thing they couldn't do: they couldn't arrest Rooksby because Elaine had already done it. She's probably a better copper than me, and her gut told her he didn't do it.'

Stamp didn't erupt or become defensive. He nodded slowly and asked, 'Did you watch the interviews with Rooksby?'

'We don't have a good enough Internet connection in Lyme Court to watch the video feed from HOLMES2, but I've read the transcripts.'

'They only tell half the story. I've dealt with Daniel Abramovitz a few times now, and he has a fairly consistent approach. This time it was different. Instead of getting his client to tell a pack of lies and stick to it, he let Dean answer every question. The lad got rattled, you could tell that. He didn't like having to explain why he got into the fight, or why Berardi needled him, but he could remember it all, right down to the Italian swear words. Then he stopped. Nothing. According to Dean, Berardi was alive. End of story.'

'Tricky. I've never run an MIT, Rod, so you're one up on me here. Why did you charge him?'

'Don't try and flatter me, Tom. I've never arrested a Deputy Chief Constable, nor do I want to. I charged Rooksby for two reasons: first, he only had to tell one simple lie. Even a Neanderthal like him could do that — he just had to keep repeating that he left Berardi alive. The second reason is the security on the Estate. You don't need me to tell you it's like Fort Knox in there. There is absolutely no evidence of anyone else being near that running track. The CPS agreed.' He finished speaking with a shrug.

Tom took out the report into Giovanni's finances and laid it near him on Stamp's desk. 'I agree with you about the security, except for one thing. There's no evidence of

Rooksby or Berardi being there either, is there? But they were there. If they can do it, so can others.'

The corner of Stamp's mouth twitched. 'That's not strictly true, Tom. We can see Dean parking his car and starting his run, and we can see him crossing the road twice during his circuits of the Estate — but I grant you, we've no idea where Berardi was going.'

'Coming. Berardi was coming from somewhere, not going.'

Rod sat up. 'How do you mean?'

Tom turned the financial report around so that it faced Stamp, then slid it across the desk. 'He was going down the hill towards his back gate when Rooksby ran into him. It had been bucketing down all morning, and Berardi had an oversized umbrella with him. He didn't retrieve it from his car, so he had taken it from home and walked somewhere fairly nearby. I think he'd been to see John Nugent. Have a look at the last page of my report.'

Rod thumbed through to the end and skimmed across it. Then he went to his computer. It took a minute to find what he was looking for. 'John Nugent was at training. We have CCTV of him leaving the estate before Rooksby returns to go for his run. He doesn't come back until the end of the day.'

'What about Holly?'

'She didn't kill him.'

Tom thought of the woman he'd met in Gary White's den. For Holly Nugent to have killed Berardi, she would have to have done a very quick change. 'No, but there is a big question they didn't answer. Neither of them volunteered the information that they'd handed over the money.'

'But it was in Berardi's house. If he had the money, what was he doing out on the running track?'

Tom said nothing. Stamp pulled his lip. 'You're right. We can't ignore this. The defence will have a field day if we don't find out what Nugent was up to. I hesitate to ask you to do any more, given your daily rate.'

'I might be able to offer a discount, courtesy of the Foreign Office.' Tom explained why Elaine had roped him into investigating the website, and concluded by saying, 'It's possible the money has nothing to do with Berardi's murder.'

'No one kills over a website,' said Stamp, in much the same tone as the one that Tom had used to say much the same thing to Elaine.

'What if someone were going to lose their job? The stuff he posted that morning was vile, and personal to those women. What if one of them saw Berardi incapacitated and finished him off?'

'Almost impossible.'

'If Dean is innocent, whoever did kill Giovanni has managed to achieve the almost impossible.'

'What are you proposing?'

'Keeping the investigation open. Allocate Elaine and me to further enquiries, and we'll pursue the financial angle at the same time as we pursue the Mother Superior.'

'But the Mother Superior didn't kill him: they were partners.'

'I know, but if we put a big enough cat among the pigeons, I reckon we'll see if one of them is a killer.'

'A killer pigeon?'

'My metaphor slipped a little.'

'I quite like DC Fraser as the big cat, so I'll let you off. Okay, Tom, you carry on. I've told the ACC that my team need the weekend off, so no matter how many nutters get killed, they're someone else's problem. Good luck with trying to interview the England captain, by the way. The national press have been trying to do it for years and got nowhere.'

Lucy needed a drink. She was also hungry, but she needed a drink more. When Holly sent the au pair out with the dresses, Lucy asked to be dropped at the pub. Grace was meeting her there, so Lucy got a bottle and two glasses in.

'It is Friday,' said Lucy, putting an empty glass in front of Grace.

'It might be Friday for you,' said Grace, 'but it's mad in the office. Now that your dad's come back in, we've got loads to sort out. It's still January.'

Lucy resolutely filled Grace's glass and topped up her own. 'So?'

'Transfer window. You can't have forgotten how mad it gets, and we've got three clients who might move next week. I've spent the last twenty-four hours telling club chief executives that we're still open for business.'

Lucy had forgotten. She knew that the window was open, in theory, but there's a big difference between reading about it in the papers and living with the knife-edge discussions and brinkmanship that would climax at midnight on the thirty-first, followed one week later by a luxury holiday to recover. 'That could be me next year,' she said.

Grace tossed her hair away. 'How do you mean?'

Lucy told her about Gianni's legacy. Grace was appalled. 'You can't! You'd die if you came to work for us.'

Us. Lucy felt it like a stab in the back. Grace was supposed to be her best friend, but when it came to business, Lucy was the outsider.

The implications of what she'd said finally dawned on Grace. 'Oh, God… No, I didn't mean it like that. I just meant that you'd hate it.'

'It's good enough for you.'

'No, it isn't. Not really.' Grace took a big gulp from her wine. 'It's great, most of the time, and I'm not going to say no to free champagne at every home match, am I? Your dad's a good boss too. That's part of the problem: I'm better off than most of my lot.'

There it was again. *Her lot.* Not Lucy's. They'd been to the same schools (from the age of nine), but nothing would change Grace's view that Lucy was from 7Bridge. Was this how the talent felt? Perhaps it would be easy to bear if Lucy had their money, too.

'What do you want, then?' asked Lucy.

'I don't know. I wish I did. I wish I could start my own business like you.'

Six months ago — six days ago even, Lucy would have taken the comment at face value, but today it just felt like Grace was saying *I wish I had a rich daddy like you.* She had to shake herself out of this; she was going to need all the friends she could get, no matter how two-faced they were. *No. Stop. Grace isn't two-faced. She's just being honest, telling it like it is.*

'I might have to close,' said Lucy. 'There's something else I need to tell you.'

Grace put down her glass. The concern in her eyes seemed genuine. 'Are you okay?'

'You think that it's Dad's money that keeps the House of Lucia afloat, don't you?'

'That's not fair. I don't mind you taking your chances: I know I would, and I know it hasn't been easy for you at home.'

'I pay a fair rent on the shop. Ask Paul. And I'm paying interest on the loan. That's not what keeps me going, it's Mama's bags. Without them, the rest of the stuff would pay the rent, but I'd starve.' She paused. 'Mama's pregnant.'

Grace's hand flew to her mouth. 'How…?'

'That's what we wanted to know. Apart from the obvious answer, obviously.'

'She must be all over the place, with Gianni … Poor Paola … Poor you.'

Lucy hadn't noticed that she'd finished her wine until she tried to drink from an empty glass. She was topping it up when the pinstriped waistcoat of Tom Morton came in to the bar. He looked around, and Lucy found herself making eye contact with the detective while holding a bottle of wine in mid-air. He looked about as embarrassed as she felt. He took two steps towards them.

'Sorry to interrupt, but have you seen DC Fraser? My colleague.'

'No scary women in here. Apart from Grace.' *Oh, my God. I said that out loud. I should have had breakfast.*

Instead of going po-faced, he stifled a laugh. 'I'll tell her you said that. She'll be pleased.'

'Don't do that. Sorry … no, I didn't mean it.'

'Take a breath, Lucy,' said Grace.

Lucy breathed. 'We haven't seen her,' she said. 'I came straight from Holly's house, and she's not on the Estate or in the Village.'

'Thanks. I'll text her.' He was about to go when something struck him. Before speaking, he looked at Grace, uncertain whether to go on.

'You can say anything in front of Grace,' said Lucy. 'I trust her.'

'I couldn't help noticing that your family is quite close to the Nugents,' said Tom. 'I don't want to take advantage of you, but how can I get to speak to John?'

'You can't.' Lucy tried to soften the harshness of her remark by waving her hand towards Tom and Grace. 'They're on their way to Southampton for tomorrow's game. Won't be back until tomorrow evening.' She took a drink from her newly-filled glass, and thumped the bottle down next to Grace. 'Tell you what, how about I send you Holly's number?'

'Lucy!' said Grace. 'You can't give that out.'

'I wouldn't want to invade Mrs Nugent's privacy,' said Tom.

'You're the police. You could just look it up. Give me your phone, and I'll send it across.'

He moved his hand inside his jacket to rub his left arm, the way he did when he was nervous. Lucy held out her hand for him to place his phone in it. For some reason, her fingers seemed to be wavering slightly. Instead of passing her his phone, he put another of his cards in her hand. 'I've still got the card you gave me in the shop,' she said. 'I want your phone.'

'There's no rush,' he said. 'You might want to speak to Holly tomorrow and get her permission. Text me her number.'

Grace spoke. 'Tomorrow. Yes, tomorrow sounds like a better idea.'

Lucy put his card in her purse. 'Don't you get the weekend off?'

'A few phone calls don't count as work. I'm off home this afternoon.'

Lucy crossed her legs, and scratched her calf. 'Will anyone be waiting for you?' She didn't care whether he was attached, of course. She just wanted to get a bit more human background. She had noticed Scarywoman's wedding ring and wondered whether her husband was a lamb to the slaughter, or whether he was even scarier than his wife. Not a nice thought.

'My mother will be there,' said Tom, 'but I doubt she'll be waiting for me.' He bent down slightly, and for one horrible moment, Lucy thought he was going to kiss her — but he put his hand on Grace's shoulder and said to her, 'I'm sure you're going to look after your friend.' *That was really nice of him, to make sure that there's someone to look after me,* thought Lucy.

'Don't worry,' said Grace. 'I was going back to work, but I think I'll get us some food, then make sure she gets a taxi.'

Food sounded good.

'Goodbye Miss Revel … Miss White. Have a nice weekend.'

'Goodbye, Chief Inspector.'

When Elaine walked into the Seven Bridges Inn, she couldn't miss Lucy White and Grace Revell. There was an empty wine bottle on the table, a second had been started, and a platter of food was being picked at. Lucy looked like she'd been crying. They didn't look up as she hurried past them in search of Tom. He was in the furthest possible corner, finishing a plate of fish and chips.

'I'm so sorry, sir. I decided to nip home and didn't realise they'd started the roadworks on the M60. That's going to be a nightmare.'

'No problem. Are you hungry?'

'I had a sandwich, thanks. Coffee?' He nodded, and she did the honours. 'Did you see Lucy White? She looked wrecked, poor kid.'

'She'd only just started when I came in. I asked Grace to make sure she got home safely. Is Rob allowed out of training camp for the weekend?'

'That's why I nipped home. Do you need me until Monday?'

'Absolutely not. No one's budgeted for your overtime.'

'You know how to make someone feel appreciated, sir. You really do.'

'Hah! Is he back already?'

'No. I went to pack a bag and put it in the car. The squad are playing a warm-up game tomorrow behind closed doors, then they're free until Monday. I'm going to drive straight up after we've finished.'

'Good. Have fun. Now tell me about Mr Hoskins.'

Elaine did so, and he told her about his encounter with DCI Stamp. Elaine was relieved that Stamp hadn't complained about her, but she was more relieved that he hadn't given her boss a hard time. She digested the news about John Nugent as she finished her coffee.

She put down her cup and said, 'I can think of ten reasons why John Nugent might give Giovanni Berardi £250k, but I can't think of one reason why he'd kill him, still less how he could have done it. And if there was a valid reason, your financial motive has gone up in smoke.'

'Which makes your mission to uncover the Mother Superior even more crucial.'

'My mission? It's your mission, with my help.'

Tom shook his head. 'I've got to get hold of John Nugent, and dig into his life a bit more. You need to stir things up in Saul's domain. I'm sure you'll find the Mother Superior without my help, but it's more important to find out whether any of them knew about Berardi's contribution to the website, and whether they could have killed him for it.'

'You mean we need to find a magician. I reckon we can get enough doubt for Dean to get off the murder charge, Tom, but I don't think we'll nail his killer. DCI Stamp and his team were thorough: there's just no conflicting physical evidence.'

'Reasonable doubt won't be enough for Rooksby. There will be so much publicity at his trial that if people think he's got away with murder, his life will be over before it's begun.'

Elaine peered into the bottom of her coffee cup. There was no inspiration to be found there. She had convinced Tom to get involved in this mess, and now she was leaving it up to him to get her out of it. 'Where do we start?'

'We could see Blackstone, I suppose, but it's been a very, very long week. Let's go and recharge our batteries.'

On the way out of the pub, they saw that Lucy and Grace had finished the second bottle and disappeared.

Chapter 13

Saturday 18 January

The road out of Throckton village goes eventually to Helmsley, up on the North York Moors. On its way, it bends a little to accommodate the track which goes to Rooksnest Farm, where Thomas Senior had been born, and where Tom had spent a good chunk of his childhood. The bits he remembered best, anyway. 'How bad is Granddad?' said Tom, breaking the silence that had lasted since they left York.

'This is the twenty-first century,' said his mother. 'You'd think it would be possible to run a hospital that didn't make its patients feel like sheep waiting for the slaughterman.'

Granddad had gone into hospital because of his chest, and had only stayed one night before insisting that Uncle Peter collect him. This weekend all the family were rallying round to get the packing done at the farm and to prepare the bungalow. Peter and his tribe had volunteered to handle the bungalow: Thomas and Co. were on packing duty.

Tom's younger sister, Diana, had been up for a couple of days and had tried to make a start, as much as Grandma would let her. 'Why can't we take the table?' was the first thing he heard when he followed his mother into the kitchen.

'Because it was built in the kitchen and it won't go through the door,' said Di.

'I'll be lost without the table. How will I cook things?' asked Grandma.

'Most people use kitchen units. With worktops,' said his mother.

'How would you know, Val? You don't need much space to open a tin,' said Grandma. *Harsh but fair*, thought Tom.

'Maybe if you had a higher worktop you wouldn't get a bad back,' said Thomas Senior.

The weather outside had turned clearer but definitely colder. The harsh weather in the run-up to Christmas looked like it might be coming back. The kitchen was as warm as ever from the Aga, but Diana was wrapped in several layers. She was an artist by aspiration (and expensive training), but did all sorts of jobs to keep the wolf (and the bailiff) from the door of her Hackney loft. She was standing between the Aga and the table, in the place that Grandma always stood.

'I've got a plan,' said Di, a little tentatively.

'Oh?' said Valerie.

'Go on,' said Thomas senior. 'It's a good job someone has.'

'Dad, can you start bringing the stuff down from the spare room? It's all packed and needs to go in the van. Tom can help me in the living room while Mum and Grandma make a start in here. You can keep an eye on each other then.'

'An excellent plan,' said Thomas. 'I'll just nip in to see Dad first, then I'll grab those boxes.'

'I'll come with,' said Grandma.

To Tom's surprise, his mother intervened. 'No need, Ma. Thomas will shout if he needs us, and I need you to make the tea while I bring stuff in from the pantry.'

They split up, and Tom found that Di had already made a good start on Grandma's collection of china figurines. He picked up a shepherdess and some newspaper, and started wrapping. 'How is he?' he asked, focusing on the china.

'Not good,' said Di. 'He hasn't got up since Thursday. I was hoping Fiona would come up this weekend and talk some sense into him.'

The other sister, his older one, was a GP in Southport. 'A crisis at the hospital, I think,' said Tom. 'She's hoping to come up tomorrow.'

Di took off her coat. 'Grandma only put on the heating when I forced her to,' she said. 'She's had the electric heater on in their bedroom.' Tom took off his own coat, then moved on to a china dog while Di started sorting books.

Grandma brought the tea through, and they paused to catch up on news, then pressed on. There was a chime from the window ledge where they had placed their phones to try and grab a signal. Di was nearest and picked them both up to check whose the message was.

'You've got a text from Lucy,' she said. 'Who's she when she's at home?'

'A witness. Pass it here.'

Diana raised an eyebrow. 'You don't usually put witnesses in your phone under their first name.' Diana had mixed feelings about being the little sister. Sometimes she felt sorry for herself: today she took advantage. *Sorry about last night!* she read from the screen. 'Either she's not really a witness or you could end up investigating yourself, Tom.'

'She is a witness. She also lost her brother last week and got drunk in public, and I need her to get me an interview with the England captain, so hand it over.'

Di held out the phone. 'What, the actual England captain? Whatshisname? John Nugent?'

Tom looked at the message: *Sorry about last night. Grace reminded me this morning that I said I'd help. Holly will see you on Monday. I'll sign you in at the Visitor Gate at 11 o'clock. Lucy.*

'Yes, the England captain, John Nugent. Only I'll be starting with his wife and working towards the man himself, perhaps via his PR.' While he was speaking, Tom text his thanks back to Lucy. He didn't mention her state of intoxication.

'Tell me now, brother dear. What on earth is this case about, and why are you mixing with these people?'

That was a very good question. It made him think for a moment. 'They're just people, like you and me, but richer.'

'I want details. Have you been on that estate they all live on? Why haven't you said anything?'

Tom was spared his sister's onslaught by a discreet cough from his father, and a jerk of the head towards the staircase. Tom followed his father upstairs, and had to force himself to swallow past the lump in his throat. What had happened?

His father held the door to Granddad's bedroom open and said, 'Welcome to the court of Lord Throckton.'

When Tom peeked around the door, Granddad was sitting up in bed, looking a lot better and holding something wrapped in a cloth in his lap.

'I'm not ill, you know,' said Granddad. 'They're just keeping me out of the way. I know what they're like.' He waved his arm towards the women downstairs.

'I don't know, Dad,' said Thomas Senior. 'What *are* they like? Don't come all *Last of the Summer Wine* just because you're in bed.'

Granddad (who had a degree in land management) leaned forward. 'She's wanted to get rid of my rosettes and cups ever since Peter took over the farm. She thinks that she can get away with it while I'm stuck up here.' He tapped the side of his nose. 'But I'm wise to her. I got Peter to put them in a safe place until we've moved, then he's bringing them down to the bungalow.' A racking cough shook him. Tom looked to his father, who looked back with a mixture of fear and resignation. Granddad coughed again, and the package slipped off his lap. Tom leapt forward to grab it, and found himself holding a heavy wooden box. It was made of varnished oak, and had a familiar design on the top: the Morton coat of arms, as granted to the original Thomas Morton in 1904 when he was created the first Baron Throckton.

Tom steadied the box and was about to lift it when Granddad said, 'Not yet. Not your turn yet.' Thomas Senior came over and took the box. It must be the Memoir. 'I wanted you to be here when I handed it over,' said Granddad to Tom. 'It'll be your turn one day.'

'But not yet,' said Tom and his father together.

Tom had forgotten about the Memoir, and tried not to think about the aristocratic title. The first baron was always known as "The original Thomas Morton", but Tom had no idea why. He knew that the Original had done some favour to Edward VII, and picked up a lot of land on the fringes of the Moors. Later in life, he had scandalised North Riding society by declaring that he was leaving Throckton Castle to his eldest child — a girl, no less. He did have two boys as well: Thomas and Alexander. The oldest got the title and little else (he had disappeared to America after the War). Alexander inherited Rooksnest Farm, and was Tom's Granddad.

When you are given a hereditary peerage, you also get a document declaring the fact; this is known as the Letters Patent, and includes a lot of small print. One of the clauses in the Throckton Letters Patent says that children born out of wedlock cannot inherit the title, even if the parents subsequently marry. Due to an administrative confusion in the State of Massachusetts, Great Uncle Thomas's marriage to Rebecca wasn't legal, so Granddad had become the second Baron last year, and collected the Memoir. All Tom knew about the Memoir was that it could only be read by the heir to the title. He hoped that Granddad would live a long time yet: he was in no hurry to read it.

'Take it, Thomas,' said Granddad. 'Go and put it in your car now, then you can get on with whatever job you've been given.'

Thomas Senior wrapped the box in its cloth and took it to safety. Tom went back to china figurines, and the waiting Diana. She wasn't going to let him leave the room again until she knew all about 7Bridge, and had extracted a promise of pictures of all the houses.

Chapter 14

Monday 20 January

'So long as you're all right, that's the main thing.' Saul took a mouthful of smoke from his cigar, and released it slowly as his mother continued to tell him how terrible the flight back from Miami had been. A theatrical cough from the door told him that Max had arrived. 'I've got to go. I'll call tonight.'

He balanced the cigar on the edge of the ashtray and went through to his office in the Estate Management suite. 'Are the police here?'

'Waiting,' said Max.

'Let's go, then.'

Tiffany showed DCI Morton and DC Fraser into the room, and there were handshakes all round. Saul had a conference table which could seat four comfortably, and waved them to it. Morton was pretty much as Max had described him, rather thin and pale, but wearing a much better suit than DCI Stamp had ever shown up in. His colleague was at the edge of what Saul would have expected from a police officer, sartorially speaking. Her blouse was acceptable, but he couldn't agree with jeans, still less with the lace-up boots. Her face was quite long, but tapered rather than horsey. Her eyes had a feral air to them — part scared rabbit and part hungry fox.

Morton spoke first. 'Thank you for seeing us, Mr Blackstone.'

'Saul, please.'

Morton gave a short smile, so short it probably hadn't registered in his consciousness. That's what public schools do for you: as well as instilling self-belief, they make social niceties second nature. His own children had the same air when they were in company.

'Our mission, if you can call it that, is to track down the author of the *SeenIn7Bridge* website. What happens to them after that is up to you, but I imagine that Princess Karida will expect them to be expelled from paradise fairly swiftly.'

'There's no need to judge,' said Saul, more sharply than he had intended. 'We're a community, not a commune. We have rules like everyone else. The Mother Superior is probably breaking those rules, that's all.'

Morton's smile was more deliberate this time. 'Forgive me. It was just a turn of phrase. I'll be more careful in future.' He turned to his partner. 'Elaine, have you got Hoskins' box?'

DC Fraser took out a small plastic box with several data sockets in the side, and put it on the table.

'Your cyber expert gave us this,' said Morton, 'in case we need to snoop on the residents, but I hope we won't have to use it. His first instinct was that the Mother Superior is based on the service side of the Estate.'

'I agree,' said Max. 'There's not a single resident or family member who hasn't been held up to ridicule on that website.'

'The staff get it as well,' said Saul, 'and the attitude is quite patronising.'

Morton considered this. 'I'm sure you've gone round in circles with speculation. It's time to take the plunge and start asking questions. Would I be right in saying that the Princess's intervention wasn't entirely welcome, Mr Blackstone? You've been very low-key before now.'

'You're right. As soon as this become police business, we could end up with all sorts of problems.'

'That applies to us as well, which is why I want DC Fraser to see the Princess this afternoon, if possible. One of my grandmother's favourite sayings is *Be careful what you wish for.*'

'Mine too,' said Saul. 'Princess Karida is expecting you. Max, have you got the reader?'

It was Max's turn to take out a piece of hardware. 'This is a fingerprint reader,' he said. 'If you register here, I can give you access through the Spa to the Hall. That way you won't need to have Beth Pedley watching you. I've also got a phone number for the Princess's maids.'

'Thanks,' said Morton. 'That works a treat. I'm sure you'll also tell your patrol officers to give us access to all the Estate. Just for a week.'

'I hadn't planned to,' said Max.

DC Fraser spoke for the first time. She had quite a strong Lancashire accent. 'It's something I could bring up this afternoon.'

Saul didn't want to fight that battle. So long as the Princess knew what she was unleashing, on her head be it. 'That's fine, Max. Just arrange it. For five days.'

'Who works here, exactly?' said Fraser.

'A lot of people,' said Saul. 'Do you want the management overview?' The police officers nodded. Saul continued, 'There are six sections in the service side: Estate Management, Security, Site Services and the Spa are all run directly by 7Bridge Estate Limited. The other outfits are under exclusive contract: catering, housekeeping and interiors.' He paused. 'Would it help if you came to the weekly meeting tomorrow morning?'

Morton and Fraser looked at each other and nodded. 'I don't like lying,' said Morton, 'but I'm happy with half-truths. Technically, I'm still attached to the Berardi case, so I might send in DC Fraser with a cover story in the first instance. Nothing cloak-and-dagger, just a little misdirection.'

Fraser looked alarmed at this, but said nothing. With that tailoring, Morton could pass for any professional, but Fraser was every inch the strong arm of the law. If she were going undercover, it would have to be a real makeover. 'Undercover as what?' he asked Morton.

'Not undercover,' responded the detective. 'That takes too much paperwork. Just with a cover story. I'll think of one overnight.'

She muttered under her breath, but Saul could hear what Fraser said: 'It had better be a bloody good one.'

Outside the Estate Office, Tom took his first really good look at the service area. He hadn't taken in more than the warehouse units on the day of the murder, and this morning he had parked in Blackstone's visitors' spot, away from the hustle and bustle.

From this angle he could see the access road from the Village, which continued past the service area on to the Spa, where Elaine had just disappeared to visit the Hall. He was surprised that the Princess and the well-heeled Spa clients didn't have a more up-market entrance than this, but then he saw the gate: security was why. In 7Bridge, luxury and privacy came a close second, but security was definitely the guiding principle.

The service area had obviously been flattened when it was constructed: a lot of the spoil must have been used to create the mound that separated it from the Estate proper. Anyone driving in would first see the car park for visitors, and its own security entrance. His mother would hate it: no one could drop in for coffee without an appointment, and no deliveries could be made without arrangement. How did online retailers cope? In answer to his question, the postman arrived. Aah. Simple: everything from packages to pallets was dropped off *outside* the Estate barrier. Someone else took it in.

What his mother would have liked – would have given a lot of money for – was the next building: Hartley Executive Catering. It presented its front door to the car park but, probably deliberately, Tom could see the back from here. It was clean, tidy and looked as if the most diligent health inspector would only find praise for their work.

The other two units were more anonymous, so Tom walked slowly past them to get his bearings. The smaller of them, nestled close to the Estate Office, was the security control; its blacked out ground floor windows giving it a menacing air the occupants no doubt cherished.

The larger building was discreetly labelled for Housekeeping, Site Services and Theafrey Interiors. Round the side, he could see that the offices were backed by a more industrial structure. What did they keep there? Sit-on lawnmowers? Sit-on vacuum cleaners to cover the acres of carpet?

He walked past catering and presented himself to Visitor Security, where he and Elaine had begun their 7Bridge adventure last week. Their communication systems must be very good, because the PO already knew that he was authorised to access the Estate.

'Do I need a badge or something?' asked Tom.

'No, sir. We've got a record of you coming in. Just make sure we know that you've left.'

'Is it possible to leave without you knowing? I didn't think there were any unmanned exits.'

The patrol officers weren't robots. Max must pay a decent wage because they all seemed as if they enjoyed their job — not something you could say about a lot of security personnel.

'It has been known, Mr Morton. A former resident once signed in most of the Chelsea team, then smuggled them out one by one in the boot of his car.'

Tom checked his watch. He was a little early. 'What about the other way round?' he asked. 'What about residents smuggling people into the Estate?'

'They don't need to, sir. Residents can bring any guest they like on site in their own vehicle. All we do is check that an authorised person is driving when the vehicle arrives at the residents' entrance.'

He thought of Hollywood movies, of professional footballers being forced at gunpoint to take terrorists on to the Estate, or other elaborate schemes. No. Gianni Berardi was killed up close and personal by someone who knew him, not by an intruder. He thanked the patrol officer and was allowed through the gate into the Estate. He walked slowly towards the gap in the mound until he saw Lucy coming towards him.

At first she was oblivious to his presence, lost in a world of music and drifting from one side of the pavement to the other. The rather shapeless dress she had worn in the pub on Friday had been replaced by leggings and fur-lined boots under a blue shift; over her top was a padded coat. Other cold weather measures included matching gloves, scarf and hat.

She came to a sudden stop when she saw him. 'How did you get in?'

'I was thinking of buying one of the empty residences,' he said. 'The patrol officer told me to wander round and have a look.'

She did a double take. 'Hah! You might be rich, but no one wanders around without permission. Are you rich? Is that why you're on this case, because you understand the wealthy?'

'You can look up a DCI's salary on the gov.uk website. I'm not rich, but I will be Lord Throckton one day.'

'Are you for real?'

'There are eight hundred hereditary peers. Why shouldn't I be one of them? That guy who plays David Archer on the radio is an earl.'

'Grandma White listens to the Archers. Don't tell me you do as well.'

'Erm, no, but my mother does. Did Grandma White buy you the hat, scarf and glove set for Christmas?'

She laughed — the first proper laugh he had seen since her father had broken the news about her brother. 'Even better,' she said, 'Grandma White bought them for Robyn. Can you imagine Robyn in a knitted hat? No, neither can I. Come on, let's go.'

They walked through the gap in the mound. At the top Tom stood to look over the Estate, but mature transplanted trees, high brick walls and twists in the road stopped him seeing much of anything. To spite his sister, he took a picture and sent it to her with this message: *Move along. Nothing to see here.* He turned to Lucy. 'In Beverley Hills,' he said, 'you can buy maps to the homes of the stars. Is there one for 7Bridge?'

Lucy had stood close to him, and joined him looking out. 'There is, actually, but it's on a scrappy piece of photocopied paper. They give it to new staff so they can find their way around. Most houses have one stuck up in the kitchen as well.'

They set off again, and Tom asked her to point things out. She reeled off the names of many Premiership footballers, and a few local entrepreneurs who had also made 7Bridge their home. When they arrived at the green, Tom looked down the path that led to the running track. There was a corresponding way through on the other side, presumably for those who only fancied a half circuit. Then he asked what the next community event would be.

'Dunno. Probably nothing now until Easter. Too cold.'

'Where did you end up on Friday night?'

Her cheeks, pink from the cold, went redder. 'I'm so sorry about that. We hit the wine bars in Wilsmlow and crashed at Grace's parents. Grace told me what I'd said to you when I surfaced next morning.'

'You didn't say anything bad. You were very helpful.'

Her eyes flicked towards him for a second, then away. 'I said DC Fraser was a scary woman, and I tried to copy your phone.'

'She is scary, sometimes.' He moved on. 'What's Holly like? I didn't meet her under the best of circumstances.'

'She's lovely. She's really caring, very protective towards her children and does a hell of a lot for charity. You don't read about that on *SeenIn7Bridge*, or see it in *Cheshire Life*.'

'And protective towards her husband, if she wants to see me first.'

'John's one of the most recognisable men in England,' said Lucy carefully. 'That's a big responsibility, and he takes it seriously. D'you know, there's not been a whiff of scandal about him? Never.' She stopped by a small drive down to some gates. 'They live just down here; she's expecting you.'

'You live down the hill and round the corner, don't you?'

'I live over the shop. Dad's house is down the hill.'

'Sorry. That didn't come out right. Aren't you coming down to introduce us?'

She looked down at the Nugents' gates, then up at him. 'You've already met. Besides, she'll want me to try on a dress for the funeral.'

They'd both forgotten Gianni for a moment, and they were both embarrassed to find themselves forgetting. There was nothing that Tom could say about the dress that wouldn't sound creepy, so he asked when the funeral was going to be.

'Thursday, at St Saviour's. It's the local Catholic church. We went to the church school there, too, but we all lapsed when Mama left. Robyn has already put her lot down for private school.'

'Didn't you go to private school?'

'Grace and I both went to Altrincham Girls Grammar, and we both bombed our GCSEs.'

'Your stepmother's fault?'

'Yeah. Spot on. It all kicked off in the spring: Mama found out about the affair and stormed off to Italy, and

Robyn said she was pregnant when she clearly wasn't and moved in.' She shrugged.

'Why did Grace underperform?'

'What?'

'I can see why you didn't fulfil your potential at school, with that lot going on, but why didn't Grace?'

Lucy balanced on one foot, tracing an invisible pattern in tarmac with her other foot. She looked very uncomfortable. After a few seconds, her shoulders lifted in a microscopic shrug. She scooped some hair back under the hat and turned to face him, ignoring his question by asking one of her own. 'What about you? Don't Barons have to go to private school?'

'I'm a Peterite.'

'Can't you get arrested for that?'

He stared at her.

'I'm so not the first person to say that, am I?' she said, pulling up the collars of her coat and hiding her nose in her scarf.

'You're the first person to say it this century, I think. St Peter's School in York is the fourth oldest school in the world. It's had two saints as headmasters, as well as three generations of Mortons as pupils. Are you sure you won't come down and help me with Holly?'

'Go on. I'll have to do the walk of shame some time.'

They stepped down the short drive to the entrance, and Lucy opened a side gate. When they got round another bend inside the property, Tom came to a sudden halt.

'Bloody hell,' he said.

'I know,' said Lucy. 'I call it *Casa Nugent*, but don't tell Holly. It makes Southfork look almost homely.'

'Do you call it Southfork as well? I thought it was just me.'

'Everyone calls it Southfork, except Mama and Dad.'

'Why is the front door open? It's freezing.'

'Welcome to 7Bridge, Tom.'

'I'm glad you're here.'

Had he gone too far? The look on her face suggested for a second that he might have done, but she grinned and led him under the portico to the grand entrance. He looked at her back, and remembered the way she had ignored his question about Grace Revell's GCSE results. Did he need to go back to it at some stage? Or could he give her the benefit of the doubt?

She should have known that there would be a return visit to Sevenbridge Hall, and she should have worn footwear with fewer laces, but Elaine loved her DMs. She even had two identical pairs, so that she could alternate them and let one pair get some air every night. Subconsciously she must have been expecting it, because she'd put new socks on this morning. Red ones.

'It was tea for you, wasn't it?' said Alia as they went through to the Morning Room.

'Thanks. We didn't get any from Saul Blackstone.'

Alia straightened a couple of cushions. 'He used to be much more hospitable when he was married.'

'I take it he's divorced.'

'Oh, yes. She left him and went back to London. They were appointed as a couple, you know. It was her job to liaise with Princess Karida, and the Princess used to go out on to the Estate.' She sighed. 'It was a mistake, such a terrible mistake.'

'In what way?'

'The Princess tries to be a good Muslim, but it is not easy for her. The man who killed her husband claimed to be a good Muslim, too. A good Muslim, the Princess believes, is tolerant. Saul and Miriam Blackstone are Jews, but not Zionists.'

'What went wrong? It sounds like both parties knew what they were doing, and Saul is still here.'

'This website that you are looking into. It first appeared about three years ago, and we all laughed a little. Then two years ago, the Mother Superior wrote that the Sultan must be very tolerant if he lets his daughter-in-law work with Jews. When someone in Ghar'aan picked it up, the Princess had to stop Miriam Blackstone's visits. She resigned, and I think she left her husband because he didn't support her enough. Please excuse me … I must make the tea.'

Elaine looked out the window, flexing her toes in her socks – because she could – and thinking about Alia — because she had to. On her last visit, the maid had been pleasant but had acted like the servant in a harem, which in a way she was. Why the sudden confessional? Elaine had made no effort to draw her out. She volunteered all that information, and then left. No personal chat, no talk about the weather, just boomph! Saul Blackstone is a Jew! It was something Alia's employer wanted to be known, but not attributably.

The Princess entered with a cheerful 'Good morning', wearing a black floor-length skirt and long-sleeved white blouse — the sort of outfit worn by the preacher's wife in American westerns. Except that the preacher's wife wouldn't be showing painted toenails on bare feet, and wouldn't be wearing a headscarf that had Arabic lettering in gold thread. Alia followed with the tray.

'Max can set up a secure messaging account for your boss,' said Karida, after the pleasantries.

'I think he'd rather I reported personally, in the short term,' said Elaine. 'If you don't mind…'

'I'm not pressed for time, if that's what you mean, and I don't mind you coming into the Hall regularly.' Karida put down her coffee. 'What is your plan?'

'DCI Morton is going to let me lead on this,' said Elaine.

'He must trust you.'

'Perhaps. Or maybe he wants me to sniff around discreetly before he takes over. He also wanted me to raise an issue before we start.'

'Just the one?'

'One big one. It's this: once we start asking questions, there's a real possibility of a backlash from the Mother Superior. If one of the national newspapers picks it up, things could get even worse. It's a real possibility. There's an English saying…'

'Let me guess: *Sticks and stones…*'

'Yes.'

'The stone-throwers and the bomb-throwers don't start with stones and bombs. They start with words.'

'I understand.'

'Do you? Do you really?' The Princess adjusted her skirt. 'I doubt that you envy my life, Elaine.' She held up a hand to forestall interruptions. 'I can see it in your face. I certainly don't envy yours. *In Sha'Allah*, we will be happy in our lives. Find this woman. Stop her.'

'As you wish, ma'am.'

Princess Karida rose effortlessly from the chair and offered a final handshake. Elaine resisted the urge to bow at the same time.

Alia didn't appear to escort her off the premises. Elaine had always been a glass-half-full kind of girl, so she took this as a sign that she was trusted, rather than a sign that she was in bad odour. As she was putting her boots back on, she missed the right foot and ended up hopping towards the wall, trying not to get mud on the carpet. When she put her hand on the wall, it gave way and she fell over.

She swore, of course, then looked up. The "hidden" door wasn't really hidden. It was rather obviously cut out of the panelling, if you looked. On the other side was a four-foot square cupboard full of the sort of things you'd need if you were going into the real world: shoes, coats, bags, and umbrellas. Lots of umbrellas. There was also a tiny cupboard full of bright colour. Elaine checked down the corridor to see if anyone was looking (and on the ceiling for CCTV), then peeked inside. She estimated the contents as 90% lycra, with added trainer. Someone had a very flash exercise wardrobe.

Beth Pedley was hovering on the other side of the door to the magic kingdom.

'Good Morning, Officer. I hope you found your way okay.'

'Thanks. Yes.'

'The receptionist told me you'd been through, but she didn't know your name. If you wouldn't mind, next time could you sign the visitor register? Just in case of fire.'

That's so lame it crawls, thought Elaine. If Beth Pedley was so desperate to know what was going on, she might have something to hide. Or she might just be a control freak. Either was possible.

Elaine promised to be good, then left the Spa. She sent Tom a text: *Game on. See you in Lyme Court.*

Holly Nugent was waiting for them in the hallway of *Casa Nugent.* Tom took a moment to check out the grand staircase, and decided that Lucy was spot on with her nickname of the property. Their hostess was either a fan of aerobic chic or had just been to the gym (probably in the back of the house). Holly was certainly a striking figure in her pink jacket and bright blue exercise leggings. The jacket was short, and the Nugent Hips which seemed to be anathema to the Mother Superior were on display. Her hair was up, making quite a pile on top of her head.

Next to him, Lucy ostentatiously removed her boots, so Tom did the same.

'Shut the door, Luce,' said Holly. 'I don't leave it open *all* the time,' she said to Tom. 'It's just easier when we've got visitors. There's no doorbell as such in these places, just a video camera that connects to the CCTV system. It's a right pain if you're upstairs. You must be Chief Inspector Morton.'

They shook hands while Lucy heaved the door closed. Holly paused for a second to look him up and down. 'Nice coat. Just dump it on the banister and follow me.'

They only went to the kitchen, but Tom got lost. It was somewhere to the right, then down a corridor, and possibly back again. The architect had probably designed the house to align the french windows with the best view. He was ushered to a six-seater round table in oak, gleaming with polish but not immaculate: young children had clearly done a lot of eating, baking and crafting on that surface.

'Tea or coffee?'

'I'd prefer tea, but I don't mind coffee.'

'Lucy, would you…'

She clearly knew her way around Holly's kitchen, and set to work, singing sotto voce as she opened cupboards.

Holly folded her hands and put them on the table. 'A lot of policemen have tried to talk to my husband over the years. None have succeeded, though.'

'Oh?'

'He's been accused of three rapes, four assaults and one count of match fixing. Every time, they spoke to his brief, went away and no further action was taken.'

'Oh.'

'That's right.' Tom had a vague memory of John being from Yorkshire, but Holly was a Londoner through and through. 'The only reason you're even in my house is that Lucy said you weren't like the others.'

'I'm sure the others were doing their job. For every false accusation, there are hundreds of real victims.'

'I know. That's another reason I'm talking to you.' She turned to Lucy, who was working the espresso machine while a mug of tea brewed. 'What did Gary say when you told him you'd arranged for the police to see me?'

'I haven't,' said Lucy.

Holly gave Tom a sharp look. 'Why did you go behind Gary's back? What's your game, Morton?'

Lucy was leaning with her back to the worktop. She had only just realised what she had done.

'I was going to speak to Mr White,' said Tom. 'It was a coincidence. I happened to see Lucy first and asked her how to get in touch with John. She clearly respects you, Mrs Nugent, because she thinks you can make up your own mind without Gary White's permission.'

'Thanks, Tom,' said Lucy, flashing him a smile, 'but there's more to it than that.' She lowered her eyes, then looked at Holly. 'Dad's in bits about Gianni. He really is. He's trying to hold it together for me and for Mama, but he's cut up about what happened. It's bad enough that Dean found out about Gianni's affair with Madison, but that's not what Tom's here about, is it?'

'No,' said Tom.

Lucy addressed Holly directly. 'He's been looking into something that Gianni was up to behind Dad's back. If Gianni was gambling again, I don't want Dad to know about it. That's all.' She turned round to finish making the drinks.

Tom said nothing. He waited until Holly was looking at him over her coffee. 'I wouldn't bother you unless I had something specific to ask,' he said. 'It's about money. Cash.'

Holly frowned. He noticed that the nails gripping her mug were neither painted nor polished. In fact they looked rather bitten. 'John doesn't gamble,' she said. 'Not at all. He used to go to the casino when he was younger – they all do when they first get big money – but he stopped when we got married. I don't think he's set foot in one since then without me next to him.'

Tom drank his tea. Holly looked from him to Lucy and shifted in her seat. 'Those dresses are back from the dressmaker,' she said. 'Do you want to nip and get them?

You'd be better trying them on at home so you can see how they go with your shoes. They're lying on the bed.'

Lucy looked relieved that there wasn't going to be a fashion show, and didn't mind being shunted out of the way. When she had gone, Holly said, 'Are you going to tell me now?'

'I think it's a question for John. If he wants you there when I ask it, then that's up to him.' He leaned forward. 'I think it's to do with the Ikedas.'

Holly put down her coffee. 'It's the first leg of the League Cup semi-final tomorrow. John's not playing, and he doesn't have to go in until lunchtime. Come about ten o'clock.'

'Thank you.'

She nodded, making it clear that he was being granted an especial favour, then she said, 'Gary's been brilliant to us. Treats us like family. Not like some of the agents. To them, we're just meat. I hope they pay for it in the next life.'

'I understand. You'll notice that I didn't take my notebook out.'

'Good.' Lucy reappeared with two suit hangers. 'Now if you'll excuse me,' said Holly, 'I'm going to the Spa. Do you want a lift with them, Lucy?'

'I'll carry them,' said Tom. 'Lucy can finish giving me the guided tour.'

They walked out together, Holly picked up a gym bag from the hallway and got into a rather modest car at the side of the house.

'She'll open the gates for us,' said Lucy, just as the cast iron barriers swung apart. Holly hadn't locked her front door, nor had she picked up any keys for the car.

As they left the property, Tom asked, 'Hasn't she got her own gym somewhere in there?'

'There's a running machine by the pool, but Holly likes to get out. She used to have a reputation for late-night exercise, especially when John was away.'

MARK HAYDEN

'"Late-night exercise"? Is that a euphemism?'

'Not Holly. No chance. When the kids were asleep, she'd leave the au pair in charge and jog to the Spa, then work out.'

They had got back to the road, and the hangers were making Tom's shoulder ache. 'Is it okay to fold these over my arm?' asked Tom. 'They're quite long, and I don't want to drop them.'

'Yeah. No problem.'

They continued their walk through the Estate. The turning to Southfork was almost the last before the road straightened to approach the rear of the residents' entrance.

'We'll go round the last corner,' said Lucy. 'As we've come this far, we might as well go all the way, if you don't mind carrying those dresses while we do it.'

When they were round the corner, Tom was faced with a difficult decision, depending on how she answered his next question — if he could bring himself to ask it. They were standing on a road that sloped down to the residents' bridge. There was a security outpost, a substantial barrier and parking spaces on both sides of the road: the running track cut through the scene. What caught Tom's attention was the car park on the left. Not only was it set much further back, part of it was zoned off with yellow markings, and it contained the most expensive collection of cars he had ever seen. He had no idea what they were, but he reckoned that all their names ended in "i". On the pavement was a metal box on a pole.

'The 7Bridge Collective,' said Lucy, following his gaze. 'Currently inactive, thanks to John. I told him about it, and he got the boys to behave. For now.'

'You can't see it from the security post, and there's no CCTV coverage, is there?'

'No. Paul called it "plausible deniability".'

'It's a nice view from here, but not as nice as Saul Blackstone's office.'

Lucy paused, staring over the trees. 'I used to write song lyrics from here, or from the top of the barrier mound, depending on how I felt. It's a shame I can't write the music as well.'

It was time to ask his question. He turned to face her, making sure his shoes scraped on the tarmac. She looked up at him.

'Why didn't you tell your dad about my seeing Holly?' he said. 'Because it's been very … easy to find things out with your help.'

'Like I said, I wanted to keep it away from him, and it was nice to be able to help. To help you.'

'That's what worried me. I wanted someone's help – yes – but I especially wanted it to be you.' He held up the bags with the dresses in them. 'You're going to your brother's funeral. You're a victim, Lucy, and victims need justice as well as support.'

She laughed. 'Did they teach you to be pompous at St Peter's? I like it better when you're funny.'

'It's hard to be serious with you, but I need to start.'

'Why? It's nice to talk, to have someone from outside the Estate who isn't after something.'

'But I am after something. Okay, if you don't like pompous Morton, I'll try this. What's worse, being stabbed in the back or being dumped after a one-night stand?'

She didn't hesitate. 'Being stabbed in the back is far worse. Being dumped is part of life's rich tapestry. By the way, you've got no chance of a one-night stand.'

'Then I'll stab you in the front. How would you feel if I arrested someone you care about? I might have to.'

'Who?'

He set his face in neutral and said nothing.

She blew out her cheeks and turned away. 'That was heavy. You didn't have to go that far.'

'It did kill the moment, didn't it?'

'Stone dead. Do I have to carry my own clothes now?'

'I owe you that much.'

They walked back up the road to Southfork. The gates here were slightly smaller and less ornate than at *Casa Nugent*. When Tom handed over the hangers, he said, 'If I do find out something about Gianni, it will have to come officially through the FLO. Would you like me to give you an unofficial heads-up?'

'You owe me that, too.'

'Thanks for your help, Lucy.'

'You're welcome. Have a nice day.'

He turned and walked away.

Isaac had thought about a security guard for Dean's appearance at the magistrates' court, but he decided that Daniel Abramovitz was big enough to handle the media, if any turned up: it wasn't a scheduled appearance. There were no cameras on the way in, but he saw that a couple of the lads in the smokers' corner had recognised Dean. Pictures were taken. He nudged Daniel and whispered, 'Watch for what happens on the way out.'

The magistrate was a little frosty when Daniel made the application for Dean to have inpatient surgery on his shoulder at a hospital in Manchester, and could he have the electronic tag taken off, please?

'The purpose of the bail conditions was to keep your client away from this area, not to unleash him.'

'If the bench wishes, I will drive Mr Rooksby to the hospital myself,' said Daniel. 'Once he's gone under the knife, he won't be going anywhere for a few days - unless he needs a scan, in which case the tag would have to come off anyway. I do like to think of how best to use public resources.'

'This is a bail hearing, Mr Abramovitz. There's no need for that attitude.'

The bench didn't wait for a non-apology from Daniel. They conferred for a few seconds then the chairman said,

'We are minded to grant your application. No one disputes that Mr Rooksby needs the medical care, and as his employer is paying, it will save the NHS some money.'

When Dean went down to get his tag removed, Daniel asked Isaac why he had come up from London.

'I've got a deal cooking on Merseyside that needs a little seasoning, but mostly I wanted to see you.'

'About Dean? It's too early to say anything. I've heard that the police have all but stopped their enquiries. If you're wanting the odds, I don't think I'll be able to give you those until I know who the Crown's barrister is going to be.'

Isaac waved the idea away. 'I'm not bothered about Dean yet. I'm more concerned about the man he's accused of killing.'

Daniel looked at the door to the holding area, where Dean was being processed, and stroked his beard. 'He's a funny one, and no mistake. The more I talk to him, the less of a clue I have about what happened to Giovanni.'

'Seriously?'

'Seriously.'

'That's not good, Daniel. That's not good. If Dean didn't kill him, who did?'

Daniel shrugged. 'Not my problem.'

'But it could be mine. Has anyone been in touch about Berardi's will?'

'Paul Warren called. He said nothing about my firm representing both Dean and Giovanni, and he's too astute not to ask questions if he knew the connection. No one else has called.'

'That's something. Do you think the police will follow it up?'

'As I said, there's no reason to think so. Unfortunately, our best contact on the Estate is dead, and there's no point trying to get anything out of Murray Cavendish because he's got little imagination and no discretion.'

Isaac nodded in agreement. Gianni wasn't just part of the big project: he was a superb spy in his own right. Murray Cavendish wouldn't notice if his wife started sleeping with Princess Karida.

'We'll have to wait. The family might do something after the funeral on Thursday.'

Dean rejoined them and lifted his trouser leg to show a bare ankle.

'Let's get you to hospital,' said Daniel, remembering not to put his arm around Dean's shoulder. 'I'll run you some interference outside: there may be media on the way out.'

'Don't worry about what they say. Just stop them barging into my shoulder. If it swells up again, they won't operate.' Dean turned to Isaac. 'I know I'm not going to be fit again until the summer, but what about next year? Daniel says that the trial may not be until September. Do you think that Trafford Rangers will loan me out to Salton again?'

'Do you think they'll want you?' said Isaac.

'If I'm fit, and my head's in the right place, they'll want me.'

'I'll see what I can do. Let's take things one step at a time. Come on… let's get you to hospital.'

Isaac went ahead to the front doors. There was a small crowd, but no TV cameras. He waved the others forward. Outside the door, they headed left, with Dean sticking close to the wall and Daniel making jokes with a couple of local reporters. Dean didn't hang his head, or pull his hoodie up: he just walked steadily towards the car park, where his parents were waiting. Suddenly, he stopped and ducked past Daniel to approach a large woman with blonde hair. Daniel spun round, unsure what was going on. Isaac hurried forward.

Instead of kissing the woman (which is what most of Isaac's clients would have done), he shook her hand. Isaac just caught him saying, 'Thanks for everything, Emily. I'll be back.'

'We know you will,' she responded, lifting her chin up. Neither of them smiled. Before the crowd of reporters and phone-wielding layabouts could re-form around them, Dean was gone again.

Isaac lingered for a second, then approached the woman. 'I'm Isaac Redmond,' he said.

'I know,' she replied. 'I'm Emily Miller — STFC Supporters Club.'

He shook her hand. 'Pleased to meet you. I see you already know Dean.'

'I do, and we're going to make sure that before the trial starts, as many people as possible know that Dean is innocent. Hopefully, some of them will be on the jury. Excuse me — I've got to get back to work.'

He watched her retreating figure. Was this the work of Dean's PR? He had sent Dean his best operator because the fallout from a murder charge is rather more serious than that from an affair. Isaac had a great appreciation of social media, but no idea how they worked. For that reason, he employed a marketing company to tell him what was happening, and a PR company to make things happen. While he waited for Daniel to return, he called Sara in the office.

'Can you call marketing and get them to do a report on Dean Rooksby? What's the consensus on his reputation at the moment? How toxic is he on a scale from rat droppings to plutonium? That sort of thing.'

'If you want my opinion, he's a demented thug, but since when has that stopped you from taking people on?'

Sara always offered her opinion: it was the price he paid for employing his daughter. 'We got him for nothing. I can already pay your bonus with what he'll bring in.'

'That's you all over, Dad. Price of everything, value of nothing. I'll get you the report before you're home.'

There had been no lunch at the Seven Bridges Inn today. Elaine had eaten *al desko* and, having raided the photocopier downstairs at Lyme Court, was now Sellotaping several sheets of A3 paper together. Once she had a big enough canvas, she drew some circles to make a Venn diagram. She labelled the left circle *About Residents*. The right circle was *About Staff*. The shared area was *Both*, obviously, but she didn't write that down. Even she could remember that.

She leaned over and collected the sheets that had churned out of the printer: eleven pages of posts from *SeenIn7Bridge*. All she had to do now was cut them up and place them on the correct circle. *Scissors,* she thought. *We have no scissors. Tom must have scissors because he's organised and he used to be a lawyer. Lawyers love stationery, therefore Tom must have scissors.* She went to look in his desk.

'There's no biscuits in there. I've hidden them.'

'Jesus! You scared the hell out of me.' How had he crept up on her? The man wears leather-soled shoes, for goodness sake.

'Good. That'll teach you to be nosy. What were you looking for?'

'Scissors.'

'Aah. If you tidy up, you might find them.'

'It doesn't need tidying. I can still see my desk.'

'No tidying, no scissors. I'll make tea.' He put down a bag from Sevenbridge Village café and took off his coat. 'Tell me about your morning while you tidy.'

It really didn't need tidying. The man was OCD, that's what he was, but he was also her boss, so Elaine started to tidy up and tell him about her visit to the Princess. At the end, Tom stared into space, rubbing his left shoulder. She got the pens he had left lying around and arranged them in geometric precision on his desk.

'See!' she said. 'All tidied. I didn't find the scissors, though.'

'What have you put the pens like that for? Have you got OCD or something?'

She tried to forgive him, because he was a man and therefore of little brain. 'Where are the scissors, sir? I need them.'

He poured the tea. 'In my briefcase. I only said you might find them so you'd tidy up.' He wandered over to her desk. 'I can see what you're going to do, but what do you hope to discover?'

She dug the scissors out of his briefcase (which had nothing else of interest in it), and cut up the first of the pages of blog postings. 'It might not tell me anything, but I've got to read them all anyway. I reckon it's possible that there might be a pattern, and this was a good way to start.'

'Good… but before you do that, can you ring Saul Blackstone and ask him to move the meeting with his staff to nine thirty tomorrow? I've got me an appointment with the England captain, and I don't want to be late.'

'What was his house like?' She paused. 'And how's Lucy White?'

'Lucy was very helpful. I couldn't have got to see Holly Nugent without her.' He sighed. 'But I had to end it with her afterwards.'

Elaine put down the scissors, which she'd just picked up. 'I hope you're joking. I really do.'

'Sort-of. I did tell her that I might have to arrest someone she cares about. She got the message. She called me pompous as well.'

Elaine cleared her throat and picked up the scissors. It seemed the sensible thing to do.

'As for Holly's house, it's incredible. I thought Gary White's place was vulgar and extravagant but the Nugents have taken it to a whole new level of naff.'

'Not to your taste, then.'

'I loved the kitchen. I'd sacrifice a lot to have a house with something like that in it.'

He left, and she called the Estate Office. Tiffany assured her that the earlier start time would not be a problem.

After an hour of carefully reading and sorting, she called Tom back in to see what she'd done. He picked up a few slips at random, read them and put them back carefully. 'Any thoughts?' he asked.

'There's not a single person on the Estate who doesn't get the treatment, as does every employee from supervisor level upwards. Berardi himself gets it in the neck a few times.'

'Conclusion?'

'I don't think Berardi wrote many of the posts, and all his contributions were relatively recent. He's not the Mother Superior.' Tom nodded encouragement. 'Either the Mother Superior is a resident who is happy to write real crap about herself, or she's on the management side and used Berardi to cover up her identity. You know — got him to write stuff about the service section to make it more realistic.'

'I agree. It's got to be one of those two explanations, and the second one is more likely. There's one issue we haven't thought about yet: how did they meet? Did she recruit him? Did he identify her and then join in the game?'

Elaine pondered her printouts. 'Saul mentioned something about Berardi having a real reputation with women, especially among the staff. There's a good chance he once had a relationship with the Mother Superior, and found out that way.'

'Excellent. I like your thinking. Use that as a strategy when you talk to them. I'll try and find a cover story that allows you to dig for gossip.'

Elaine swung on her chair, then put her feet on the desk. He frowned at her, and she took them down. 'Sorry. If the Mother Superior killed him, it can only be for one reason: he was threatening to expose her. He posted three really horrible things on the day he died. Could that have been a threat?'

'Could have been. You need to get home. Leave these here, and I'll have a proper look.'

Elaine stood up and stretched her back muscles. 'Do you fancy a drink? Bit of company for both of us.'

He smiled. 'That's actually a very nice idea, but one of us would have to drive.'

She hesitated, then dived in. 'We could hit the Northern Quarter, then you could crash in our spare room.'

He weighed it up. 'We're here all week. Have you got anything planned for Wednesday night?' She shook her head. 'How about I move hotels for one night? Then we can do the job properly.'

'You're on. Goodnight, Tom.'

On her way out, he threw one last comment.

'Besides, Elaine... if we leave it for two days, it will give you a chance to tidy up at home, too.'

There were no scented candles, and no glass of wine. Juliet Porterhouse had made a resolution to do without both when she was having a midweek bath. To her, a shower was a way of getting the body clean, whereas a hot bath also cleansed the mind and the soul. Now that she was alone again, and her youngest daughter had an en-suite, she could indulge herself with a bath every evening.

The resolution to do without candles and wine had come after reading one too many articles in her own newspaper about the effects of middle-aged, middle-class alcoholism. She didn't consider herself remotely near middle-aged (fifty being the new thirty), but she was resolutely middle-class.

Her phone was in a specially-lined wicker basket on a stool next to the bath (present from older daughter), and programmed to make no sound or vibration to incoming texts or emails (courtesy of elder daughter's boyfriend).

Voice calls were different. She had already sent two to voicemail, but when *Tom Morton* showed up on the screen, she wiped her hand and answered it.

'I'm not disturbing you am I?' said Morton, with his cultured northern accent. She wasn't going to mention the bath to a policeman. Definitely a case of Too Much Information.

'Don't worry. I wasn't busy. How are you? No problems with the trial, are there?'

They had come together professionally before Christmas, and thanks to an off-the-record interview with Morton, she was sitting on a goldmine of background. When the trials were over, she was going to get a front page and at least four inside the *Sunday Examiner*. Not only that, she was going to cover the trials themselves: one in the eye for the Old Bailey boys on the paper.

'No. All proceeding slowly, as you would expect.'

While he was on the phone, she chanced her arm. 'Have you any way of getting in touch with Conrad Clarke? I'd love to hear his side of things.'

'Hah! You'll be lucky. Try talking to him and you'll get some very strange people knocking on your door. Anyway, I heard he's gone underground.'

Something in his voice made her think that Morton was laughing at a private joke. She made a mental note, then waited to hear what he wanted.

'Fancy a trip to Manchester?'

'No, but I might come anyway if you make it worth my while.'

'I might need some plausible deniability. If I asked you up on Wednesday, could you make it at short notice?'

'Hang on… let me check.'

She didn't check her diary. She did a frantic Google of *Morton* and *Manchester* instead. There was one hit: Tom had given evidence at the inquest of Giovanni Berardi.

'I should be free,' she told him. 'Let me know.'

Of course she would be free. Juliet Porterhouse would crawl to Manchester over broken glass to get the inside story on the 7Bridge murder. She got out of the bath and headed downstairs for a glass of wine.

Chapter 15

Tuesday 21 January

A few months before leaving Leicester, Elaine and Rob had watched an episode of *Location, Location, Location*. It wasn't their normal thing, but Rob (who had time to study the TV guides) had said that it was featuring flats in Manchester. The two couples on screen had been told, in Kirstie's inimitable head-girl way, that they shouldn't be thinking about central Manchester, and that they should get real. Rob was about to receive a generous signing-on fee, so they started their own search as close to the centre as possible.

Before she left for 7Bridge that morning, Elaine looked around their new flat. It looked tidy to her. Well... perhaps she might get the vacuum out tonight, in case Morton did come over. Then again, it would be dark when he arrived. She could just turn the lights down. She set the alarm and left.

Her boss was waiting in his car at the Estate service area because it was too cold to stand outside. He waved her into the passenger seat and said, 'I've had a think. I reckon that we can legitimately link the money found in Berardi's house with *SeenIn7Bridge*, but only if we hint that he may have been involved in blackmail. That way, we can play it down. The main thing is that the staff don't think we're conducting a witch hunt.'

She mulled it over. She wouldn't have done it that way, but it might work. She nodded, and they made their way to the Estate Office conference room, where the weekly meeting was already under way. Tom went in first, and while he was meeting and greeting, Elaine took a look round.

Saul sat at the head of the table, with Max Nolan very conspicuously at his right hand. Two chairs had been left empty on his left, then there was a ring of five women. Accident? Design? Statistical probability or statistical fluke? Elaine quickly shook hands with Saul then took the empty chair at the corner.

Saul restarted the meeting. 'I think most of you have recognised our guests already, even if you haven't met them. This is Detective Chief Inspector Morton, from London, and his colleague DC Fraser from South Lancs. When he's finished outlining his purpose today, could you all give a brief introduction, so he knows who you are and what you do?'

Elaine looked uneasily at the group round the table: all women, apart from the ex-army security chief and their male boss. Several analogies flashed through her mind: a primary school with a male headteacher, a convent with a priest, a herd with the alpha male, and a harem. Back to the Princess, who pulled the strings from inside the Hall. None of any of this made for a healthy environment, in her opinion. She shook her head and concentrated on what Tom was saying.

'…That's why we are still investigating certain matters connected with Mr Berardi's death. I believe you are aware that he was associated in some way to the *SeenIn7Bridge* website…'

Elaine looked around the room. Several of the women looked at each other, or down at the table. This was not going to be a popular topic.

'…Our enquiries have to consider his relationship with one or more of the residents.' He paused and did a survey of his own. 'You can rely on our complete discretion in this matter. I've investigated too many cases of misconduct not to realise how devastating leaks can be for some people. Mr Blackstone assures me that you are the same.'

'You mean he's got us over a barrel,' said one of the women. She was the most expensively and informally dressed of the group. A cashmere sweater was co-ordinated with pearls and a floaty cardigan. Her hair was delicately highlighted to match her delicate complexion.

'Thank you, Anthea,' said Blackstone. 'If you'd let Inspector Morton finish.'

'Yes. We're particularly interested in any information you can provide on Berardi's relations with the residents. Preliminary enquiries will be handled by my colleague, DC Fraser. Formal statements may follow.'

Blackstone nodded to the woman on Elaine's left. She was wearing loose trousers and a baggy top. It looked like she might actually get her hands dirty at some point, because Elaine could see rough patches on her palms, and two of those blue plasters that chefs use.

'Sonia Hartley, of Hartley Executive Catering. We provide catering for residents in their homes, for the Hall, the Spa and canteen facilities for the staff. As far as the residents are concerned, most of the talent work to a nutrition plan provided by their club.'

Elaine spoke for the first time. 'The talent?'

'It's what they call the residents who earn money,' said Anthea, the woman who had spoken before. 'All the legal residents are men, and most are professional sportsmen. We had a woman tennis player once, but she retired and left. And a singer from one the girl bands. She left, too. The women on the Estate are universally known as WAGs, even when they have their own careers.'

'Thank you for that clarification, Anthea,' said Blackstone. 'Natasha?'

'Hi. I'm Natasha Thompson of 7Bridge Domestic Services, also known as Housekeeping,' said the next person. White blouse, chain store suit. A little older than the others, probably. 'We provide all indoor services except maintenance.' She smiled. 'Most people think of us as the cleaners, but all the nannies and au pairs are appointed through us, as are the secretaries… Basically, anyone who works indoors. We also do the laundry.'

It was Anthea's turn next. 'Anthea Godfrey.' Being Anthea, she stood up and leaned across Sonia and Natasha to shake Elaine and Tom's hand. 'I run Theafrey Interiors. My mission is to make sure the residencies look, and work, exactly as the residents would like them to.'

Next in line was Beth Pedley. Before she spoke, she stifled a yawn. '…Excuse me. Beth Pedley, manager of 7Bridge Spa and housekeeper at the Hall, in case DC Fraser hasn't already told you.' Her remarks were addressed solely to Tom. All three of the previous speakers had looked at both police officers equally. 'My part of the Estate is the only section open to non-residents, but most of the WAGs are Spa members. We have some personal trainers who work in the residencies, but most of the women come to us.'

The last woman to speak was the shortest - shortest hair, shortest in height, shortest jacket.

'Vanessa Grafton, site services manager. We look after all external and internal maintenance, including residency gardens. That's it.'

'And that's it for me too,' said Tom. 'If you'll excuse me, I'll see you later.'

'Who would you like to see first?' said Blackstone, after the door had closed behind Tom.

Elaine looked at the notes she had made. 'Beth and Natasha, please.'

'Does it have to be immediately?'

'No, but very soon.'

'Here,' said Sonia Hartley, passing over a business card with a note on the back. 'The canteen's upstairs in my building. Help yourself to a late breakfast and hand this over at the till.'

That suited Elaine down to the ground. 'I'll be back in half an hour,' she said.

There was strictly no admittance to anywhere other than the canteen within Hartley Executive Catering. There was no receptionist — just a buzzer guarding the doors to the kitchens and offices. Upstairs, Elaine pushed through double doors into a modest space full of tables, and playing host to a wide cross-section of people. Perhaps infected by Tom's neatness bug, she had a quick look: there wasn't any dirt anywhere. Spotless was the only word.

She made her way slowly across the room. Patrol officers were clustered together, as were cleaners and a couple of women wearing tabards from the Spa. They didn't look like they did the treatments: they probably changed the towels. A couple of people were wearing suits — but mostly it was uniforms, and mostly it was women. The sense of unease that had started in the Estate Office continued to build, but she couldn't quite put her finger on it.

The breakfast was hot, tasty and plentiful. If Tom were planning another meeting in the Seven Bridges Inn, she would have to stick to water. On her way back to the conference room, she had a good look at the other buildings. When she arrived, Beth was sitting in the same seat, checking her phone.

'Ms Pedley?' said Elaine, pointing to a chair.

'Mrs.' The other woman gave a sigh and came over to sit nearer. While Elaine was taking out her notebook, Mrs Pedley continued 'What exactly are you after, officer?'

'We're in a difficult position,' said Elaine. 'We think a crime may have been committed, but we're not sure who the victim might be.' It was true, but also as vague as possible.

Mrs Pedley was having none of it. 'In other words, you're on a fishing expedition, backed by Saul. I'm happy to answer any specific questions, but I don't gossip. That's one of the reasons I'm in charge of housekeeping at the Hall: the Princess values her privacy. As you've seen.'

'The Princess is aware of our investigation. Perhaps we could start there. Do you talk to her much?'

Mrs Pedley smoothed her hair. 'Naturally I talk to the Princess.'

In her notebook, Elaine wrote: *Beth Pedley is a servant. Only sees PK to receive orders or complaints. Ambitious?* Then she asked, 'How did Giovanni Berardi get to know about this business with the pool maintenance guy?'

'That's what I mean: someone gossiped. Only three or four of my staff knew what was going on. One of them had too much to drink at the staff party and ran their mouth off when one of Gianni's girlfriends was listening. To get in his good books, she told him. The person who had too much to drink has been dismissed, but I can give you her contact details.'

That was harsh. 'Do you lose many staff like that?'

'She was lucky. Occasionally I remind them that the 7Bridge Estate will pursue anyone who leaks information through the courts. It stops them talking to the press.'

'Yes. I suppose that the WAGs need to know they can confide in the staff.'

She was given a strange look by Mrs Pedley. 'The Spa members come for exercise, cleansing and pampering, not psychotherapy. Do you have a Spa membership?'

Elaine hadn't been to a spa since her hen weekend, four years ago. She did use the gym in Leicester, but not the spa. Why would she? 'I'll be specific, then. How many of your staff did Giovanni Berardi have relationships with?'

'Three relationships I got to hear about. All of them have since left. How many one-night stands there were is anyone's guess. I do know that Saul warned him off a couple of years ago: he was told in no uncertain terms not to take staff into that place of his in the woods.'

That was interesting. As well as everything else, the Estate management also tried to regulate the residents' sex lives. It was a shame they hadn't stopped Berardi having a fling with Madison Greenwood. He might still be alive if they had nipped it in the bud.

Elaine wasn't floundering, but she didn't know where to go next with the brief that Tom had given her. Beth Pedley played a crucial role in the interface between the Hall, the Spa and the residents on the Estate. She was going to have to take instructions on this one.

'Thank you. One final question: have you ever heard any of the residents say anything about Mr Berardi that wasn't connected to his recreational habits?'

'When he stopped gambling, I heard that he worked very hard for his father. Other than that … no. Shall I send Natasha in?'

'Please.'

Tom hadn't slept well last night, for several reasons. He left Elaine to her fate in the Estate Office, hoping that the bitter wind coming down from the Peak District would wake him up, and banish thoughts of Lucy, Holly Nugent and Dean Rooksby (going under the knife today, he had learnt from HOLMES2 this morning). He signed in through the security barrier and drew his gloves back on. Being a bloke, they didn't match his hat or his scarf. There he was again: thinking of the splash of colour he had seen in Lucy's outfit yesterday. Walking along the same path wasn't going to help him forget her, either.

Because he didn't have to keep pace with her shorter legs, he opened his stride and got to the green with too much time to spare. He turned left and joined the running track. It was exactly a week since Gianni had had his fatal encounter with Dean. The air was too cold for running, in his opinion, but two women passed him as he descended past the memorial flowers marking the spot. They ran together, but one of them accelerated as he got closer, so that no one would have to move off the path. He vaguely recognised the slower runner, and although the faster one was a stranger, the colours of her top looked familiar. When they had passed, he looked round and saw the 7Bridge Spa logo on her back. Was she staff? If so, what was she doing on the Estate? If she was a resident, why was she wearing that top? He lingered a second to see which way they went, but the two women disappeared round a bend, the slower one having put on a spurt to catch her partner.

He hadn't quite realised how few general access points there were, and he had to do an enormous loop to get to the front gates of *Casa Nugent* even though he had passed the back some time ago. In the end, he only just made it. He buzzed the intercom and heard the lock release. A young woman with long blonde hair in a ponytail, tight jeans and bare feet was waiting at the front door.

'This way, please,' she said, with a distinctly East European accent. When he bent to unlace his shoes, she added, 'Not necessary in this room.'

Last time they had turned right. This time they turned left and entered what Tom would have described as a ballroom, if he'd been in a stately home. The ceiling was higher than most modern houses, and the room was split into zones by strategic placing of furniture. On the right, four leather couches were placed at angles in front of an enormous white screen, which was itself surrounded by speakers. A space at least five metres square on the left was finished in pale oak, and there was a lighting bar hanging from the ceiling. The wall at the end held a metal plate full of sockets and connections. Tom didn't like dance music, but he recognised a dance floor when he saw one. Beyond the wooden floor, the walls were black and windowless.

'Over there,' said his guide, pointing to the far corner, and a pool of daylight.

He crossed the room and saw a formal dining area: black chairs up to a black table. The backs of the chairs were high and narrow, with Japanese overtones. Seated with their backs to the sliding doors were Holly and John Nugent.

Holly remained seated when he arrived at the table, but the England captain stood up to shake his hand. Tom didn't often feel dwarfed or humbled, but John Nugent made him feel both. He towered over Tom by at least four inches, made more obvious by his ramrod-straight back and shoulders that strained at his training top. His hair was short, and flecked with grey, like the stubble on his face. When they shook hands, Tom could feel the restraint in Nugent's grip — the knowledge that he was by far the stronger but wasn't going to rub the other man's face in it.

Tom reached for his warrant card, but Nugent waved it away. 'So you're what a senior policeman looks like,' was his opening remark.

'Not yet. I'm strictly middle management .. thank you for seeing me. I'm very grateful.'

'Cut to the chase. I've got to be at training soon,' said Nugent, pointing to a seat.

Tom took the time to remove his overcoat. 'Your house is very warm, Mrs Nugent. Very welcoming on a day like this.' Holly flashed a quick smile but didn't offer to take his coat. Tom laid it across his knees. He forced himself to meet Nugent's gaze. 'Because Holly is here, I assume you don't mind her knowing what's going on.'

'Why should I? What *is* going on? You wouldn't tell her anything.'

'I was the first police officer to search Giovanni Berardi's house, and I found a lot of money on the table. Do you know anything about that?'

'What makes you think I do?'

'It was a great deal of money, Mr Nugent. So much money that you couldn't have misplaced it.'

'So?'

The England captain's eyes were a steely blue, and hadn't wavered since Tom looked at them. He bit the inside of his lip, reached into his pocket and opened his notebook. He only had one advantage in this contest, and he had to use it carefully.

'The money, all of it, is in secure storage. The investigation team asked me to look into where it came from. There was nothing like that amount in Mr Berardi's accounts, so I dug deeper. It's what I'm good at.' He looked up and gave Nugent a smile, then he tapped his pen on the notebook. 'I traced those notes back to your account with Praed's bank in Leeds. It's unofficial at the moment, but I know the records are there. I can get them with a warrant.'

Nugent cracked. He glanced at Holly, and Tom knew that this was the first she'd heard of it. Nugent licked his lips. 'It was commission.'

'Really? What for?'

'For putting the deal together with Kaito Ikeda.'

'That's not how the deal was structured. I've seen the contracts.' That was a lie, but Tom knew the paperwork would back him up.

'No. It was a personal bonus. He wanted paying in cash.' Nugent's voice rose a couple of tones. 'I told him that he had to pay tax on it.'

'I'm sure you did. What was the exact amount?'

'How much did you find?'

'Please, Mr Nugent. I know how much you withdrew from the bank.'

'It was two hundred and fifty grand.'

Very interesting. If Nugent were telling the truth, where had the other fifty thousand disappeared to? Tom didn't press the point just yet; he had a more important question. 'When did you make the payment?'

'Does that matter?'

'Yes, it does, Mr Nugent.'

Nugent looked at his wife, then at Tom. There was no going back now. 'I paid him on the day he died.'

'Jesus Christ, John! What are you telling me?' Holly's response was immediate and instinctive. Whatever she had known about the money, this was news to her.

'Nothing,' said Nugent. 'It was just a coincidence.'

Tom waited to see if either of them was going to take it further. They weren't. He jotted a couple of notes in his book, then said, 'Because you had contact with Mr Berardi shortly before his murder, a formal statement will have to be taken by the MIT — that's the major incident team. I'll be honest, Mr Nugent, the first thing they'll ask is why you didn't come forward earlier.'

Nugent had seen this coming. For the first time, he gave his answer looking down at the floor instead of across into Tom's eyes. 'I didn't say anything because I'd left the Estate well before it happened. I went to training a bit early. I stopped in the Collective car park, ran round to Gianni's house, then jogged back to the car. I'm on CCTV leaving the Estate at half past eight. There's no way back in.'

'Why so early?' asked Tom. 'Why that morning?'

'I don't like having that sort of cash around, even with the security here. As soon as Gianni emailed me from the airport, to tell me he'd signed the contract, I made arrangements to pay him.' He looked up. 'Another reason I didn't tell the police was that I felt guilty. If I hadn't paid him that day, he wouldn't have met Dean like that. He'd still be alive.'

Holly put her hand on John's shoulder. 'And you've been carrying all this around? John, no wonder you had a stinker last week. You should have told me.'

John patted his wife's hand. 'I'm sorry, love, but you've had so much to cope with yourself… that's all.' He looked at Tom. 'If you're not taking my statement, I'd better get going.'

John Nugent had withheld information from the police, and they would have to make another appointment to see him, presumably through his solicitor. Tom didn't like it, but he was prepared to live with it. Before he let Nugent go, he wanted one more reaction. 'So, just to confirm what you said, Mr Nugent … You withdrew £250,000 from the bank and paid it all to Giovanni Berardi on Tuesday morning of last week, as commission for his work on the Miyagi New Engine deal. Correct?'

Nugent nodded.

'Thank you,' said Tom. He stood up, then added, 'Japan must mean a lot to you.'

He caught it: just a flicker of Nugent's eyes towards his wife, and the fact that he didn't answer Tom's question. Instead, Holly leapt into the breach. 'It's a new start, Mr Morton. It's a great big adventure, and we're ready for it.'

Tom smiled and stood back. John kissed his wife and shook hands with Tom. 'Back in a second,' said Holly, following her man to the door.

Tom went to look out at the garden. An area of stone flags, not unlike the one behind Southfork, was battened down against the winter. He could imagine it in high summer — the doors open, perhaps a hundred people milling in and out, partying and dancing.

'Is he in trouble?' asked Holly, returning from the hall. She was wearing jeans today, and outdoor shoes that looked as if they were box fresh.

'No. If he had been interviewed before – and if he'd changed his statement – that would be different. The law does not require you to come forward. I promised you I'd be discreet, Mrs Nugent, and I will tell DCI Stamp myself. Do you know what my day job is?'

She ventured a smile. 'You mean this is a hobby?'

'Absolutely. My normal role is to investigate police corruption and misconduct in public office. If anyone from Stamp's team leaks John's memory lapse to the media, I'll be down on them like a ton of bricks.'

'Memory lapse. I like that — but it won't wash, will it? He'll have to think of a better excuse than that before they interview him.'

She was pleading with her eyes. Holly knew what John had done, even if her husband didn't realise it himself, and Holly was desperate to minimise the potential effect. If Tom antagonised either of the Nugents, life could get difficult. He didn't want the Football Association ringing Leonie.

'Do you remember what Lucy said when we came round yesterday?' he asked.

'What? About not wanting Gary to know?'

Tom nodded, and said, 'It's a lame excuse, but it's better than having a "memory lapse".'

'Thanks, Tom — I mean Inspector Morton. Sorry, that's talking to Lucy. She calls you "Tom". Why's that, I wonder?'

This was very dangerous ground indeed. 'I met her at a bad time, and I tried to be sympathetic. Perhaps I should have stopped her, but that would have been rude.'

'Mmm,' said Holly. She had a small charm between her teeth — one of two or three on a necklace that he hadn't seen before. She dropped it out of her mouth and asked if he wanted tea.

'That's very kind, but I'd better be going.' Something about the shape of the charm was ringing bells, but he couldn't place it. Then he remembered. On a whim, he tried it out when he left. Instead of goodbye, he put his hands together and said, '*Namaste*.'

Holly started to reciprocate, realised what she was doing, stopped, then carried on. '*Namaste*, Inspector. What made you say that?'

'I saw the charm on your necklace. My sister went through a phase of incorporating religious symbols in her art, and I remembered. My ex-wife was into serious yoga. Briefly. One of your charms is the *aum* sign.' He nodded to her, and left a slightly amused, slightly puzzled Holly Nugent behind him.

He walked around the corner and called the number he'd been given for Max Nolan. Yes, Max could see Tom straight away. He strode through the Estate, and as he descended from the mound, he saw Elaine walking from the Hartley building to the Estate Office. She didn't notice him.

Max Nolan's command post was exactly what Tom expected: sometimes the predictable is reassuring. It was almost bare of ornamentation, the military memorabilia were discreetly displayed, and the biggest splash of colour was an A4 photograph of his wife and children, taken against the blue background of a holiday swimming pool. There was a laptop on his desk, but no array of monitors. Tom got the impression that Max spent most of his time in the CCTV room or out on the Estate. Perhaps he spent a lot of time looking for holes in the fence.

'Out of curiosity, what would have been your approach to the Mother Superior issue?' asked Tom.

'Not my problem,' said Nolan. 'I told Saul that it wasn't a threat to the residents' security, so I'd have left it.' He paused for a moment, and Tom saw something behind the military mask. 'But Saul sees the bigger picture, so he says. He says there's more threats to security than kidnappers and paparazzi. That's why he decided to bring you in originally: the antics of that 7Bridge Collective mob were going to cause an embarrassment.'

'I think we can forget about that problem. Lucy White promised to sort something out.'

'She probably didn't need to. Now that Gianni and his Maserati are no longer with us, there's no one who's really up for it.'

Maserati? Tom didn't remember a Maserati, or the repayments for one in Gianni's financial records. He added it to his mental list of loose ends, shook his head, then said, 'I need two things, Mr Nolan. First, I need a list of any female residents who have ever had biometric access to the Hall, and then a complete record of when they went through. I'll take a download rather than a printout.'

There was no raised eyebrow, no questioning or dispute. Nolan simply said, 'And the other thing?'

'I passed a woman on the running track at 09:45 this morning, roughly at the spot where Berardi was murdered. She was wearing a 7Bridge Spa top. Can you tell me who she is?'

Nolan picked up the phone and pressed a well-worn button. 'Dave, can you look something up for the police?' He offered the handset to Tom. 'Tell him what you just told me.'

Tom repeated the description, and was told he'd have an answer in five minutes.

'That download,' said Nolan. 'It won't take long to prepare - there aren't many women on it - but I can only hand it over on a memory stick, with an encryption program. How quickly do you want it?'

That was a fair compromise. They were giving him some quite sensitive information without a warrant, so he should take precautions. 'After lunch will do.'

'If I'm not around, ask for Dave. Aah, here he is.'

A patrol officer stuck his head through Nolan's door. 'It's one of the personal trainers from the Spa,' he said. 'Kirsty, I think her name is. She works with Claire Roebuck a fair bit.'

That was why he half-recognised the woman — in the last image he'd seen, she was wearing a lot less clothing.

'Claire Roebuck: your resident pagan,' said Tom. 'Last seen running naked around the Christmas tree.'

Dave snorted and quickly ducked out of the room. Nolan was not amused. Tom thanked him for his help, then said, 'If I'm making jokes about Mrs Roebuck, wouldn't you say she's lost a bit of security?'

'It's a point of view,' said Nolan.

Tom stood just inside the doors, where it was warm, to send a message to Elaine: *Reaching a dead end here. Need a change of approach. Going for a walk via the residents entrance. See you in the pub. TM.*

As well as the tasty breakfast Elaine had enjoyed in the canteen, it seemed that Hartley Executive Catering also did barista-grade coffee. Natasha Thompson was shown into the conference room carrying two takeout cups embossed *HEC*. She put one in front of Elaine and said, 'I was getting one for myself and didn't want to look mean.'

'Thank you. I'm starting to get a feeling for life in 7Bridge. Would I be right in thinking that it's not an option for residents to provide their own staff?'

Mrs Thompson stirred two sugars into her coffee. 'Pretty much. Even though quite a few of the residences are owned by Trafford Rangers and other clubs, Saul has the final say on who moves in. He makes it clear that all staff have to be approved by me. Very few of them bother.'

'So that gives you and your team unique access. It's the same with cleaners the world over — they get to see everything, and they're often the worst paid.'

She gave Elaine a grim smile. 'Vetting staff is my top priority, DC Fraser — and by the way, I pay my cleaners more than the living wage, and I look for long-term loyalty.'

Despite the slap down, Mrs Thompson's attitude was still far more helpful than Beth Pedley's. Elaine backtracked. 'As I said, I'm getting a feeling for the place, but I'll always be an outsider. Has your company had the contract for long?'

'Since the Estate opened. I had a business with my husband, but the contract for 7Bridge required exclusivity, so we split the existing business in two so that I could have the Estate operation as a separate concern, and he kept the original company. I have a bigger turnover than he does now.' She gave a smile. 'Though he blames me for stealing his best staff, and for using his business like a training ground. He's right.'

'Can you tell me about the *SeenIn7Bridge* posting that Giovanni Berardi made on the day he was killed? The one about the Border Force raid.'

Mrs Thompson turned her cup round to centre the logo in her hands. 'Someone tipped off the Border Force. Until the posting on the website, I thought it was a rival company, but now I think Berardi did it. He'd think it was funny: he could be very childish like that. The women arrested were all on probation with the Estate business. We'd had a lot of sickness after a bug went round, and I was very short-staffed. The women had all been working for my husband, and he had done due diligence on their paperwork.' She shrugged. 'The trouble is … the people traffickers have a lot of experience at forgery. Two of staff they took away are back at work already. We won't be prosecuted, but I don't want a repeat of my interview with Saul, that's for certain.'

'One last question: how do you and your staff get around the Estate?'

'We share buggies with Max's mob: it would be impossible otherwise with all the equipment we have to carry. That's one of the few things where Saul overruled him, actually. When it rains, which it does a lot round here, we get priority.'

'Thanks for the coffee, and your time.'

Elaine had decided very early in the interview that Natasha Thompson wasn't the Mother Superior. Something about the way she held herself, the way she knew what was important and the way she had no secrets did not fit the profile of the author of *SeenIn7Bridge*. Beth Pedley was a different kettle of fish altogether, but Elaine wasn't sure if that meant she was the snake in the grass or simply a woman on the make who thought she could do a better job than Saul.

She made a few notes and was working out what to ask next when Tom sent her a text. She responded, *Me too. Good Idea. Enjoy the walk. I'm going to the Spa. EF.*

Lucy did try to see the good in Robyn. She really did. It was just that there wasn't much. Robyn had given Lucy's father three more children, and was an efficient hostess, but that was it. As far as Lucy could tell, Robyn rarely gave Dad any pleasure any more, if she ever had: she had certainly never done anything good for Lucy.

'The priest will let you read a prayer. He'll want you to read a prayer,' said Robyn. 'My mum read one at my gran's funeral.'

Deliver me from my daughter, O Lord, was probably the prayer, if Robyn's mother had any sense. Actually, she did. That was something good about Robyn: her mother. 'I just can't,' said Lucy.

'There's time to change your mind. He's not coming until this afternoon.'

The details of the funeral were spread all round them on the kitchen table. Dad had promised to sort out the funeral, but that was before Newcastle United's striker had torn his anterior cruciates. They were now trying to buy one of Dad's up-and-coming players, but the player wanted to stay on the south coast, and his current club wanted too much money — so Dad was in Geordieland and Robyn was in charge.

'Show me the food again,' said Lucy.

'Don't worry about that. Sonia will do exactly what I tell her.'

Which was precisely Lucy's concern. If there wasn't a hint of Italy in the food, Lucy might actually kill her. She'd had enough. In desperation, she checked her phone; there was a one-word text from Holly: *Shoes??????*

'I've got to go out. Serious wardrobe issue,' said Lucy.

Robyn bridled a little. 'Well, if you're happy to leave me in charge all of a sudden… These Orders of Service have to be confirmed by two o'clock.'

'Fine. Just make sure they've got the proper version of the "Our Father" in them.'

'What's "Our Father"?'

Lucy was already heading out. 'The Lord's Prayer.'

When she reached the central road, she could just see a familiar Crombie overcoat disappearing on to the green, alone. At least John hadn't been arrested. She didn't have time to think about Tom Morton today — either what he'd said about Grace's GCSEs, or about the man himself. But when she arrived at *Casa Nugent*, Holly had other ideas.

'He sticks to his guns, does your detective.'

'He's not my detective, Holly. He's just a policeman who's been on the emotional intelligence course, that's all. He's after someone to arrest for something.'

Holly narrowed her eyes Lucy could feel herself going red. She changed the subject. 'That Gucci dress you sent is gorgeous, and the length works for me, but I need heels. Mine are suede and they just won't do.'

'We'll go out. We should get something in Knutsford.'

'No time,' said Lucy. 'Do you remember the Boxing Day Ball?' Holly nodded. 'Ellie was wearing new shoes that day. I bet they fit.'

'Wait here.'

'It's all right. I know where they'll be.'

'No, I'll get them. Ellie's moved her stuff around a bit. Go and put the kettle on.'

'Leonie must allow you a very big expense account,' said Elaine, when Tom finally arrived at the Seven Bridges Inn.

'I've just been talking to her, as it happens.' His face looked raw from the cold, and he fumbled the buttons on his coat: he must have been standing, talking on the phone, with no gloves on.

'Oh, yes?'

'Yes. What do you fancy?'

'Nothing, thanks. I had brunch in Sonia Hartley's excellent canteen. If Max Nolan had any vacancies, I'd be tempted to work there just for the food.'

'Fair enough. I'll do without as well.'

He returned from the bar with a pot of tea and half a pint of bitter. 'Tell me how you got on. You can skip further details of the breakfast.'

Elaine told him about her interviews, and that she was sure Natasha was innocent. She said that something was off about Beth Pedley, but she wasn't sure what it was.

'Mmm… I agree. I'm afraid that things have got more complicated: that money came from John Nugent, and he handed it over just before Berardi died.'

'What? You don't think he…?'

'No. Not only does he have an alibi, he wouldn't have drowned Berardi. If John Nugent were the killer, he would have broken his neck. Single-handed.'

'He made a big impression on you.'

Tom gave her a funny look, then said, 'The complication is financial. John Nugent swears that he gave the whole £250,000 to Gianni. I don't think he's lying, so there's £50,000 unaccounted for.'

'Did the patrol officer take it?'

'No. I made him switch on his chest-cam before we entered Berardi's house. It wasn't him, so I reckon that's what Berardi was doing out in the rain — handing over the fifty grand to someone.'

'Do you think they hung around and killed him?'

'I don't know, Elaine. I really don't. What I do know is this: Rod Stamp will have to try and track it down, because the CPS can't take Rooksby to trial with that loose end dangling. Even I could have a field day with that sort of reasonable doubt, and I'm no advocate.'

Elaine wasn't sure about Tom's conclusion. If she were on the jury, and she was given a stark choice between a violent footballer in a jealous rage, and an unknown person who might have been given some money, she'd go with the footballer every time. She picked up on something Tom had slipped in to his comment. 'You said DCI Stamp will have to look into it. Why not us?'

'It's nice having a team of two, but we're specialists. This calls for the resources of the MIT. Rod will have to move the time frame back by twenty minutes or so and see if anyone could have met Berardi. You know the drill: trace, interview, eliminate. It could take days.'

Elaine felt like the purpose had drained out of her day. If they weren't looking for the person who killed Berardi, why were they messing around with the Mother Superior? That really was a job for a private detective, not a police officer. She sighed. 'Shall I arrange interviews with Sonia, Anthea and Vanessa?'

'That's what I rang Leonie about. I think we're in danger of running headlong into trouble if we persist at the moment. I think we should suspend our investigation until after the funeral. We'll start again next week.'

'And do what in the meantime?'

'How do you fancy a trip to Rome? If you take unpaid leave on Friday, you can watch Scotland take on the might of Italy. I'm sure Rob will be grateful for the support.'

That was the best thing Elaine had heard in days. The delight lit up her face – she could feel it from inside – and then she remembered that it was only Tuesday. 'What about tomorrow and Thursday?'

Tom had the decency to look a little guilty. 'Sorry. I can't keep you away from ACC Schofield any longer. There's a major trial starting next week — part of the ongoing historical sex abuse inquiry. Schofield says that when/if you're not needed with me, you've to report to Operation Rewind.'

'Sir, that's… never mind. Whatever.' Elaine reordered her list of Jobs from Hell. It now read:

(3) Fraud
(2) Professional standards
(1) Historic sex abuse.

There was a lot of (1) in South Lancs, for some reason.

'Are you still speaking to me?' he asked.

'Of course. Why?'

'I'll have to take a rain check on your offer of company tomorrow. I'm going to have to see someone else.'

'Not only are you sending me to Operation Rewind, you're seeing someone behind my back.' The look on his face suggested that she'd overstepped the mark. 'Sorry, sir. Who is it?… If you don't mind me asking.'

'I'll let you know if it works out. If we're going to make progress, I need to find out a few things that will mean ringing alarm bells. We need some plausible deniability.'

Elaine had never liked that phrase. It stank, and she wasn't sure she wanted to work like that. She tried to think positively: she might find her niche in Operation Rewind, and putting in solid hours with SLC rather than CIPPS had to be good news.

Before then, there was always the paperwork. Tom asked for a lift back to the Estate service area, and on the way over, Elaine asked him whether he thought they'd ever get any answers to Gianni Berardi's murder.

'I think that depends,' he said, 'on whether I'm right about the Mother Superior.'

She glanced over at him. 'We've talked about this before. You didn't reckon the website had anything to do with his death.'

'It doesn't. Directly. But while you're on the flight to Rome, ask yourself this: how long would it have taken Saul and Max to figure out Berardi's involvement after those last three posts were made? Remember, he didn't know he was going to get beaten up and killed when he made them. When you've thought about that, ask yourself why he made them, and why he made them on that day.'

They were very good questions. Elaine had been working towards the same questions last night when she laid out all the posts on the Venn diagrams. She had no idea. 'What are you not telling me?' she asked when they had arrived next to his car.

'You've got all the facts, Elaine. Working out the answer might keep you amused when the Scottish scrum collapses on Saturday. See you later.'

In fact, she had finished at Lyme Court before he returned, and left him a note:

Berardi was spying for the Italian Football Association. He was killed by England's 007 — John Nugent, who is going to Japan because he was trained there as a Ninja. Enjoy your mother's cooking. EF.

Chapter 16

Wednesday 22 to Saturday 25 January

Dean's shoulder was strapped up so tightly that he could barely move his other arm either. Last night he had been fed by a nurse. It wasn't an experience he was keen to repeat, and certainly not with his mother. Once she knew he had survived the operation, she reverted to worrying about the wrong thing.

'When's Mr Abramovitz coming to see you, love?' she asked.

'Never mind him. It's the surgeon I need to see.'

'I thought it went well.'

'They always say that; it just means that they didn't chop my arm off by mistake. The important thing is whether I'm going to get full mobility. And when.'

'I know that, but you need to talk to Mr Abramovitz, too.'

'If I did talk to him, Mum, I wouldn't ask about manslaughter.'

'I've been looking it up on the Internet. If there's an element of self-defence, and if you plead guilty, they could cut the sentence to a year or so, with remission.'

He had no option but to close his eyes, because he couldn't move anything else without risking the microsutures holding his shoulder together. He counted to five.

'I didn't kill him, Mum. I'd rather serve life in prison than admit to something I didn't do.'

'Don't say that, Dean. Don't say it.'

He tried desperately to change the subject. 'Have the press left you alone, now?'

'Yes. I don't know what the Ice Maiden did, but it seems to have worked.'

She meant his PR. When you got to know her, the woman was probably very pleasant. Dean hadn't got to know her, so he couldn't argue about the nickname. The Ice Maiden was effective, though, and not a single reporter had rung the private hospital or attempted to get past the front desk. The same could not be said for other intruders.

'You must be Mrs Rooksby,' said Isaac, slipping into the room like a shadow. He held out his hand. 'Isaac Redmond. So pleased to meet you at last.'

His mother had never really liked Gary White, but she took a shine to Isaac straight away. 'Thank you so much for what you've done for our Dean. It's really good of you.'

'My pleasure, my pleasure.'

'He still gets twenty per cent of my wages, you know. And he charges extra for the PR services,' said Dean.

His mother sniffed.

'I'm sure you need a break,' said Isaac, putting his arm ever so gently into Mum's back. 'I need a word with your boy. Won't take long.'

'Can you get me tea in a mug with a straw?' said Dean. He didn't want her hanging around either.

Isaac pulled up a chair. 'You have a good friend in Emily Miller. She's working hard for you.'

Dean pointed to the teddy bear on the window ledge. It had arrived in Stoke with his stuff from 7Bridge on Saturday morning. 'She gave me that on Boxing Day. Her devotion to Salton Town is utter and total.'

Isaac shook his head. This was clearly something he didn't often come across. 'I want to ask you something, Dean, while you can't hit me.'

'Not funny, Isaac.'

'You haven't heard what I'm going to ask yet.'

'You're my agent. You can ask me anything you like, so long as it's not, "Did you kill Berardi?" because I've already answered that.'

Isaac pulled his lip. 'I'm coming round to your point of view on that one, which is why I want to know if Berardi was up to anything. Beyond the obvious, I mean.'

Dean stared at his agent for a long second. 'If I didn't know about Madison, I'm hardly likely to know about anything else, am I? He could have been plotting anything, the devious little git.'

Isaac held up his hands. 'Okay, okay … I just wondered what he'd been up to — whether he'd been doing anything different lately.'

The only reason Dean had slept last night was drugs. They were starting to wear off, bringing pain and clarity in equal measure. 'Why do you want to know? I thought you and Gary White were rivals.'

'We are, but you're on my team now.'

Dean wanted to shrug, but settled for rotating his right hand. Isaac didn't notice. 'With, like… hindsight, I reckon that Madison did talk a bit more about him before I found out. Especially at Christmas. She said he put a lot of effort into that thing with the Japanese and John Nugent.'

'What Japanese?' If Isaac had been an insect, his antennae would have been quivering right now.

'I don't know. None of my business, but Madison told me that Berardi was all over them at the Nugent Ball. If you look up the pictures online, you'll see them. I don't think there were many other Japanese people there.'

'Thanks, Dean.' Isaac stared at the window for a second, then jumped up when he heard footsteps. He ushered Mum back into the chair next to Dean's bed, made small talk for a couple of minutes, then started to leave. Dean was grateful he that could hold the plastic cup and take his own drink, and it was only when Isaac put his coat on that he remembered something else.

'Tell you what…' said Dean. 'Berardi moved heaven and earth to bring our wedding forward. I wonder why that was. Perhaps Madison had already dumped him.'

'Perhaps,' said Isaac. 'Look after him, Mrs Rooksby. See you, Dean.'

There was a church in Sevenbridge Village, but it was the parish church. Saul didn't give any thought to the significance of that until Max reminded him that St Saviour's was both Roman Catholic and on the way to Macclesfield. That made his mind up, and he asked Max to come with him.

'Why?'

'Security. Put the Estate on lockdown for the funeral: only residents and long-serving staff to enter or leave. You can keep an eye on the mourners while I represent the Princess.'

'Are you not going for your own sake?'

Saul shrugged. 'I probably would. For Gary. I can't say that I miss Gianni for himself.'

'I'd better give the orders and get changed. Have you got a spare tie in a respectable shade?'

Saul went through to his private rooms and fetched a couple of ties. 'Keep them. Which way is the cortège coming on to the Estate?'

'In through the service gate; out through the residents'. Mourners from the Estate have been asked to join the cortège at Southfork.'

'Don't call it that. Is there any family coming from outside?'

'Two cars. They're being booked in half an hour before.'

'We'll go in with the funeral cars. That way we can keep an eye on things.'

There hadn't been a frost the night before – which was good – but the wind had turned round to the east again, which meant snow. Probably. Saul drove his Mercedes slowly through the security gate behind the funeral cars, and paused for Max to jump in.

'Status?' asked Saul.

'All good.'

'Tell me if I'm wrong, but this is only the second funeral of a resident, isn't it? There was that boy who crashed his car, but that was before my time.'

'That's right. You know which house he lived in, don't you?'

'No.'

'Dean Rooksby's, or what used to be Dean's. The talent can be superstitious: let's hope that word doesn't get round or you'll be bringing in the bulldozers.'

'Don't tempt fate. It could easily happen.'

They followed the cars, then waited at a discreet distance until the family had been seated and other residents had joined in. Saul noticed that Holly Nugent was being chauffeured by an off-duty patrol officer. 'Isn't that…?'

'Gavin. Yes. Gary asked me if he could be available. Apparently there was an argument between Lucy and Robyn. Lucy wanted Holly in with the family. Robyn didn't. This was the compromise.'

Saul drove patiently after the cortège for nearly half an hour until they reached St Saviour's. When they entered the church, he was surprised to find how empty it was, relatively speaking. Young people's funerals are normally standing room only. There were almost as many wreaths as mourners, and the front of the church was covered in blooms.

The front row was split between family (on the left) and White-Berardi staff, plus Holly Nugent on the right. Saul had been to a fair few Jewish funerals, and some Church of England, but this was his first Roman Catholic one. He found the liturgy dreary, and the hymns uninspiring. Few of the congregation sang.

One of the prayers was read by Gary, who did his best, but the eulogy was given by the priest. You could get anything subcontracted to India these days: call centres, software engineering, data processing, word processing — and now it seemed you could get sermons written there too. The priest said nothing about Gianni that couldn't have been written in Mumbai using an article from the *Evening News*.

There was a final moment of bathos when they stood to say the Lord's Prayer. 'Contrary to what it says in your Order of Service,' said the priest, 'the prayer to Our Father finishes after "Deliver us from evil", but the doxology is permitted in the Ecumenical version.'

Saul had absolutely no idea what he meant, and neither did the congregation. It must have meant something to Lucy, because she was whispering to her father and pointing a finger at Robyn.

Very few joined in with the prayer, and a great many of the (mostly female) congregation held back from the interment. There was a narrow strip of Astro Turf from the path to the graveside that was barely big enough for the family. Saul walked round the outside. He pointed at the mourners huddling by the church and whispered to Max, 'They don't want their heels to sink into the mud.'

'Or say the wrong thing.'

At the grave, the priest said very little, and didn't attempt a repeat of the Lord's Prayer. At the end he informed the mourners that they were welcome to join the family at the parish centre, which was over the road.

'Look,' said Max. 'Beyond the lych gate.'

'The what?'

'Over there. That's where the paps are waiting: they can get shots of everyone crossing the road.'

'Go and keep an eye on things. I'll join you shortly.'

Saul was the last at the grave. He said his own prayer for Gianni, because he hadn't felt like joining in the circus inside the church. On his way out, he stooped to look at the wreaths. After the fourth one, he realised what was going on: every sponsor that Gianni had got for his clients had sent a wreath. Only a few had sent actual people, and none of the clients themselves were here. Training took priority.

Gary and Lucy were greeting people at the door, and Saul was at the back of the queue. Max came over and said, 'I'm a little worried about what happens when the reception committee has finished. I'm going to man the door and keep it private afterwards. You go ahead inside.'

The paparazzi had gone, but they had left behind the celebrity trackers, fans and gawkers who had seen on their phones that Holly Nugent, Sheena Cavendish and others were gathered here. Saul hated them: did they have no self-respect? Did they have nothing better to do with their lives? 'Good thinking, Max — and get a couple of the team up here to take over from you. I won't be long.'

By the time Saul got to the front of the queue, Lucy looked very fragile, and even Gary was starting to wilt. Saul had seen Gary force a smile and clap a few men on the back, but Lucy was very subdued. Most of the mourners had to be introduced to her.

Gary looked over Saul's shoulder and saw that he was the last in line. He breathed an audible sigh of relief. 'Thanks for coming,' he said.

'Gary … so sorry … so very sorry.' He paused. 'Princess Karida has asked me to convey her deepest sympathies to you and all your family.'

'Pass on our thanks.'

'Saul,' said Lucy in a clipped voice. They barely knew each other, so he aimed for dignity, and simply bowed his head. Lucy nodded back.

He looked up, and the first thing that struck him was that there were two camps in opposite corners. Holly Nugent was at the centre of one and Robyn White in the other: about a third of the guests milled around between them. He looked to see which way Gary and Lucy would go.

Gary adjusted his suit, then headed towards his wife and other relatives. Lucy took a step towards the door and peered out as if waiting for someone else to appear. He'd never seen her looking so smart before, not since she was a child. She stood on the threshold for a second, then turned.

'Were you expecting someone or just getting some air?'

'I was just checking to see if the police came.'

'If they hadn't made an arrest, they might have come.'

Lucy wasn't wearing a coat, and Saul couldn't tell whether the shiver was from the cold or from something inside. 'I don't think we've seen the last arrest yet.'

Saul knew what DCI Morton was up to, but why was Lucy concerned? *Please, God, do not let her be involved with the Mother Superior like her brother was*. It was his second prayer of the day. Now that the Princess had called down the wrath of Scotland Yard, the police would want to arrest someone to justify their time here.

'You're tall,' she said. 'Can you see where Grace Revell is?'

'With Paul Warren and his wife … I presume it's his wife. Over there, next to the Italian flag.'

'Thanks.'

Saul began a slow circuit of the room, picking up one glass of wine to be sociable. The first person who stopped him was one of the senior managers from Trafford Rangers. 'We might be buying a new midfielder next week,' he said. 'From Spain. Is Dean Rooksby's place ready to use?'

'It's empty.'

'This could be quite a big buy. Very big. Can you get it redecorated and given the premier treatment? If he likes the Estate, we'll be looking for somewhere bigger in the summer.'

'I'll get Anthea started as soon as you email confirmation.'

The manager looked at the door. 'I'll nip out for a smoke and send it now.'

Saul continued round, reaching the Italian flag. It was hovering over a selection of antipasti and cheeses that would have had his mouth watering in summer. He nodded to Paul Warren and was about to move on when Gary came over.

'Saul, can I have a word?' He motioned for Paul to join them, then led the way to a quiet corner. 'Keep this quiet, Saul, but I wanted to ask about Gianni's residence.'

That was quick. Saul had expected this conversation, but not at the funeral.

'It's your house, Gary — on your land, obviously. We had no problem with Gianni living there, but that was after a special application. The same would apply if you wanted to use it again.'

'I was thinking of offering it to Lucy,' said Gary.

'Oh? She would have to become a resident,' said Saul. 'We'd welcome her with open arms – you know we would – but that's a lot of money for her.'

'Keep this quiet, too. Gianni left her his shares in White-Berardi. He had twenty-five per cent of the stock. I've asked her to come on board … join the firm.'

Warren's moustache was doing that thing — the one that showed he wasn't comfortable. 'I don't think Lucy knows her own mind yet,' he said.

'I'm not going to push her,' responded Gary, 'but I wanted to make sure there were no obstacles from the Estate Office first.'

'I'm sure the Princess would agree with me.'

'Good man. Thanks.' Gary patted Saul on the shoulder and moved away, leaving Saul with Paul Warren. Neither man knew what to say.

Saul was going to say something about the service but Warren spoke first.

'We're going to dissolve the 7Bridge Collective,' he said. 'It seems so pointless after what's happened to Gianni — and besides, it was mostly his idea in the first place.'

'I'd forgotten about that,' said Saul, nodding to himself. 'It's what brought DCI Morton amongst us in the beginning. I wonder if he ever filed a report. We haven't had the bill, yet.'

'He seems to have disappeared,' said Warren. 'He never said goodbye, so maybe he's coming back.'

Saul knew that Morton would be back on Monday, but he wasn't going to give up that piece of information. 'Does he need to say goodbye? Perhaps he'll just fade away. Is Lucy likely to move back on to the Estate? I gather there's still no love lost between her and Robyn, judging by that business with the Orders of Service.'

The relief that comes at a funeral had got to both of them a little. Warren snorted into his moustache, and coughed. 'Lucy's had a bad time. Really bad. Not just Gianni, but this business with her mother.'

'What business?'

They both turned and looked at Paul's wife, their last known location for Lucy, but Mrs Warren was on her own. Saul scanned the room, and saw that Lucy and Grace had gravitated towards the bodies orbiting Holly Nugent.

'She's going to have a little baby brother,' said Warren. 'Allegedly.'

Saul finished the champagne and picked up two shots of grappa from the Italian table. He passed one to Paul, who demurred at first. 'I need someone to drink a toast with,' said Saul. 'I'll get Max to send some drivers over if you're worried.'

Warren accepted the shot glass. 'To Gianni,' he said.

'To the memory of Gianni, and to all the White-Berardis,' said Saul, and they drained their glasses.

Saul saw the first people starting to leave, so sneaked out behind them. Outside, he lit a cigar, then checked his phone: the email from Trafford Rangers had arrived. He would have to get moving on that. When Max came over, Saul knocked the end out of his cigar and put it in the aluminium tube. He held out his phone in one hand and his car keys in the other. 'Your choice, Max: drive us back or talk to Anthea.'

Max took the keys and strode off down the road. Saul dialled Anthea's number, then followed Max towards the car.

On Saturday morning, Tom bit the bullet and drove the short distance round the ring road to Haxby, and asked about joining the rugby club. During his chat to Leonie the other day, he had become more and more convinced that she was looking to keep him out of London, but why? She knew he had been rattled by the Jigsaw case, and that he had put down few roots in London, but was she being sympathetic or manipulative?

Tom liked to see both sides of things. His ex-wife had said it was one of his biggest failings: he saw it as a strength. You could argue that Leonie was making the most of the situation. Tom was a valuable asset who would enhance CIPPS' reputation outside the south east, and who was happy working away from a home base for prolonged periods. On the other hand, he had bagged a big scalp, he was young and he deserved a senior position in the organisation. Stuck in York, he was no threat to her.

Either way, he wasn't going back to the Lambeth office for a while yet, so he put his New Year's resolution into action and went to Haxby. The club steward pointed him in the direction of a man in the corner. Tom went over and introduced himself. The man said his name was Craig Capstick, then looked Tom up and down.

'You're at that difficult age,' said Capstick.

'Difficult for what?'

'Too old to get in the first team; too young for the Vets. How old are you?'

'Thirty-four.'

'I'm the Vets captain, for my sins. Come back after your next birthday and I'll snap you up. Not that we play many matches at this time of year. Too cold by half.'

'Thanks for the vote of no confidence,' said Tom. 'You know how to kick a man when he's down, don't you? I was hoping to get in the second team.'

Capstick considered this. 'Can you make training regularly? It's on Tuesdays and Thursdays at seven o'clock.'

'I'll try.'

'If you turn up for three weeks straight, they'll give you a couple of run-outs as a replacement. After that, it depends how good you really are.'

Tom had never played club rugby, so he didn't know how typical this reaction was. Unless he got something more permanent in York, he couldn't commit to the training, but he would be thirty-five before he knew it. 'What are the bus services like from town?' he asked.

'Very good. They run quite late.'

'Then can I join the club and see how it goes?'

Capstick shouted across the bar, 'Application form!' Then he said to Tom, 'Are you a person of good standing who is not likely to bring the club into disrepute?'

'More or less.'

'Then I'll nominate you this minute. It's £90 for playing members, but you don't have to send the cheque until after the next committee meeting.'

'Thanks. What can I get you?'

'Bass. Only thing worth drinking.'

Tom bought two pints and took the application form from the steward. They chatted for a short while as more men drifted in. Capstick introduced him to a couple of people, and Tom decided to stay for the Italy v Scotland match on the big screen.

At half time, Italy were leading a dour match 3-0. Tom sent a text to Elaine: *My mother cooks better than your front row can scrummage. Hope Rob gets a game 2nd half. I will have news on Monday. See you Lyme Court 10:00. TM.*

Before the game restarted, he got a reply. *Rob coming on soon. Scotland not my team. Can I really join CIPPS? Not going back to Op Rewind. Enjoy the weekend. EF.*

What had she done now? Surely she couldn't have alienated the Operation Rewind team as badly as she fell out with DS Jepson. Not in two days.

All but a handful of the Haxby crowd were cheering for Italy. Tom got a very strange look from Craig when he cheered Rob Fraser's appearance on the pitch. 'His wife works for me,' said Tom apologetically. 'If her husband plays well, she's in a better mood.'

Italy tired towards the end, and Rob scored his maiden try for his country; Scotland won 17-9. After the game, Craig offered to buy him a drink, but Tom declined and made his apologies.

'Don't worry, Tom,' said Capstick. 'Your secret's safe with me.'

'Which one? I've got a few.'

'The fact that you're a copper. Well, you must be if Elaine Fraser works for you. I looked her up on the ScotWAGs site.' Tom had no idea that such a thing existed. Did Elaine know? Capstick continued, 'You can keep my secret as well: I'm an estate agent. Neither of us has got a profession to brag about, but if you need somewhere in Haxby, let me know. See you soon.'

Tom would argue about that the next time they met. Even after Plebgate, the police still had a better reputation than estate agents, surely? On the way through Haxby he saw that half of the *For Sale* boards had Capstick & Co. written on them. Not so much of a secret, then.

It started to snow later, but that didn't deter Thomas Senior from driving them out to Throckton: nothing would make them miss Grandma's housewarming. What impressed him most was the contribution Diana had made. Within ten minutes of arriving, Grandma had drawn him aside and told him that she couldn't have managed without his sister. 'But don't tell Fiona that,' she said. 'It'll only cause ructions.'

This was exactly the sort of thing Fiona probably should hear, but Tom kept his counsel. Granddad looked a lot better, and managed most of the evening before Fiona led him to bed. Shortly after, Juliet Porterhouse called. She had rung this morning to confirm that the information he wanted had been emailed to a private account, so what did she want?

'Do you read the sports section, Tom?' she asked. It was Saturday night, of course. She had just put the paper to bed (did they still say that?) and was no doubt in/on her way to the pub. Tom usually read the *Sunday Times*, not the *Examiner*, but promised to do so tomorrow.

'We pride ourselves on our rugby coverage,' said Juliet, rather deliberately. 'And on page seven is a wonderful picture of Elaine Fraser leaping in the air to celebrate her husband's try. That wouldn't be *your* Elaine Fraser, would it?'

'She's not mine, but yes, that's her.'

'Make sure you keep a copy for her. Bye.'

What was that all about? Tom tried talking to Uncle Peter about how they were settling into the farmhouse, but after the third time Peter had said, 'Ask the wife,' Tom gave up.

The snow was thickening, and the party broke up. Diana said she was coming back with them, then returning to London tomorrow. 'Fiona's staying over,' she added.

Perhaps word had got to his older sister after all.

Chapter 17

Monday 27 January

'Was it that bad?' asked Tom.

'What? The trip, the game or working on Operation Rewind?'

'I assume you enjoyed seeing Rob. We both know the game was dire, so that leaves Rewind. What happened?'

Elaine sank into the chair by Tom's desk and looked at him. She seemed happier and brighter than she was last week, but there was a shading round the eyes that he hadn't seen before. Could have been lack of sleep, but he saw something deeper.

'It was bad, Tom.' She sighed. 'You see victims all the time on patrol and in CID, but this was different. I spent two hours supporting one of their DSes in an interview. This poor bloke had had his life wrecked – completely wrecked – in the children's home he was sent to. Nothing can fix him, not even the thought of justice: the abuser is dead. The Rewind team were after the care home manager, but this bloke barely remembered him.'

'I'm sorry. You don't know how you're going to react to these things until you see them.'

'C'mon … cheer me up. Let's forget Rewind and tell me you've got something on Berardi or the Mother Superior.'

Tom had stacked up the reports, printouts and folders on the desk. He moved them slightly to one side, then said, 'I can do this on my own. Not easily, but I could do it. I'm saying that because it could go horribly wrong, and I want to give you the option to back out now. Even if we succeed, the only person who will give us any credit is Leonie.'

She reached over and adjusted the files again, back to where they were. 'You asked me for 100% commitment.

I'm not going to back out now. What's the worst that could happen?'

'Do you want me to answer that?'

She frowned. 'I was joking. You mean things could get really, really bad?'

'If I've miscalculated, we could both be asked to resign to avoid a diplomatic incident.'

She whistled. 'Wow. That's too good a chance to pass up. Count me in.'

He passed over a folder. She opened it, glanced inside then leaned across to hit him with it.

'Oi! That's assault,' he said.

'And this is harassment,' she responded, chucking down the image of her celebrating from yesterday's *Examiner*. She picked it up again. 'Please tell me you don't have a laminator at home. That would be very sad.'

'My mother has one. Before I start, did you give any thought to those questions I asked you last week?'

'I did. There's only one sensible answer: Giovanni was preparing to leave the Estate. The money was deposit on a house outside, and he wanted everyone to know what he'd been up to.'

'It's the most likely explanation for now, but you might change your mind. Here's what I found out after I abandoned you to Operation Rewind. First, Gianni had a Maserati.'

She whistled again. 'Rob looked up the price for one of those. That's serious money.'

'It is, but Berardi didn't own the car. It was leased, and it was taken away the day he died. I had to do some digging, but the lease payments were being made by a well-known soft drinks company. The marketing department there believed the car was leased to Owain Marshall, and that this was part of his sponsorship deal. Marshall plays for Merseyside United, in case you didn't know, so somehow

Berardi ended up with a very expensive car that should have been allocated to someone else.'

She frowned. 'It could have been a commission payment.'

'Too much, and it sticks out like a sore thumb. This is where it gets dangerous: I think that the source for most of the Mother Superior stories is Holly Nugent, and that Berardi was blackmailing John to keep it quiet.'

'No. Never. She gets more stick than anyone.'

'Have a look at this. When I stood you up last Wednesday, I was meeting a reporter from the *Sunday Examiner*. We have a professional understanding. She did some digging for me, and she tipped me off about that picture of you as well, but she's good. We owe her a big favour now.'

'We owe her a favour? As in you and me?'

'Possibly. I'll come to that later.' He slid over the first of Juliet's reports for Elaine to read.

Holly kept it quiet, but she was three years older than John. Before they met, she had worked as a dancer in various exotic clubs. It was long enough ago for few pictures to have survived, and Gary White had bought off their owners. Holly's career had ended when her then boyfriend was cautioned for domestic violence. She had met John shortly afterwards through a Trafford Rangers community programme when Holly was working as a carer to disabled children to fund herself at college. It was well known that she was estranged from her family in south London.

Elaine put the folder down. 'Why has none of this come out before?'

'Gary White is a very powerful man, in some ways. Newspapers won't write about Holly because they'd lose access to players in Gary's stable. Magazines won't write about her because they'd lose access to the players' wives. Most of this stuff is out there somewhere.'

'I'll buy it for now, as a working hypothesis.'

'It gets worse. Have a look at this.'

The other folder contained only one piece of paper: an offer from an Oxford college to Kareena Patel Al'Khabaat for a place to study English Literature, dated seven years ago and including the phrase *...subject to the successful conclusion of your studies at St Mary's School for Girls.*

Elaine studied it for a second, turned it on a slight angle, then frowned. 'Who...?'

'Instead of taking up her place at Lonsdale College, Kareena accepted an offer of marriage from the Crown Prince of Ghar'aan. She changed her name, too. There's more to Princess Karida than she would like us to know about.'

'How did your reporter friend get hold of this?'

Elaine hadn't noticed, but there was a new piece of equipment in their little rented office. Tom picked up the letter and fed it into the shredder. 'One of Juliet's colleagues prepared a story on the Princess some years ago. John Lake, or one of his colleagues in the Foreign Office, convinced them not to print it. What you've just seen doesn't exist.'

Elaine looked peeved. 'How can we operate like that?'

Tom smiled at her. 'You'll get used to it. We pick up a lot of things in CIPPS that we can't prove or document. The key is to use the information without using it.'

Elaine opened her mouth, paused, then said, 'Very Zen, sir. One of our instructors used to say *You do not conquer the mountain, you turn it into meadows.* I didn't understand him, either.'

'It's not Zen we need to focus on, but we've got our plan of attack now.'

She cheered up. 'I like the sound of that. Who do we go for first?'

'Saul. I need to ask him a question, then it's over to you. I'm going to trust you a lot, Elaine. I'm going to let you loose on the Princess.'

Her eyebrows shot up. 'That is a lot. Is there no way you can get access, if it's this important?'

'No. The only other choice is Leonie, and I'm sure of one thing: you'll focus on answers rather than chat-up lines.'

Elaine grimaced. 'She can't be that bad, surely?'

'I'd rather not find out. I'll give you the full story after I get my answer from Saul.'

'Am I not included for that one?'

'Horses for courses. You've got a special mission: get the breakfasts in, before we're barred.'

The last thing Saul wanted to do on a Monday morning was talk to Anthea Godfrey, which was why he looked on DCI Morton as a gift from God. The police officer seemed slightly taken aback at the effusiveness of his welcome, and although he accepted coffee, he declined the pastries.

'I was hoping to sample Sonia's legendary canteen breakfast,' said his visitor.

'Even better. Tiffany!' The assistant pivoted on her heel. 'Get two vouchers for our guest to go with the coffee.' He turned back to Morton. 'You've caught me in a good mood. I went to London for the weekend, saw my parents, my children and my brother. When I came back on the train earlier, there were fourteen – fourteen – emails from Anthea Godfrey about Dean Rooksby's house, as well as two voicemails and three texts, all expecting a meeting this morning.'

Tiffany poured the coffee, and Morton said, 'I take it there's a problem.'

'Hah! If only there were one problem. Trafford Rangers want to move a new player in on Friday. Anthea's favourite decorator is snowed in, the curtain fabric is out of stock… I could go on, but I won't. How can I help you?'

Saul drank his coffee and waited for the detective. He looked a little embarrassed, for some reason. He opened a folder from his briefcase, then thought better of it and put the folder away. Finally, he looked up. 'You may prefer Anthea after I've asked you this question.'

'I doubt it.'

'Why did you and Miriam really get divorced?'

Saul was glad he'd put his cup down. Morton must have been talking to some serious gossipmongers if he was asking that question. Worse, he had come in specially, which meant that there must be another agenda underneath. Saul did not like where this conversation might go. The first problem was that there were at least three different versions of why he was getting divorced, and without knowing which one Morton had picked up on, he couldn't tell where to divert the blame. 'Who have you been talking to?' he asked.

Morton gave him a bland look. 'Does it matter?'

'It's nice to know who's been spreading stories when the stories get to the police.'

Morton looked down at his cup. 'I got divorced last year. My wife had an affair.' He looked up again.

He shifted in his seat. Morton hadn't struck him as someone to get hard-assed unnecessarily, and his position wasn't very strong, either. Saul decided to bluff this one out. 'I'm sorry about that,' said Saul, 'and they say it's good to share, but Miriam and I had reached the end of the road.'

'There's something else you and I have got in common, you know. I used to be a lawyer, too, although I suppose we both still are, technically.' Morton smiled. Saul wasn't sure he liked that. The other man continued. 'So I bent the rules a little and checked with the family court. You started the proceedings, not her. I presume you're still arguing about the financial settlement.'

Now it was Morton calling his bluff. He could be outraged at this invasion of privacy, throw the man out and lodge a complaint, or he could answer his question. The only thing that stopped him answering was that one question usually led to another. Time to change direction. 'I always wondered why the Mother Superior never mentioned my divorce. I presume you don't think that Miriam is behind the website, so what does my marriage have to do with finding the Mother Superior?'

'Miriam had an affair, didn't she?'

'Why are you pushing this?'

'Because the Mother Superior was very kind to you. You might want to return the favour.'

Saul had a good poker face. He knew that, because the patrol officers had stopped inviting him to their game some years ago. He didn't give anything away to Morton, but he could feel the tension gripping his chest muscles.

And then he realised that his silence had answered Morton's question for him. The policeman finished his coffee and fastened the straps on his briefcase before continuing. 'When I sent DC Fraser to see the Princess last week, she returned with a lot of bits of information. I like to call them jigsaw pieces.' He paused and smiled at some personal joke. 'It's taken me a while to realise which bits fitted into which puzzle.' He made eye contact, and held it. 'The reason it took a while is that I needed time to get to know you. Princess Karida said that your wife left you because you wouldn't support her after the business about her being Jewish and being barred from the Hall. I don't believe that for a minute. I know you're not a frum, but you wouldn't stand for an insult like that.'

Saul closed his eyes. Morton had brought it all back again. The pain, the humiliation … and the knowledge that he couldn't share it with anyone. He pinched his nose and tried to breathe slowly, to let the image of Miriam go out of his head so that he could focus on the here and now. Morton wasn't doing this to humiliate him, so what was his game?

'I'm not proud of it,' said Saul, 'but what's it got to do with you?'

'It's the order of things that made me wonder. Princess Karida barred your wife from the Hall before you separated, and I think she did that because she cared about you. For some reason, you agreed to look like the bad guy, when it was your wife who was in the wrong.'

'What of it?'

'I don't want to pry, I really don't — but we both know that the Princess's access to the outside world is limited. So how did she know what was going on? You must have figured out already that Giovanni Berardi wasn't involved with *SeenIn7Bridge* for long, and you must have figured out that there were – are – two other people. One to provide the gossip, and one to write it up.'

Saul laughed. 'It had crossed my mind. From reading the text, you might think that the Mother Superior was a man, but the attitude is very … female.'

'The Mother Superior isn't a man, but the writer is someone with limited experience, who's led a sheltered life and who has drawn most of their inspiration from reading books rather than the Internet.'

No. This couldn't be right. No way could Kari be the Mother Superior. Surely? 'You can't be serious, Morton. That's madness.'

'I agree. It's very odd, but you would have found out the same thing yourself. Neil Hoskins said that the internet traffic was coming from outside the residents' part of the Estate network. If we got GCHQ on to it, I'm sure they could track it back to the Hall. They're very good at things like that.'

'Why would she do it? And why would she get you to find her out.'

'I have no idea. That's why I'm sending Elaine in to get the truth.'

This could devastate the whole community. More seriously, if it got back to Ghar'aan, it could put Kari in all sorts of danger.

'What if you're wrong?'

'That's why I need your word that you won't say or do anything until I say so. If I'm wrong, you don't want to be dragged down with me. If I'm right, you'll need to be on hand to pick up the pieces. Can I have your word?'

He meant it. His eyes were locked on Saul's, and there would be no equivocating here. 'You have my word.'

'Then I'll be going.'

Morton was halfway to the door when Saul said, 'If the Princess is the writer, who's the source?'

'I might be wrong, Saul. If I am, I don't want to ruin anyone else's day.'

He left. Morton's eyes were blue, in a typically English sort of way, but when he had asked for Saul's word of honour, something red glinted at the back of them. Now they were gone, Saul wondered if he could ring Max and get Elaine Fraser's biometric ID removed from the system. He looked at his computer, and a little red light blinked on the side of the unit. Maybe that was what had reflected in Morton's eyes, or maybe it was a warning. The winking light also reminded him of the Recording light on the POs' chest-cams, and of his personal CCTV project. He went back into it for one last look, and decided that he couldn't ignore it, even if they had arrested Dean Rooksby for something totally unconnected.

Saul grabbed a cigar from his den and his outdoor gear. On the way out of the office he told his PA that he would be on the Estate, and that she should get Max to find him urgently if necessary. She gave him a strange look.

He ducked into the security office and grabbed a radio, something he rarely did, and left word where he was. The duty officer also gave him a strange look.

He paused inside the smoked glass for a minute, until he saw DC Fraser emerge, zipping up that vibrant red jacket she always wore. When she had passed, he went into the canteen and found Morton finishing a hearty, if very unhealthy, breakfast. He frowned very deeply when Saul approached him.

'I've got something to show you,' said Saul. 'Fraser is going to be a while yet. Let's walk off that food on a tour round the Estate. I've got a radio in case there's a crisis.'

'Okay,' said Morton, pushing his plate aside. 'Let's go.'

When push came to shove, Elaine just couldn't face the full English: she was far too nervous. The smell, however, was too appetising for complete abstinence. She ordered a sausage butty and tucked in while she waited for Tom to return from seeing Saul. They had come in separate cars, so she hadn't had a chance to discuss the strategy for confronting the Princess, and wondered what Saul could add to the mix.

'Couldn't you wait?'

Jesus! Tom had appeared behind her again. Where had he come from? 'Sorry, sir, I wasn't as hungry as I thought.'

He showed her two complimentary vouchers. 'Gift from Saul. I don't think we need to declare them. You keep one for later, but I'm going to cash mine in now. Some of us had to cross the Pennines on nothing but toast.'

He collected a plate full of goodies and tucked in. 'I'm sure it's the Princess,' he said between mouthfuls. 'Saul's wife had an affair.'

'Who with?'

'Don't know, don't care. The important thing is that the Mother Superior laid down a cover story, and that happened after Miriam was barred. She cares about Saul.' He moved on to his fried egg, dipping a hash brown into the runny yolk.

'So how do I tackle it, sir? I don't want to ruin everything.'

'You won't ruin things. Well, unless you hit her, that is.' He waved his fork around. 'Avoid violence, that's my tip. I know how I'd handle things, but you're not me.'

She drained her tea. The sausages had been peppery, and were starting to repeat on her already. 'Do you have any more words of wisdom, or shall I get going?'

Tom pointed expansively towards the exit and grinned at her. He was enjoying this far too much for her liking. Elaine stood up and reached behind her back. She unclipped the extensible baton she'd been carrying for days and put it on the table. 'For the avoidance of temptation, sir. Besides, you might need it.'

'Oh, yes?'

'If this goes pear-shaped, you'll have to answer to Rob.'

'Thank you, Constable, I'll look after it for you. On second thoughts, I'll do you a swap. Here.' He put down his cutlery for a second, fished out a card and jotted something on the back. 'Good luck.'

Elaine left the canteen and strode towards the Hall. Once through the perimeter security gate, there was a path through the gardens that shortened the distance a lot, but it still gave her enough time to fret. When she signed in to the Spa reception, she was none the she was no closer to having a plan. Thankfully there was no sign of Beth Pedley.

Elaine stood in front of the massive connecting door and squared her shoulders. How would Tom handle this? She considered his style. He would make an appointment, ensure there was tea on the table, then manoeuvre his opponent like a chess match. She looked again at the note had written on the back of his card: *Imm Rules V, para 159. Also A&I 2006, Sect 15*. Did the man ever stop being a lawyer? She didn't have time for this.

She pressed her finger on the biometric lock. The door clicked. She swung it open and marched down the corridor. 'Hello … anyone home?'

Ahead, and to the left, she heard the crash of crockery, and what had to be a Hindi curse. She followed the sound. Alia ran out from a doorway and banged right into her. The maid stifled a scream and backed off.

'Where is she?' said Elaine.

'I… What do you want?'

'She's here somewhere.' Elaine took a step forward and folded her arms. Alia backed into the doorway, and Elaine saw a small pantry behind her. A china cup was in pieces on the floor.

Alia pulled herself together. 'If you'll excuse me, I'll see if the Princess is available.'

'Take me to her.'

'You can't…'

Elaine pulled out her warrant card. 'Take me to her, or I'll arrest you for obstruction. It's cold out there, and those sandals won't protect you.' She added a smile, just to show she meant it.

Alia got the message. 'She's in the gym. Turn right at the other end of the corridor and listen for the music.'

Elaine stood back. 'After you. It would be rude to barge in. Besides, I don't want you to get on the phone.'

Alia tried to maintain some dignity as she walked down the corridor, so Elaine closed the gap until she was nearly kicking her. Alia stumbled, then ran round the corner and knocked at a door. She pushed it open and cowered in a corner. Elaine strode past her and into a small private gym with a resistance machine against the wall, a rowing machine and a treadmill that faced the window. Princess Karida had her back to them, and headphones in.

It was warm in the Hall, but even Elaine would have felt underdressed in the Princess's outfit: a professional-grade sports top and tiny briefs. Most of the sportswear in the cupboard was less revealing than this. Why? Elaine shrugged to herself, and took one of the few chances to do a Morton: creep up on someone while wearing big boots. She walked past the running machine and pulled out the safety cord.

Karida didn't just flinch, she jumped away from Elaine, caught her foot on the frame of the machine and fell heavily in a heap. This was too good to be true, so Elaine planted her Doc Martens in front of Karida's face, then offered a hand to help her up.

At this point, the public school upbringing reasserted itself. Karida crawled away from Elaine, while pulling out the earbuds and adopting an expression of outrage. 'Get out of here! Get out of my house.'

The Princess had backed into the rowing machine. There was nowhere else to go. Elaine took a step forward, then squatted down in front of her. 'Or what? You'll call the police? Sorry, I'm already here. You could call a patrol officer, I suppose.' Elaine held up her thumb. 'Except that they put my biometric in the system, so I'm invited.' She leaned forward, her nose inches from the daughter-in-law of the Sultan of Ghar'aan. 'There's another choice. You could put some clothes on and explain why the fuck you sent my boss to chase his arse looking for the Mother Superior when she's right here.'

She held it there for a second or two. Karida was trembling as her sweat chilled against the metal of the rowing machine, and terror changed the healthy smell of exercise into the stink of fear. Then Elaine stood up, stood back and offered her hand again. 'You could order tea while you're at it.'

Karida stayed on the floor, but looked her in the eye. 'Get out of my house. Get yourself out of my house now.'

Elaine's world lurched on its axis. Was Tom wrong? Had he sent her in here to destroy her own career, or had she just mucked up again? She remembered his face, blue eyes glinting with fun as he tucked into his cooked breakfast. He would back her every step of the way, she knew, but she had to back herself. From far away at his training camp, she heard Rob's voice: *If you dinnae believe in yourself, why should anybody else?*

She hitched up her belt. 'My car is down at the Estate Office,' she said. 'It's a long walk there, in the cold. With what you're wearing, you might get hypothermia. I'll take pictures too, you know. I don't need the money, so I'll resign after I've booked you into the police station. Then I'll put the pictures on the Internet. Last warning.' She reached round and took out some plastic wrist ties. 'These hurt a lot more than handcuffs.'

Karida looked at the ground. 'I expected you to come back with evidence, not violence: this is England, not Ghar'aan.'

'I've never met my boss's grannie, but I know her favourite saying: *Be careful what you wish for*. God knows why, but you made a wish that someone would find out what you were up to, and we did. We could have got evidence, but I was a bit pissed off at being used like a servant, so I left my boots on. Here, get up.'

The third time she held out her hand, the Princess took it. Elaine was surprised how much muscle the woman had built up. Well, there wasn't much else to do in here, was there? 'One question for starters,' she said. 'Why didn't you just stop writing it?'

Karida was shivering in earnest now. 'It's not me who needs the help to stop doing this. It's Holly.'

'Aah. Put some clothes on. I'll see you in the Morning Room.'

There was no sense in keeping up the aggression. Besides, she didn't think she could. Elaine took off her boots and left them outside the Morning Room. She took off her coat, too, and realised she was sweating as much as the highly-buffed Princess. She sent Tom a quick text: *Victory. I think*. When Karida didn't show up immediately, she wondered if she'd blown it. Could the spoilt brat actually have locked herself away, and called security? She was tempted to go running after her when Alia brought in the tray.

'The Princess sends her apologies. She felt the need of a shower, but she will be along shortly.'

Elaine could live with that, provided the woman didn't go for a sauna first. She looked out of the window for a moment, then sat down and made some notes. Karida appeared shortly afterwards, her hair tied back to keep it dry, her Olympic running kit replaced by leggings and a tunic. She sat down and poured herself a cup of tea, then took a deep breath and poured one for Elaine as well.

'You can put the notebook away,' said the Princess when she had put down the teapot.

Elaine put the notebook on a side table, near at hand. Karida passed her tea, then sat back.

'How much do you know about me?' asked the Princess.

Was she fishing for information, or just enjoying the moment? 'I know you're probably more British than Ghar'aanian. I can find out the rest, if I have to.'

Karida ventured a smile. 'You're not wrong. People in Britain – if they think about Ghar'aan at all – lump us in with the Gulf States, but we're not like that. Ghar'aan is physically closer to Gujarat than to Saudi Arabia, and there has always been a big Indian minority there. My family – my father's family – owned a lot of land on the main island of Ghar'aan. We bought it off the British Government when the naval base was closed down. I was born a Hindu, in India, and my father only took me to Ghar'aan when he divorced my mother. He remarried a junior member of the royal family, which is why my name is hyphenated. My branch of the family all had to convert to Islam, at least in public. My father sent me to school in Britain.'

'Go on.'

'He sent me to a strict Catholic girls school. I don't know what he thought I would do with a third religion. They're not like cars: you can't drive the one that suits you.'

'I wouldn't know. My father brought me up to be a good atheist,' said Elaine.

'Lucky you.'

'From the sound of it, yes. How did you end up marrying the Crown Prince?'

'Football.'

'What?' Elaine had expected some tale of palace intrigue, not football. In her experience, football was rarely the answer to any sensible question.

'My father loves football, and when the Sultan bought Trafford Rangers, he got himself on the board. It meant he could see me, too. I used to go a lot. The Crown Prince was at Cambridge, and Sevenbridge Hall used to be the royal family's little pied-à-terre in the north, before it became my home in exile. We met in the directors' box.' She shrugged, and Elaine's antennae twitched.

'You got pregnant.'

Karida blushed, for the first time since they had met. 'Yes. The Crown Prince couldn't believe his luck — he had a westernised girl hanging off his every word, but he had reckoned without my father. As soon as I told Papa what had happened, he announced it to the Sultan. I wasn't consulted.' She drank some tea. 'I wasn't pregnant, either, but it was too late.'

This was filling in a lot of gaps, but Elaine sensed a yawning chasm of confusion. She tried to create a bridge over it. 'What's your long game, Kari? You're bright, you're in a strong position, you grew up fast. You must have started *SeenIn7Bridge* for a reason.'

'Must I? When Miriam was still with Saul, I used to use the Spa. That was the whole idea of building it, so that I could have a social life. That's when I met Holly, in a yoga class.'

Elaine put two and two together, and realised what Morton had been on about with his biometric logs and his obsession with women's fitness. 'You had private classes in the Hall, didn't you? At night.'

'We did. The teacher was very good at yoga, and very spiritual too. She helped me see how false my position was.

One night, Holly brought a bottle of wine. I shouldn't have, but I did. In the morning, I discovered that we'd given birth to a monster: we'd created the Mother Superior.'

'That's not very spiritual.'

'It made sense at the time. The Mother Superior was supposed to point out the vanity and shallowness of life in 7Bridge.'

Elaine thought of all the vitriol that had been poured on residents, on staff, on the Princess herself and especially on Holly. She put down her tea. 'What went wrong? Why not just stop?'

'Holly. I couldn't stop her once we'd started, and after she told me about Miriam Blackstone, I became even more isolated.'

'Why did you stop seeing her? According to my boss, Holly hasn't been into the Hall for over two years.'

'You don't have children yet, do you?'

Elaine had everything she wanted, and more. She would have to wrap this up soon or she would overload. She would give the Princess one more moment of confession. 'Not yet, but we're going to have them one day.'

Karida looked out of the window. Were they tears, or was the water running out her hair where it had been caught in the shower? 'My original plan was to leave here, to start again with nothing — to become a fitness instructor, maybe, or to go to university. Then my son started walking, and talking, and I knew I couldn't leave him. On his fifth birthday, we were summoned to Ghar'aan. The Sultan told us that his brother was being made chairman of Trafford Rangers, and that he would be in charge of my son's education. On that day I realised that I would not be allowed to take my son with me. I must stay with him until he is old enough to look after himself.' She looked back at Elaine. 'Ever since then, I have been trying to stop Holly, but I can't. And then she got Berardi involved, and I had no choice. I ordered Saul to bring in someone who could get proof. Then Berardi was murdered.'

Elaine leapt on the statement. 'You think his murder was connected to the website?'

'I have no idea, Elaine.' She looked up, to see if Elaine would object to the use of her first name. She didn't. 'That's why I wanted DCI Stamp to look into things officially, and why I got the embassy to bring you and DCI Morton on board: you can go to Holly and say, "We know who you are." I don't know how good your memory is, but I told you that I wanted the Mother Superior found and stopped. I didn't say I wanted her expelled from the Estate. It would destroy her.'

That was enough for Elaine. She had to get going before she started to feel sympathetic, and that would never do. As it turned out, the answer to her next question knocked that on the head anyway. 'Could you give me some proof? Something with which to confront her?'

Karida gave the laugh, the little tinkly laugh they teach girls in rich people's schools. 'That's not going to happen. There's never going to be anything connecting me to *SeenIn7Bridge.*'

Elaine felt her nostrils flaring, like an enraged bull. 'You don't have diplomatic immunity. I checked. I'm afraid that murder is a more serious matter.'

A shadow flashed across the Princess's face, just enough to show there was something haunting her. *The murder of her husband, perhaps? Who cares.*

'I had no connection to Berardi. I don't know what Holly had gotten herself into, Officer, but it was nothing to do with me. At all.'

This was now officially above Elaine's pay grade. She stood up and held out her hand. 'Thank you for your help.'

Karida stood, too, and shook hands. 'Good luck. And goodbye.'

Elaine picked up her boots on the way out, and checked the carpet as she headed for the connecting door. There were no stains. She texted Morton: *All done. Where are you?* His response came before she'd finished tying her laces. *Meet me at the crime scene, where it all started.* What on earth was he up to now?

When Saul Blackstone had interrupted his breakfast, Tom thought for a moment that the man had gone back on his word, but no, Saul had something to tell him. Tom was stiff after the drive down, and the walk round the Estate sounded like a good idea.

They walked in silence until they were through security, then Saul asked if Tom had any children.

'No. We were getting close to thinking about it, but my ex-wife got cold feet. If you can call a Russian with a murky past "cold feet". What about you?'

They walked slowly over the mound. 'Two,' said Saul. 'Twins. They finished their A levels up here when we split up, then both went to different colleges in London. One lives with Miriam, the other with my parents.'

They arrived at the crossing point, where the southern arm of the running track crossed the main road through the Estate. 'I want to show you something about the spot where Berardi died,' said Saul, 'but we'll take the long route.'

'Fine.' They were about to turn right when Tom got the first text from Elaine. 'Looks like I was right about the Princess.'

Saul stopped and stared at him, blinking. 'In the name of the Lord, why?'

'I think we'll have to wait for Fraser to return before we get an answer to that question. Do you or Max have any contact with the security services?'

'We keep in touch with counterterrorism from time to time, but not really. Apart from the business with the 7Bridge Collective, we have a good relationship with the police.'

It was too cold to be standing around without good reason, so Tom set off round the track. 'This could go in several ways,' he said. 'It may not ever become public, depending on what happens next.'

'I still can't get over it. First she creates this website, then she asks the Foreign Office for help in closing it down. Madness.'

Tom hadn't been round this way before, and he found the view much less appealing than the western circuit. Round here, most of the track was hemmed in by a twelve-foot-high security fence rather than trees and river. He commented on this to Saul.

'Room to expand, if necessary. The Estate Office owns all the land between here and the back of the Village. The Princess has said that if we get a few more residents, we'll build a community centre or something.'

For conversation, Tom asked about Anthea Godfrey.

'Don't get me started,' snorted Saul. 'I don't know how she got the job, I really don't. The woman's a nightmare to deal with. It's not often that I quote contractual terms at people, but with her it's the only thing that gets her off her backside.'

They got to the northern crossing point, by the Residents gate and the Collective car park. There were fewer cars than before, and Tom was going to mention this when he got his second text. He told Elaine to meet them up the hill. When they had crossed the road, Tom asked what was on Saul's mind.

Blackstone stopped, and pointed to the lamp standards with the useless CCTV cameras. 'We have a lot of foxes around here,' he said. 'And very few stalkers or robbers. Those CCTV cameras are on a separate system to the others because there's never anything on them. The hard disk records forty-eight hours of nothing, then overwrites it. In fact, they only record high definition for a ten-second loop, unless they're triggered by movement. Do you see those lights?'

Tom nodded.

'They come on when someone walks – or runs – past them in the dark. On a typical winter's night, the recorded images on this system consist of foxes and random lights, when the cameras are at the right angle.'

Tom thought he could see where Saul was going with this, but wanted to be sure. He looked from pole to pole, trying to work out what it would be like at night.

Saul continued 'On the day Gianni was murdered, it was early and it was raining. Heavily. A lot of the motion sensors were triggered because it was so dark. It got me thinking, and I asked for the footage, but I'm no expert. It took me a long time to work out what was going on.'

'Have you told DCI Stamp's team?'

'I only cracked it after your visit this morning, when you got me thinking the impossible about the Princess. If you look a bit earlier than the murder, when it was even darker, you can see that several people were on the track at different points, judging from the way that the lights go on and off. It would take a small team to plot them all, though.'

He was on to something. This could help them see whether Berardi was out and about when Tom reckoned he was handing over that missing £50,000. It might even help narrow down a list of possible recipients. Tom had two candidates in mind, but wasn't sure what to do next. He heard a shout from up the track, and saw Elaine emerge from a buggy. 'Can you excuse me for a moment?' he said to Saul.

Blackstone nodded, checked the wind direction, then moved downwind to light a cigar.

'Well?' said Tom to Elaine when she half jogged up to him.

'You were spot on, both times: Princess Karida is the writer, and Holly is the source. She admitted it, but she wouldn't give me any proof.'

Elaine went through her meeting with Karida, and Tom could sense that there was something she wasn't telling him about the way that the Princess had been persuaded to confess, but he left it out for now. Elaine finished her account with a question. 'How are we going to tackle Holly?'

'First of all … well done. That was excellent, Elaine. I think I can see a way ahead, now, but I'm not sure where it leads.'

He turned to the side, as did Elaine. They stared over the river, towards Manchester, as did Saul. Tom had to play his next move very carefully: they could easily be kicked off the Estate if he got it wrong. He pulled his lip, and looked sideways at Elaine. She had turned in a different direction, perhaps towards the north-east. Was she thinking of Rob in Scotland? Did that explain the smile playing on her face? He made up his mind.

'Saul!' he shouted. The Estate manager started walking slowly towards them. To Elaine, Tom said, 'You've come out on top against a member of royalty already, so a mere DS shouldn't pose you a problem.'

'You're joking, sir. I can't go and see Jepson.'

'Yes, you can.' Saul had come into earshot. 'Mr Blackstone, does the MIT have the same footage as you?'

'Probably not. I have more.'

'Then could you take my colleague, explain to her what you've just told me, and show it to her on screen?' He turned to Elaine. 'Go and see Jepson or Stamp, and explain it to them. Then find out how they got on looking for that missing £50,000. Text me when you've finished. If I don't reply, go back to Lyme Court and write up what you've done today.'

'Is that it?' She looked at Saul, uncomfortable with his presence. 'Shouldn't we work out our next step, and probably inform John Lake about what we're doing?'

Most of the time, Tom would have agreed with her. Police work rarely moved on impulse: it was simply too dangerous for that. Today was different. Today was about catching people on the hop, before they could close ranks or change their minds.

'The Princess isn't going to say anything to anyone, and Leonie would rather know at the end of things. That way she won't have to make any awkward decisions. I'm pleased that we've cracked the Mother Superior question, but…' He looked at Saul, who had been as interested in their conversation as Elaine was reluctant to share it. 'Mr Blackstone, I think you've guessed that Giovanni's death was more "complicated" than it might have appeared at first.'

'You think there might have been someone else involved?' asked Saul.

'Yes. No matter how important she thinks she is, Princess Karida's problems are a lot less important than a murder enquiry. I need to plan our actions with that in mind.'

Elaine looked peeved. Tom could have sent Saul away again, but he wanted to keep the Estate Manager involved, just a little bit. He looked directly at Elaine before saying, 'I'm going to see Lucy White. I need her to do one last favour.'

'It's Holly, isn't it?' interrupted Saul. 'That's why you wanted to know about her visits to the Hall. Holly is providing the gossip for *SeenIn7Bridge*.' He nodded to himself, and the corner of his mouth twitched. 'It makes sense. She's the queen bee on the Estate, no matter what Robyn White thinks of herself.' His eyes sparkled. 'You could say that Holly is the mother, because Karida is certainly superior.'

Saul had given his word once. Tom didn't need to ask for it again to ensure the man's silence. 'You're right. It's Holly.'

'You don't need to go through Lucy to see her,' said Saul. 'I can get hold of her for you.'

'I'm not going to see Holly yet. I need Lucy's help to see John Nugent first.'

'Oh,' said Saul.

'Sir? Shouldn't I—' said Elaine.

'No,' said Tom. 'You put your career on the line this morning to do something I couldn't. This one's on me alone. I'll let you know how I get on.'

He left them before Elaine could object again, and was dialling White-Berardi as he walked up the slope. He asked to speak to Paul Warren first.

'Mr Warren … sorry to bother you. I have a small favour to ask of Lucy. Do you know where she is?'

'Should I be there?' said Warren.

'That's up to her, I think. She's more than capable.'

'I know. That's what worries me. She's gone back to her shop today.'

'Tell her I'm coming, then you can ask her whether she wants your help.'

Tom was desperately hoping that she didn't want Warren's help. This was mostly because he didn't want Gary White to hear about his interest in John Nugent, but a part of him wanted to see Lucy again just because, well, just because she was Lucy.

Chapter 18

Monday 27 January

The last of Mama's handbags were huddling together for protection like sheep in the fold. If Lucy opened her doors, the she-wolves of Cheshire would soon pick them off. She had tried spreading them out in the display and she had tried mixing other stock in with them, but the fact remained that the House of Lucia had been started with Mama's handbags, and without them the cupboard looked very bare.

She had updated the displays after Christmas, and had earmarked some stock for disposal in a mini sale, but she couldn't face lifting the shutters and going back into business, because she had no idea whether the shop had a future.

Everyone seemed to be telling her that it was her choice, but she didn't want to choose. After the funeral, she had been knocked right off balance by Dad's suggestion that she move into Gianni's house. There were so many reasons to refuse that she had run out of fingers trying to explain it to Grace on Friday night.

First, Robyn would hate her for it; second, she hated the house; third, it was Gianni's place: could she ever forget what he'd been up to in the bedroom? And who with? (*With whom*, Grace had said, topping up their wine).

The fourth, fifth and sixth reasons for saying no all grew out of money, like weeds in shit (*Eeuw*, said Grace). She couldn't afford to be a resident unless she gave up the shop and went to work for the business. Grace was saying nothing about that, probably because she was dead against it.

Later on in the evening, one of her exes had turned up at the bar, and told her that he was now selling EU-compatible exhaust upgrades for classic cars. She could feel her eyes glazing over the minute he said "EU".

On Saturday afternoon, she had asked Dad to take her to the airport for a £180 return trip to Milan. He did so, without asking why, or when she was coming back. Mama was the same — she welcomed her, looked after her, showed her the image from the scan (normal), but refused to talk about whether she might be designing any more bags. Lucy had flown back from Milan on Sunday evening with no more idea of what to do with her life than she had had when she flew out.

She stood in front of the display of handbags and put her fists on her hips, beating herself to the rhythm of the music playing quietly over the PA. It wasn't fair. None of it. They expected her to be grown up and make decisions about her future, when she wasn't sure that any of it was right. When Paul rang, she leapt at the phone to distract herself.

'I've had a call from your favourite detective,' he said.

'Oh?' She wished people would stop calling Tom her *favourite detective*. It was getting annoying.

'He wants to pop round for a quick chat.'

'Now? Did he say what for?'

'He's on his way over from the Estate, but he didn't say what it was about. Look, Lucy, there comes a point where we have to consider what they're up to. I don't know who's authorised Morton to go digging around like this, but we can't afford to let the police have unlimited access to our affairs.'

That was it, in a nutshell: was she a part of "our affairs" or not?

'I think perhaps I should pop down and see what he wants,' continued Paul. 'Just because he's been nice to you, it doesn't mean you have to be nice back.'

Yes it does, because the only decision I have to make is whether to talk to him, and that's an easy one. She didn't say that. What she did say was, 'If I'm going to join White-Berardi, I'll need to stand up for myself. Tom Morton isn't the most difficult challenge I'll face, is he?'

Paul laughed. 'Probably not. If he asks anything not directly connected to you personally, point him in my direction.'

'Thanks.' Lucy turned off the music and put the kettle on. If she had known he was coming, she might have downloaded some choral music to wind him up. *No, that's going too far,* she thought. *I don't want to give him the impression I care.* By the time the kettle had boiled, there was a knock on the back door.

He looked cold, as if he'd been walking around outside a lot, and something was troubling him. He started to unbutton his coat. 'You might want to leave that on,' said Lucy. 'I haven't put the heating on very high because I'm not open for business.'

The coat stayed on, but he did finish unbuttoning it. The slightly retro suit he had been wearing last week, with the broader pinstripe, had been replaced by one in a darker blue. Otherwise, she couldn't tell the difference. His shoes showed traces of both a high gloss polish and an outdoor walk. 'Come through,' she said, passing over a mug of tea.

He looked round the showroom on his way to the couch, just as he looked round every room she had seen him enter. Policeman's habit or natural curiosity? Tom was a man who didn't give much away.

Lucy made some inane comment about business, then forced herself to shut up and listen. Tom put down his mug and slid his right hand up his jacket. Lucy couldn't take it any more. 'Are you okay? You keep rubbing your left arm, and you've been doing it since we first met.'

He jumped, and looked guilty. 'Sorry. I'm fine.' He paused, and decided she was owed an explanation for this behaviour. 'I had a skin graft there before Christmas, and it got infected. The wound has healed but people, mostly my mother, keep telling me I rub it when I'm distracted.'

Why should he get to ask all the questions? There was something big he wanted to talk about. She could tell that. She had been studying the way his eyes wandered, the way he moved his cup around, and the way he rubbed his arm. These were all signs that he was working up to something. Usually they would be followed by an intense stare that she found both scary and compulsive.

'What happened?' she said.

'I didn't look after the graft properly. I didn't change the dressing often enough, and it got infected.'

'I guessed that. What happened in the first place that warranted the graft? You weren't getting rid of an embarrassing tattoo, were you? Maybe your ex-wife's name in a big heart?'

This shocked him even more. 'God, no! I wouldn't—' Perhaps the rudeness of her question made him tell the truth. 'I was in a car that got blown up.'

Oh My God. Lucy put her hand to her mouth. *Who was this man? How did he get to that situation?* The look on her face embarrassed him even further. Tom looked down, and put his left hand on his right, perhaps to stop himself rubbing the wound again.

'It's a long story,' he said. 'I jumped out just in time, and escaped with burns. The other two men in the car weren't so lucky. At least they didn't feel anything.'

This sort of thing didn't happen to people she knew. 'Were they police officers? It must have been terrible.'

'One was a drug dealer, the other a terrorist, and both were murderers. As I said, it's a long story.' He shrugged, and picked up his mug.

Lucy made a promise to herself: she would find out all about that story before the end of the day. For now, there was nothing more to be said, so she waited.

He took a deep breath. 'There have been some developments. Quite a few, actually. I need your help, but I don't want to put you in a difficult position.'

Here it comes, she thought. *He's going to look up now.* He did, and the blue in his eyes caught some of the glow from her lighting scheme. She could see little flecks of red reflected in them. 'Let me be the judge of that,' she said.

'The police keep a lot of secrets,' he said. 'It's part of the job, but that doesn't mean I like it. When it comes to witnesses – and especially victims like you – I try not to ask them to keep secrets, because that's the first step on the road to evil.'

'Evil?' She tucked her legs underneath herself and leaned on the arm of the couch. 'Small word, big idea.'

'Very big,' he said, venturing the ghost of a smile. 'But it's what happened to Gianni. Evil is the only word to describe it.'

She brushed her hair aside. 'I never like the way he slept around, but he didn't deserve what happened to him. You could call that evil, or you could call it misplaced macho aggression.'

Something was troubling him very deeply. He hadn't dropped his gaze, but his right hand snaked up to his arm again. 'If I tell you something,' he said, 'you could pass on that information and I could get in serious trouble.' She was about to say that she could keep a secret, but he pulled out his right hand and held it up to stop her. 'Let me finish. I could go ahead with my investigation – carry out my orders and file a report – but someone could get hurt. The only way I can see of limiting the damage is to ask for your help.'

'You want me to write you a blank cheque? Give you my help without knowing why? That's a very big favour, Tom.'

He sat up in the chair, and leaned towards her. 'I know. This isn't a negotiation, it's a plea for help.'

'Who is it?'

He rubbed his lip. 'I need your help to see John Nugent, on his own, because the person I'm worried about is Holly.' He finished speaking and slumped back.

Holly? My God, what has she been doing? Surely she couldn't have been sleeping with Gianni. Not Holly. She looked around the room, to avoid his gaze for a moment. *How wrong can a girl be?* She had thought he was easy to talk to, because he wouldn't ask her to make decisions, but this was a massive one. She tried to empty her mind, to silence the competing voices, and finally she closed her eyes. All she could hear then was Tom's voice: *I need your help.* If she didn't trust this man today, would she ever trust anyone again?

She opened her eyes. 'I'll do it, but you have to tell me why afterwards.'

He breathed out. 'Of course. I just need to see John, on his own, as soon as possible.'

'Easy. He played yesterday, so today's a day off. He's gone out with the little one — a boy. He's taken him to an indoor adventure playground thing. If you let me come with you, I'll keep an eye on the lad. If I'm there, he won't get too suspicious.'

'That's too much to ask. You could face a huge backlash if it goes wrong.'

'Is Holly really in trouble?'

'I believe so.'

Lucy stood up with as much grace as she could, given her short legs and the low couch. 'Then let's go. I owe Holly quite a lot, and this is the least I can do.'

'What are you doing here?'

It was offensive and hostile, but it wasn't a complete refusal of entry. *Glass half full*, Elaine told herself. *She hasn't thrown you out. Yet.* She didn't bother smiling at DS Jepson: no point in wasting energy. 'There's something I need to show you,' she said, holding up the DVD that Max Nolan had given her. 'And my boss has a few questions.'

'What?'

'What questions or what's on the DVD?'

'Don't be clever, Constable. It doesn't suit you.'

Elaine bit her lip. This was one situation where thinking like Tom might be an advantage. He would never put himself ahead of an investigation, or let his ego get in the way of a result. 'Did you have any joy locating Berardi's missing £50,000, or in identifying who he gave it to?'

It was a direct question. Tom was entitled to know the answer, and DS Jepson would only get up Rod Stamp's nose by refusing to answer it.

'We've narrowed it down to two people,' said Jepson. 'A patrol officer called Gavin, and that fitness instructor called Kirsty.'

'Oh?'

Jepson finally gave in and sat down. She didn't offer Elaine a seat, but Elaine could live with that. 'We spoke to Claire Roebuck, and she says that when Kirsty arrived on the day of Berardi's murder, she had clearly been running: she was soaked through. She brought a change of clothes in a rucksack. There was easily room for the money in there. Gavin the patrol officer was on duty, and he never activated his chest-cam, so it's difficult to pin down his movements.'

'This might help,' said Elaine, offering the DVD. 'Saul Blackstone has some ideas that might help you.' She explained what Saul had discovered, and how it might be used with other information to build up a picture. Jepson didn't say *Thank you*, but she did offer some more information in return.

'We've checked out Kirsty and Gavin. Both deny receiving money, but both of them are hiding something. We've looked at their financial records, but nothing obvious sticks out.' She looked towards Rod Stamp's office, which was currently empty. 'The boss thinks they're both living beyond their declared income, but so do a lot of people with zero-hours contracts and flexible payment arrangements. Rod actually said on Friday that if he had the budget, he'd get DCI Morton to look into them.'

'Thanks,' said Elaine. 'Keep us posted.'

The nod of agreement she got in return was grudging, but genuine. Perhaps there was a way back into CID that didn't involve Operation Rewind. *Glass Half Full Fraser*. It wasn't a bad nickname, just a tad clumsy.

She had turned her phone to silent during her visit, and saw a missed call from Tom when she checked it. He had left her a voicemail telling her to meet him at the Manchester office of Abramovitz & Co. *Typical Morton*, she thought. *Nothing about Holly or John Nugent*. She had to look up their address on her phone and trust to the satnav, because she had no idea where she was going.

On the way to the play barn, their destination was all they really talked about. Tom drove. Lucy gave directions, and explained that John Nugent had a half share in the business.

'It's one of the local farmers who decided to diversify. Somehow, John got to hear about it and put up half the capital. He goes there regularly, and Holly buys a lot of food from the farm shop. There are other benefits, too.'

'Such as?' said Tom, to make conversation. They were both anxious to talk about anything other than what they had shared for a moment in the House of Lucia. At least Tom was. He guessed that Lucy felt the same, by the brightness in her voice.

'John's tried hard to be a normal dad. That's easy to say, but not so easy to do. He guards his privacy, but he doesn't want his children brought up in a bubble. He brings them all here, apart from Ellie.'

Did Tom detect a note of disapproval?

Lucy continued, 'You'll see what I mean when we get there. Just do what I say.'

'I wouldn't dream of doing otherwise,' said Tom. He glanced to the side: she was sticking her tongue out in his direction, until she realised that he was looking. Then she turned to look out of the window.

'Follow the brown signs,' she mumbled.

To avoid an awkward silence, Tom said, 'I may need to get in touch with the Ikedas, just to check something. To save me asking … do you have a contact number? And how did Gianni cope with the time difference?'

She turned back, eager to be helpful. 'The best thing is to Skype both of them together. Kaito understands a lot more English than he speaks — then Mitsumi can translate his answers.' She looked through the windscreen. 'He trusts her with all his business affairs. Believe me: negotiations went a lot more smoothly after they started dating.'

'Damn,' said Tom. 'I don't have access to Skype, or any other video conference system.'

Lucy smiled. 'Are you in Saul Blackstone's good books?'

'More or less.'

'Then use his system. He talks to the Princess all the time, and I know Gianni used it a few times too.'

This fired off several warning rockets in the back of Tom's head, but he couldn't follow up on the emergencies now. 'I might do that,' he said. 'Do you know if they stay up late in Japan?'

'I've got Mitsumi's mobile number,' said Lucy. 'I'll forward it to you. Text her in advance.'

'Thanks.'

Tom drove into the farmyard, and discovered a variety of land-based leisure opportunities, including a petting zoo. Not having children of his own, and with Fiona's kids being a long way away, he didn't know that such places existed. Lucy got out and walked towards a barn with five metre-high pictures of jungle animals on the outside. Tom followed.

'It's a clever set-up,' said Lucy. 'You can't get past the barrier without children under eight. That deters paparazzi and journalists.'

'Not some of the ones I've met,' said Tom.

She turned to face him. 'It does round here. No one wants to be caught exploiting children just to catch the England captain off duty. They also have a membership scheme: once John arrives, only members are allowed in afterwards.'

'What on earth for?'

'Have you never heard of celebrity trackers?' He shook his head. 'Some people, as soon as they see someone famous, use an app on their phone to tag the location. If everyone knew John was here, a lot of people would flock to the place, just to take pictures of him with their children.' She shoved her hands in her coat pockets, and pursed her lips. 'Some people would take their kids out of school just to get through the door.'

'I guess I'm not used to being round celebrities,' said Tom. Something – nerves, maybe – pushed him to say, 'Is that why you never went out with footballers? You must have seen enough of them.'

'How dare you?' said Lucy, but she laughed. 'My dad would have killed me when I was younger, and when I was old enough to decide for myself, I discovered that I was too short, too clever and had too much self-respect to become a WAG.' She went inside, holding back the strongly-sprung door for him to follow. 'You wait here. I'll go and find him. If anyone looks at you, try not to be a policeman.'

Inside the front door, a short tunnel had been made with childproof barriers to a height of four feet, with netting above. You couldn't get in without tearing down the netting or being admitted through the security gate. You could see what was going on, though. A large open area was occupied by parents, grandparents and au pairs. Many of the tables had buggies next to them, and lots of toddlers zoomed back to their base for refreshments before returning to the end of the barn.

The whole wall was occupied by a huge structure made from padded metal beams, plastic poles, slides, nets, rollers, chutes and crash mats, and filled with ball pools into which toddlers dived. Tom had never seen anything like it, and if he ever had children, he would bring them here. If he won the lottery, he would build one in his back garden. From barely toddler through to should-be-at-school age, children climbed, slid, dropped and jumped around the structure. Not one single child looked bored.

Lucy was talking to a member of staff at the counter, who pointed around the corner, then admitted her. Tom watched her cross the recovery zone, and couldn't help admiring the way she moved, dodging children and tables as if she were on the dance floor. She disappeared from view, and the room seemed to get a little darker. Tom realised that three young women were staring at him from the counter. He nodded and smiled, on the basis that a policeman would frown and take out his warrant card. The staff lost interest.

The back of Tom's neck prickled, and he looked around the room. John Nugent was watching him from within the barn, a frown on his face. He stood still, more deeply rooted than the fixtures on the climbing frame. Lucy reappeared at the counter and waved him forward. When he got to the end of the tunnel, the gate buzzed and Lucy ushered him through. She pointed towards John, then squeezed his arm. 'Good luck.'

Tom crossed the floor, with the memory of Lucy's hand on his arm tingling like magic dust had been sprinkled on him. Halfway over, Nugent turned and walked through a Staff Only door. Tom followed and found himself in a small pen at the back of the barn, with John Nugent and a young woman smoking a cigarette. She stubbed it out and fled back inside. The little pen was a wind trap, freezing cold — but something made Tom unbutton his coat. He thrust his hands in the pockets, to stop himself rubbing his arm.

'How can I help?' said Nugent in a totally neutral voice.

'My colleague DC Fraser went to see Princess Karida this morning,' said Tom.

Nugent's face gave away nothing. That said it all to Tom: if he had no idea what Tom was going to say, he would have been curious at least. Either that, or Nugent was a dead-hearted sociopath.

'Before I say any more,' said Tom, 'I understand your position.' Nugent frowned. 'I understand that the whole of the FA, along with half the country and half the government, is desperate for England to win the European Championship.' He tried a smile. 'Even I'm behind you, though I'd prefer us to win the rugby World Cup. However, I'm afraid that MI6 don't care much for football.'

'So?'

Tom sighed inwardly: clearly Nugent wasn't big on context. 'Princess Karida has made a statement to the police that she herself was behind the *SeenIn7Bridge* website, and that she ran the website in partnership with your wife.'

Nugent cracked. He turned his face away and swore under his breath.

Tom pressed on. 'The Princess regrets her actions, and wishes to stop. She alleges that your wife is preventing her.'

'She's not breaking the law,' said Nugent. 'This is none of anyone's business but ours.' He was gritting his teeth as he spoke, but Tom could see the fear and pain in his eyes.

'That's why I mentioned MI6,' said Tom. 'In their eyes, oil is more important than football. If they think Holly's activities are threatening the Princess, they'll stop her all right. Believe me: I've dealt with them before.'

'What are you talking about? Are you saying that they'll get the SAS to fake an accident? That's stupid.'

'This isn't TV, Mr Nugent. They'll just get GCHQ to rub out all trace of the Princess's involvement, then get their friends in the press to smear Holly's name so badly that the Princess can throw her off the Estate. You must have realised this might happen.'

He launched himself at Tom, who had no time to react other than pulling his hands out of his pockets. Nugent slammed him back against the barn and pulled his lapels up, lifting Tom on to his toes. Tom could feel the power quivering in Nugent's shoulders as he thrust his face into Tom's.

'If anything happens to Holly, I'll hold you personally responsible. Do you hear that? You'll end up like Berardi, only worse.'

Tom had found something in his coat pocket: Elaine's baton. He fumbled the button and clicked the spring. There was only one shot he could make, because he was pinned against the wall, so he brought the baton up in an arc and smacked it into Nugent's face.

The footballer staggered back, with blood already coursing from the wound to his temple. Tom raised the baton. 'I haven't told them!' he shouted. 'They don't have to know.'

The door cracked open, and Lucy stepped out. How much had she seen? Nugent looked from Tom to Lucy, and panic replaced the anger in his face.

'What are you doing?' said Lucy, turning from man to man.

'It was a misunderstanding,' said Nugent. 'I slipped on the floor and cut myself.'

Lucy looked at Tom's baton, still raised in the defensive position, and then looked him in the eye. She expected an explanation, and he had promised her one. Not only that, Tom couldn't afford for Nugent to stay in denial.

'It's Holly,' said Tom. 'She…'

'No!' said Nugent. 'It's not true.'

Tom lowered his baton. 'She's the Mother Superior.'

Lucy stepped between the men, but turned to Nugent. 'Tell me it's not true, John, and I'll believe you.'

Nugent looked over her head at Tom, who nodded slightly in Lucy's direction.

'Yeah, it's true,' said Nugent. 'She needs help.'

Lucy took a step forward and put her hands on Nugent's chest. 'Oh, my God … John, what's been going on?'

The blood hadn't stopped running. It had trickled down his cheek, and was now dripping on to his shirt. He rubbed it it with his hand, and smeared it across his forehead. He didn't know what to say next.

'Mr Nugent?' said Tom. The other man looked up. 'If you give me your word that your wife will stop today, then this goes no further, provided you answer a question. I can keep her name out of my report, but only with your co-operation.'

Lucy turned and looked up at Tom, one hand still on John's chest. 'He's telling the truth, John. If you do what he says, he'll keep his side of the bargain. I'll help, too: you know I will.'

'What do you want to know?' said Nugent.

'Gianni knew about Holly didn't he?' said Tom. Nugent nodded. 'And he was blackmailing you, not her.' Another nod. 'You agreed to start talking to the Ikedas in exchange for his silence, and no doubt other favours, too. So tell me this: what was the £250,000 for?'

'I don't know for certain, but he owed money. He'd pawned something, or borrowed the money against security, or something like that. All he said to me was, "Now I get back the Crown Jewels." That was when I handed the money over. Next thing I knew, he was dead.'

Tom's stomach lurched. He suddenly knew exactly why Gianni Berardi had died, and who was responsible for his death.

'Thank you, Mr Nugent. I need to leave, Lucy. Can you stay with John? Get him cleaned up and work out what you're going to say to Holly.'

Lucy nodded.

Tom looked up at Nugent. 'I'm only going to say one thing: get out of the Estate now. This week, if possible. I don't know your wife at all, but I think it's poisoned her.'

'Poisoned?' said Nugent.

'Yes. I think she's been bitten by something poisonous, and the only antidote is to get her away.'

Tom couldn't bear to stay another second, because he had to find out whether he was right about Gianni's killer — and it could be the worst thing he had ever discovered. He opened the door to the play barn and found a sturdy middle-aged woman on guard inside the door, protecting John's privacy. 'Have you got a first-aider?' asked Tom.

'Yes. What's happened?'

'Nothing, really — but Mr Nugent needs some attention before he comes back inside. Thank you for your time.'

She stared down at his hand. The baton. *Oops.* He retracted the handle and shoved it in his pocket. He took out his phone as he headed for the exit.

After the five-star luxury of the private hospital, arriving at the Manchester offices of Abramovitz & Co was like being bumped down from first class to economy, but Dean didn't mind. In fact, he was more chilled and relaxed than he had been since Boxing Day, when he crashed into that Turf Moor goalpost and knackered his shoulder. Being arrested for murder hadn't helped either.

On Saturday morning, the consultant had come to see him. *How about that, eh? Consultants making weekend visits.* It was proof that Dean still had it, and he was determined to hang on to it. Even better, the doctor had told him that the operation was an unqualified success — and that, provided he didn't tear the sutures, he would be good as new in no time. The consultant attempted humour by saying that Dean should avoid unarmed combat: Dean had gritted his teeth in response. By this morning, Dean could already feel more mobility in his shoulder than he had experienced in weeks.

Things got even better on Sunday, when Gus Burkett and his wife dropped by on their way to Tatton Park. Not only had Gus agreed to a selfie (now on the STFC Supporters' website, thanks to Emily), his mentor and manager had officially given Dean his support, and said that the Salton Town chairman wanted a meeting with Isaac on Monday.

And so, here he was, sitting in the reception area of Daniel's law office, waiting for Isaac, Daniel and the chairman to thrash things out. Unfortunately, whatever they decided, he would still have to go back to the magistrates' court this afternoon and have his tag re-fitted, then Mum would take him back to Stoke.

The law-office might not have five star furniture or fittings, but it was certainly busy. The reception area was just that — an area on the fringes of an-open plan office. Most of the staff here seemed to be women who sat down and ate a lot, judging by their size. The receptionist herself had got through two doughnuts in the time that Dean had been waiting. He was watching her out of the corner of his eye (to see if she would make it through the whole box) when a cold blast from the door announced a visitor, and Dean sat up straight.

The new arrival was pretty unmistakable, even though he'd only met her once before: you tend not to forget the person who arrests you for murder. Even without the arrest to jog his memory, he would have recognised the policewoman anywhere, especially as she was still wearing those great big boots and that huge red mountaineering jacket. She was a striking woman underneath the clobber as well, and, in a weird way, she reminded him of Madison —

if you could imagine his ex-fiancée being photomanipulated to become six inches taller, stretched like a rubber band. Even her face looked as if it were too long.

The policewoman said something to the receptionist, then walked over to the chair next to Dean, while looking at something on her phone. She sat down, turned to acknowledge him, and nearly jumped out of her seat.

'Shit! Sorry … excuse me, Mr Rooksby. I wasn't expecting you to be here.'

'I wasn't expecting you either. Does Daniel know you're coming?'

'Who?'

'My lawyer.'

'Oh, no. We're not here to see him. That would be bang out of order. I mean, that wouldn't be appropriate. We've got an appointment with another one of the partners.'

'We?'

'My boss is on his way. I'll leave you in peace.'

Dean was enjoying watching her squirm. If she was that bothered about being next to him, she couldn't be that bad. 'You were pretty quick off the mark the other week, when you jumped in the ambulance with me. Why didn't I see you again in the hospital?'

She took a deep breath and calmed down. 'I happened to be first on the scene, that's all. Once the major incident team had been called in, they took over. I've been doing other things since then.'

'So have I.'

She looked him over, appraising him, and he shivered slightly.

'You're looking better,' she said, '…if you don't mind me saying.'

'I've had an operation. There's a long way to go yet, but I'm on the mend.'

'Good. You were in a pretty bad way when we first met.'

'I wouldn't call it a meeting, exactly. You arrested me.'

'I'd just seen Giovanni Berardi. What did you expect me to do?'

There was something about the way she said it — something not quite what he had expected. Whatever game this woman was playing, it was beyond Dean. He decided to keep it simple, and give the line he'd practised with Daniel. 'I'm not sorry for what happened between us, but I didn't kill him.' The effect was spoilt slightly when he tried to fold his arms, and his shoulder twinged.

She folded her own arms. Was she taking the mick? 'Then who did?' she said.

'I don't know.'

She unfolded her arms, and half turned towards him. 'Apart from the obvious, did Giovanni do anything odd? Anything you thought was out of the ordinary?'

Since he had been charged with murder, Dean had asked himself this question at least six times a day. Usually, he was trying to see whether he should have spotted signs of Madison's affair, but there was one other thing.

'What's your name?' he asked. 'I was a bit preoccupied last time.'

'Detective Constable Fraser — South Lancs Police. I haven't got a business card, but you can see my warrant card if you want.'

'I'll remember.' He checked her ring finger: she was married. 'Look, Mrs Fraser, you can tell your boss this: the only thing that Berardi did that I couldn't explain was just after Christmas. On the Sunday, he came round and told Madison that he could bring our wedding forward — sort it all out. Why would he do that? It's none of his business, and I can't see that he had anything to gain.'

She frowned, but said nothing because Daniel Abramovitz appeared. They didn't recognise each other, so Dean had great fun making the introductions. Mrs Fraser went red, and stood up. Daniel puffed out his chest and was about to get angry, when this posh bloke in a Crombie stepped between them. Where on earth had he come from? How long had he been there? Dean stayed seated: he didn't want to risk his shoulder.

'Excuse me, Mr Abramovitz,' said the new bloke. 'I'm DCI Morton. My colleague and I are here to see your partner, and she was being polite. She asked about Mr Rooksby's health and was entirely professional, I assure you.'

Slightly deflated, Daniel turned towards him. 'Dean? Is that true?'

Why did this Morton bloke lie? If he'd been here all along, he must know about the rest. Morton looked at him in a steady way, not begging, as if it were in Dean's interest to go along with the story. 'Yeah,' he said to Daniel. 'She was just being nice.'

Daniel had to have the last word. 'Don't do it again,' he said to the detectives. 'C'mon, Dean.'

Dean stood up slowly and followed him through the office. Daniel had his own space, with glass walls and a view of the canal. Isaac was in there, but there was no sign of the Salton Town chairman.

'He left by the back door,' said Daniel, when Dean asked him about it. 'We have a special exit and entrance for clients who wish to remain discreet, but it's good news. He's going to get his media people to work with your PR. They're going to test the waters and see whether it would be good for the club or not.' He gave Dean an evil grin. 'Judging by the way you've got Emily Miller cheerleading for you, that shouldn't be a problem.'

The thought of Emily in a cheerleader's outfit was too much for Dean, and he shook his head to clear the image. 'That's great. Thanks, both of you.'

'No problem,' said Isaac. 'Tell him the other good news, Daniel.'

The lawyer frowned. 'It's not news, exactly, but I've been in touch with the CPS. They're not keen to set a date for the Plea and Directions hearing.'

Daniel had explained to him that Dean would remain on bail until the CPS had sorted out their paperwork, then a date for his full trial would be set — so he understood what Daniel was saying, even though he couldn't see the significance of it. 'So?'

'Normally, if you'll forgive me, a case like yours would be a simple one. The CPS would want to get the trial scheduled as soon as the courts are free, but they're stalling. I think the police are still turning over rocks, and whatever's crawled out isn't to their taste.'

Dean mulled this over for a second. Perhaps the appearance of Mrs Fraser in reception was a sign that not all the police were happy with the way things were going. Things really were looking up.

'I want you to come in with me at first, then take the kids away,' said John Nugent, on the threshold of *Casa Nugent*.

'Are you sure?' said Lucy. They hadn't spoken on the way back from the play barn, because the little lad in the back wasn't daft: he already had difficulty believing that Daddy had fallen over and cut his head. When the Range Rover pulled up under the canopy, the boy had dashed off to see Mummy, and Lucy knew that Holly would emerge in a moment to find out why her husband had a big dressing on one side of his face.

'Yes,' said John. 'If Holly refuses to admit what she's done, we could go round in circles for days. I don't think your policeman friend will give us that long.'

'He's not my friend,' said Lucy automatically. 'He's just a friendly policeman.'

'Whatever,' said John.

Lucy still couldn't believe it, even though she knew it to be true. How could Holly have done all this? Last year, when she had read: *Another lamb to the slaughter: welcome Madison Greenwood, airbrushed to perfection, then trussed up like a Sunday Roast*, Lucy had thought the Mother Superior was an out-and-out bitch, with no feeling at all — but if it were Holly, how could she write: *Loud peals echoed around 7Bridge today as Thunderthighs Nugent was seen jogging off the Christmas pudding?*

It was madness: pure madness. And that was the only explanation: something in Holly's head didn't work the way it should do. Lucy shivered. She had admired Holly for all sorts of reasons, and that hadn't changed, but she could never look at her in the same way again. No wonder she wanted to go to Japan. Lucy had turned Tom's idea round in her head too: Holly had been poisoned by something in 7Bridge. It was a bit OTT, but it made sense, in a biblical sort of way.

They had made it through the front door, and were by the staircase when Holly came running out of the family quarters. She stopped in horror when she saw John's face. 'Oh, my God, John. What's happened?'

'It's over, love,' said John.

'What?' Holly looked from John to Lucy in bewilderment.

For a mad moment Holly must have thought that her husband was telling her that they were getting divorced, and that he was running off with a younger model. Yeah, right: like that would ever happen.

'I've had the truth beaten into me,' said John, attempting a smile. 'This copper hit me with his baton to convince me I had to stop lying. It's time for the truth: you've got to stop doing the website, love. Completely.'

Holly put her hands on her hips. 'What copper? Did someone do that to you?'

Lucy could see what John had meant: she was in denial. Holly hadn't heard the part about the website, just the bit about John being hit over the head. John wasn't helping matters, either. This needed bringing out into the open, and quickly.

Lucy took a deep breath, and said, 'The police have been to see Princess Karida. They've issued John with a warning that you have to stop writing the Mother Superior stuff, Holly.'

'No, no,' said Holly. 'That's crap. Complete crap.'

John stepped in. 'No, it's not, love. I've known about it for ages, and Lucy's telling the truth: the police know too.'

Holly pulled at her hair, dragging the curls down on one side. 'No, you can't. You can't.'

John looked uneasily at Lucy. Although she hated the word, Lucy could only describe Holly as being on the edge of hysteria. 'Take her upstairs, John. I'll go through to the kids.'

John took his wife's arm, and led her up the stairs, until she collapsed on the third step. He leaned down and scooped her up with a grunt.

'Remember what Tom said,' added Lucy. 'The sooner you get out of here, the better.'

'Yeah, right,' said John, disappearing along the corridor.

I must let her off the leash more often, thought Tom, as he watched Elaine recover from her encounter with Dean Rooksby and his lawyer.

'Sorry, sir,' she muttered when they were left alone.

'Don't apologise,' said Tom. 'You were entirely within the codes of practice. And I think you got some good information there.'

'What? The stuff about the wedding? Where does that fit in?'

'A good question. I've been over and over Madison Greenwood's statement, and the MIT simply didn't push her far enough. Not that I blame them or anything. They asked plenty of questions about the affair, so they weren't going soft. Now that I know what Berardi was up to, it makes sense in one way, but prompts another question.'

'How do you mean?'

'According to Madison's statement, she had a final fling with Berardi before Christmas, then broke it off definitively — but she kept seeing him socially, including the Nugents' Boxing Day Ball, when Berardi was hosting the Ikedas' visit. Why? According to Madison, Gianni threatened to tell Dean about the affair unless she kept seeing him. But why get involved in her wedding plans?'

Elaine lifted her head. 'If he's anything like some of the blokes I've met, he thought he'd get back inside her knickers if he persisted.'

'Not a nice image for a Monday morning, Constable.'

'It's not nice being on the receiving end, either, but sorry.'

Tom gave her a hard stare. 'I don't think that was his motivation. He might have been doing it to torture her, but I don't think he actively enjoyed cruelty. I think there's another agenda at work here, but I don't know what.'

The receptionist called them over, and Tom decided to divide their forces again. 'You don't need to see this bloke,' he told Elaine. 'Go back to Lyme Court and get hold of Madison. Ask her about the wedding business. She's a witness, not a suspect, so get her to speculate. It all goes in the stockpot.'

She looked at him for a second. 'You mean, "It's all grist to the mill"?'

'I do, but I like to make my own clichés.' He paused. 'When I had my own house, I used to make my own stock, too.'

Elaine stood up. 'You're really worrying me now, sir. I'm leaving before you get too personal.'

Tom took off his coat and draped it over his arm. A junior admin assistant led him upstairs to a small office with a view of a brick wall and too little ventilation. The lawyer who greeted him – without leaving his seat or shaking hands – could have used some air as well.

When Tom was an undergraduate, one of the lecturers had referred three times to the image of lawyers in *Bleak House*. Intrigued, Tom had borrowed a copy and found it fascinating, if slightly scary: did he really want to enter the same profession as Mr Tulkinghorn, the monstrous attorney? Well, yes, he did, but he vowed to quit if he ever found himself drying out like an old deed locked in a box too long — which is exactly what he did seven years ago when he joined the Met.

While he was still a keen young solicitor, Tom had coined the phrase *Tulkinghorn's Syndrome* to describe lawyers who dried out and reverted to the nineteenth century: the man opposite Tom clearly had a bad case of it. It was so bad that Tom had to write the man's name in his notebook twice, and then still couldn't remember it.

'Yes?' said the lawyer.

'I understand you acted for Giovanni Berardi in drawing up the final version of his will.'

'I did. I notified the executor of this fact once the inquest had been opened.'

'Did you act for Mr Berardi in any other matters?'

'I've already spoken to DS Jepson, and told her that I only acted for Mr Berardi in that one matter. We talked about a number of issues, but as I didn't charge for my time, nothing was written down.'

Tom's eyebrows shot up. Had he heard the man correctly? *Because no fee changed hands, the conversation had never happened.* That seemed to be the gist. He shook his head to clear the fog that seemed to be encroaching.

'Can you remember nothing of the topics that you discussed?' he asked.

The lawyer looked at his watch. 'They may have touched on enforceable covenants arising from articles of incorporation,' he said smugly. Tom had no doubt that if he asked the man to explain, he would be charged a fee. The good news was that Tom knew that this was connected to the shares in White-Berardi. The bad news was that it piled up more circumstantial evidence against persons other than Dean Rooksby.

'One last question,' said Tom. 'How did Mr Berardi come to you? I can see that he wouldn't want Paul Warren to know about the change to his will, but why did he come to you?'

A flicker of emotion moved over the lawyer's face — the first that Tom had seen since entering the room. 'He was recommended to me,' said the other man.

'By whom?'

'I admire your grammar, Inspector, but I can't answer your question because we don't record these things. Customer satisfaction surveys and suchlike are not our forte. You said it was your last question, I believe.'

He was obfuscating, and he made little effort to hide it, but Tom was fairly sure that something else he'd seen today answered the question. He made a point of jotting down in his notebook the following observation: *The Lawyer refused to say who recommended his services.* Then he crossed out "refused" and substituted "declined". Much better.

He thanked the lawyer and headed for 7Bridge, and rang ahead to the Estate Office to ask if he could borrow Saul's secure videoconference connection.

Chapter 19

Monday 27 January

Elaine ducked out of the law office before anyone else could detain her. She was doubly relieved. First, to get away from the embarrassment of being caught talking to Dean: second, to avoid Tom's interview with the other lawyer. Knowing Tom, the discussion would soon be full of references to this Section of that Act, and the implications of Wallace v Gromit in the court of Claymation. And he would expect full notes afterwards. She smiled at the approaching traffic warden and jumped into her car.

It was only when she passed a deli that she remembered it was a long time since the sausage sandwich in the 7Bridge canteen. Since then, she had endured a showdown with royalty and round two with DS Julia Jepson: no wonder she was hungry. She picked up lunch for her and something for Tom, then she remembered that he hadn't told her about his meeting with John Nugent. Damn.

While eating her sandwich in Lyme Court, she re-read all the HOLMES2 material on Madison Greenwood (and the *SeenIn7Bridge* stuff for dessert). According to Madison, she had been lonely and isolated when she and Dean had moved to the Estate, and Gianni Berardi had singled her out for special attention. He had introduced her to the other WAGs, got her membership of the Spa sorted — even got her the internship with Anthea Godfrey. Generally, he had shown her a good time while Dean was trundling around the country with Salton Town.

Elaine had glanced at the STFC fixture list earlier during the investigation: they certainly earned their wages in the Championship. Salton Town were playing twice a week for most of August and September, only stopping for an international break in October. No wonder Madison had felt lonely, and by introducing her to the other 7Bridge women selectively, Gianni had made her feel that open relationships were the rule rather than the exception. *Yeah, right*, thought Elaine. *That had clearly been a message that Madison was eager to hear.*

According to her statement, Madison had regretted her actions immediately, and only continued the affair sporadically, until finishing it in December. There was a brief statement that she had only agreed to accompany Gianni to the Boxing Day Ball because Holly had asked her to be his escort. There was no mention of wedding plans.

It took a while to track her down. Madison's phone was switched off, and no one answered the landline at her house. She dug around until she found Mrs Greenwood's mobile, and finally got an answer. Her daughter, it seemed, was working as a tour guide at the Potteries Museum. The museum staff passed on a message, and Madison was on the line ten minutes later.

'How do I know you're a police officer?' she asked. 'All I've got is your mobile. The press are still after me, and I can't afford the risk.'

It was a good question. Elaine wasn't at a police station. She was in a rented office, so Madison couldn't call her back. She went for the direct approach.

'This might be distressing, Madison, but do you remember the moment you saw Gianni's body? I was there, in a red coat. It was me who arrested Dean, but I've been off the main enquiry since then.'

'Oh. You could still be press, though.'

Elaine pinched the top of her nose. This could be difficult. 'Why don't you call the enquiry team? They can verify that this is my mobile number. But, please … this is quite important.' She kept her fingers crossed, because the last thing she wanted was a call from Julia Jepson asking what was going on.

She heard a sigh from the other end of the phone. 'Send me a selfie, holding up three fingers on your left hand.'

'Pardon?'

'Take a picture of yourself, holding up three fingers on your left hand.'

'That's what I thought you said. What on earth for?'

'So I know it's a real picture. Then if you're not DC Fraser, I can get you arrested for impersonating a police officer.'

This was surreal. She could sympathise with Madison — after all, a Scottish rugby reporter had once caught Elaine off guard and to discover the real reason Rob had missed training (shut his fingers in the car door while drunk, as it happened). But this was bizarre.

'How about this, Madison? I'll do what you want, and I'll take a picture of my warrant card.'

'Good. I'll call you back.'

Elaine felt ridiculous, but complied. Madison had the grace to sound a little sheepish when she finally agreed to talk.

'It's about Gianni,' said Elaine. 'I spoke to Dean this morning…'

'You've spoken to Dean? How is he?'

The neediness was palpable. Elaine swallowed hard, thinking of how the cocky young footballer she'd met today had behaved. If Dean Rooksby thought of Madison at all, it wouldn't be with affection. 'He's had an operation. He seems much improved.'

'Good. About his shoulder, I mean.' She hesitated. 'Has he admitted anything else?'

'I'm afraid I can't comment on that, but I'm not expecting him to enter a guilty plea … put it that way.'

'Oh. How can I help?'

'Dean claims – off the record – that Gianni pushed you to move the date of your wedding forward, and that he did so after Christmas. Is this true? And if it is, then why did he do it?'

'I've wondered that ever since. I don't know why.'

'So it's true.'

'Yes. The day after the Ball, he said that he was going to up his game: he was going to be organising more things, become much more central to the Estate's way of life. He said that he could get the Princess to be a guest, and that I'd be welcome at the Hall once I was a married woman.'

Elaine nearly tore through the page on her notepad writing this down. What game was Gianni playing? Was he blackmailing everyone on the Estate? If he was putting pressure on the Princess, then Kirsty or Gavin were strong contenders for a starring role in *Who Will Rid Me of This Troublesome Italian?*

'Did he say anything else, between then and the day of his death?'

'More of the same. He was going to be making connections all over the place, and he thought that Dean was going to be the next big thing at Trafford Rangers after John Nugent retired.'

'Did he put any pressure on you to resume your … relationship?'

'Not after Dean proposed. I think he was back-pedalling — trying to be more of a friend. He was good fun. I enjoyed his company.'

'Thank you for your time, Miss Greenwood. You've been most helpful.'

'What's this all about, anyway?'

Elaine had some idea of where her boss was going, but she wasn't entirely sure. 'In a major enquiry,' she said to Madison, 'we have to follow every lead, even if they go nowhere.'

She ended the call and stared out of the window, towards the canal. If all this came out in court, during Dean's trial, it would create a lot of doubt. He would probably get off now, but they were nowhere near finding any evidence that would allow the CPS to prosecute anyone else.

'Come through to my den,' said Saul. 'There's someone who'd like a word with you.'

Tom followed the Estate Manager into his private space, and tried not to gag at the lingering cigar smoke. Saul opened a window when he saw the look on Tom's face, then pointed to a visitor's chair, which had been placed at the side of a leather-covered partners' desk to get a view of the large monitor.

On the screen was a richly brocaded chair, currently empty. Saul sat down and took the mouse, locating a microphone icon on the screen and clicking it from *mute* to *broadcast*.

'He's here, ma'am,' said Saul. Tom had a fairly good idea who would be online, and he was right. A very regal-looking woman, dressed in pink silk with a blue headscarf, sat down in front of her monitor and looked at them.

'Princess Karida, I presume,' said Tom.

She said nothing for a moment, her eyes flicking from one part of the screen to another. 'You're not as intimidating as your psychotic sidekick made out, Inspector.'

Tom tried to keep a straight face. 'Who would that be?'

'DC Fraser, as well you know. She had me believing that unless I co-operated with her enquiries, I could expect much worse from her boss.'

Because there was a little window at the bottom of the screen, Tom didn't have to turn aside to see Saul's reaction: he was horrified. Tom smiled at the Princess, 'There's more ways to kill a cat than choking it with cream.'

Saul looked even more horrified, but the Princess said, 'Is that another of your grandmother's sayings? I've already been treated to one this morning.'

'Someone please tell me what's going on,' pleaded Saul.

Tom waited. After all, the conversation wasn't his idea.

'We had a visit from DC Fraser this morning,' said the Princess. *Is that the royal We?* wondered Tom. 'As a result of that, it was discovered that the Mother Superior is one of the residents, who had help from a third party. DC Fraser assured me that pressure would be put on this person to cease their activities, and thus end the problem.'

Good heavens above. What is the woman playing at? Tom looked at her poised, elegant face, and at Saul's creased brow. Karida smiled, and Saul burst out laughing.

'What's so funny?' she asked.

'Is this the story?' said Saul. 'I know what's been going on, thank you very much, but if this is the official version, then so be it.'

A cloud of wrath descended over the on-screen image. Before she could take out her anger on her employee, Tom stepped in.

'As you say, steps have been taken. If you want the matter concluded to your satisfaction, I suggest you contact your embassy and advise them of our successful mission, and how pleased you are with our … personal service.'

'Touché, Inspector.' She smiled, and a hint of green flashed in her eyes, or maybe it was a fault on the camera. Either way, she was astute, attractive and almost certainly dangerous. 'I think we're all agreed: this matter is closed.'

'Almost,' said Tom. 'The resident we're talking about may be leaving. If she does, she will take her secret with her. And I have one other question.'

The Princess looked a little disappointed to hear about Holly. 'If that's what she wants, so be it. What was your other question?'

'Do you have anything to do with a personal trainer called Kirsty?'

The Princess grimaced. 'She did some work with me after Holly stopped coming to the Hall. I believe she handed in her notice to Beth Pedley this morning. That's what Saul tells me.'

'She may have been working for Berardi. You're well rid of her.'

'Thank you, Inspector.' Her eyes moved to her left. 'Saul, we'll speak tomorrow.' She leaned forward, and the screen went blank.

Tom leaned back, and turned to his right. He pushed his chair away from Saul's personal space and said, 'I don't know what game she's playing, but it's a long one, and it's not centred on 7Bridge.'

Saul frowned. 'What do you mean?'

'The next time you're seeing your twins in London, arrange a visit with John Lake from Security Liaison. It might be good to have him as a friend, because I think the Princess has her eyes set on a much higher prize than being queen bee in this little hive. I think she's looking at a regency in Ghar'aan.'

Saul rubbed his chin. 'John Lake? I might just do that.' He slapped his thighs and stood up. 'I'm off for a walk, before it gets dark. I've got the Ikedas' video location in the address book here,' he said, pointing to an icon. 'Take your time, and if you need any refreshment, just shout very loudly for Tiffany. In fact, I'll get some sent through.'

Tom thanked his host, and sent another text to Japan. By the time Tiffany had brought him some tea, he was trying to make contact on screen. It worked first time.

He had no idea what to expect, but the silk pyjamas and the emperor-sized bed were a little alarming. Mitsumi Ikeda and her husband were lounging against the headboard, and their end of the conversation appeared to be based on a small device propped on a pillow between them. Both of them bowed as best they could. Tom felt obliged to bow back.

'I'm very sorry to disturb you,' he said. 'Thank you so much for waiting up.'

Mitsumi inclined her head. 'Lucy said that an important policeman wished to speak to us. Anything which will help the police with their investigation into the death of Berardi-*san* is important to us.'

Tom looked more closely at her while she was speaking. Mitsumi wasn't as young as he had expected, and her face was obviously used to having a serious expression on it. 'Even so,' he said, 'I've never spoken to a witness in bed before, especially one on the other side of the world.'

Mitsumi's eyes flicked to Kaito, and a sly grin appeared. 'My husband likes to play games late into the night. Anything which brings him to bed early is appreciated.'

'Erm … thank you, Mrs Ikeda. I believe that you spoke to Detective Sergeant Jepson while you were in America. I've read your statement, and it was very helpful.'

'*Arigato*,' said Kaito, smiling and nodding.

'My husband says that he was glad to help.'

Tom got the feeling that Mitsumi was elaborating a little, but he pressed on. 'Can I ask you a general question?' She nodded back to him. 'If I may say so, you did very well to sign John Nugent to your company. How did you get to know Giovanni Berardi? How did you get so close to John Nugent?'

She blinked, then turned to her husband. Tom sat patiently for about two minutes, watching two Japanese newlyweds in their pyjamas, in bed, having a full and frank exchange of views in a language that was completely beyond him. At one point, Kaito shook his fist at her, and she slapped his wrist, and things got very intense. Then they stopped. Mitsumi turned back to the camera.

'Forgive me, Inspector. Some of this I did not know. It happened before I met my husband.' She closed her eyes. 'Do you know the football player Owain Marshall?'

Tom knew the name: it was on the lease agreement for Berardi's Maserati. 'Yes, another one of Gary White's footballers.'

Mitsumi shook her head. She had loosely pinned up her hair, and some of it dropped down. Kaito leaned over and brushed it out of her face. 'No, Inspector, that was the problem. Marshall-san is a client of Isaac Redmond.'

Tom jerked forward. How had he missed that? Probably because Marshall lived north of Liverpool, not on the Estate.

Mitsumi continued. 'My husband met the Merseyside United team when they played in Japan, and he met Mr Redmond there too. Mr Redmond introduced my husband to Mr Marshall and they talked about a deal, but it was no use.'

'Why not?'

Mitsumi lowered her eyes. 'My husband does not like Merseyside. He only cares for Trafford Rangers.'

Aah. A fanatic. 'What happened next?'

'Nothing, for a long time. Then Mr Redmond called my husband. He had a young lady with him in London who translated. Mr Redmond said that he had a friend who could put Kaito in touch with John Nugent.' She waved her hand in annoyance. 'This I did not know. It happened two days before we met, and on our first date I had to translate an email from Gianni. I did not know that this was all new.'

'Has your husband ever spoken to Mr Redmond since then?'

Kaito had been dividing his attention between his wife and the camera, but he answered this question before Mitsumi could say anything further. 'Redmond say "Never again." He say we never speak again until Nugent-*san* is in Japan.'

Tom bowed to the screen. 'The police are very grateful for your help. Another officer may be in touch soon. But not during the night, I hope.'

The couple bowed. 'Please give our regards to Lucy,' said Mitsumi.

'I shall,' said Tom, and severed the connection.

He sat back and cradled his mug of tea. This was bad news in all sorts of ways. He sent a text to Elaine: *On my way over*.

He bumped into Saul on the way out. 'Do you know a patrol officer called Gavin?'

'Sure. He's an ex-trainee with Trafford Rangers. Broke his leg at eighteen years old:never walked properly since. He was Gary's client, and Gary got him a job here while he decides how to spend his compensation money. He's been with us a while now. Good officer.'

'Thanks.'

Tom was thinking so hard that he walked past his car without realising. When he had doubled back and got in, he put the radio on to distract him. It didn't work.

Elaine had the kettle on back at Lyme Court, and even held out a sandwich bag when he took his coat off.

'I'll swap you,' he said, taking the baton out of his coat pocket. 'Sorry … I haven't cleaned the blood off.'

'Nice one, sir.'

'I'm serious. It was only a flesh wound, but I did use it on the England captain.'

'Sir! Has he complained?'

'Self-defence.'

She stood there, still holding the brown bag. Tom put the baton on the desk, and took the sandwich. 'You first,' he said. 'I'm hungry.'

Lucy spent the rest of the afternoon trying to distract two increasingly worried children, then had to collect a third from Infants, and later Ellie from the bus stop. She knew what time the infant school finished, and Lucy wasn't insured for the Nugents' cars, so she had called her dad.

'I don't know how you get landed with this sort of thing,' he said when she climbed into the BMW. Because of his own young tribe, there were two child seats in the back already. The youngest Nugent played happily with two dinosaurs, and the next one watched a video on her iPad as Gary drove through the Estate and on to the main road. He put the children's favourite music on the system to give them some relative privacy.

'Sorry, Dad, but there was a crisis, and Holly asked me step in. Don't worry, they're paying me. Unlike Robyn,' she added. She rarely missed a chance to get in a dig at her stepmother.

Dad surprised her by biting back, something he rarely did. 'Phoenix and the boys are your family too, even if you don't get on with their mother. You should care about them as much as you cared about Gianni, God rest his soul.'

Lucy flushed, grateful for the gathering darkness. 'Yeah, well … I've got nothing against them, have I?'

'Robyn has a lot to cope with. You should cut her some slack.'

And Robyn has a lot of help, too, she thought.

'Besides,' said Dad, 'do you want to spend the rest of your life working for babysitter money? I had a look through the shutters this morning. You've got hardly any stock left, and I reckon Mama's going to have other things on her mind, as you no doubt discovered at the weekend.' He paused and let this sink in, just to show he had been thinking about her, then he added, 'Is she okay?'

'She's fine, and so's the baby. So far.'

He was getting close to the small prep school where Holly had lodged her second child. It was more expensive and exclusive than the one patronised by Robyn. He slowed down to give him more time.

'I can tell you're not keen on joining White-Berardi, love, and I can understand that, but does that shop really have a future?'

'I don't know, Dad — but if I don't try and make a go of it, where will I be?'

'How about this? instead of joining the firm, why not quit while you're ahead? That shop is worth a lot more now than when you took it over. A hell of a lot more. The auditors would be quite happy for the company to buy back the lease for much more than you paid, and that would wipe out your debt too. You'd be in profit then.'

She turned to look at him. This was interference, yes, but it was welcome. Dad was giving her a real option, but there was a big problem. 'But I'd have no capital, beyond what I could get for selling the stock, and some money in the bank. I'd be no better off than when I started.'

'That's where you're wrong,' he said confidently. 'You've got a profit-making business under your belt – a real feather in your cap – and that's not all. You've got the shares that Gianni left you, and they're worth a lot.'

She shot straight back. 'I wouldn't sell them.'

'I know you wouldn't, and that's why Robyn came up with this idea.'

Robyn? Since when did Robyn have thoughts about Lucy's future, unless it was about getting rid of her?

'Robyn suggested that we could either buy them off you at a fair price, or you could use them as collateral for a loan, and we'd lend you the money. That way, you'd still get the dividends.'

It was a tempting thought. Very tempting. Her dad parked outside the school, and Lucy prepared to collect her charge (luckily, Holly had registered her with the school as an appropriate adult). She put her hand on the door handle and her father added, 'It's like the Crown Jewels, isn't it? Kings and queens used to pawn them, only nowadays they put them in the Tower of London and charge a fortune to visitors.'

When they returned to the Estate with all three children in the back, Dad said, 'I'll walk home and you can keep the car for the evening. That way you can collect Ellie from the bus stop later.'

'Thanks a million, Dad,' she said, planting a big kiss on his cheek.

'Ugh,' said the middle Nugent. 'Kissing … ugh.'

Lucy turned round. 'I'll kiss you later.'

'No! Urgh!' they said, giggling.

There was still no sign of John when she got in. That was when she ordered the pizzas, in desperation. Holly wouldn't be worrying about her children's diet today. Finally, at five o'clock, John came downstairs looking exhausted. 'I need to speak to your dad,' he said.

Hearing his voice again sparked a jolt of realisation in Lucy's brain as it put two things together. At the play barn she had been thinking about Holly, about the wound on John's face, and about the baton in Tom's hand. She had barely registered John's comments, until she heard his voice again, and remembered what her father had said: *the Crown Jewels*. Gianni had said he needed the money to get back the "Crown Jewels" and Dad had said the same thing. Was it a coincidence, or were they both talking about Gianni's 25% stake in White-Berardi?

That was a very uncomfortable thought, and it sat uneasily in the back of her mind as she asked John what he wanted Dad for.

'It's going to be a tough call — convincing him that the England captain needs to up sticks and leave, just like that. I may need some help.'

'Don't look at me,' said Lucy.

John looked desperate, and Lucy realised that Holly's mental health, possibly her life, might be at stake. She didn't want her father putting pressure on John to stay on the Estate if it meant putting Holly at risk. She knew someone who owed her a favour, and would definitely keep his mouth shut.

'Shall I call Tom?' she said. 'The friendly policeman. He might convince Dad, if no one else can.'

John flopped down on the same step where Holly had collapsed earlier. 'You can call the Pope if you think he'll help out,' he said.

Lucy pointed up the stairs. 'Shall I…?'

'No. She won't see anyone at the moment.' He sniffed. 'Is that pizza? Good choice, Lucy. Order a pepperoni and a Hawaiian, would you? And a bottle of red wine.'

He clambered to his feet and walked back up the staircase.

Lucy took out her phone, and a shadow moved by the doorway to the family kitchen. Ellie stepped forward.

'What's going on, Auntie Lucy?'

Lucy had never seen a child so afraid in her life. 'I need your help, Ellie,' she said. 'Things are going to be difficult tonight.'

'What do you think?' asked Elaine, when they had both finished bringing the other up to speed on their separate adventures.

'What do you think?' responded Tom. 'I'm the boss. I get to go last.'

She gave him a look. 'Giovanni Berardi was a chancer, a philanderer, a manipulator, a blackmailer, a schemer, a gossip, a spy. All in all, a double-dealing back-stabbing bastard. Not bad for someone in their twenties. I'm surprised he lived that long.'

'Brilliant. Thank you, Elaine. I know which piece I'm missing now.'

She stared, open-mouthed. 'I'm sorry, sir. I didn't mean it to come out like that. I was just giving my gut reaction first rather than go over the facts. I'll start again.'

'I'm being serious,' he said. 'You could have summed it up in one word, though: Gianni was a compulsive gambler.'

She swallowed. 'That's two words.'

'So it is.'

'Why does that make a difference? His gambling, I mean.'

'How did he pay off his debts so quickly?'

'I don't know. I doubt that he did it with a big win; compulsive gamblers never quit while they're ahead.'

'They don't. When he died, he had nothing of value except his shares in White-Berardi, and that cash in his house. According to John Nugent, Berardi wanted the cash so that he could "get back the Crown Jewels". The "Crown Jewels" must be his shares, and they must have been in hock for a loan.'

'Hock?'

'Security. Who would have lent him that sort of money, and taken the shares as security? It certainly wasn't a bank.' He leaned forward to reinforce his point. 'Gianni was murdered on the day he collected that money. It has to be the trigger.'

She blew out her cheeks. 'It can only have been Isaac Redmond who loaned him the money, or someone from White-Berardi.'

'I doubt that it's Isaac. According to the Ikedas, Isaac only got access to Gianni last year. The gambling debts were paid off before that.'

'You've met him more than me: do you think it's Paul Warren?'

'No. That only leaves Gary.'

'His father? Surely that's impossible. Psychologically and physically impossible.'

'I'm not sure about the psychology, but I saw him very soon after the murder. If he was the killer, how did he get rid of the clothes so quickly? He was spotless when I saw him.'

'He would have known that we had no warrant to search his house. He could stash them and then get rid of them.'

'I know. Without that forensic evidence, we'll never pin him down.'

'What shall we do?'

'For now, nothing. No one's going anywhere, so let's get everything written down from today. A lot has happened, one way and another.'

They both switched on their computers and began entering the reports. Tom was nearly finished when he looked up and saw it was dark. 'More tea before the last lap,' he said, standing and stretching. At that point his phone rang: it was Lucy.

'Hello,' he said. 'I've put you on speaker.' Right now, Tom did not want anything connected to Gary White to be said without a witness.

'Oh,' said Lucy in a small voice. 'Who's there?'

'DC Fraser.'

'Okay.' The disembodied voice rallied a little. 'She knows what's going on with Holly, right?'

'She does.'

'We've got a problem. My dad needs to be convinced that this is so serious that John and Holly have to get out of Dodge asap, and we have to do it without telling him that Holly is the Mother Superior.'

Tom cringed. That wasn't like Lucy: she must be under a lot of pressure to reach for the cliché jar. 'I see. How can I help?'

'I'm still at *Casa Nugent*. Dad's coming over soon. It would really help if you could be here … put the sort of pressure on him that you did on John. Without the baton, obviously.'

Elaine stifled a snort. Tom was torn. He had a duty to help Holly, for Lucy's sake. She had risked a lot for him. How that would affect Gary he had no idea. 'We'll come,' he said.

'We?' said Lucy. 'Wouldn't that be a bit … scary?'

'DC Fraser has other strengths. She can make the tea and look after the children.'

Elaine's stare bored into him. He would pay for that later.

'Thanks, Tom — I mean DCI Morton.'

When Tom had put his phone in his pocket, Elaine said, 'Scary? Really?'

'She calls you Scarywoman. If the cap fits…'

'I'm on overtime, right?'

'Yes. And antisocial hours. Let's go.'

The gates to *Casa Nugent* were open, as were the double doors. Tom walked under the canopy and into the house. A slight figure appeared from his right — a young girl wearing baggy clothes. How old could she be? Ten? Twelve?

'You must be the police,' she said. 'I'm Eleanor Nugent.' She folded her hands in front of her, pressing the fingers towards the floor. 'Lucy said I should show you through to the dining room or the kitchen. My parents will be down shortly.'

Tom decided on twelve going on thirty. 'Thank you, Miss Nugent. I know the way to the dining room, but I got lost going to the kitchen. Perhaps you could take my colleague with you.'

The girl jerked her head in a fast nod, but said nothing. Elaine looked at him, concern all over her face. She was right: this was a very strange household if they thought it appropriate to send a child to act as footman. Tom nodded his head towards the family zone, and Elaine followed in the precisely laid heel-and-toe footsteps of Eleanor Nugent.

The door to the party room was ajar, and Tom slipped through. He took the route round the right so that the carpet would absorb the sound, and so that the fireplace would screen him from the dining area. At the far end of the room, Lucy and Gary White were sitting at the table, both with a drink in front of them. Tom slowed down to hear what they were saying.

'We're going round in circles,' said Gary. 'If you won't tell me what's the matter with Holly, let's change the subject.'

Lucy had her arms folded, and was sitting away from her father. 'All right,' she said. 'Tell me about the Crown Jewels.'

Tom froze, one foot in the air.

'What you talking about?' said Gary.

'Gianni owed a lot of money to the casino, didn't he?'

'That's ancient history, love. What's brought this on?'

'It's not that ancient. It was only a couple of years ago. Where did he get the money from to pay it back?'

'I don't know. Honest.'

She lunged forward. 'Don't lie to me, Dad. You loaned it to him, didn't you? And you took his shares as security.'

'What else was I to do? He could have wrecked the business if he carried on gambling. The only way I could stop him was to bail him out and bring him home. What do they call it…? An intervention … that's right. I told him, "You've got to stop, Gianni, and you've got to live on the Estate." I told him, "If I bail you out, I want it paid back with hard work." And he did. Paid in full.'

'When?'

'Why do you want to know that?'

'Just tell me, Dad. When did he pay you back?'

'Six months ago, I think.'

'No, he didn't. That money on his table, on the day he died … that was the repayment, wasn't it?'

Gary put his hand to his chest. Tom couldn't see his face properly, but under the lights, he could see sweat glistening on the bald head. He didn't answer his daughter's question.

'Did you see him, Dad?' She put her hand on his left arm and shook it. 'Did you see him on the day he died? Did you?'

'Leave it, Lucy. Stop there. You can't ask me that.'

She released his arm, and put her hand in her mouth. 'Oh, God, what have you done?' She scrambled back, knocking over the chair. With a bump, she backed into the French windows.

'Calm down, Lucy. The police are coming. In fact, you'd better leave now. We can talk about this later.'

Lucy was terrified. Not physically, Tom could tell that, but every other aspect of her world had come apart at the seams. He stepped forward a pace.

'I don't think there's going to be a "later", Mr White.'

'What the fuck?' Gary scrambled to his feet, turning his head from Tom to Lucy. 'Did you set this up? Have you sold me out, Lucy?'

She was sobbing, shaking her head and still biting her knuckle to stop herself speaking.

'If I know your daughter,' said Tom, 'she'd rather get on a plane and leave the country than see you again. Not because she hates you, but because she's frightened that she'll give you away.'

Gary stared at Tom, flicking his eyes over Tom's shoulder to see if there was anyone else coming. He took two steps forward. Tom braced himself, ready to scream for help. He hoped it wouldn't come to that.

'Where are the clothes?' said Tom. 'Who helped you get rid of them?'

Gary tensed his fists.

'It was Robyn,' said Lucy. 'She went to Southfork before she came to the office. On the day that Gianni died. He must have told her to hide them before she joined us.'

Instead of launching himself at Tom, Gary spun round to face his daughter. 'Leave her out of it.'

It clicked into place: Lucy wouldn't accuse her father of murder, but she was happy to implicate her stepmother in a conspiracy. Tom stepped forward, into Gary's space. The other man stepped back and raised his fists.

'Fifteen years,' said Tom. 'Probably. Half off for good behaviour, definitely. Tell me where the clothes are now, and I give my word that Robyn won't be prosecuted for perverting the course of justice.'

Gary flicked a smile. 'How do you know we didn't burn them?'

'Because you're not a career criminal, Mr White. You suddenly found yourself with a bag full of blood-stained evidence. Normal people are so scared of it being discovered that they can't throw it away. Normal people watch TV and see the police searching through bins and rubbish bags. You've hidden those clothes, probably in the grounds of your house, but they are still there. I saw your barbecue: it's gas. Perhaps if it was the summer, and you had a fire pit…'

'What's going on?'

All three of them turned to find John Nugent standing by the door.

'Go and get my colleague from the kitchen, sir, please,' said Tom. 'And take Miss White with you.'

'I'm all right, John,' said Lucy. 'Quickly, go and get the policewoman. For Holly's sake, please.'

Nugent took two steps back, then turned and ran.

'Where are they?' said Tom.

'Where do you think? Bottom of the septic tank. Every other house is on mains drainage except us. Don't make Lucy watch this … please.'

'I don't think I can stop her.' He took a deep breath. 'Gary White, I am arresting you on suspicion of murder. You do not have to say anything, but it may harm your defence if you do not mention when questioned something which you later rely on in court. Anything you do say may be given in evidence. Do you understand that?'

'Yeah.'

'Gary, did you kill your son?'

'Stepson. In the end, the little git forgot he was supposed to be family. He was going to ruin everything.' He shrugged.

'Dad. No. Please, no.'

Elaine ran into the room, followed by John Nugent. Tom turned to Lucy. 'You've seen enough. Please, take John out and explain that he must put Holly first, no matter what happens.'

'Gary?' said John. 'What's going on?'

'Go on, son,' said Gary. 'Do what he says.'

John Nugent had spent most of his life doing what Gary said, and tonight was no different. Lucy ran across the room, avoiding her father and grabbed John's arm on the way. Elaine opened her arms in a *What?* gesture.

'Mr White,' said Tom. 'You have been cautioned. Do we have your permission to search your property for items relating to Giovanni Berardi's murder?'

'Yes, yes — but get me out of here first.'

'DC Fraser, would you escort Mr White to my car? I'm going to make a phone call.'

'Sir.'

'The bastard's going to win after all,' said Gary.

'Who?'

'Isaac bloody Redmond, that's who. He'll be on the phone to Paul by nine o'clock tomorrow, with an offer on the table by noon.' He gave a bitter snort and moved towards Elaine. As he went past Tom, Gary hissed, 'If you go back on your word about Robyn, I'll kill you. Got that?'

'I never go back on my word, Mr White.'

As Elaine led Gary through the double doors, Tom dialled Rod Stamp's number.

'Rod, are you at work?'

'Just leaving now.'

'Take your coat off. You're going to have a busy night.'

Chapter 20

Tuesday 28 January

Elaine liked trains, but she didn't obsess about them. It was a good job she liked them, because both her father and her brother were locomotive drivers. Since Dad had taken early retirement from the network, he had been the principal volunteer driver on a heritage railway, so she had certainly experienced her share of steam and smoke-filled platforms. They looked good on TV, but the reality was a lot smellier.

Freezing fog was creeping under the canopy and sending its fingers to tweak her nose as she waited for the train from Euston, clutching Tom's Post-It note in her gloved hand. He had passed it to her just before midnight, telling her that she needed an early night.

'What for?' she had asked.

'Early start, Constable.'

'I'm not going to like this, sir, am I?'

'That depends. You might get on famously.'

'Who with?'

'With whom.'

'Whatever.'

She looked at the note: *08:45, Platform 5, Man. Piccadilly.*

'You're collecting Leonie,' he had said, 'then bringing her to Lyme Court. You can collect breakfast as well.'

So there she was, freezing her tits off in the gloom, waiting for the Deputy Director of CIPPS. The train was ten minutes late.

She walked back into the relative warmth of the concourse, but the bustle of commuters made her head throb, and she couldn't face any more coffee. She went with the flow, trying to unkink her muscles in a circuit round the station, then resumed her position as the red Pendolino glided towards the buffers with a textbook braking manoeuvre. There was a flood of suits dashing towards the exit when the doors were released, followed by older travellers, and then the suitcase brigade.

Elaine was standing at the end of the first class section so that Ms Spence would have to pass her (Tom said that CIPPS' expenses policy was quite rigid about travelling in standard class seats). The last two out of first class were a middle-aged man and a much younger woman, fussing about who should carry the cases. She heard her call him *Dad*, then he turned, and she recognised his face from the research she'd done last night: Isaac Redmond was in town.

Gary was right, she thought. *The vultures are definitely circling.* She shivered again and turned her attention back to the standard class carriages. She had also looked up Leonie (discreetly), and saw her boss's boss approaching, wheeling a case and talking to another woman.

Leonie looked much better in life than on her driving licence. She was swaddled in several layers on top, but they all stopped at the waist, so as not to hide her tailored trousers and killer heels. She must have a high pain threshold to have travelled from London in those. Leonie had a slightly pixie face and clear skin that made her look years younger than forty-two, an impression that was accentuated by the blue clip holding back her fringe. Elaine was unsure how to respond. Tom was clearly wary of his boss — but for the life of her, Elaine couldn't see why.

Leonie was saying something funny to the other woman, who gave a smoker's laugh in response. She was clearly older, and had a style all of her own. She wore a long woollen coat in green, and was busy wrapping a red scarf round her neck against the cold. Her brown knee-length boots looked old and comfortable, but expensive, like her hair. Leonie's was a light brown, immaculately bobbed to shoulder length: the other woman's was long and wild, but still had that salon shine. What it didn't have was dye: most of it was grey. When the women were ten feet away, Elaine held out her warrant card.

'DC Fraser, ma'am. DCI Morton sent me to collect you.'

Leonie stuck out her hand. 'Leonie Spence, and don't call me *ma'am*. I'm your boss, not your senior officer. I prefer first names.' She gestured to the other woman. 'This is Miss Juliet Porterhouse, of the *Sunday Examiner*.'

They shook hands, and Juliet said, 'I recognised you from the picture.'

'Don't,' said Elaine. 'It will only encourage him.'

'Who?' said Leonie. 'What picture?'

'We're in the Transport Police car park,' said Elaine. 'This way.'

She marched off, her cheeks burning as she heard Juliet telling Leonie about the photo of her in Rome. It had been funny, and quite touching, when Tom had presented her with the laminated copy — but hearing Leonie ask Juliet whether Elaine had been wearing a Scotland shirt was a little creepy. She shuddered, and accelerated towards the exit.

The reporter was still with them when she arrived at the car, and Leonie said, 'Can we give Juliet a lift to Wythenshawe?'

'Of course, ma'am, but we're going to Lyme Court. It's where DCI Morton set up our base, and he's meeting us there.'

Leonie frowned, either at the accidental use of *ma'am*, or at the unexpected destination. 'How far out of the way is it?'

'About twenty minutes.'

Leonie smiled. 'That's okay. Let's go, Constable.'

With a reporter on board, they couldn't talk about the case, so Leonie amused herself by asking what it was like being married to an international athlete. Elaine couldn't decide whether the innuendo was about Rob's wealth or his sexual prowess. Judging from the way that Juliet snorted, she guessed the latter.

'I wouldn't know,' said Elaine. 'I've never been married to anyone else. Suits me well enough.'

Leonie gave her an appraising look, and changed the subject. Elaine was feeling slightly nervous when Juliet got out of the car: was Leonie going to do something *really* unpleasant, like put her hand on Elaine's thigh?

When the boot slammed down, Leonie heaved a sigh of relief. 'God, I hate being nice to the press. Gets right up my nose.'

'You seemed to be making a good job of it, if you don't mind me saying.'

'Careful, Elaine. Never confuse the job with the person who's doing it. Juliet Porterhouse is much nicer than Paul Ogden, my boss, but I know who I'd rather have behind me in a fight.'

Elaine kept her peace.

'How's Tom?' said Leonie.

'Tired, I imagine. He was still going when he sent me home last night.'

'But he's been okay, mostly?'

Elaine locked her hands on the wheel and stared ahead. 'It's been a pleasure to work for DCI Morton. He's a very good boss.'

'I know that, dammit, I'm worried about him.'

'He's fine, Leonie.'

There was a pause, then her passenger shifted around. 'He hasn't told you, has he?'

'Told me what? He's told me about his divorce, his dad's knighthood and his mother's cooking, but that's about all.'

Leonie sighed. 'Have you noticed anything about his left arm? The top part, especially.'

Elaine shifted in her seat, and checked her mirrors. 'I've noticed that he rubs it when he's thinking, or stressed.'

'If he doesn't want to tell you, then you'll have to dig it out for yourself. It's not a big secret. Well, not all of it. Anyway, has this Gary White person confessed yet, or are we looking at a disaster?'

'I think they're playing chicken. Gary won't confess until he's certain that his wife isn't going to be charged with assisting an offender, and Rod Stamp won't give that assurance until they've drained the septic tank and found the clothing. They'll be doing that around now, I imagine.'

'Eeuw. Gross. Honest opinion: did Gary do it?'

'Absolutely. One hundred per cent. I saw the look on his daughter's face five seconds after he confessed to killing her brother.'

'Oh. That can't have been a pleasant sight.'

'Even worse for Tom,' said Elaine. It slipped out before she could stop herself. Leonie picked up on it straight away.

'What's she like? Young? Pretty?'

Damn and double damn. Elaine wondered how to row back from this one … then she remembered her orders, and took a sharp left into a lay-by with a chuck waggon. 'Sorry, Leonie. With taking Juliet to Wythenshawe, I forgot about getting the breakfasts in. Did you eat on the train?'

Leonie gave her a level stare, then decided not to push the point about Lucy White, much to Elaine's relief. 'Just a bacon sandwich for me,' she said. 'I presume Tom will have the kettle on.'

'Always,' said Elaine, then she jumped out of the car before Leonie changed her mind.

The phone call to Mama had been the hardest part. After that, everything else seemed straightforward.

Lucy had been forced to call the landline in Italy when Mama's phone went to voicemail, and then she had to negotiate with Enrico, telling him that it was important without giving anything away. Mama didn't believe her at first, which made it ten times worse, and then she had screamed and dropped the phone. The next hour was even more surreal than the moment Dad had confessed: Mama kept coming back to the phone, crying, going for a lie down, shouting instructions to Enrico and asking questions that Lucy couldn't answer. Finally, she heard Enrico tell Mama to take a sedative. He came back on the line and said that he would look after her, and Lucy had to trust him.

All that had happened in the sumptuous surroundings of Holly's Principal Guest Bedroom. As soon as John had told his wife about the arrest, Holly had rallied: finding someone in deeper shit than herself had brought her back down to earth.

Unfortunately, Lucy reckoned that Holly had also gone back into denial about being the Mother Superior — and now the England captain had gone AWOL from training, and the press were smelling a rat. Dealing with that sort of crap was Dad's job, but Dad was in jail.

She and Holly had sat up until the small hours with a bottle of wine. Then she'd crashed out until Ellie stuck her head round the door, already in her school uniform. To Lucy's mortal shame, she had been forced to borrow some of Ellie's clothes before she left. The top was big enough, but the leggings were a little tight in the wrong places. She had said that she'd get some clothes from Southfork, but the whole property was sealed off by the police.

It was going to take a long time before she could adjust to Dad's guilt — if he was guilty and not covering up for Robyn. In fact, that would be him all over: it was much easier to believe that the evil stepmother had killed Gianni, and that Dad was taking the blame. Much easier to believe that than to believe that Gary White had held his son face down in a puddle and drowned him.

'How is he?' she asked Paul when he picked her up at ten to nine.

He looked composed on the surface, but his eyes seemed to have disappeared inside his skull. Lucy had no idea what he was thinking. 'I don't know,' he said. 'I only saw him for a short while, before a criminal specialist took over. I don't think the police were happy about me being there at all, but Gary insisted…'

'What? What did he insist?'

Paul's moustache moved from side to side. The car was still stationary. 'He told DS Jepson that I had to be there, or the deal was off.'

'What deal?'

Paul sighed. 'A confession, I'm afraid.'

'Did he…?'

'He didn't talk about what happened with Gianni. All he wanted to do was to talk about how I should deal with Isaac Redmond.'

'How could he! How could he think about that at a time like this?'

Paul turned to face her, and she could see the pain and exhaustion now that his eyes were in focus. 'He said that it was his only weapon, his only lever. If he didn't get the right deal, there would be no money for Robyn, and he'd never see Phoenix and the boys again.'

The coffee that had been Lucy's only breakfast started to rise in her throat, and she loosened her seat belt. She made an effort to swallow, and said, 'Did he say anything about me or Mama? Anything?'

Paul put his hand lightly on her shoulder. 'The first thing he said to me when they brought him into the room was this: "Lucy's lost her dad tonight. Time to step up to the plate, Godfather." I think he'd been rehearsing it on the way over.'

If Paul hadn't been such a nice bloke, she would have hit him for repeating that. Lucy didn't need a father figure. She needed her dad. You can't resign from being a father … not really. She let go of the seatbelt, and it snapped back into the reel. 'Let's go.'

He drove out of the Estate and dropped her at the front door of White-Berardi, where a uniformed police officer was keeping the pavement clear of the media. He said he was going to park the car at the end of the Village rather than risk an ambush in car park.

Lucy dashed across the pavement and up the stairs. Alone in the middle of the office stood Grace. Lucy was bracing herself for sympathy from her friend, but all she could see was cold fury.

'You and your fucking family,' said Grace.

Lucy recoiled from the venom in her friend's voice, and stood with her mouth open.

'Isaac Redmond's on his way over to close us down, and I'll be out of a job by lunchtime,' continued Grace. 'I've heard about those shares Gianni left you. You'll be all right and I'll be unemployed, thanks to your brother and your father.'

Lucy latched on to the only thing in Grace's tirade that made sense. 'I'll insist that they keep you on. In fact, I'll insist that they make you office manager. I owe you that much, after you bombed your GCSEs to keep me company.'

It was Grace's turn to stand open-mouthed.

'I was talking to someone last week,' said Lucy. 'He made me realise that I probably dragged you down with me after Mama left and Robyn moved in.' She shrugged. 'I've always wondered why you didn't come to sixth form college with me.'

Grace collapsed on the nearest chair. 'It wasn't you,' she said. Her shoulders started to heave, and sobs dragged themselves out her throat. 'It wasn't … you. It was Gianni. I was pregnant when he went to Italy.'

Oh shit. 'Did…?'

'I had an abortion, of course.'

'Then why did you come here to work?'

Grace turned to face Lucy, mascara streaming down her cheeks. 'To be near him again. To get him out of my system. I don't know. It doesn't matter now, does it?'

'Is everything okay?'

Lucy whirled round to find Paul standing in the doorway.

'Not really,' said Lucy. 'I think Isaac might have to wait downstairs for a while. By the way, where is everyone?'

'So this is what you've been spending my money on,' said Leonie, looking around the two-room rented office in Lyme Court.

'To be accurate,' said Tom, 'part was paid by the 7Bridge Estate, part by the Foreign Office and part by SLC. I haven't been a drain on CIPPS budget since I started back in January. You should give me a bonus. And Elaine. By the way, what have you done with her?'

Leonie waved a hand towards the door. 'She's reheating the breakfast buns in the kitchen. She's a bit different to Kris Hayes.'

'In some ways. They're both good coppers. Elaine's just a bit older — a bit more experienced in CID. She's a bit more volatile, too.'

'Hmm. We'll finish this conversation later. Here she is.'

No one spoke during the ritual consumption of the breakfast rolls, and Leonie excused herself afterwards. Tom raised an eyebrow to Elaine, who shook her head in response.

'Don't ask,' she said. 'I have no comment to make whatsoever about Ms Spence.'

'Wise move.'

'There is something you can tell me,' she said, wiping the last of the red sauce off her mouth. 'A few days ago, you said you'd done a deal with Juliet Porterhouse. I met her this morning.'

'Eh?'

'She was making friends with Leonie on the journey up from London. Have they met before, do you know?'

'On my last case.'

Elaine gave him a look that said *I know something, but not everything.* Tom kept a blank face, until he realised that he was rubbing his left arm. Damn. Elaine had noticed too, but she changed the subject. 'A few days ago, you said that you'd done a deal with Juliet — an interview with her about 7Bridge in exchange for information.'

'I did.'

'You also said there was a forfeit in case we couldn't deliver.' Elaine leaned into his space and continued. 'What was it?'

'I promised to put her in touch with former Squadron Leader Conrad Clarke, a man I'm not sure even exists in this world any more.' It was an honest answer, but not one that would make any sense to Elaine.

'Oh,' she said.

'And for you…'

'For me? What did you sign me up for? Without my permission, I might add.'

'An interview, obviously. With their *Examiner Life* Sunday magazine, talking about life as a rugby wife. That sort of thing.'

'I could live with that, I suppose,' she said, and then she saw the smile lingering on his lips. 'What? What else?'

'I also promised a photograph. In uniform.'

Elaine raised her arm to hit him, but heard Leonie's heels tracking down the corridor. 'Later,' she scowled.

Those were two conversations he wasn't looking forward to. Tom topped up their mugs, and was about to start speaking when his phone rang: it was Rod Stamp.

'My boss has come up,' said Tom. 'Do you mind if I put you on speaker?'

'Fine.' Rod paused while Tom made the adjustment. 'Good news, Tom. He's just confessed.'

'Brilliant. What happened?'

'We found a package in the septic tank. Luckily for us, he'd wrapped it pretty well, so the inside won't be contaminated. Forensic won't open it until later, but simply having it was enough. It allowed us to threaten him — to tell him that we could now arrest Mrs Robyn White, who would grass on him to save her own skin. Either that or he had to trust us and make a full statement, which he's doing right now. You were right about everything, more or less.'

'Thanks, Rod. How much more input do you want from me … us.'

'According to the FLO, you seem to have had more contact with the firm than anyone. Can you follow up the Isaac Redmond angle? I understand he's in a meeting with Mr Warren and Miss White this morning.'

'No problem.'

'And one other thing. You'll have to tell me what Berardi was using as blackmail over John Nugent.'

'I wasn't joking, Rod. That information really is a national security issue. I can give you the name of someone in the secret service, if you want, or you can take the Deputy Director's word. Leonie?'

She leaned towards the phone. 'I'm afraid so, DCI Stamp. Now you have a confession, that information is going to be sealed under the ninety-nine year rule.'

'Well, bugger me,' said Stamp. 'Now I've heard everything. It's official: the England football team are protected by MI5.'

'MI6, but never mind,' said Leonie.

Tom thanked his colleague and disconnected the call.

A smile played around his boss's lips. 'So, Tom, you were right about everything. You'd better tell me about it too.'

'Almost everything,' said Tom. He took a long preparatory draught from his mug, and sat back in his chair. 'It was all about the family business in the end. Gary White had brought up Gianni from a few months old – never treated him as anything but a son – until Berardi betrayed the family business by selling out to Isaac Redmond.'

'Go on,' she said.

'If it had been the other way around, if Gianni had killed his father, then his defence team would be finding a psychologist to testify that he had an addictive personality disorder.' Elaine pulled a face. 'I agree. What can't be argued is that Berardi *was* addicted to risk. For years he satisfied that through gambling, but addicts never win.'

'No, they don't,' said Leonie.

'When Gary bailed him out, with a £200,000 loan, he took Gianni's shares as security and made him toe the line. After that, Gianni got his thrills from driving and a lot of casual sex.'

'Bit of a cliché.'

'Quite. And just as unsatisfying, which is why he started to raise the stakes. Gianni knew that unless he could get the £200,000 cash, he would forever be in his father's debt, and have no choice about what to do in life. If Gary foreclosed on the loan, Berardi would have no assets whatsoever. So he did a deal with Isaac Redmond, Gary's biggest rival.'

Leonie looked puzzled. 'That's a big risk to take, for potentially very little reward. Redmond wasn't offering shares in his own business.'

'Gianni didn't use his shares. I may never find out all the details, but Redmond was paying the lease on a Maserati, in exchange for information and access. Gianni used his own instincts to identify the Mother Superior and put the squeeze on John Nugent.' Tom shuddered inside. 'It was just a good job he didn't try blackmailing Princess Karida.'

'Mmm,' said Leonie. 'Well done to both of you. This has really put CIPPS on the map in the North West.'

'Thank you,' said Tom. 'There should be at least another two weeks' work out of this yet.'

'Good, but that's not why I've dragged myself up here.'

'I thought you missed me,' said Tom.

She stared at him for one second. Then two, three, four. Then she grinned. 'In your dreams, Inspector.' She sat up straight and adjusted the clip in her hair. 'Didn't you tell me you had a sister who lived in Southport?'

'I did. I do.'

'Is she political?'

Tom tilted his head on one side. 'She's a doctor. It's impossible to work in the NHS and not be political to a certain extent. She's also on the parochial church council.'

'But she's not active in any political party?'

'She's a GP, a mother of two and involved in the church. She doesn't have time for party politics. Nor does her husband.'

'Then she should be good for local knowledge. I'm off to see ACC Schofield shortly.'

'Good luck,' mumbled Elaine. Leonie ignored her.

'Something's kicked off at the other end of SLC's patch; something to do with that by-election they had before Christmas. After yesterday, I'm sure he'll realise what good value we offer.' She smiled at Tom, then turned round to look at Elaine. 'You don't have to answer now, Elaine, but I'm sure Tom will want to take you with him if I get the job for us.'

'If it's a choice between DCI Morton and going back to Operation Rewind, put my name down for Southport now.'

'Fine. Can one of you take me to Wythenshawe? That's where I'm meeting him.'

Saul shook his head sadly and said, 'No matter how much you offer, they will offer more. The Ghar'aanian royal family will never share 7Bridge with you. Sorry, Isaac.'

Saul wasn't enjoying this. He wasn't enjoying it at all. When the news broke about Gary's arrest last night, the only response from the Hall had been an ominous silence, until Isaac Redmond appeared on the scene this morning and placed a bid to take over White-Berardi Ltd, including its 20% stake in the Estate.

Saul had been given his orders, but was disobeying one of them. Instead of dealing with Isaac by phone, he had invited him over to the Estate Office, where they were sharing lunch and a cigar.

'I know…they can…afford it,' said Isaac, keeping his cigar going, 'but why did they let Gary have the stake in the first place?'

'I wasn't here then, but I believe that they needed a magnet — someone to start the community off, and to act as a draw for other talent. Gary was very good at that.'

'He was. Still is, I suppose. After all, he's not dead, is he?'

Saul said nothing.

Isaac got his cigar glowing and continued. 'Gary White knows more about football — and more about the way footballers think - than I ever will, that's for certain. I like to think I'm better on the business side, and on selling the dream. It's a shame we had to be rivals. Why won't the royal family let me buy Gary's stake?'

'Do you need me to spell it out?'

Isaac looked at the end of his cigar. 'Yes, I do.'

'J-E-W. The royal family will never sell to one of us.'

Something clouded behind Isaac's eyes, and his nostrils flared. 'Then what are you doing here?'

'Trying to get out. I made the mistake of believing the hype, and thinking that it could be different. I sometimes think Miriam started that affair because it was the only way she could escape.'

Isaac finished his coffee and puffed on his cigar. 'How well do you know Paul Warren?'

'Well enough. He's very astute, as I'm sure you've discovered. A little too easy to bluff, in my opinion — which is why he worked with Gary rather than on his own.'

'He's run out of gas,' said Isaac. 'He doesn't know it yet, but when the deal is signed, he's going to grind to a halt. He's got no future with me beyond his local knowledge.'

'Shame. He's a good man.'

'He is, and he'll be hard to replace. I'd need a qualified lawyer who knew the area and the people involved.'

Isaac looked carefully at him, and Saul returned his gaze. Saul didn't like doing business on a nod and a wink, but sometimes you have to play the game. 'How can I help?' he said.

'It would be really useful to know how much the Princess will offer before they call my bluff.'

It was time for Saul to do the same. 'If I come on board with you, I won't force Paul out. He has to walk.'

'He will. Leave that to me. You'll have to accept this woman Grace Revell as your office manager. At least to begin with.'

It was a good deal, even though no salary had been mentioned. Saul would get out of the Estate, he would have a job where he could use some of his connections and he would be poised to return to London, if he chose. He held out his hand. Isaac tapped the ash off his cigar and shook on the deal.

'My instructions were simple,' said Saul. 'I was to double your opening bid, then go as far as three times your first offer. Then I was supposed to call back for further instructions. I'd stop at three times if I were you. The White family will let the rest of the business go for much less when they see what the Princess is offering. I understand Paul has shares, so he'll get a nice lump sum. Should help you convince him to walk away.'

Isaac nodded.

Saul went to his cupboard and pulled out two glasses and a bottle of Polish vodka. He poured two small measures and passed one to Isaac. There was no toast, as such, they just clinked glasses and downed the vodka in one. Saul put the empties on the tray and relit his own cigar. 'What about Dean Rooksby? He must be thrilled.'

'Funnily enough, he isn't. Pleased, yes, but not thrilled. He always knew he hadn't done it. He has to go before a judge to get the case dismissed, but they're removing his electronic tag on Thursday. Dean will go far, mark my words. My first challenge will be dealing with John Nugent.'

'Oh?'

'Sorting him out might be your first job for me, Saul. There's something horribly messy going on with John Nugent, but Lucy White seems to think she knows someone better placed than you to make things happen.'

'Have they told you what the problem is?'

Isaac frowned. 'No, they haven't. I knew he had issues at home, which is how Berardi got a foot in the door, but I've no idea what's going on. Do you?'

'Yes, but I gave my word not to tell anyone. If Lucy can't resolve the issue, let me know straight away.'

Isaac stood up and held out his hand again, this time with more conviction. 'Deal,' he said.

'Deal,' said Saul.

Word of Tom's role in the case must be spreading. When Elaine and her boss arrived at the White-Berardi office, the constable on duty visibly straightened his posture. 'Are you going in, sir?' The young officer didn't so much as glance in her direction.

'Yes,' said Tom. 'Have you had many problems with the press? They don't seem to be around.'

'Round the back, sir. It's too much of a traffic hazard here, so Mr Warren said they could congregate in the back car park. He promised them a statement this afternoon as well.'

'Right. Thanks.'

She followed her boss into the building and up the stairs. He lingered at the top, and she joined him by the glass door that opened into the office. 'Busy,' he said.

He was right. The old White-Berardi staff were seated at their desks, all speaking loudly on their phones. The exceptions were Paul Warren and Grace Revell — who were standing in Gary's office, talking to two women. 'I wonder who they are,' said Tom, pointing at the newcomers.

'The dark-haired one is Isaac Redmond's daughter; I haven't seen the other one before. No sign of Isaac himself.'

'Aren't you well briefed? Nice work. Come on.'

Tom walked through the office without being challenged, and approached the glass-walled command room. Grace saw them coming and stepped outside.

'Thanks for coming,' she said. 'Lucy said she was going to get hold of you, but I didn't think she'd get you here that quickly.'

'She didn't,' said Tom in a flat voice. 'We're here to continue our enquiries. Is Mr Redmond around?'

'He's gone to see Saul Blackstone. Shouldn't be long.' She took some of her hair (which looked rather lank today), and twisted it into a braid. 'Lucy said she was going to ask for your help. Something to do with Holly Nugent.'

'Aah,' said Tom.

'Sir?' said Elaine.

He stepped away from Grace and half whispered to her. 'I made a promise to John Nugent in exchange for his testimony on the cash payments. It looks like I'm being asked to keep that promise.' He shrugged. 'It was worth it.' He turned back to Grace. 'Where is she?'

'Gone to her flat to get changed.' She pointed at the unknown woman in the office. 'Isaac brought his chief PR consultant. She said that Lucy had to support Paul when they make a statement to the media.' Elaine looked more closely at the woman. She hadn't been on the train with Isaac, and wherever she had materialised from, the journey hadn't affected her immaculate suit, hair, makeup or poise.

'We'll go and see her,' said Tom. 'The flat's above the House of Lucia, isn't it?'

'Yeah.' Grace was about to continue, but something struck her. She altered her stance, sticking out a hip and letting go of her hair. She placed the hand on her waist and said, 'The video entry phone doesn't work. Press two short and one long on the bell, then she'll know you're not reporters.'

'Thanks,' said Tom, and led the way out down the back stairs. 'If you weren't here, Elaine, I'd have called you in before I made this visit.'

'I'm sure that wouldn't have been necessary,' she said.

'Sometimes you have to play by the rules,' he said, and opened the back door.

An army of cameras flashed at them, then stopped when they realised who it wasn't. Some of the reporters recognised Tom and started shouting, 'DCI Morton! Can you…?'

Tom ignored them all. Except for Juliet Porterhouse. He made eye contact with her, and nodded, then he pressed through the throng until he came to the barrier that separated Lucy's properties from the White-Berardi car park. A second police officer was on duty there, and Tom had to show his warrant card before being admitted.

He pressed the bell, as Grace had suggested, and the lock buzzed open straight away. Elaine followed him upstairs, until they both stopped dead at the entrance to the living room. It was impossible to believe that Lucy owned both the flat and the sumptuous boutique downstairs. The wallpaper had mould growing on it next to the chimney breast and the gas fire looked like it should be condemned. The smell of damp in her nostrils was a barrier which Elaine had to push through to get inside. Lucy herself was standing, shivering, next to the window that overlooked the car park. She was wrapped in a dressing gown.

She looked up, and her hand flew to her mouth. '*Ohmygod* … it's you. I thought it was Grace. That was her special ring on the bell.'

'She told us to do that,' said Elaine. Tom appeared to have been struck dumb.

Lucy's mouth set in a line. 'I'll have words with her about that later.'

Tom coughed. 'We need to talk, Miss White, but it can wait.'

'Is Isaac back?' asked Lucy.

'No.'

'Then we've got ages.' She picked up some keys from the top of a mahogany-effect sideboard, whose plastic veneer had peeled up where the chipboard underneath had swollen. 'This key opens the front door of the flat. That remote will lift the shutters on the shop and disable the alarm. I'll see you in five minutes.'

Tom took the keys and left without another word. Elaine felt the sticky embrace of the carpet as they crossed the room, and couldn't wait to get outside. From the landing, she caught a glimpse into the only bedroom: a single mattress lay on the floor, and the rest of the room consisted of mobile hanging rails stuffed full of clothes. She was glad that the door to the kitchen was firmly closed.

The shop was as cold as the flat, but Elaine still breathed a sigh of relief when they went inside. Tom dropped the keys on the shop counter, then disappeared. Elaine was taking a closer look at the handbags when Tom reappeared with a fan heater. He turned it on, then disappeared again.

The stitching in the bags was exquisite, and the colours distinctively bold. Elaine took one down and felt her hands glide over the leather. It was brash and confident, but took no shit. Exactly the image of herself she wanted to project.

'They're on special offer,' said Lucy from the doorway. Elaine nearly dropped the bag as she fumbled it back on to the display.

Lucy had opted for a white blouse and black trousers. She had also put her hair up. None of these decisions was the right one, in Elaine's opinion. Perhaps Lucy had been hoping that Grace was coming round to help her choose an outfit.

'Coffee,' said Tom, emerging from the back room with a tray. Lucy slumped on to one of the couches. Remembering how cosy they were, Elaine hooked an upright chair from the dressing table and placed it with her back to the display of bags. Tom and Lucy were avoiding eye contact with each other. This could be very embarrassing. Elaine cleared her throat and four eyes locked on to hers.

Her boss finally found his voice. 'We need to talk to Mr Redmond,' he said, 'but Miss Revell advised me that there was unfinished business with Holly Nugent. How is she?'

'In denial. She thinks that it will all go away if she ignores it.'

Elaine was bursting with curiosity, and decided that if she upset both of them they might start talking to each other. 'Why did she do it?' she asked. 'She must really, really hate herself.'

Lucy flinched back, and Tom's eyes darkened. Lucy turned her body completely towards the opposite couch and said, 'Holly took so much shit when she started her domestic violence campaign that something inside snapped. I think one part of her believed that her whole life on the Estate was a lie. At the same time, she was determined to be the best possible member of the community. I think trying to live two lives sent her a bit loopy.'

'Would that be a technical term?' said Tom with a smile.

Lucy smiled back. 'I did business management at uni, not psychology, but I really believe that she won't get better until she can start living a different life — and that has to start now.'

'What does John say?'

'We came up with a plan. John is going to fake an injury that needs specialist treatment in Japan. They all go over, but Holly and the kids never come back. John returns in time for the end of the season, and to lead England to glory in the European Championships. Afterwards, he announces that he's signed for Kaito Ikeda's local team.'

Elaine couldn't resist it. 'It's a good plan, apart from the bit about leading England to glory.' The other two stared at her, and she looked down at her notebook.

'There's a big, big problem, though,' said Lucy, turning back to Tom.

'Only one?'

'It's enough. Trafford Rangers will never agree to this: they want John to honour every last minute of his contract. Even when he doesn't play, he's worth a fortune to them in merchandising.'

'And you think we can help?'

Elaine was pleased that Tom still included her in the conversation, but her pleasure didn't last long.

'You managed to get something over on the Princess before,' said Lucy. 'I'm sure you can do it again.'

'No, no, no,' said Elaine. 'I can't go back in there.'

Tom sat back, and rubbed the top of his left arm. Elaine noticed that Lucy had noticed. In fact, Lucy seemed to know why he was doing it. Just how close had those two got? This could get beyond embarrassing if he'd crossed the line somewhere.

'I don't think Elaine can do it,' said Tom. Lucy's face fell, but Elaine felt relieved. 'But I know someone who would relish the challenge.' Lucy perked up again. He turned to Elaine. 'Can you give Leonie a briefing tonight? Tell her what to expect, in broad terms. I'm sure she'll have her own tactics.'

Elaine didn't fancy a one to one chat with Ms Spence, but she quite liked the idea of Leonie vs Karida. She only wished someone would sell tickets.

'What about you?' said Tom to Lucy. As he did so, his eyes flicked up towards the ceiling and the flat above them.

Lucy went deep red. 'I'm not proud of it,' she said. 'I ran out of money after I did the shop. There was no point doing one bit when it was all a mess.'

Elaine disagreed. She would never live like that, no matter how little money she had.

'Sorry,' said Tom. 'We'll leave you in peace.'

'We'll be in touch,' said Elaine on the way out. Tom and Lucy had failed to say goodbye. It didn't look like either of them could bring themselves to do it.

Chapter 21

Thursday 30 January

Dean lifted up his trouser leg and examined the skin underneath. There was a slight rash, but that would fade, like the story of his arrest. The magistrate had just given him unconditional bail, in advance of a crown court hearing. 'You say I don't have to turn up again?' he said to Daniel.

'The next hearing is a formality – but it has to be in front of a judge, not a magistrate. You don't have to go – but most people in your position would want to be there, just to see the look on the Crown Prosecutor's face when he says they got it wrong. The judge always says something nice, too. It helps keep the compensation bill when down you sue them for wrongful arrest.'

'Stuff the compensation. Just make sure they cover your costs. I don't care about the rest.'

'Are you sure?'

'I only spent one night in the cells, and I was injured anyway. They won't give me much money, and it's not worth the bad press.'

Daniel gave him a sharp look. People always did when he showed them that his brains weren't all in his feet. 'There is one more thing you can do,' he said.

'What's that?'

'Take this and sell it. Send the proceeds to Emily Miller and tell her to spend it on something to benefit the supporters.' He held out an envelope for Daniel to take.

'Why don't you give it to her yourself?' said the lawyer.

'She might get the wrong idea. Take a look.'

Daniel opened the envelope and saw the engagement ring inside, the one that Madison had returned to him.

'Aah,' he said. 'I see what you mean. Leave it with me. I have a cousin in London who should give you a good price.'

'I thought you might.'

Daniel gave him another look, and held out his hand.

Dean shook, and thanked his lawyer for everything. Then he walked out of the magistrates' court. Outside there were no cameras, but there were a couple of reporters, one of whom had a decent-looking phone. Dean looked around and saw Emily, with an old man who looked like her dad. He was wrapped up in an STFC scarf.

'Here, mate,' said Dean to the reporter. 'Do you want an exclusive?'

'You what?'

'Follow me, and get ready to start recording.'

He strode over to Emily, trailing the reporter in his wake. She looked surprised, but recovered and introduced the old man. Dean was right: it was her father.

The reporter caught up with them and held up his phone. Dean eased father and daughter apart, stood between them, and turned towards the camera.

'I'd like to thank all the supporters of Salton Town who stood beside me over the last few weeks. It reminds you that football really is a family, and I'll do my best to repay that support next season.'

It wouldn't be on the news, but it would be on social media — and that was better because with any luck it would go viral. His PR had told him not to do anything like this, but where was she today? Gone to 7Bridge to hold John Nugent's hand, apparently. He hoped that Johnny realised how lucky he was. Dean certainly did.

While the camera was still focused on him, he turned and gave Emily a big kiss on the cheek. Before she could react, he patted her father on the shoulder and jogged across the road.

His new Range Rover, courtesy of Isaac, was waiting in the car park. By the time the exit barrier had risen to release him, Dean had bonded his phone with the Infotainment system and told Siri to find him a premium estate agent in Salton. He quite fancied one of the flats converted from the old Salton Main Hall and like his career, they would only increase in value. Yes, one of those flats would do nicely. Until he was re-admitted to the promised land, one of those flats would do very nicely indeed.

'Do you fancy Southport?' said Tom.

Elaine was about to lower a slice of pizza into her mouth. 'Sounds good,' she said, then thought of something and put the pizza down. 'Do I have to meet your sister? And did she inherit your mother's cooking gene?'

'Maybe … and no. In that order.'

Elaine nodded and carried on eating.

Tom had finished, so he stood up and started clearing away. They were due to leave Lyme Court tomorrow - Friday - but there wasn't much else to do apart from paperwork.

'If I let you work from "home" tomorrow, can you get up to see Rob?'

'Oh! Yes please. I mean … thank you. That would be great. When do you want me back?'

He looked down at his calendar, to avoid the eye contact he knew would be coming. 'I've got to go to Earlsbury again next week. How about you working out of the MIT office on Monday to Wednesday? There are quite a few actions to complete. I should be able to catch up with myself by Thursday. Obviously, I'll come back here in the interim if anything urgent comes up.'

'I don't think Julia Jepson will be making me a cup of tea in the near future, but at least I'm not barred. That's fine, sir.'

His phone rang with an Unknown Number. It was probably a PPI call, but he was obliged to take it anyway.

'Hello, Inspector. It's Holly Nugent.'

Tom put down the pizza box and gave the call his full attention.

'Thanks for what you did,' said Holly, 'but I need to see you. It's important, and private.'

'I don't really do private. It doesn't work very well for me, but I'll certainly see you. Where are you?'

'We're staying in a hotel, near the hospital where John's being treated for his mystery injury. The paps are camped outside, and it's terrible here. I didn't think I'd miss the security, but I do now.'

'Where is it?'

'Can you meet me somewhere outside?'

'If that works better for you, and it's not too far.'

'Do you know the First Bridge?'

Tom thought he hadn't heard properly, so he repeated what she'd said.

'Yes, that's right. The First Bridge is down the river from Sevenbridge, not far from Wilmslow. It's by a nature reserve. I'll see you there at three o'clock, if that's okay.'

'If that's what you want.'

Tom debated taking Elaine with him, but it was a public place, after all. However he told her what was going on. She shrugged, and they both got back to work.

According to the map the First Bridge was well off the beaten track, and Tom was glad of the brown signs that pointed to the First Bridge Wetlands and Walking Trail. The car park was small and deserted. The bridge itself was closed to vehicles, and very old. Tom walked up to it, winding his scarf around his neck to keep out the cold. From the top, he could see what must be the second and third bridges further upstream — they were also old and not in regular use.

A black 4x4 came down the lane and pulled up by the wooden posts that allowed cycles but not cars on to the bridge. In the passenger seat, he could see Ellie Nugent. Surely Holly hadn't brought all the kids with her? The rear windows were blacked out.

The car only stopped a second, and the door opened on the far side. With a roar of diesel, Holly pulled away. Standing in the road was Lucy. *Oh dear.*

He should have walked to his car and ignored her, but that wasn't going to happen. He waited on top of the bridge as she danced between the bollards and skipped up the incline. She kept her hands in her pockets and stood on his left, by the parapet.

They looked up at the second and third bridges for a second, until Lucy broke the silence. 'We were going to drive away if Scarywoman was here.'

'Don't call her that. She's a good police officer.'

'You're right. Sorry.' She took a deep breath. 'When you had your interview with John…'

'You mean when he put me up against the wall, and when I whacked him with Elaine's baton.'

She smiled. 'That one. Yes. You said that Holly had been bitten by something poisonous.'

'Did I?'

'Yes. Like Eve, in the Garden of Eden.'

'It was only a metaphor. They break down if you push them too far.'

'But it got me thinking. Was Gianni the serpent in Paradise, or was it Dad? Who was worse? Gianni for what he did when he was alive, or Dad for killing him?'

'Don't go there, Lucy. You're not God. Only God can make judgements like that, and I don't think there is a God.'

'I thought you went to church a lot.'

'I like some sacred music, and I understand where it's coming from, but I don't believe in an almighty God.'

'What do you believe?'

'I wish I knew. If it helps you come to terms with this, my mother would say that you should try to forgive both of them. I don't agree. My younger sister would say that you have to remember the good that they did, and honour them for that.'

She thought about it for a while. 'Gianni could be a right pain most of the time, but he knew how to live in the moment. He brought a lot of pleasure to a lot of people. That can't be evil.'

'That's good — and your father's not dead. Just missing for a few years.'

'That's going to need a bit more thought.'

He turned to face her. 'I hear you've become very rich now that the Princess has bought out the White-Berardi stake in the 7Bridge Estate.'

She pulled a face. 'Blood money.'

'It's still money, though. You don't have blood on your hands.'

'Even if my father does, you mean.'

'I have no idea how you're going to deal with this, Lucy. I wish I could help, but I can't.'

She didn't flinch, or look hurt. She just smiled and turned back to the view. 'You already have,' she said. 'Holly's off to Japan tomorrow, thanks to you. I had a long talk to Mitsumi last night. She's going to introduce Holly to a therapist. If Holly can recover, so can I.' She paused. 'I'm going to put the money from the sale of the Estate shares into trust. For my children's education.'

'That's quite a strange thing to do.'

'You're right. It's still money. I'd hate to give it away now and change my mind later.'

'Fair enough. I'd probably do the same. What about the money from the sale of White-Berardi itself?'

'By the time I've paid off the loan on the shop, there's enough to afford a flat and a car. That's it: my inheritance. I'm going to look for a job, starting Monday.'

'And I'll be on another case.'

She turned back, and slowly stretched out her hand towards his left arm. He flinched inside, but didn't draw away. She placed her fingers on his coat, right above the spot where he'd had the skin graft.

'I know there won't be a trial, but will I see you at the sentencing?' she said.

'Not necessarily — it's DCI Stamp's responsibility. On the day it happens, I could be anywhere.'

There was a shirt, a jacket and a thick wool coat between her hand and his arm, but he could feel the heat penetrating the cloth. Or was it just his imagination? He didn't move to take it away.

'In that case,' she said, 'I'll see you when I see you.'

'I hate to be practical,' said Tom, 'but do I need to give you a lift? We're in the middle of nowhere.'

She flashed him a smile. 'Holly's waiting by the main road. She made me come.'

'Then thank her.'

'I will.'

She slid her hand down his sleeve, over his watch, and gripped his fingers. He felt the cold bite through. She gave them a squeeze and let go. She walked backwards for two steps, then turned on her heel and jogged down the slope. When she got to the bottom, she leapfrogged the bollard and did a shuffle in the gravel. Then she shoved her hands in her pockets and walked quickly down the road. The warmth from her touch lingered on his arm until she disappeared round the corner.

Knowing he might regret it, Tom ran down the bridge and vaulted on to the bollard, balancing for a second before jumping down again.

'I'll see you when I see you,' he shouted, aiming his words over the trees.

He probably wouldn't, of course, but it made him feel a lot better to think that he might.

***

Tom, Elaine and Lucy's stories continue in the second Tom Morton novel, *Another Place to Die*. Keep reading for a sample.

This is the first Tom Morton Book, but it isn't the first to feature him. If you want to know how he got that burn on his arm, and how he came across Sqdn Ldr Conrad Clarke, you can read all about it in the *Operation Jigsaw Trilogy*.

The *Jigsaw* trilogy is a thriller, and a few years older than this book. Check it out and judge for yourself.

The End.

Author's Note

Thank you for reading this book; I hope you enjoyed it. If you did, please leave a review on Amazon. It doesn't have to be long. Reviews make a huge difference to Indie authors, and an honest review from a genuine customer is worth a great deal.

If you came to *A Serpent in Paradise* after reading the *Operation Jigsaw* trilogy, then I hope you enjoyed the slight change in style, and that you didn't miss Conrad too much.

Dedications should speak for themselves, but this one deserves a footnote. I wrote, and published, the *Operation Jigsaw* trilogy before summer 2014. Those books included the character Kate Lonsdale, Tom Morton's cousin.

Kate Lonsdale is entirely fictional and I hope resembles no one but herself. One of the starting points, however, was my own cousin – Kate Burge. I still find it hard to believe, but my cousin, the real Kate, was tragically killed in an accident on the Isle of Man in 2014. I doubt that anyone who knew the real Kate will ever read this, but as I publish the book, I offer a silent prayer in her memory.

In this book, all the characters are fictional and so are most of the places and organisations.

Please turn over for a short extract from the next Tom Morton Book.

Another Place to Die

by Mark Hayden

A Tom Morton Book — No 2

The Perfect Place for Death…

Matt Cross is a pillar of the community in Southport: family man, entrepreneur and environmentalist. Everyone is happy to take his money, drink in his bars and forget where it all came from, until Matt is found murdered next to a statue in the woods behind his manor house.

DCI Tom Morton and DC Elaine Fraser are reunited to take on the case, and Tom finds himself in an abandoned building, with a team of misfits, facing a wall of silence.

Available now from Amazon for Kindle.
Print Version available 2017.

Prologue

Last December

When Kingsley saw the man with the gun, he slammed on the brakes. His mountain bike skidded on the farmyard cobbles.

The man with the gun looked round. 'You all right, lad?' he said with a dense Scouse accent.

'What are you doing here with that,' said Kingsley, pointing to the gun. It was a shotgun, broken and resting in the crook of the man's left arm. 'And what are you doing on my land?'

The man raised his eyebrows and looked around the farmyard at the ancient cottage, at the even more ancient barn and at the concrete pads where modern buildings had once stood.

Kingsley studied him. He was dressed like a gentleman farmer, with an old Barbour jacket and Hunter wellies. Underneath the outfit, the man was tall, broad and altogether bigger than Kingsley, though he must have been a couple of decades older, probably in his fifties.

He was smiling when he turned back to face Kingsley. 'Congratulations, Mr Laidlaw,' he said. 'A great victory on Thursday. Good luck in your new job. I'm sure you won't miss teaching.'

So the man knew who he was, but that didn't explain the gun, or what he was doing in the farmyard.

'Are you moving to London?' said the man.

'You still haven't said what you're doing here,' responded Kingsley. His heart rate hadn't slowed after the ride, and was getting faster if anything. His legs started to shiver.

'Just checking the place out,' said the man. 'I am your landlord, after all.'

'No you're not. Andrew Mallinson owns this land, and you're not Andrew Mallinson.'

'Andy Mallinson is my agent. I'm Matt Cross. You've met my wife, Layla.'

The shivers shot up from Kingsley's legs into his back. 'I thought she was a widow,' he blurted out, then cringed back.

Instead of being offended, Cross burst out laughing. 'That's a good one, that. I'll tell her that when I get home. Makes me wonder who she's been spinning that yarn to. I didn't think the Sustainable Lancashire Party was full of swingers, but you never know.'

'She just never mentioned you, that's all,' said Kingsley. He couldn't get on his high horse about trespass, because Cross was on a public footpath, but that didn't explain the firearm. He pointed to the gun and said, 'What do you need that for?'

'I've been to Another Place,' he said, jerking his head behind him, towards the open fields.

What? Crosby is in the other direction, thought Kingsley. 'You've taken that gun on to the beach? Are you mad?'

Cross laughed again. 'Don't be soft. It's a private joke. I've been looking for rabbits in Northridge Copse. They're over-running the woods, but it's too cold for most of them to be about. Bugs Bunny lives to breed another day. You still haven't told me if you're moving to London with our new MP.'

'I don't know,' said Kingsley. 'Penny hasn't decided whether I'd be more useful to the party down in London or up here getting ready for the local elections in May.'

'Fair enough. Doesn't really matter in the short term. It'll be a couple of years before the development starts.'

Talk of development made Kingsley look towards the neighbouring property, Northridge Farm.

He couldn't see the UGAS drilling tower from here, but he thought about it night and day. UGAS wanted to frack the rocks deep underground to release shale gas. It was opposition to this project which had propelled Penny Markland to victory in the parliamentary by-election.

'What development?' asked Kingsley.

'If we can send UGAS packing, then I can develop Quaker's Fold. I would have done it two years ago if they hadn't discovered that gas. You can't build new houses next to a gas plant.'

Kingsley swayed on his feet. It was impossible. This couldn't happen. No way would Cross be allowed to build on greenfield land at the edge of a village: it stood against all planning principles. 'You'll never get permission.'

The shotgun was slung casually over Cross's arm, as if it weighed nothing. Kingsley had never been so close to a firearm before, and he kept sneaking glances at the weapon. He could see that there were no cartridges in the breach, and Cross had been careful to keep the barrels pointed away at all times. As soon as Kingsley blurted out the words *you'll never get permission*, Cross took his hands out of his pockets and snapped the gun closed.

Kingsley's eyes were riveted on the motion of Cross's hands as the gun swung round. The heavy wedding band on his left hand was matched by an embossed signet ring on the right. Both rings glinted in the afternoon sun, and contrasted with the dark burr of the stock and the bright red rubber cushion on the end. For a fraction of a second, Kingsley looked into the deep black pits of the barrels, and he couldn't help but flinch.

Cross put the gun down, very carefully, and said, 'We'll see 'bout dat,' turning up his Scouse accent by a couple of notches. He gave Kingsley a cheerful smile. 'I thought you'd be grateful, anyway, what with me winning the election for youse.'

'Penny won it, with help from me. And Layla, I suppose.'

Cross stepped forward, and if his feet hadn't been around the bike, Kingsley would have stepped back. As Cross moved into his personal space, Kingsley could smell gunpowder and death around him.

Cross patted Kingsley on the shoulder. 'Who got that tape recording, eh? And who got it printed and shoved through every letterbox in Southport, eh? Enjoy the moment, Kingsley. Layla tells me you worked hard on this campaign, but that was only one battle. You need to focus on the local elections if we're going to win the war. See you later.'

Cross picked up his gun, then walked through the yard and up the path. Kingsley watched him carefully, trying to hold on to the feeling of triumph that had swept through him in the early hours of Friday morning in the leisure centre. Slowly, the pile of ballots for Penny had grown larger than the stack of votes for her Liberal opponent until he had conceded defeat.

On the Monday before the election, a tape had emerged of the Liberal candidate giving his real views on fracking. He had said that he was against it in public, but on the tape he said that his party would never vote against anything that lowered gas prices for consumers, and that if he wanted to be a shadow minister, he wouldn't be voting against his party. And then the candidate had called the electorate *nimbies*.

Somehow, the Sustainable Lancashire Party had come up with boxes of leaflets, and volunteers from Liverpool had come up to deliver them. Cross had said he was behind it, and Kingsley wasn't going to argue. He vowed to start a new campaign: The Quaker's Fold Action Group. *QUAG*. He quite liked the sound of that. He also made a promise to get Matt Cross personally. Two could play dirty in politics.

To read more of Another Place to Die, *search your Amazon store for the title or for Mark Hayden.*

Printed in Great Britain
by Amazon